ZACHARY TYLER LINVILLE

Nerdist

Published by Inkshares, Inc., San Francisco, California, as part of the Nerdist Collection
www.inkshares.com

Edited and designed by Girl Friday Productions
www.girlfridayproductions.com

Cover design by David Drummond
Cover images: © Sean Pavone/Shutterstock; © ChrislovaArina/Shutterstock

ISBN: 9781941758854
e-ISBN: 9781941758861

Library of Congress Control Number: 201595895

First Edition

Printed in the United States of America

To my great-grandma, Mammaw Mag. You taught me to read, and opened the door to thousands of worlds.

PROLOGUE

Bustling crowds pushed their way through the subway station. Last-minute shoppers, arms full of bags, rushed to the next department store. There were the usual commuters, already looking forward to kicking back with a glass of eggnog and enjoying the holidays. A few families fought the crowds, laden with suitcases and duffel bags on their way out of town. Christmas carols floated through the air, mixing with the bells of volunteers dressed as Santa asking for donations.

"Jimmy, hurry up, the Q train is pulling in," Meghan snapped, grabbing the sleeve of her eight-year-old brother's coat. "Mom's going to be furious if you make us miss our flight."

"Hold on, I dropped my MetroCard." Jimmy yanked his arm from Meghan's grip and reached for the yellow card on the ground. A black-gloved hand swooped in, picked up the card, and held it out. Jimmy looked into the face of a tall businessman, clean-cut with salt-and-pepper hair and a curious smile. "Thanks."

"Jimmy!"

"Coming!" Jimmy spun and raced after his sister, shoving the card into his front pocket. He jumped through the doors of the train right before they closed. "Sorry."

"It's okay, just take a seat." His mother motioned to the seat next to Meghan. People pushed in around them as the train pulled away. "Wipe your mouth; you still have some chocolate on it."

Jimmy reached up and rubbed his face.

"I'll get it." Jimmy's mom removed her glove and rubbed at the chocolate. It proved to be stubborn, and she licked her finger to remove the smear.

"Is Dad going to be at Grandma and Grandpa's when we get there?"

"No, we'll meet him in Atlanta during our layover, and then we will fly together to your grandparents."

"Cool." Jimmy leaned back and closed his eyes as the subway rattled on.

Meanwhile, the tall businessman maneuvered through the crowd. He threw change into a donation bucket and excused his way past people. As he reached the stairs leading to the street, he carefully removed his left glove, making sure to flip it inside out. He threw it into a garbage can and then disposed of the right glove as well. He climbed the stairs and disappeared into the winter evening.

1. ASHER

After

Asher crouches, tightening his grasp on the baseball bat.

"Did you hear it too?" he whispers over his shoulder.

"Yeah, it sounded like it was coming from the left up ahead," Wendy whispers back, her hand resting on the pistol in her side holster.

Asher takes quiet steps forward through the fallen leaves and sticks, his green eyes searching through the trees for a sign of movement. He counts to thirty, hairs prickling up the back of his neck and his heart thumping. A bead of sweat slides down his temple.

"It must have just been a rabbit or a squirrel," he says, standing and running his fingers through his messy brown hair in relief. There is a snap behind him, and he turns, his body going rigid. He wraps both hands around the bat and pulls it close.

"It can't be one of them, can it?" Wendy asks.

"I don't know. I think it's hiding. It's just as cautious as we are, and they don't hide."

A scream reverberates through the woods. A large shape darts out from a tree and disappears into the foliage.

"There it goes!" Asher says.

Wendy hushes him.

"What do we do?" Asher asks.

"Did you get a good look at it? I couldn't make it out."

"No, it was too fast, but it *was* hiding. I don't think it's one of them."

"We need to get out of here. If it was one of them, there could be others. And if it wasn't, something screamed. Something nearby. Let's go."

They cut a slow and steady path in the opposite direction of the scream. Asher keeps watch to their left and behind them while Wendy watches the right and takes the lead. They stop for a break after an hour passes without any other disturbances. Wendy leans against a tree and pulls a water bottle from her belt, a relic of her marathon training, and takes a sip before handing it over.

"Thanks." Asher squirts the warm water into the back of his throat.

"We should be thanking the screamer back there—they might have just saved us from having to protect ourselves." Wendy takes the bottle back and clips it onto the belt.

Asher pulls a protein bar from his pocket and snaps it in half, devouring his portion. The bar helps dull the hunger in his stomach but isn't enough to add meat to his bones, which are starting to show through his skin. He believes they are nearing the highway; the trees are more spread out, and light easily filters through the branches. He asks Wendy what she wants to do. She glances up, her bright-blue eyes reflecting the patches of sky showing through the treetops, and takes a moment to chew her half of the bar. She says they need to continue to the highway to gauge their location. The afternoon is creeping into evening, and they need to find a place to camp before nightfall. Nodding, Asher crumples the wrapper and tosses it. He has been following Wendy's lead for two weeks, ever since they finally abandoned the university.

Each time he has asked her questions about their destination, she's refused to answer. He has stopped asking now—without having any family left or anywhere else to go, and having let go of his best friend days after the outbreak—it doesn't much matter where she takes him. He owes her his life, and he clings to her.

"Hold up," Asher says, dropping to retie his shoelaces. Wendy keeps walking, her eyes darting from the right to up ahead. Just as he pulls the laces tight, Asher spots a man lurching from a thicket of trees toward Wendy's left. Jumping to his feet, Asher yells, "Watch out!"

Wendy spins and comes face-to-face with a blood-covered middle-aged man, his teeth bared. He lets loose a guttural howl, and he closes his hands around her throat, lifting her off the ground. Kicking, she feels her foot connect with his knee with a crunch. His fingers loosen, and she pulls herself free as he wobbles and loses his balance. Both Wendy and the man crash. Rolling away, Wendy pushes herself to her hands and knees, but he grabs her foot as she tries to stand, causing her to crash onto her face.

Asher reaches the struggling pair, raises the bat, and brings it down with all the force he can muster. It connects with the man's head in a thump. Asher hits him again, sending out a spray of blood as the body goes limp. Wendy jerks her foot away from him and brushes the dirt and leaves off her front as she gets to her feet, panting.

"I'm so sorry," Asher says, the color gone from his face. "I thought you heard me when I stopped to tie my shoe. I should have been more alert, surveyed the area better before I stopped—"

"It's fine. I'm okay. Let's just not let it happen again. I should have listened to you better."

"Let me see your neck—did he get you?"

Wendy pulls her hair up from her neck, turning her head from side to side. Asher leans in close and inspects it, but there aren't any scratches.

"It'll probably be sore, but it's not scratched. I don't see any blood."

She lets her long blonde hair fall around her shoulders.

"Thank you for bashing his skull in," Wendy says. She grabs her bag and hefts it onto her back. They check their shoelaces and continue.

It only takes a few minutes to reach the tree line and emerge from the woods at the bottom of a steep slope. The air is still and silent as they begin their ascent, slipping and sliding on the grass while trying to maintain a foothold, the undernourished muscles in their legs straining from exhaustion. Asher reaches the guardrail first and grabs it before offering Wendy his other hand to pull her up and over the top onto the asphalt.

The highway is a graveyard of cars and trucks and buses in all conditions. They are packed closely together. A thin layer of dust and pollen covers them. Several have doors hanging open or shattered windows.

Many have been crashed into one another, while others appear pristine, as if waiting to be purchased and driven off the lot.

Asher shields his eyes from the sun reflecting off the cars and surveys their surroundings. Vultures circle above, a common sight these days; two swoop down fifty yards away. They squabble over some kind of remains. Aside from the birds, there is no other movement.

"Which direction do you want to go?" he asks.

"This way." Wendy begins walking into the sun along the side of the road. Asher looks to the east, the downtown Orlando skyline visible over the horizon, but he follows Wendy west. He suspects she has a specific destination in mind.

"That guy looked fresh, right? How fresh?"

"I don't know, maybe a day or two? The blood was dried, but I don't know that it was his. And he was strong, human strong."

"At least we're going the opposite direction he came from," Asher says.

"Let's check the cars for supplies." Wendy makes a sudden turn from the shoulder into the maze of vehicles. She tries the driver's side handle on a truck and laughs. "Gotta make sure nobody breaks into your car when the world goes to shit." None of the other doors open, and she moves on to the next car.

A little further down the road, Asher looks through the windows of cars, gagging when he checks the backseat of one. The opposite window is smashed; a mixture of glass and dried blood covers the body of a young man. His face is forever twisted in a scream, and a large chunk is missing from his neck. Asher turns away, bumping into Wendy.

"What is it?" Wendy asks, looking over his shoulder into the car.

"It just caught me off guard," Asher says, lifting the handle of another car. The door creaks open.

"Yeah, well, it's not something I think either of us expected to get used to. Anything good in there?"

A small cooler is wedged behind the driver's seat. Asher climbs into the passenger seat and waves Wendy over. He lifts the cooler free. The lid pops off, and a few cans of soda and a couple of moldy sandwiches spill out. Wendy gets in the backseat, throws the sandwiches onto the floor, and hands a couple of the sodas to Asher.

"Jackpot," Asher says, popping one of the cans open. Wendy follows suit and they tap the cans together before each takes a long draw. Asher lets out a loud burp, sending both of them into fits of laughter before Wendy lets out an even louder burp.

"I don't even drink soda," Wendy says.

"But it's like the forbidden fruit now," Asher replies. "The idea of never having a soda again makes it irresistible."

The sky darkens, and raindrops pitter-patter against the windshield and roof.

"We can wait it out," Wendy says. Asher slings his backpack into the driver's seat and closes the passenger door just as the rain picks up. Within seconds, they can't see beyond the windows.

"April showers . . ." Asher trails off as thunder rumbles. "At least if anything was tracking our scent, the storm should wash it away. I can keep watch—get some rest while you can."

"Thanks," Wendy says, pulling off her own backpack and placing it on the seat as a pillow. Asher stares out the windshield, waiting to hear Wendy's breath even out as she settles into a slumber. He roots through the items in his bag and finds a small yellow notebook. His pen is nearly dry. He licks the end, trying to get it flowing again. Asher scribbles in the notebook, poised and ready to wake Wendy if needed, but her screams never come. Today, only the waking world is a nightmare.

2. ASHER

Before

It was his second shift at Cup o' Joe, the café inside the university's library, and Asher had made his third drink of the day incorrectly. Coffee was coffee; why did there need to be different levels of foamed milk? And he didn't get the difference between putting the espresso in first or last. He spooned extra foam on top of the light brown liquid just to fill the cup, and then snapped the lid on before anyone noticed.

"Café au lait for Stacey?" A pretty red-haired girl approached the counter and took the cup from him. She smiled at him as their fingers brushed against each other. He watched her stop at the sugar stand and pop the lid off. "Shit."

She was going to notice he made it wrong. She looked up, locking eyes with him; he blushed. But with another quick smile she poured a sweetener packet in, stirred the drink, and disappeared into the stacks.

"Yo, Earth to Asher. Can I get a caramel macchiato?" Dale nudged Asher and handed him a paper cup.

"Yeah, sorry." Asher turned back to the espresso machine as Dale manned the register. When nobody was looking, Asher peeked at the cheat sheet under the counter and read the ingredients for the drink.

"Just take a breath. It's only coffee." Dale patted him on the shoulder and placed another cup on the counter. "These are college students; most of them are hopped up on amphetamines right now anyway."

***

Asher scrubbed against the permanent stains in the steaming pitchers, hopelessly attempting to rid them of the smell of burnt milk. Dale finished counting down the register and slid Asher's cut of the tips, a meager $6.78, across the counter. Asher abandoned the pitchers and shoved the cash into his pocket as Dale flipped off the lights and locked up. They passed the empty librarian's station, thanked the security guard holding open a door, and parted ways.

"Hey there."

Asher jumped at the voice and stumbled into a bike rack.

"Oh my God, I'm so sorry. I didn't mean to startle you." Stacey, the pretty redhead, rushed forward and grabbed his hand to help him up.

"Oh, umm, h-hi. Sorry, I didn't expect anyone to be out here at this time of night." Asher stood and straightened his clothing. "It's Stacey, right? Asher," he said, sticking his hand out.

"You remembered." Stacey smiled and blushed, but returned the shake. "I read your name tag. And sorry again."

"Don't worry about it."

"I just finished a study group, and I knew the coffee shop was closing, so I thought it might be worth it to wait around until you got off work. It's kind of embarrassing in retrospect."

"No, no, not at all."

"Really?"

"Yeah, I've never had anyone wait around for me before. Hold on one second." He bent down and finished unchaining his bike. "Maybe I can walk you home? Do you live in a dorm?"

"No, I drove here—my car is in a garage across campus." Stacey pointed off into the distance. "All of the good garages were full, so I had to park in the boonies."

They laughed nervously. "I hear you. I didn't even bother getting a parking pass this year. Figured I could get some needed exercise while helping the environment. No offense or anything, though! I'm not like a hippie, I don't have a problem with people driving, I drive everywhere, well, except to class and work now, but that's because of the parking situation, and now I'm rambling . . . umm, a save would be appreciated right about now."

"No offense taken. But since you can't walk me home, could a gal get accompanied to her car? It's not safe to walk across campus alone these days. Unless you have to go the other way?"

Asher pulled his bike free of the rack. "Ladies first."

"And my mom said chivalry was dead."

They walked along, chatting, for ten minutes under the streetlamps before reaching the parking garage.

"Thanks for the talk. I'm glad you decided to wait for me to get off work," Asher said.

"Me too. Not to be too forward again, but could I get your number?"

"Do I have much of a choice? You know where I work." A glimmer of confusion and remorse crossed Stacey's face. "Kidding! I'm kidding. It was a joke, sorry."

"Oh! I thought maybe you concluded I was creepy after all."

Stacey punched Asher's number into her phone and hit Call. Asher held up his own phone, her number lighting up on the screen. Stacey climbed into her car and started it. "So there's this party tomorrow night at an apartment in my complex. Would you like to come with me?"

"Definitely, consider it a date. Just text me the details."

"A date, huh? Who said anything about a date?" With a smirk, Stacey began to back out of the parking space. Her taillights disappeared around the corner, and Asher pedaled off across the dark campus.

***

Asher could hear music and voices through the door. He took a deep breath. I could still back out, he thought. I'm not going to know anyone here; I could have gotten sick at the last minute. Shaking off his nerves, he stepped forward and knocked on the door. A tipsy brunette opened it. She was wearing a tank top and shorts a size too small. Her face was done up with makeup.

"Do I know you?"

"Uhh, no. I was looking for—"

"There you are!" Stacey emerged from the crowd, red Solo cup in hand, and pushed her way toward the door. "He's with me, Margot."

"He's cute." Margot stepped to the side and Asher slipped past her. He awkwardly hugged Stacey. When she kissed him on his cheek, he was hit with the distinct odor of tequila.

"What took you so long? I thought you were going to be here an hour ago."

"Yeah, sorry, I had a hard time figuring out what to wear," Asher lied, motioning to his blue jeans and plain T-shirt.

"Aw, that's adorable." Stacey giggled and took his hand, dragging him into the kitchen. "There's a bunch of drink options. I'm having a margarita, but there's wine, vodka, beer, rum, or some kind of punch stuff with fruit in the cooler. I think there are a few more things in the fridge."

While Stacey prepared another margarita, Asher settled on a cider.

"I want to introduce you to my friends." Stacey again grabbed his hand and dragged him through the crowd, past sliding glass doors that led to a balcony swarming with frat types playing beer pong. She pushed open a door at the end of the hall and Asher followed her into a bedroom. One group of people lounged on a bed playing a drinking game involving dice, and another group stood next to a large wardrobe. The room as a whole took on a different atmosphere than the rest of the party—the music was quieter, allowing people to have actual conversations. "Hey, guys, this is Asher, the guy from the coffee shop I was telling you about."

Asher waved. He recognized one of them, a blond boy with deep-brown eyes from his American History class. He had the classic "boy next door" vibe. As he noticed Asher, his face lit up. "I know you! Well, I don't know you, but we have class together. Professor Bernstein. I'm Ellis." Ellis extended his hand. When Asher shook it, he felt a shock-like jolt shoot up his arm.

"Who wants to play a drinking game?" Stacey asked, surveying the group and taking another gulp of her margarita.

"Whoa, why don't we slow it down a bit?" one of Stacey's friends said, trying to grab the cup from her. Stacey danced backward and out of her reach.

"I'm fine—it's a party. Why don't you all get on my level, Michelle? Now about that game."

"I'm down. I'll grab a deck of cards," replied one of the guys, stepping out of the room. The rest of the group migrated from the bedroom to the dining room, inviting others to join them. The guy with the cards flubbed an attempt at shuffling and then spread them out into a circle on the table. Asher sat, and Stacey quickly plopped in the chair on his right, leaning slightly into him.

"Do you mind if I take this seat?" Ellis motioned to the chair directly next to him.

"Yeah, of course, go ahead."

"Thanks."

Stacey leaned forward and pulled a card from the circle. "Two. That's you." She grabbed Asher's forearm and gave it a light squeeze. He sipped from the bottle of cider, his eyes locked on Stacey's grin. "Now it's your turn to pull a card."

He grabbed the closest card and flipped it over. "Seven."

"Heaven!" Three people yelled and thrust their arms up. As the last to do so, Asher drank again.

Ellis was next and chose an eight. "I guess that means I need to choose a date." His eyes moved from person to person in the circle and fell on Asher. "So what d'you say? Be my date?" Ellis smiled and batted his eyelashes.

"Your date?" Asher stiffened, a bit caught off guard.

"Relax, it just means that when I have to drink, you have to drink. Are you new to this game?"

"Yeah, I guess so. To both things—being new, and your date."

"Cheers." Ellis lifted his cup and tapped the rim to Asher's bottle.

***

Several rounds into the game Asher got up to snag another drink. He felt slightly fuzzy, but he was still the most sober person at the party.

When he returned to the table, Stacey's friend Liz readjusted her glasses and pulled a card signifying a round of Never Have I Ever.

"Three fingers up, bitches. Umm . . . never have I ever gone skinny-dipping."

"Seriously? What loser hasn't gone skinny-dipping before?"

"C'mon, that's a cheap shot."

A round of complaints, insults, and protests filled the air until everyone but Liz, Ellis, and Asher folded a finger down.

"Don't worry, Liz, looks like you aren't the only loser here," Ellis said with a smile and another wink. Next up was Corey.

"Never have I ever kissed a guy."

"What the hell, what's next? 'Never have I ever had a vagina?'" Liz asked and punched Corey's arm. Asher watched all of the girls put down a finger, and with the exception of Liz, who still held up two fingers, they aimed their still-standing middle fingers at a laughing Corey, who drank in response. "All right, all right, let's keep going."

"Never have I ever hooked up with a professor."

"He was a grad student!" Stacey yelled, picking up her cup and chugging the remainder of her drink to a round of cheers and applause. She stood up and bowed before stumbling toward the kitchen. Ellis used this chance to lean over to Asher.

"So how's your date going?"

"Is she all right?"

"Stacey's a good girl; don't let them fool you. She's known most of the people here since high school, so she's very comfortable around them and they all give each other crap. And the guy they're talking about really was a grad student. He wasn't teaching one of her classes, so try not to think any less of her."

"I wasn't going to—"

"I'm just yanking your chain." Ellis got up for a bathroom break, leaving Asher confused and shifting in his seat while waiting for Stacey to return.

***

The party started to wind down, making it easier to navigate. Almost everyone had blundered off, leaving behind cups and bottles on every surface, and a painting on the living room wall had been knocked askew. Asher waited with Liz outside the bathroom door for Stacey to emerge.

"How're you doing in there, sweetheart?" Liz asked after knocking on the door. "Come on, it's not every day you have a cute boy willing to listen to you puke and still wait to walk you home." A muffled sound came through the door followed by the toilet flushing. Stacey stumbled out, her face pale and her hair pulled into a disheveled ponytail.

"I'm never drinking again."

"Uh-huh, haven't heard that one before." Liz said, trying to help support Stacey.

"I'm fine—I can walk on my own."

"Would you like to hold my hand at least?" Asher asked, offering a hand to Stacey. She accepted with a smile.

"I'm sorry for drinking so much. I let my nerves get the best of me."

"Don't worry about it; it happens to the best of us. Maybe if I hadn't been so late you wouldn't have been so nervous." He guided her toward the front door, kicking trash out of the way before Stacey tripped, and as they walked through the living room, Asher noticed Ellis speaking on his cell phone out on the otherwise-empty balcony. He sounded as if he was in a heated discussion, but Asher couldn't make out the words. When Ellis caught sight of Asher leading Stacey through the front door, he ended the conversation and rushed to assist. Asher used his body to support Stacey down the stairs, and he was one landing down when he heard Ellis's voice.

"Hey, Asher, wait up." Ellis jogged down the stairs and placed Stacey's free arm around his shoulders. "I hope I'm not interrupting your romantic date, just figured I could help, seeing as Stacey lives two doors down from me."

"Thanks, I appreciate it. I didn't know which building to go to, and I don't think I'll be getting much help from this one," Asher said, nodding at Stacey, who seemed to have passed out while stumbling along. "Everything okay with you?"

"What? Yeah, of course, why wouldn't it be?"

"It seemed like you were having a pretty intense argument when I saw you on the balcony. Not that it's any of my business."

"Oh, you heard that? Yeah, it's nothing; thanks for asking."

Ellis guided them along the sidewalk, but his attitude was less enthusiastic than it had been. Not knowing him that well, Asher decided not to push the issue by asking any additional questions, and they carried on in silence. While walking along the fenced-in pool, Stacey suddenly lifted her head.

"I think I'm going to be sick again." She pushed the guys away and stumbled through the grass and to a bush, falling to her knees and retching loudly.

"Should we help her?" Asher asked.

"Nah, she did this to herself. Plus, better out than in." They stood and waited for her to finish. When she did, she twisted and sat on the ground.

"I hate these shoes," Stacey said, pulling them off and standing. She grabbed both shoes and threw them as hard as she could. They landed in the pool.

"You're going to want those in the morning." Ellis jogged to the gate and entered the pool area.

"I'll help you," Asher said. Stacey trailed behind them. The guys stood at the edge and gazed down at the shoes lying on the bottom of the pool while Stacey collapsed onto a lounge chair. Asher looked around. "Is there a net?"

"I think they keep it locked up with all the pool supplies so the students can't damage anything." Ellis kicked off his shoes and pulled his shirt over his head. He turned to Asher. "You ready?"

"Ready for what?"

"To not be a 'loser' anymore." Ellis dropped his pants. He was completely nude. "Never have we ever been skinny-dipping." He dove into the pool, leaving Asher standing with his mouth hanging open. Asher glanced back at Stacey, but she was passed out on the lounge chair. Taking a deep breath, he unbuttoned his shirt and dropped it. "Come on, slowpoke," Ellis called. "Why're you so scared? It's not like you have anything I haven't seen before." To help put Asher at ease, Ellis held his breath and dropped underwater. Asher quickly undressed and jumped into the pool.

3. RICO

Before

Rico swayed to the music with his eyes closed. He was overcome by a sense of euphoria; he felt the rhythm and beats of the electronica music in every inch of his being. A hand slipped into his wavy black hair, and he felt a body press up against his, hips grinding. He opened his eyes and saw Chloe staring at him with a smile—her blue eyes gleaming from the multicolored lasers flashing around them. She held the spliff to her lips and inhaled before pressing her lips against his and exhaling. He breathed the smoke in and blew it out his nose. He placed a hand on the back of her head and pulled her in for a longer kiss.

***

The show ended, and Rico and Chloe stumbled from the arena and through the streets looking for his car.

"Do you have any idea where you parked?" Chloe asked, giggling.

"It has to be in this lot," Rico answered. This was the fourth lot they had searched. They reached the end of a row, and Rico buried his face in his hands and laughed. "I don't have a clue."

"Maybe we shouldn't have taken those pills." Chloe pushed up against Rico and they resumed making out against the trunk of a car.

Chloe slid her pale hand up the back of his shirt and along his brown skin, and he slipped his fingers into the waistband of her skirt.

"I remember where it is!" Rico pulled back from the kiss. He led Chloe to a fifth parking lot where he repeatedly hit the panic button on his keys until an alarm sounded. When they reached the SUV, Rico picked Chloe up and spun her. He plastered another kiss on her and unlocked the doors. Instead of getting into the driver's seat, Rico opened the backseat door and pulled a lever on the side, dropping the seats down and climbing in. He looked out the open door, inviting Chloe to climb in and shut it.

Within seconds, Rico had Chloe's top over her head and tossed it into the front seat, then quickly lost his own shirt as well. Rico climbed on top of Chloe, and with their faces pressed against one another and hands in constant motion, their bodies molded together. Chloe slipped out of her skirt while Rico unbuttoned his jeans and shoved them down to his ankles. Suddenly, flashing red and blue lights filled the dark interior of the SUV.

"What the hell?" Chloe pushed Rico off her and searched around for her clothes. There was a knock on the window and a bright flashlight shined through the glass, blinding them.

"Miami PD. We need you to step out of the car," a deep voice demanded.

"Are we being arrested? We're being arrested." Chloe started to break down, wrapping her arms around her knees to cover up as she cried.

"It's fine," Rico reassured her. He pulled his jeans up and opened the door without buttoning them.

"Out of the car," the officer repeated. Rico stepped out, holding his hands up. The officer lowered the flashlight, allowing Rico to see his face.

"Matty?" Rico asked, squinting and tilting his head. "Oh, thank God."

"Enrico Martinez, I thought I recognized your car. Who's the girl?" Matty nodded at the open door.

"Just a friend. I'm glad it's you, though. I'm sorry if we were causing any problems, we'll be out of here in thirty seconds," Rico said. Matty shined the flashlight into his face. Rico threw up his hands to block the light. "What are you doing?"

"You're blitzed right now, aren't you?"

"No, I'm not," Rico lied.

"Hands on the car." Matty forced Rico to place his hands against the hood. He patted the boy down before reaching into one of Rico's front pockets and pulling out a small baggie with two white pills in it.

"It's not what it looks like," Rico pleaded.

"You know the drill," Matty responded, and read Rico his rights, placing cuffs on him. "Miss, you need to get out of the vehicle right now."

Chloe emerged, makeup streaked down her face, and wearing Rico's shirt. The shirt was big on her, landing midthigh. Matty focused the light on her eyes, discovering they were equally as bloodshot as Rico's. He placed her in handcuffs too. He and his partner led the two of them to the back of their escort car and shut them in before calling for a tow truck.

"I can't go to jail. My parents are going to kill me," Chloe choked, tears pouring down her face.

"Don't worry, they'll call my dad. He'll get us out of this," Rico said, and hoped it was true.

***

They were able to convince the police to allow them to put their clothes back on, but they had to wait in the cruiser and watch the SUV get towed.

"Can we speed this up please, Matty?" Rico asked once they were on the road, the annoyance in his voice obvious.

"It's Officer Rhodes," Matty sneered. Rico rolled his eyes and slouched back into his seat.

They reached the station and were led inside and separated. Hours later a different officer came and retrieved Rico, leading him down the grimy hall, the officer's boots squeaking on the linoleum as the fluorescent lights flickered overhead. The high from the pills and spliff Rico enjoyed during the show had worn off, and his wrists were sore from the tight cuffs. The officer pushed him through a door, and Rico saw his father standing at a desk in sweatpants and an old college T-shirt, talking to Matty. The two laughed, but the smile disappeared from Rico's dad's face when he spotted his son. Matty came around behind Rico and unlocked the handcuffs.

"Thank you again, Matty," Antonio said, shaking Matty's hand.

"I'm sorry, but it was for Enrico's own safety. I couldn't allow him to drive," Matty answered.

"I appreciate it. We'll see you for the game on Sunday?" Antonio asked.

"Of course, Andrea and I will pick up some wings." Matty smiled. Antonio grabbed Rico by the arm, his fingers digging into his son's biceps, and pulled him through the station.

"What about Chloe?" Rico asked his dad.

"She's not our problem," Antonio said, shoving Rico through the front door.

"We can't just leave her here," Rico said.

"Either you get in the car with me right now, or I will march you right back into this station and have Matty re-cuff you." Antonio glared at his son. Rico glanced from his dad to the station door, conceding defeat and following him through the parking lot. Antonio's black sports car was sleek and immaculate; there wasn't a speck of dust on the dashboard and the new-car smell was pungent. Antonio started the ignition and Rico glanced at the radio clock to check the time: 4:37 a.m. "This is the last time I save you, Enrico. You should be ashamed of yourself."

Neither Rico nor Antonio spoke until they pulled up to a modest suburban house, the lawn well kept but simple. Antonio asked where Rico's mom, his ex-wife, was.

"She's working overnights," Rico answered. He reached down to unbuckle his seat belt, but Antonio grabbed his sore wrist.

"She's been leaving you unsupervised to run around and do what you want at night? I'm having a talk with her; she's going to start working days again."

"That's the thing, Dad." Rico loaded the moniker with as much anger as he could. "When you run off with your client and file for a divorce, you don't have a say in what she does anymore." He yanked his arm free, released his seat belt, and slammed the door behind him. He stomped up the driveway without looking back and punched the code into the garage door. The door slid up and Rico slipped underneath it, quickly hitting the button to close it.

Rico checked himself in the bathroom mirror. His exhaustion showed on his face, and even though he felt completely sober, his eyes remained red. He peeled his foul-smelling shirt and pants off and brushed his teeth while in his boxers. The medicine cabinet hinges creaked as he grabbed eye drops. The alarm clock read 5:24 a.m. by the time he climbed into bed and pulled the covers up over his head.

It felt as if his eyes had just closed when the comforter was ripped from him.

"Get up." Melissa swatted the top of Rico's head. "C'mon."

Moaning and rolling over, Rico mashed a pillow over his head with one hand to block out his mom's voice. He patted around the bed searching for the sheet.

"Nope," Melissa said, yanking the pillow out of her son's grasp and tossing it through the open door and down the hall.

Rico checked the clock; he'd only been asleep for forty-five minutes. "Mom, please."

"Don't 'mom, please,' me. Get up." Melissa grabbed the corner of the comforter and dragged it down the hall with her, ensuring he could not try to go back to sleep. Rico rolled onto his back and stared at the ceiling. He sat up, grabbed a T-shirt from his dresser, and followed his mom to the kitchen. Melissa stood at the coffee pot, measuring grounds into a filter, her back to Rico as he plopped into a seat at the table. A few minutes later, Melissa retrieved two mugs from the cabinet, filled them with steaming coffee, and set a mug in front of Rico. She sat opposite him and waited.

"I take it I'm not going back to bed anytime soon?" Rico asked.

"Maybe you should have thought about that before getting arrested and having your car impounded," Melissa snapped. Rico looked down at the coffee mug, his face red from embarrassment. "How do you think I felt getting off a twelve-hour shift to a call from your father?"

"Why'd you even answer? We don't need to talk to him," Rico exclaimed.

"This isn't about who does or doesn't need to talk to him. This is about the fact that you were caught naked with some girl in a public parking lot high out of your mind. You're lucky it was Matty that caught you; someone else might not have released you so easily." Melissa slammed her hand down on the table. "Dammit, Rico. How are we supposed to make this work when I can't trust you?"

"I'm sorry, okay? I didn't mean to get arrested," Rico said.

"I'd hope not! I doubt many people hope to get arrested. What if you'd gotten behind the wheel and killed someone? What if you'd killed yourself? What were you thinking?" Melissa demanded.

"I wasn't—that's the thing with drugs, you don't have to think. That's why they're so great," Rico said, raising his voice.

"I can't keep doing this. First you get suspended from school, and then last month you steal beer from a gas station, and now this. When does it end?" The anger dissipated from Melissa's voice and was replaced with desperation. A tear slid down her cheek. "Do you blame me?"

"What?" Rico asked.

"Do you blame me for your father leaving?"

"Of course not. He's garbage," Rico spat.

"You can't stay angry at him forever. I get that you're upset, and you have every right to be. But he didn't abandon you—he left me. And I've let him go because this is the way things have to be now. You have to let your anger toward him go as well. You can't keep acting out in revenge," Melissa explained.

Rico drank a large mouthful of coffee to avoid talking. He'd heard this same speech time and time again for the past year. Every time he landed in hot water it was the same story. Swallowing, he said, "I want him to feel the same way he made us feel."

"I wanted that for a long time too, I really did. But keeping that inside will destroy you, and I don't want you to become the same bitter person I was, and that he still is." Melissa finished her coffee and got up from the table. "I'm too wired to go to bed, and you're not getting out of this scot-free. Gather up the laundry and start a load in the washer, and then get the lawn mower out because the grass needs to be cut. I need to vacuum."

She opened a hall closet and removed a vacuum cleaner, her relaxation ritual of a complete-house scrub down in full effect. The coffee made Rico jittery and alert, even though his mind and body were calling for bed. He knew better than to protest his mom's orders.

The entire morning was spent on house and yard work. Melissa finally retreated to her room and after a few moments Rico heard the water running from her bathroom. He stopped midway to his own bathroom at the sound of the doorbell. He was surprised to see Antonio twice in one day.

"Where's your mom?" his father asked, stepping through the entryway.

"She's in the bath," Rico answered.

"I tried calling her again; she didn't answer. You look like death." Antonio sized his son up from head to toe.

"Thanks, do you need something?"

"You better watch your tone when speaking to me. I came by to tell you I picked your car up from the lot."

"Cool, can I have the keys?"

"No, you can't. Until you prove that you're responsible and deserving, it will be staying at my house. Are we clear?"

"Crystal. If that's what you came all the way over here for, then you're welcome to leave now." Rico crossed his arms.

"Tell your mom to answer her phone." Antonio opened the front door and stormed out, slamming it and rattling the picture frames on the wall. Rico locked the door before finally closing himself into the bathroom and turning the hot water up as high as it would go. Once the bathroom was full of steam, he stepped under the scorching stream in an attempt to scrub away the past twenty-four hours.

4. RICO

After

Rico awakes to gentle rocking. He sits up, disoriented. His brain starts to wake up, and he recognizes the interior of the boat's cabin. Slipping out from under the blankets, he tucks them tightly around the small body next to him. He reaches under the bed and feels for the loaded shotgun before unlocking the cabin door and peering up the steps to the deck.

The early morning sun warms his face. A seagull flies overhead and dives into a wave, emerging with a small fish. The boat rocks and tilts in the water adding serenity, long forgotten, to the morning. Rico sits in the captain's chair, placing the shotgun on top of the steering control panel, and pulls his knees up to his chest. He stares out across the vast open ocean, his back to the coastline.

"Rico?" A small hand curls around the edge of the cabin door, holding it slightly open, a sliver of a face and a hazel eye illuminated by the light filtering down the stairwell.

"Hey, kiddo. It's okay, you can come up," Rico says. The door opens and a young boy emerges, steadying himself with the handrail. His bare feet slide along the wooden deck, and he wraps his arms around Rico's waist.

"I woke up and you were gone."

"I'm sorry, Jayden. I didn't want to wake you up." Rico ruffles the kid's already messy hair, which has turned a lighter brown during their week on the boat and in the sun.

"I thought they got you."

Rico drops down to one knee and pulls Jayden in tight. "I promise you, they're never going to take me away from you."

"Pinky promise?"

Rico holds out his pinky and Jayden wraps his own tiny finger around it. They shake.

"I'm hungry," Jayden says.

Rico laughs at the boy's ability to shift focus, never fully allowing the fear in. He retreats to the cabin and realizes their food supply is nearly exhausted. He grabs the last fruit cup, a small package of cookies, and one of three bottles of water. "Eat the fruit before the cookies."

Jayden takes the food and sits against the starboard side. He slurps the juice before grabbing pieces of diced pears and oranges. After finishing the fruit, he tears into the package of cookies, offering it out to Rico.

"I want pizza," Jayden says, bits of cookie tumbling from his mouth.

"Don't talk with food in your mouth," Rico responds.

Jayden swallows the mouthful. "Where are we going? When are you going to take me home?"

"I've told you, kid, I can't take you home."

"Because of the aliens?"

"Yeah, because of the aliens."

Rico waits for the kid to push the subject, to finally reject the explanation given for those *things* that have taken over the land. Try as he might, Rico knows he can only shelter Jayden from the truth for so long. However, Jayden reaches into the package and pulls out another cookie, seemingly satisfied with the answer.

"How long do we have to stay out here on the boat?"

"You ask a lot of questions."

"I'm a kid; I want to know things." Jayden rolls his eyes.

"Curiosity killed the cat." Rico smiles, but it disappears when the realization of his words hits him. Rico looks out at the coast. They are close enough to make out lifeguard stands along the deserted beach and the dark windows of the buildings just beyond the sand. The only cars in the street are motionless.

Rico buckles Jayden into a life jacket before putting his own on. They need supplies. The boat sputters but doesn't start. Rico tries again, but nothing happens.

"Dammit." Rico slaps the steering wheel.

"What's wrong?" Jayden asks.

"Nothing," Rico lies.

"Is it broke?" Jayden asks.

"No, no, it's not broken. I think we're just out of gas. We'll get some when we land. Can you do me a favor?"

Rico directs Jayden down into the cabin to retrieve their shoes, the gas can, and duffel bag. Rico opens up the storage well and drags out the life raft. He drops it overboard as it auto-inflates, unfolding and expanding enough to easily carry them to and from shore with supplies.

"I got 'em," Jayden calls, returning to the deck.

Rico accepts the gas can and the duffel bag. "Okay, listen to me, I'm going to pick you up and lower you into the raft. When I put you in, I need you to move to the side so I have room to get in too, do you understand?"

"Yeah."

Rico lifts Jayden and slowly lowers him over the side of the boat until his feet touch the raft's bottom. The current and waves move the raft to and fro, and Rico only releases his hold when Jayden assures him he's balanced. Rico quickly dashes across the deck and retrieves the shotgun.

"Here, hold this for me." Rico extends the gun sideways to Jayden so the barrel isn't pointed at either one of them. "Be careful, careful. Don't put your hands near the trigger—steady it. Let it point out over the water not down at the floor."

"I've got it," Jayden says, wrapping one hand around the barrel and one hand around the stock. Jayden sits down and scoots backward to give Rico space. Rico sits on the side of the boat, lowering himself feet-first until he's in the raft as well.

After taking the shotgun back from Jayden, Rico moves to the front of the raft and lays the gun across his lap. He grasps the oars and lowers them into the water. Rico uses less strength to row as they come closer to the beach, the current pulling them forward, but he is forced to remain focused and determined to keep the raft straight and prevent it from capsizing. A wave swells up under the raft, lifting it.

"Jayden, hold on tight!" Rico yells, shoving his feet into the crevices to gain traction and stability. The wave crashes, spilling water into the raft and flooding the floor as another wave catches them. They slam back down, taking on additional water. Rico hops out over the side, his shoes filling with water, and grabs the front of the raft, dragging it up to the dry sand. An odor undercuts the briny air. Decay.

"C'mon." Rico holds out his hand.

"Can I take my shoes off?" Jayden asks. "I like walking in the sand."

"I don't know; we need to see what we can find and get back to the boat," Rico answers.

"But my shoes and socks are all wet."

"I'll tell you what, let's move quickly and gather up as much as we can. If we get back to the beach and the sun is still out, we'll hang out and have a picnic and you can take your shoes off," Rico offers.

"It's only the morning, we have all day," Jayden counters.

"Exactly, so there's a strong chance we'll be back here with plenty of sunlight. Deal?"

"Deal."

Rico holds out his fist, offering his pinky. He leads the kid farther up the beach, keeping watch. He turns his attention to a building across the street, having caught movement in his peripheral vision. But it is nothing more than a curtain flapping in an upper-level window, caught through the open window by the sea breeze. An unsettling feeling takes hold in the pit of his stomach, the feeling of being watched, and Rico hurries the boy along, eager to return to the boat.

5. ASHER

Before

The summer sun had warmed the pool so that it felt like bathwater. Asher held his breath as he sank until his bare butt touched the bottom. Without any noise permeating the water, Asher was able to shut off all thoughts and relax as he drifted, and he felt at peace for the first time in a while. It did not last long; his lungs began to burn. He kicked off from the bottom and gasped for air when he broke the surface.

"Oh good, you didn't drown. You had me worried for a minute that you hit your head." Asher was startled to find Ellis merely a foot away and quickly splashed backward in surprise.

"Sorry, I didn't realize you were there."

"When you didn't resurface, I got a bit worried, wanted to make sure the alcohol didn't do you in."

"Yeah, thanks."

"So this is what all of the craze is about? Skinny-dipping doesn't feel much different to me, although I guess there is a bit of an exhilarating thrill at the thought of it. It's a shame Stacey's passed out, she's missing a free preview of things to come." Ellis dipped back below the water and swam laps. Asher, confused about the proper etiquette in the situation, retrieved the shoes. He placed them next to the pool and leaned against the wall, looking up into the star-filled sky.

"It's a good thing we're doing this tonight, and not when the moon is actually full; that's when the crazies come out."

Asher jumped from shock again. "Jesus, can you stop doing that?"

"Jesus is here? What's he doing?" Ellis rapidly spun around as if to catch a glimpse. "Is he walking on water? Is he invisible? Why can't I see him, does that mean I'm going to hell?"

Asher couldn't help but laugh. "Not actually Jesus. You. You keep sneaking up on me."

"You just make it so easy to do." Ellis rested his back against the edge and started to float his body toward the surface. Asher cleared his throat as a precaution before Ellis's body broached the surface and Ellis sank back down. "It's like we're on our own little date since Stacey passed out. And think, you didn't even have to buy me dinner first to get me naked." He knew Ellis was joking, but Asher fidgeted regardless. After a moment of awkward silence, interrupted only by Stacey's snoring, Ellis spoke up again.

"What's your favorite color?"

"Uh, blue, I guess."

"You guess? It's your favorite color."

"Blue."

"Attaboy. I'd say mine is green."

"What are you, a leprechaun?"

"You've got jokes now, do you? Yeah, watch out, I'm going to steal your pot of gold."

"Good luck, you'll probably find it before I do."

"Favorite movie?"

"That's a tough one. Maybe *Jerry Maguire*."

"'You had me at hello.'" Ellis mocked Asher's response by making a crying face. On an impulse Asher lunged forward and shoved Ellis under the water. Ellis reemerged sputtering water and laughing. "You're out of your mind! I don't think we can be friends anymore."

"Oh, we're friends now?"

"Not anymore, you nearly killed me."

Headlights crossed over their heads, and Asher spotted a security guard pulling up in a golf cart. Ellis saw the look of fear on Asher's face and followed his eye line out to the parking lot. "Dammit." He quickly hoisted himself out of the water and ran for his pile of clothes.

"Who's in there? The pool's closed," the security guard called out, approaching the fence to investigate.

"Asher, hurry up," Ellis hissed, pulling up his pants. Asher rushed to follow suit, pulling on his boxers and shoving his arms through his sleeves without buttoning up his shirt. He threw his pants over his shoulder and snatched Stacey's shoes. Each guy grabbed one of Stacey's arms and lifted her from the lounge.

"Whasgoinon?"

"Shh, don't worry about it. C'mon, we gotta go."

"Stop right there!" the guard yelled, a flashlight illuminating their worried faces. The guard had yet to enter the fenced-in enclosure and was on the opposite side of the pool, granting the three an opportunity to wobble through another gate.

"Sorry, sir! It won't happen again, promise!" Ellis called over his shoulder as they escaped across a patch of grass toward his building. "We're up on the third floor."

They took their time crawling up the stairs with Stacey supported between them, as Ellis guided them to Stacey's front door.

"Stacey, wake up. Wake up, we need your keys." Ellis tapped her on the cheek and she opened her eyes.

"Why are you guys so wet?"

"We went swimming. We had to recover your shoes. Remember you threw them in the pool?"

"I hate those shoes."

"We know. Now c'mon, where are your keys?"

"My shoes?"

"No, your keys."

"I hate those shoes."

"Yeah, you told us."

"Let me just check her purse," Asher said. He rooted through the debris, shoving aside her wallet, phone, and old gum wrappers as change rattled around until his fingers touched rigid metal. He tried three keys before finding the right one. The apartment was pitch-black and smelled of vanilla. They tiptoed in order not to wake anyone, pausing in their tracks when Asher's weight elicited a loud creak from a loose board.

Ellis took charge, using his free arm to find the wall and navigate through the dark. They stumbled to the bed and settled Stacey in. Asher dumped the shoes on the ground, and, as they left the room, Stacey said, "I'm sorry for ruining our first date."

"Don't worry, I had fun."

"I was really nervous; I thought you wouldn't like me."

"I think you're great—get some rest."

"Next time I won't be so nervous. I'll stay sober."

"Sounds like a deal. G'night."

They slipped out of the room and closed the door. Asher locked the front door from inside before they stepped out onto the landing between Stacey's and Ellis's apartments. He secured the door behind them.

"Thanks for all of your help tonight. I appreciate it."

"No problem, it was cool getting to know you. Are you good to drive?"

"Yeah. I only had a couple of drinks, and it's been like an hour since we left the party?" Asher checked his watch. "Shit, it's almost four."

"I've got a couch you could crash on just to be safe."

"Thanks, but I need to change into something drier anyway."

"Cool, well, drive safe."

Asher descended the stairs and walked to his car while Ellis unlocked his front door and disappeared inside.

6. ASHER

After

"It's so freaking humid," Wendy complains, swatting away a mosquito. The storm has finally abated and they continue down the road, utilizing what little sunlight remains. Wendy's shirt is soaked with sweat. "I'm going to sweat to death before anything else."

"What I wouldn't give for a dip in a swimming pool," Asher responds, a bead of sweat dripping into his eye and blurring his vision.

"I'd settle for a hair tie. I'm about to take my knife and hack it all off." Wendy holds her hair up on top of her head. "Not to mention it's nasty and smells from not being washed."

"I don't think it looks too bad," Asher says, ignoring the matting in her once-shiny hair.

"Want to trade?" Wendy smiles but releases her hair. "Hey, look in this one!"

Asher trots over to the SUV while Wendy tests the handles. He sees a case of water and several other grocery bags in the trunk and circles around to try the remaining handles. None of them gives.

"There's too much stuff in here; we can't leave it," Wendy proclaims. They observe their immediate surroundings. They haven't encountered any threats since the man in the woods, their path along the highway thus far clear of danger. Asher lifts the baseball bat up over his shoulder as if preparing for a pitcher to throw a ball. He swings the bat with all of his strength at one of the windows, causing a shattering clamor, magnified in the disturbing silence. He preps the bat once more, swings, connects, and sends glass fragments tinkling to the ground.

Wendy unlocks the door and climbs over the seat into the trunk, hefting the bags through to Asher. He sifts through the goods, separating the useful on the seat from the useless on the floor, while Wendy pulls water bottles free from the plastic casing, replenishing the supply in her running belt.

"The bread and eggs won't be of any use, but there's some canned fruit and—" Asher glances up, his words catching in his throat. "Wendy, get down."

"What?" Wendy asks, maintaining her focus on the stream of water transferring between bottles. Asher grabs her by the shoulder, the ends of his fingers turning white as he squeezes harder than intended. His face is pale and he stares past Wendy through the back windshield.

"Lie down. Now," Asher whispers, giving her a light push. He slowly pulls the door shut, more glass shards falling out and bouncing against the ground. The door closes with a soft thump.

Six of the turned are visible through the back windshield. The closest is four feet from the back of the SUV and stumbling slowly forward. Her stringy hair is ripped out in patches and flesh is missing from her left cheek, the wound scabbed over and grisly. Her flesh has begun to gray, and her searching eyes are sunken in. The soiled clothes she's wearing are dark and soaked, but Asher's unable to tell if it's blood or the storm.

Lying on the floor of the trunk, Wendy reaches down toward her calf and pulls a hunting knife from the sheath strapped to her leg. She scoots her body up against the tailgate of the trunk, her foot hitting the case of water and crinkling the plastic. Asher looks down at her and shakes his head. The bodies angling forward don't react.

Asher lowers his backpack, freeing his arms. Sliding down in the seat, he keeps his gaze locked on the approaching woman and her companions. He opens the carton of spoiled eggs. He waits, counting his breaths in his head, until the woman is inches from the back windshield. Asher sits and launches the first egg through the broken window, over the roof of the car parked next to them. It splatters against a car in the far right lane.

The woman's head jerks, searching for the source of the commotion. Asher sends a second egg flying, and it cracks inches from the first. The woman screeches, changing course toward the broken eggs. Asher grabs a third egg and throws it. He watches all six of the infected drift from the car, following the lead of the woman.

"Stay here," he whispers.

"What are you doing?" Wendy asks, sitting up.

Asher crawls forward, sending a fourth egg sailing across at his target. He leans out the window, placing both of his hands on the top of the car to lift his weight. The roof is still wet from the rain and, as his butt clears the window frame, his left hand slips. He loses his balance and falls backward from the SUV, twisting to brace himself. He lands on the broken glass and pavement, left arm first, his feet knocking loudly against the door. As he looks up, he locks eyes with the infected man trailing the pack.

Ignoring the stabs of pain in his arm and the droplets of blood forming on his skin, Asher staggers to his feet, wasting no time in flinging the door open and snatching the baseball bat. When he spins around, he is forced to confront Scabbed Cheek, the egged car now abandoned. Asher jumps into the fray, kicking his foot and sending her sprawling backward into one of her companions. Glass crunches under his feet as he abandons the SUV for the car parked next to it. All six sets of eyes bore into him as he pounds the bat against the hood before disappearing around the side of the egged car. He drops down to a crouch on the overgrown shoulder and glances around for any previously unseen infected. A body lies several yards away, the face covered in blood and the throat torn out. There aren't any flies buzzing above it and the sky is absent of vultures; it's a fresh kill, the pack having feasted on the corpse until Asher shattered the window. Asher regains his feet and looks through the car's windows. All six infected continue toward him.

Asher darts east, doubling back a few cars behind them to approach the group from the rear. He edges up behind the last member, bringing the bat down on the man's head. He crumples to the ground. Asher smashes the head once more before bringing the bat sideways across the jaw of a female and sending her crashing into a car. The other four have turned their attention toward him, allowing Asher to see that the next closest threat is the most freshly turned—his cheeks remain rosy, but his eyes are consumed with rage and hunger. Pus bubbles from the bite wound on the man's hand when he reaches out.

Asher swings the bat upward, catching the man under the chin and snapping his head backward. The man collapses to the ground with a gurgle in his throat. Asher stomps his foot on the man's neck, stopping the noise. The fourth and fifth members of the pack go down easily, their bodies already weakened and starved. Scabbed Cheek is nowhere to be seen. Asher jogs toward the SUV—his pounding feet on the pavement cover the noise of a foot being dragged across the surface. He catches the sound too late and is caught off guard when a force knocks him. Asher has allowed the woman to gain the upper ground; a large truck had blocked her presence, and she sends both of them into the side of a car. He pushes away from her hot and rancid breath.

He grabs her clothes and thrusts her back, her teeth inches from his face and her hands trying to find purchase on his shoulders. Suddenly, her force lessens and her body goes slack, dropping in front of him. Wendy stands next to him, her raised hand holding a blood-covered hunting knife. Asher watches the blood run from the wound in the woman's temple, mix with her stringy hair, and pool around her head.

"Thanks," Asher pants, bending over with his hands on his knees.

"Don't try and be the hero again," Wendy answers, turning her back to him and walking away.

7. ASHER

Before

Asher rolled onto his back at the sound of his phone, the sun hitting him fully in the face through the window. He squinted, and snippets of the previous night slipped into his mind. The phone vibrated on the nightstand again—two text messages, both from Stacey. He tapped the screen and opened the messages. The first, at 9:00 a.m. read, Im so so so so sooooooo sorry about last night. The second text: pls tell me u forgive me and that I didn't do anything 2 embarrassing. He smiled and typed a response.

A: Don't worry about it. You apologized enough last night. Besides, it was kinda cute to be your knight in shining armor. At least you didn't puke ON me, lol.

S: OMG. Was I rly that bad?

A: Nah. How're you feeling today? Hungover?

S: Dead. Im in bed w/ covers over my head. Can't move or I'll vom. Again.

A: I saw plenty of that last night.

S: Ugh. Im going 2 kill myself.

Asher threw the blankets off. He was slightly hungover as well. He shuffled to the bathroom, stepping on his discarded clothing, and turned the shower on. He popped an aspirin and stepped in. The shower was too hot, scalding his skin at first touch, but he was too tired to bother changing it, instead resting his forehead against the cooler tiles to alleviate the throbbing in his head. It was relaxing in a sense, the steam clearing his sinuses and the water opening his pores. By the time he stepped out of the shower and toweled off, his headache was gone. His eyes were still red from the chlorine and his stubble was more noticeable than was allowed at work, but it was a Saturday. There wouldn't be any managers at the coffee shop; only students had the pleasure of the weekend shifts.

**

Asher pulled into a parking space in front of Stacey's building and grabbed the shopping bag off the passenger seat. A guy emerged from a car a couple of spots down. He was tall and pale with dark hair and a scowl plastered on his face. Asher locked the car and headed to the staircase, and the stranger followed, hanging back a few paces, his hands shoved in his pockets and looking down at the ground as he walked. But when Asher stopped at Stacey's door, the other guy continued and knocked on the door two apartments down before opening it and walking in. Stacey answered in sweatpants and a ratty T-shirt, her hair pulled back, and dark circles around her eyes. Seeing Asher, however, gave her a spark and her eyes lit up.

"What are you doing here? I look a mess," she said with a weak smile. "Come in." He stepped over the threshold and lifted the bag.

"I can't stay. I have work, but I wanted to make sure you were feeling better and drop off a hangover kit." He handed the bag over, and while Stacey looked through it, he named off everything. "There's aspirin for the headache, ginger ale for the nausea, a lemon-lime sports drink for rehydrating, and I would have gotten you a burger but the gas station didn't have any, and I'm not sure a gas station burger would be any good. So . . ." He felt sheepish, standing with his arms crossed, the smell of vanilla overpowering his senses. His headache had reemerged.

"Wow, what did I do to deserve this?" Stacey stood on her tiptoes to kiss his cheek. "Thank you, this is so sweet."

Asher blushed, awkwardly hugging her. He thanked her for inviting him to the party and explained that he had fun and enjoyed Stacey's presence even if she didn't remember everything. He advised her to get some rest and excused himself for running out, but he needed to get to work before he was late.

"Maybe I'll feel well enough to go get that burger when you get off work?"

"Yeah, just let me know." They hugged once more, and Asher left. Out on the landing he glanced toward the door the stranger had entered, then returned to his car.

***

The weekend passed for Asher in a blur of work, homework, and texting with Stacey—who remained too unwell to make good on dinner. He arrived early to campus on Monday, washed the sweat from biking to campus in the day's heat off his forehead, and sat outside his next class with a book.

"Strawberry-banana or mango-pineapple?"

Asher looked up and saw Ellis, a cup in each hand.

"I figured you were probably tired of coffee, and I don't care for it in the first place. So I got smoothies. But I didn't know what kind you'd like, so I picked up options." Ellis sat next to Asher. "So, what'll it be? Strawberry-banana or mango-pineapple?"

"Strawberry-banana. Thank you."

"Don't worry about it. What're you reading?" Asher flipped the book, displaying the cover: *Juliet, Naked* by Nick Hornby. Ellis raised his eyebrows. "Naked?"

"Not like that."

"Either way, I haven't heard of it; is it any good?"

"I'm not very far into it, but I love it so far," Asher answered, returning it to his bag.

"Are they making a movie of it? I'm more of a movie guy."

"Not sure. But there are movie versions of a few of his other books. You should check them out."

"Have you seen them?"

"I've read all of his books, but I've only seen a couple of the movies."

"We'll have to watch the rest, then," Ellis said. The door to the classroom opened and students poured out. Asher and Ellis stood and entered the empty room. Asher paused, unsure if he should take his usual seat toward the back of the room or if he was supposed to sit toward the middle with Ellis. Thankfully, he didn't have to decide. Ellis found the desk next to Asher's usual spot and sat. Asher settled in as Ellis asked about the rest of his weekend. He told Ellis of Stacey's hangover and his work schedule.

"What about you?" Asher asked.

"Relaxed at home a bit Saturday and cleaned the apartment. I lead an adventurous life. Yesterday I just went to my parents' house for family dinner."

"Your parents live nearby?"

"Yeah, they're professors here. My sister and I get free tuition, but neither of us wanted to live at home. I have my own place, but Ivy has a roommate. Our parents wanted us to get a full college experience, as long as we show up to dinner once a week."

"That's cool, sounds like your family is close."

"For the most part. What about yours?"

"They're all in Small Town, North Carolina. We're pretty close as well, I guess, but I needed some time and distance to myself, y'know?"

Professor Bernstein entered and called the class to attention. Asher sat back and drank the rest of his smoothie while Bernstein droned on about colonial settlements. Asher nearly dozed off, but Ellis nudged his shoulder. They hung back from the rush of students shoving toward the door when the lecture ended, neither of them in a hurry.

"I don't have your number." Ellis handed Asher his phone to key it in.

"Send me a text so I have yours. What are you up to tonight?" Asher asked.

"Group project, and then I have dinner plans. You?" Ellis replied.

"Just studying, I have an exam tomorrow."

"Sucks. Good luck on your exam, though hit me up if your brain needs a break." Ellis held the glass door open. Asher thanked him for the smoothie and promised to take him up on the offer. As he unlocked his bike chain he felt his phone vibrate.

E: This is Ellis! Now you have my number.

8. RICO

Before

"Chloe! Wait up!" Rico rushed down the high school hallway. He reached out to stop her.

"I'm going to be late to class," Chloe said, shrugging his hand off. He pushed past another student to walk alongside her.

"We have four minutes until the bell rings. I tried calling you all weekend," Rico said. Chloe stopped and faced him.

"My parents took away my phone. Some people actually get in trouble when the police arrest them." Chloe rolled her eyes and continued down the hall. Rico chased after her, arguing that he tried to convince his father to assist her.

Chloe ignored him and opened a classroom door. Rico followed her and sat at the same two-person lab counter. Students flowed into the classroom and took up their assigned seats. Mr. Evans stepped out of his office as the bell rang, the conversations dying into silence. Chloe slid off her stool and pulled a note from her purse. Rico watched as she walked to the front of the classroom and handed the note to Mr. Evans. He glanced up to look at Rico.

"Ethan, can you and Rico swap seats? I apologize for the switch up." Mr. Evans placed the note in his lab coat pocket, turning to the board and writing out the lesson plan. Chloe returned to her seat without glancing at Rico. Rico marched to the back of the classroom and took the vacated seat Ethan left behind. Mr. Evans ignored Rico's behavior and launched into the lecture. Everyone hurried to take notes. After class, the bell rang and Rico shoved students out of his way to be the first out the door.

He caught sight of a familiar face entering the boy's restroom and ducked in after him. The bathroom stank of urine, the garbage can was overflowing, and the floor was crusted with dirt. Rico bent over and searched under the stall partitions. In the very last stall, for the disabled, he saw a pair of boots. Rico tapped his knuckles against the door and heard the lock turn. Doug, in his full combat glory of boots, baggy jeans, and a camouflage T-shirt, stepped back.

"Rico Suave, my main man." Doug clapped Rico on the back. "What can I do you for?"

"The usual." Rico pulled his wallet out of his back pocket.

"I heard you got busted this weekend," Doug said, accepting the money. He bent down and unzipped the main compartment of his pack, pulling out a sandwich bag of pills.

"Don't worry, I didn't sell you out," Rico said.

"I'm not worried, I've got you and you've got me." Doug handed over a smaller bag with six pills inside. He heckled Rico about ditching Chloe, the story having spread across the school.

"It's not true. People need to keep their mouths shut. Chloe won't even talk to me right now, but—" Rico was cut off by the one-minute bell. Doug held his hands up, only meaning to relay the rumor before leaving Rico behind for class. Rico pocketed the baggie of pills and followed Doug. Only the stragglers remained in the hallway, scurrying to beat the final bell. Rico fingered the pills in his pocket, his mind far from school. The bell rang, and he hurried away from the restroom. He left the building, stepping into vibrant sunlight.

***

Halfway into his walk home, Rico popped a pill. He put his headphones on and turned up the volume. When he slipped through the door, he was in a state of delirious euphoria. Melissa was passed out on the couch with the television on, and Rico sneaked to his room without confrontation. He allowed his thoughts to fade away, his mind enraptured by the drugs and music, and went from dancing alone to nodding off on the floor. Light no longer filtered through his window; the moon had replaced the sun. He was coming down from his high and his stomach began to grumble. An open energy drink rested on his bedside table.

There was a note on the kitchen counter from his mom, telling him a plate of food was waiting in the microwave and that she'd been called in to work. He chugged the drink while he reheated the meal. His phone was devoid of any missed texts or calls from Chloe, and, even though he was not expecting any, his heart sank. There was a text from Doug, though, containing only an address. Hitting reply, he typed: No car. Give me a ride?

He was shoveling food into his mouth when his phone beeped with a text: 10 minutes. Rico finished his meal and dropped the dish into the sink without rinsing it. He changed shirts and checked his pocket for the five remaining pills. A horn blasted, and he grabbed his keys and rushed out. Doug was waiting, windows down on his junker car and rock music blaring.

"Hurry up," he screamed through the open window. Rico hustled down the driveway. Doug handed him a blunt, and Rico placed it to his lips, inhaling deeply. Doug shifted the car into drive and pulled away from the curb, asking about Rico's SUV. Rico explained the story.

"You weren't in History today," Doug said, supporting the argument against Rico's sense of responsibility.

"Okay, Dad." Rico took another drag of the blunt before passing it back.

"I'm just saying. I don't want my best customer to get the boot. Again." Rico turned up the music, drowning out Doug's voice. He leaned his seat back and closed his eyes until the car came to a halt, and Doug killed the engine. The radio cut off, but it was replaced by music emanating two houses down from where they parked on the car-lined street. Rico recognized several vehicles from school and other parties.

An unfamiliar guy standing inside the door thrust red plastic cups into their hands and directed them to the kitchen. A crowd surrounded the keg, and nobody seemed to have intentions of moving.

Rico squeezed his way through, reaching for the tap. He filled the first cup and traded it to Doug for the empty one. Rico looked around, but there was no sign of Chloe.

Doug left to make his business rounds, patting his bulky cargo pockets with a wink. Rico walked the main floor of the house before stepping out the sliding doors to the backyard. Another crowd stood around the pool, shouts and laughter carrying from the swimmers. Sheila, Chloe's best friend, leaned against the pool slide talking to a boy from another school. Rico was halfway to Sheila when she looked at him, her expression souring.

"Well, look who had the nerve to show his face," Sheila sneered.

"Hey, Sheil." Rico ignored her tone and asked, "Is Chloe coming?"

She excused herself from the boy before addressing Rico again. "Even if she was going to be here, what makes you think she'd have anything to do with you? What, getting her locked up wasn't good enough for you?"

"Are you the one going around telling people I did that?"

"So what if I am? It's true, isn't it?"

"Forget it. When you see her, will you just ask her to talk to me?"

"Good luck with that," Sheila said, turning back to her suitor.

Rico downed his beer as he walked away from the pool. He swallowed another pill and tossed the empty cup in a bush. He headed to the living room, drawn by the music. People swayed back and forth, conversation impossible. He felt hands against his hips and smiled.

"You showed up." He opened his eyes expecting to see Chloe, but instead an unknown girl was pressed up against him, dancing.

"Oh. Hi." The girl couldn't hear him but continued dancing with him. She leaned forward, planting a kiss on him, and he smelled the liquor on her breath. Rico stepped back, and a sudden urge to leave overcame him. He walked off without an excuse and found the bathroom.

Rico washed his hands after flushing the toilet and opened the door, coming face-to-face with Sheila again.

"I wonder how interested Chloe will be to see this," she said, holding up her phone, showing a photo of Rico and the girl kissing. Sheila smiled, her impish features exaggerated by her delight, and she left Rico standing in the open doorway.

9. RICO

After

Rico and Jayden cross the street from the beach, approaching a surf shop. Shattered glass from the front door covers the ground, crunching under their shoes with each step. Rico pokes his head through the broken door, surveying the store. He sees clothing racks, several of which are knocked over, an empty drink cooler, scattered surfboards, and other beach supplies. An eerie stillness fills the stale space.

"Are we going in?" Jayden asks.

"Yeah, but don't let go of my hand." Rico steps through the door, tightening his hold on Jayden. They slowly walk through the store, listening for any sound other than their wet shoes. Rico finds men's and boys' clothing and searches through a T-shirt rack for dry alternatives.

They stand side by side, admiring the matching Day-Glo lettering that reads "Daytona Beach" down their torsos. They also wear new board shorts and water shoes. Rico packs their wet shoes and pants into the bottom of the duffel bag for safe measure along with a bottle of sunscreen. They explore the store a little more, taking candy bars and bags of trail mix, but otherwise find nothing else of use.

Rico leads Jayden from the store, shotgun over his shoulder, and Jayden proudly carries the empty gas can. The stink of decay lingers, but if Jayden is bothered by it he lets it go; only Rico scrunches up his nose when it hits in waves. A clattering noise ahead stops Rico near the edge of a run-down building, and he instinctively pulls Jayden behind him.

"What is it?" Jayden asks.

Rico quiets the boy, whispering, "Stay here."

Rico creeps forward and peers around the corner. A bald-headed man in ragged clothes bumbles around the alleyway knocking into garbage cans and spilling rotted trash, his back to the entrance. Rico relaxes his grip on the shotgun. He steps into the alleyway, kicking a crumbled soda can, the aluminum scraping against the cement.

The man turns around, and Rico sees his face. He has shock-white eyebrows and loose, wrinkled skin. The moment his bewildered eyes settle on Rico, his expression contorts into wrath. The elderly man bares his teeth and growls. Rico cocks the shotgun and secures the stock against his shoulder. He looks down the barrel, his aim slow and calculated until the man's head is locked in the sight. The figure shambles forward, but Rico is unable to pull the trigger. He lowers the gun. Although the man's clothes are tattered, they are covered in dirt, not blood. The look of confusion when he first turned around replays in Rico's mind, almost a sign of humanity before it was replaced with anger. Rico sees somebody's father, a grandfather, moving too slow to pose an actual threat.

"What's wrong with him?" Jayden asks from Rico's side.

"Jayden, I told you to stay put."

"Did the aliens get him?" Jayden asks, ignoring Rico's reprimand. Rico grabs Jayden's hand and pulls him from the alley and in front of the next building, shielding him once more. They watch until the elderly man steps out of the alley and continues into the street, having already lost track of his prey.

"We need to keep moving—let's find a gas station," Rico says.

"Are we the only ones the aliens didn't get?" Jayden asks.

"I don't know, kiddo. I'm sure there are some other people too, and we'll find them," Rico answers, hoping he is right. In the street, the mangled body of a teenage girl lies in a pool of blood. Rico steers Jayden away before the kid catches sight of the corpse. A horde of the infected block the path in front of them.

For once, Jayden remains quiet, but his hand begins to tremble in Rico's. A rancid smell drifts from the horde, repugnant, and Rico's stomach flips. It's a mixture of old blood, rotting flesh, body odor, and human waste. The infected mill around in different states of haggard anger, snarling and growling while bumping or pushing one another. Rico and Jayden watch, momentarily unnoticed. Rico slowly bends to Jayden's level.

"Look at me," Rico whispers, trying to get Jayden to turn away from the group in front of them. The boy's face is ghostly and his hand continues to shake. "Hey, look at me."

Jayden faces Rico, his bottom lip quivering, his eyes wide and filling with tears.

"I'm going to get you out of here, I promise. We're going to be safe, okay, kiddo?"

A tear slides down Jayden's face, but he nods.

"Now close your eyes and trust me," Rico whispers. He releases Jayden's hand and lifts him. The front of Rico's shirt becomes wet and warm as Jayden wraps his arms around Rico's neck accidentally knocking him in the head with the gas can, and Rico realizes Jayden peed himself out of fear. "Did you close your eyes?"

Jayden nods, burying his face into Rico's neck. Rico whispers for Jayden to keep his eyes closed, his own eyes on the body of the teenage girl in the street. Her face is unidentifiable, flesh is torn from her right arm, leaving only bone behind, and the remains of her intestines spill from her stomach. One of her legs is missing. Picking up his pace, he hurries past the body and away from immediate danger.

They cover several blocks without encountering any additional threats, and Rico allows Jayden to open his eyes and walk again. The kid launches into a plea to go home, and Rico assures him they will return to the boat as soon as they replenish their gas supply. He ruffles Jayden's hair to try to perk him up, but Jayden stares at a pothole and puffs out his chest, fighting off tears.

A large gas station occupies a corner at a traffic stop, but Rico looks on in dismay. A car, which looks to Rico like it had been engulfed in flames, has smashed through the storefront and destroyed the entire façade and most of the interior. Abandoned cars are stationed at each pump, but none of the pumps work. Rico slams his fists against the last pump and kicks the beat-up station wagon parked near it.

"Dammit."

Jayden drops the gas can, the hollow reverberation taunting Rico, and sits on top, creating a dent. Rico stifles a desperate laugh and, instead, a sob of frustration escapes his chest. Hot tears spill from his eyes, splashing on the ground as they drop from his chin.

"There's gas, just not here—" Rico stops midsentence. A skeletal hand materializes from under the station wagon, quickly followed by another hand with bloody fingertips where nails once were. The first hand reaches out farther, landing inches from Jayden. Jayden follows Rico's gaze downward, spotting the hand. He jumps up with a scream, backing away from the gas pump and the woman emerging from under the car, who is dragging herself inch by inch. "Jayden, shut up!"

Rico picks up the shotgun, aims it at the woman, and pulls the trigger. A loud shot rips through the air, and the woman's face explodes. Her head drops down to the cement but her hand twitches and moves forward. Rico fires off a second shot into the top of her head and the hand stops. He drops the shotgun and grabs his chest, trying to steady his breathing. He turns to check on Jayden, but the boy is gone.

10. ASHER

Before

The words floated nonsensically around the page. Asher closed his eyes, taking a break from his reading and forcing himself to breathe evenly. He glanced at the clock; it was only 8:17 p.m. He had been studying for hours, but it felt like days. He pushed away from the desk for a snack break to give his mind a rest. He opened the bedroom door to the sound of explosions and war machines. Derrick and Mark, his two roommates, lounged on the couch playing a video game and drinking beer.

"Yo, A, want some beer?" Mark said.

"No thanks, I'm studying for an exam," Asher answered, crossing the hall to the kitchen.

"Have a drink with us. Beer break," Mark retorted.

"I'm good, but thanks."

Cheap beer, a bottle of ketchup, and a jug of milk were the only items in the fridge. Asher grabbed a granola bar from the pantry and joined his roommates on the couch. "Let me play a round."

"You'll mess up my kill ratio," Mark said, refusing to pass the controller.

"Whenever you play you end up shooting me, not the other players," Derrick added. "Dammit, sniper got me."

"That's not true. Besides, I'm excellent with a gun," Asher protested.

"A gun in real life and a gun in a video game are completely different things," Derrick responded. "And who the hell lets you have a gun?"

"I was raised with a gun in one hand and a Bible in the other," Asher answered, with an exaggerated southern accent. He launched into a mock tirade, saying, "The South will rise again!" while texting a message to Ellis.

A: Taking you up on that study break offer. How was dinner?

"You guys don't mind if Renee comes over later, do you?" Mark asked. "She's been texting, so I told her to just come over when she gets done with class."

Derrick and Asher consented, and Asher resumed studying. Periodically, Asher checked his phone, but there was no response. It wasn't until he was nearly finished with the chapter that it vibrated.

E: It was good, went to this great Mexican place. So full!

A: Nice. Mexican sounds delicious. My fridge is just milk and beer. lol.

E: What more does a college student need? Haha. How goes the studying? Super smart yet?

A: Hey! I've always been super smart, just getting smarter! Hard to concentrate though with WWIII going on in my living room.

E: WWIII??

Asher told Ellis that Mark and Derrick spent more time playing video games and drinking than anything else. Neither of them worked, and between the two, only Derrick regularly attended classes. Asher also explained his third, unofficial roommate was Mark's girlfriend. Renee's willingness to keep the apartment clean didn't hurt, though, and she provided an out when Asher needed a break from the war sounds. Ellis asked Asher's last name, and after Asher texted back, Clarke, the messaging abruptly ended.

Seconds ticked by, and Asher gave up, resuming his reading and scratching notes on index cards to stay focused. When his phone beeped again, it was a Facebook request from Ellis Williams.

Asher accepted the friend request.

E: Nice profile picture ;)

A: Thanks.

The picture had been taken at Mark's last birthday. Renee was in hula skirt and coconut bra, her arm around Asher. He was wearing a sailor hat and had an inflatable hippopotamus inner tube around his waist. Asher felt an inclination to learn more about Ellis and abandoned any pretense of getting schoolwork done to scroll through Ellis's profile. He clicked through profile pictures but stopped at the third one. It was a picture of Ellis with the stranger Asher saw at the apartment on Saturday, except, in the photo, the guy was smiling instead of frowning and looked genuinely happy. The phone vibrated again.

E: Looks like someone is quite the ladies' man. Has Stacey seen all of these pictures?? ;)

A: lol. No, we aren't FB friends. They're all just friends.

E: uh-huh.

E: just messing with you. When are you two going on your second date?

Asher hadn't spoken to Stacey since the previous day, and they had yet to schedule their rain-check burger date. He teased Ellis about being a bachelor; other than the one picture, Ellis was alone in all of his profile pictures, and when prompted, Ellis responded that girlfriends weren't his "thing." For the second time that night, Asher's text was met with silence. He shifted uncomfortably in his chair, wondering why he had sent the last text. He never used words like "bachelor," and he couldn't explain what made him do so tonight. His fingers hovered over the screen as he searched his brain for a way to change the subject without trying too hard, but nothing seemed adequate. Another silent minute passed, so Asher tossed the phone across the room and onto his bed. He continued his note-taking.

He finished a section and arched in his seat to stretch before calling it a night. He carefully packed his school bag for the next day, the first mundane task in his nightly ritual before bed. Water from the faucet muted the sound of the phone vibrating while Asher brushed his teeth. He was burrowed under the blankets, patting his hand around the mattress for his phone so he could set his alarm, when it vibrated with a second text.

E: Hahaha.

E: Actually, no. I have a boyfriend, Brandon. We've been together almost a year now.

Asher felt a knot in his stomach; his mind jumped from the night in the pool to the smoothies the next morning. Asher reopened Ellis's profile and found a profile for a "Brandon Thomas" after a quick search. Brandon's profile picture was the smiling image of him with Ellis. Brandon was the upset guy Asher had seen before. Asher realized minutes had passed with Ellis's admission going unanswered. He wasn't sure what to say or how to handle the situation, but he composed what he perceived to be a neutral response.

A: That's awesome! Congrats on the almost anniversary. My brain is like mush right now, so I'm going to crash. Talk to you later.

E: Goodnight, sleep tight!

A: Don't let the bedbugs bite.

E: And if they do, bite them too.

Without the light from the phone, the room plunged into complete darkness. Asher, however, was unable to fall asleep and lay in bed for hours, tossing and turning. Each time he was on the verge of nodding off, a fact for his exam would randomly resurface or an explosion from the living room would rock the apartment and the cycle would start again.

Asher's phone alarm shrieked. He didn't recall actually falling asleep, but when he tried to press Snooze he noticed a text waiting for him, sent only minutes prior.

E: Good luck on your exam!

***

"Hey, Dale." Asher tied his apron and stepped behind the counter. Dale was perched at the register as usual, ringing up a student, and quickly waved back. Asher grabbed the cup for the student's drink, a skinny vanilla latte. Asher called out the name and handed off the drink. Dale approached him, reminiscing about an art exhibit he'd visited during the weekend, and the two chatted during a lull in business. Lunchtime was never busy because most students were either in class or eating in the union.

Dale switched modes and started quizzing Asher on drink recipes. Asher was finally getting the hang of the technical terms behind each drink, and their conversation was interrupted on occasion by the opportunity to actually make a drink for a customer. As the end of Asher's shift neared, he heard someone by the pickup counter. Ellis approached with a smile.

"Hey," Asher said. "Do you want something to drink?"

"Nah, I'm good, thanks. I had to pick up a book before my Comm class, and figured I'd stop to see how your exam went. I tried texting you."

"Yeah, we aren't allowed to have our phones out while working. It was good, though. I guess all that time spent studying paid off. You sure you don't want anything? My treat." Asher grabbed an empty cup and waved it. "I'm actually getting pretty good at this."

Ellis chuckled and answered, "I guess just an iced tea?"

"Boring." Asher scooped ice into the cup.

"Sorry, I'm just a simple guy. I know what I like and I go for it without needing any frills or thrills," Ellis said. Asher stiffened, his mood prickling and his friendly demeanor slipping. He slid the drink across the counter and Ellis took a sip. "Perfect. Thanks."

"No problem. Consider it thanks for the smoothie," Asher said. "What time is your class?"

"Four. I'm going to go sit over there and read. I need to prep for a presentation." The space next to a row of computers was filled with large overstuffed chairs and side tables. Students filled most of the other chairs, but several seats remained unoccupied.

"I'll keep things dull so as not to be distracting," Asher said, looking more toward Ellis's left ear than his eyes.

"I'm sure that'll be a struggle." Ellis rolled his eyes. "When does your shift end?"

"In an hour. I'm going to pick up lunch, head home, and crash."

"And you say I'm the boring one," Ellis huffed, turning and taking claim of a nearby chair. Ellis glanced up at Asher and mouthed, "Get to work," before opening the book.

***

Asher stuffed his apron into his bag, his shift over, and saw the three text messages he'd missed while working: one from Ellis asking about the exam, one from his mom also asking about the exam, and the last one from Stacey. He clicked on the text from Stacey.

S: Hey, haven't talked in 2 days. Hope everything is going well. Maybe we can grab lunch or something soon??

He answered her text, asking what time and day would work for her, and pushed through the back door at the exact moment Ellis stood from the armchair and stepped into his path.

"Off to class?" Asher asked, playing with the dangling strap of his bag.

"I'm not feeling well." Ellis coughed into his hand. "Wouldn't want to spread it to a classroom of people."

"I can grab you a hot tea if it'd help," Asher offered before noticing the growing smirk on Ellis's face.

"I was thinking something more like a hot slice of pizza. You did say you needed to grab food before going home."

**

They entered a small restaurant, wedged between two bars, in the strip mall across from the campus. It was early afternoon, but a group of five sat shoved into a booth with two empty pitchers and one still half full of beer. Asher's tennis shoes stuck to the floor. They approached the counter and placed their orders: sun-dried tomatoes and goat cheese for Asher, and Ellis ordered prosciutto and spinach. Ellis insisted on paying, and afterward, not wanting to sit near the booth of five that had started seeing who could burp the loudest, they pulled up stools at the bar.

"Look, I'm sorry if I made things weird last night," Ellis started, obviously noting Asher's change in disposition toward him.

"No, I should be the one saying sorry. I'm just not really used to being around someone that's . . . you know . . ."

"Gay? You can say it. I'm still just a person."

Asher looked around the bar, feigning interest in the dozens of bumper stickers covering the surface, wishing their food would arrive. He could hear his mom's voice nagging him to remember his manners, and he looked at Ellis, searching for something to say. He fumbled a second apology.

Ellis granted him a reprieve, and they questioned each other as they had at the pool. Asher teased Ellis for naming a required reading book from high school as his favorite, *The Catcher in the Rye*, but was caught off guard and impressed by Ellis's grasp of the book and his intellectual display—how the message of people being unreliable resonated with him. He couldn't explain why he was surprised, Ellis had already said his parents were professors, but Asher was used to Ellis acting like a goofball.

"What about you?" Ellis asked.

"That's a bit harder for me, because I do like to read a lot." Asher thought for a moment. "I guess I would have to say *Alice's Adventures in Wonderland.*"

"And you make fun of me for liking a book I read in high school," Ellis retorted.

"It's about reexamining life through someone else's eyes and accepting things that are different to you but are perfectly acceptable if you can open your mind to other possibilities," Asher explained.

"Wow. That's the deepest acid trip ever," Ellis teased.

"Shut it," Asher said, lightly pushing Ellis off his barstool. "If you grew up in a small, close-minded town in North Carolina, you'd be thankful for a book teaching people that the world is crazy and zany and there isn't anything wrong with that."

"Crazy and zany, eh?" Ellis burst out laughing and Asher rolled his eyes. At that moment their pizza slices arrived and conversation died out. Finally, Ellis spoke up again. "North Carolina. How was that?"

Asher swallowed before responding, giving himself time to contemplate the best way to answer. He tried to shrug it off as being fine, but Ellis pushed him for details and asked why he left the state to go to school. Asher finally got going. His perfect brother, Brady, was everything parents could want in a kid: star of the football team, prom king, class president, and always eager to please. Brady received a free ride to college, married his high school sweetheart, and was now running a factory while his wife stayed home with their two precocious babies. Many of Brady's friends remained in town or moved back immediately following school, the same men that, alongside Brady, taunted and tormented Asher as a kid. Asher told Ellis about a time he was chased through the hunting woods behind his parents' house and hid among tree roots for four hours while Brady and his friends got belligerent in the garage off of whiskey.

"It'd be nice to be able to go home whenever I wanted, for a meal or something, but it was for the best. I just needed to get away and be out on my own. Everyone I grew up with got accepted into the same college, and I did too, but I knew if I went there it would be high school all over again. And like you learned from *The Catcher in the Rye*, some things are just better left in the past. Coming here was my way of making a new path." Asher set his slice of pizza down while processing the change of tone in the conversation.

"High school was that bad?" Ellis asked. Asher remained quiet for a second.

"That's one way to put it. My parents said they were proud of me, but there were times I saw the disappointment in their eyes when I didn't want to play sports and when I wanted to write instead of following in Brady's steps. And even without Brady and his cronies, high schoolers can be brutal. But I pushed through, and I made myself excel academically to help me escape, and now I'm here." Asher sighed. "Sorry, I don't want to be a downer."

"You're not a downer. I like learning more about you. I can't imagine what growing up like that was, but I'd be lying if I didn't say I'm glad it brought you down here." Ellis slapped Asher on the back. "What's your favorite dessert?"

"Chocolate, or something lemony."

"That was a quick response." Ellis laughed.

"What can I say? I know what I like," Asher said, mimicking Ellis.

"And when you know what you like, you should go for it," Ellis teased.

"Oh yeah?"

"Cupcakes!" Ellis exclaimed, wiping the grease from his hands and standing up. "Come on, we're going to another of my favorite places. It's my treat."

11. ASHER

After

"Should we stay on the highway or go back into the trees?" Asher asks, shoving the last can into his pack.

"There's only going to be tree cover for a couple more miles. And at least we can see longer distances on the road," Wendy answers, buckling her refilled belt.

"We didn't encounter any of them for two days traveling through the woods; a couple of hours on the highway, and we ran into six," Asher counters.

"And we ran into one before we got to the highway, and something caused someone to scream right before that. There's not a safe option as long as we're out in the open. There're thousands of cars along the highway, even more people at one point. We don't know how many of those people are alive, how many are dead, or how many are infected. I'd rather see them coming than listen for a branch to snap."

"You're right," Asher agrees. "So what are we waiting for?"

Asher takes the lead, continuing into the setting sun. They cover distance at a brisk pace, no longer stopping to search through vehicles, their backpacks bulging and weighted with supplies they've already scavenged. After three miles, the trees lining the highway end and are replaced with overgrown shoulders. Colorful weeds peek out above the long grass. Service roads run parallel to the highway, separated by chain-link fences, and backed up with cars. Strips of brown buildings are farther off, beyond the service roads. They spot a grouping of ravished tents in a building's parking lot, abandoned now even by the vultures. The sun begins to set, painting the sky with vibrant oranges and reds, while they cover an additional four miles.

"It's hard to believe something so beautiful can still exist." Wendy smiles.

"I don't think so; I look at you every day," Asher responds.

"Smooth," she laughs, shoving Asher to the side, her cheeks flushing.

"We should call it a day, find one of these cars to stay in," Asher suggests. "There's a school bus up ahead, worth the risk?"

"Tough to say. On the one hand there could be a lot of them on it, and if they're children I'm not particularly looking forward to that encounter. On the other hand, if it's empty, the windows are high enough to crack without anything getting in and it offers an elevated vantage point."

They increase their pace, wanting time to search the bus and move along if it doesn't pan out. Asher steps up to the emergency exit door and peers through the bottom windowpane. Crumpled cans and torn food wrappers litter the floor, but otherwise the aisle and space beneath the seats are clear. Asher raps his knuckles against the glass and listens. Nearly half of the windows are already partially down. They check out the side of the bus, but it's hard not to notice the blood smeared and splattered on the inside of the glass.

"Oh my God, look," Wendy whispers, pointing. A thick trail of dried blood leads from the front doors of the bus to a pile of scorched bodies. Limbs, torsos, and heads stick out at odd angles. Most of the body parts are larger, but there are numerous child-sized bodies mixed in as well. Tears well up in Wendy's eyes. No smoke billows from the stack; there are no signs of any hot embers. The bodies are old and cold.

"Somebody cleared out the bus before we got here," Asher says.

"They could still be on the bus," Wendy says, displaying a level of fear Asher has yet to see from her. "We need to keep moving."

"Whoever did that would be long gone. Nobody is going to stay in the same spot for too long. They would have exhausted their supplies and moved on. They probably used it for a night like we plan to, maybe two."

"Okay," Wendy says, nodding.

Asher tells her he will board the bus and verify it's safe before Wendy follows. She's visibly shaken, and they can't risk her vulnerability. Although Wendy protests, he forces her to agree. She offers the gun, but he refuses it; she'll need it if there's no chance for his own escape and he tells her to run.

The rubber lining between the door panels is warped, allowing Asher to slip his fingers through and tug against the doors until the connected handlebar next to the driver's seat comes loose and the now unsecured doors swivel open. He grasps his bat, leaving his bag with Wendy, and ascends the steps. The aisle remains clear, but Asher doesn't notice the thin fishing line strung between two seats. His shoe catches and a string of cans attached to the end of the line jingle against each other. He silences the cans and calls out to Wendy, telling her he's okay. As he moves toward the back, he checks the seats row by row. Trash is piled into the seats and the vinyl covering is hacked off of most of them.

A squeak, like rubber twisting on the floor, carries out from under a seat in the middle of the bus. The hairs on Asher's arm rise and he is swept with the sensation of being watched. The sound seems to come from almost directly behind him, and he lowers his body to check under the seats once more. On his hands and knees, ducking his head down, he meets a pair of eyes that are wide with fear. Before Asher can register what is happening, his eyes are flooded with a burning liquid, and he shoves himself up and backward, crashing into a seat frame and hitting his head on the support. He falls to the ground between two seats. He wipes and claws at his eyes.

"What the hell?!" Asher screams, kicking his legs out to ward off his attacker. Snot pours from his nose as the feeling of flames licking at his face intensifies. The bus shakes and groans and he hears stomping coming up the stairs.

"Asher?" Wendy calls out. In his moment of panic Asher forgot to tell Wendy to run, but she wouldn't have abandoned him even if he had.

"Wendy? Wendy, be careful! Someone else is here." Asher lowers his hands and tries to open his eyes. His vision is blurred. He reaches out to find the bat, but it's nowhere within reach. Instead, he rolls onto his stomach and, using his hands to drag himself along, he low-crawls under the seats toward Wendy's voice.

Wendy stands at the top of the steps, her gun drawn, her feet firmly planted. She crouches down, catching the light hitting the fishing line, and looks under the row of seats to her right. The space is empty, so she turns to the left and spots Asher pulling himself along on the ground, his face contorted in pain, his skin blazing red and wet, his eyes clamped shut.

"Whoever you are, show yourself," Wendy yells down the bus. "I don't want to hurt you, but I have a gun."

"Drop the gun," a deep voice demands from outside. Wendy risks a look through the door and sees a tall man stepping forward, approaching the bus with the pistol in his large hands aimed directly at her. Acting on impulse, she jumps the fishing line and runs a couple of feet before throwing herself into a seat.

The bus shakes more forcibly as the man storms the stairs.

"Tonya, are you okay?" his voice booms.

"I'm okay; they didn't hurt Marie or me," a woman answers from the back of the bus.

Asher freezes on the ground, unaware of Wendy's location. He is caught between both exits, defenseless.

"Please," Wendy says, her voice catching in her throat. "We don't want to hurt anyone. Please let us go."

"Who are you?" the man asks.

"We're just kids," Asher answers. "It's getting dark and we need a place to stay. We didn't know anyone was here."

"Why did you have a gun drawn?"

Wendy explains the situation, but the man demands she turn over the gun, even when they offer to leave the bus.

"Okay, I'll give you the gun. But will you promise to let us go?" Wendy asks.

"Yes, he'll let you go," the woman, Tonya, says loud and clear.

Wendy bends over in the seat, lays the gun on the ground, and shoves it hard toward the front of the bus.

"Do you have any other weapons?" the man asks.

"I have their baseball bat," Tonya announces.

"You can't send us out there without any weapons," Asher says, aghast. "We'll die!"

Wendy offers their food and water supplies in exchange for their remaining weapons. Without any sort of blunt instrument, they know they'll be prey for anyone or anything they cross paths with. The man doesn't acknowledge the offer but orders them into the aisle of the bus.

"Please, sir, be reasonable," Asher pleads, feeling his way onto a seat. Wendy follows Asher's lead but grabs his arm to alert him to her presence. The man towers over them, his broad shoulders and muscular body making it difficult for him to stand within the aisle. An unkempt beard hides his dark face, but it's short enough to suggest he was clean-shaven when the outbreak became full scale.

He seems surprised when he sees them and immediately lowers his gun. "You really are just kids. Are you alone?"

"Yes, sir," Asher answers. Wendy nods.

"What about your families?"

"We were students at the university; my family is in North Carolina. At least, they were before . . ." Asher's silence fills in the blank.

"Kansas," Wendy adds.

"What happened here?" he asks Tonya.

"I saw them approaching and hid with Marie. I could hear them talking through the windows and the girl mentioned a gun. You weren't back yet, and I was afraid, so when the boy found me I sprayed him in the face with the pepper spray." Tonya's voice carries from the back. Wendy looks over her shoulder, but the woman isn't visible.

"Here." The man takes a step forward. Wendy lunges in front of Asher, lifting her arms in defense. "I'm not going to hurt you; we need to flush his eyes," he says, and holsters his gun before unclipping a water bottle hanging from his belt.

"I have water," Wendy replies, placing a bottle of her own in Asher's hand.

"Lean your head back and rinse your eyes," the man instructs. "It's not going to wash it out completely but it'll help." Asher listens and empties the lukewarm water into his eyes. He begins to see better, but his eyes still burn. He lifts up the bottom of his shirt to wipe the remaining water and snot from his face.

"Can we go now?" Asher asks, but the man remains in their path rather than stepping aside.

"You two should stay here," he answers.

"You told us we could go," Wendy says.

"I did, but look how dark it is. Soon there isn't going to be any light, and his eyes are messed up. You can't take your chances out there."

"How do we know we're safe in here?" Asher asks.

"You don't. But I think this whole thing has been a misunderstanding. Tonya, give the boy his baseball bat back."

The woman reveals herself, standing from the last seat. Her braids are pulled back from her face. She steps forward, lifting the bat in offering. Asher is tentative about reaching out for it, half expecting for her to tighten her grip and swing. She relinquishes it and returns to her seat, walking backward with her brown eyes on them.

"I didn't pick up the gun when you slid it forward, but I'll give you two options. If you don't trust me, which I understand because we know nothing about each other, you can retrieve the gun and get off of our bus and take your chances, armed, out there. Or you can leave it where it is, as will I, and stay the night and we'll figure out the next move in the morning."

Wendy faces Asher and they silently confer. Asher nods, and although the man witnesses the exchange, Wendy relays they've accepted the invitation, as long as she can retrieve their packs from outside. The man tells them to relax and catch their breath, disappearing from the bus and coming back seconds later with their packs. He returns the bags without any further questioning.

"Thanks," Wendy says.

"You're welcome. I'm Todd."

"Wendy."

"Asher."

"Wendy, Asher, welcome to our bus."

12. RICO

Before

Rico sat, doodling in his notebook, at a picnic table during the lunch period. Chatter buzzed as everyone socialized while eating, but he was unable to bring himself to contribute. It had been a week since Sheila took the picture of him at the party. He was unsure if she had shown it to Chloe or not, but either way, Chloe was continuing to ignore him. He checked across the courtyard where the two girls, engrossed in laughter, leaned against a giant mural, but he couldn't help noticing that Chloe's smile was missing something. Her head turned, and for a second their eyes locked before Rico looked down at his doodle.

"Earth to Rico." Doug's voice snapped him out of his own thoughts.

"What?" Rico asked.

"Underground rave this weekend—they're texting out the info tomorrow night. You in?"

"Does a zebra have stripes?" Rico asked.

"Huh?" Doug scrunched his forehead.

"Yeah, I'm in." Rico dropped his notebook inside his bag and abandoned the table.

The halls of the school were silent as he wandered toward the library. It was even quieter in the library, and he knew he would not be bothered; most students avoided the place unless working on a project.

He found his usual far corner empty as expected and sank onto the ground against the bookshelves. The bell ended lunch but Rico ignored it. Soft footsteps padded across the carpet and Rico looked up, surprised to see Chloe round a bookcase. He remained stationary and silent, waiting for her to speak, but she stared down at him and chewed on her bottom lip.

"Do you want me to leave?" he asked.

"No, I came here to talk to you. I figured when you left lunch this was where you were coming," Chloe said.

"Don't you have class?"

"Don't you?"

"Touché. So, what's up?"

Chloe sat across from Rico and tossed her purse next to his bag.

"I wanted to say I'm sorry." She looked down at her old manicure, the paint long since chipped off, and picked at a piece of dead skin hanging from her cuticle. Rico searched her face, but she continued apologizing without looking up, saying she knew she was just as responsible as he was for getting arrested and understood he didn't have the power to get her released.

"Wow. That's very grown-up of you," Rico said.

"Forget it, I shouldn't have even bothered." Chloe reached for her purse but Rico's arm shot forward, catching her.

"Sorry. I guess I've been angry as well because you've been ignoring me. I really am sorry that you got in so much trouble. Did they book you?"

Chloe told Rico that the police had taken her mug shot and fingerprints. She was released to her parents and only had to complete community service hours rather than serving any time. Rico proposed a peace offering to Chloe, agreeing to volunteer for community service in a show of support, and shouldering some of the punishment as well. He wanted to spend time together, to mend their relationship, and pointed out that the time would pass faster with a friendly face nearby.

"Is it true your dad took your car away?" Chloe asked.

"How did you know?"

"People talk. And I've passed you walking to school when my mom drops me off. They don't trust me anymore to ride with Sheila."

The mention of Chloe's best friend made Rico uneasy, but he realized that Chloe was only speaking to him because she hadn't seen the picture on Sheila's phone.

"Maybe after you finish your hours they'll trust you again. That's another reason I should do them with you too. It'll show my dad that I'm responsible enough to get my car back."

Chloe smiled, conceding to working her community service hours with him. They spent the remainder of the period talking and laughing as quietly as they could to escape the librarian's attention. By the end of the period Rico was hopeful things were getting back to normal, and he kissed Chloe. The bell carried through the library. They left holding hands and smiling like children.

Rico stood at Chloe's locker after she excused herself to go to the restroom.

"You never learn, do you?" Rico turned to see Sheila staring at him.

"You know, you really shouldn't sneak up on people all the time," Rico said.

"Did you forget I still have that picture of you?" Sheila threatened.

"No, I didn't forget. But I know you didn't show it to Chloe, so for that I say thank you."

"I didn't show it to her because she was already hurt enough and you were leaving her alone. But I saw you two walking down the hall holding hands. You need to stay away from Chloe. You're poison, and she's just going to get hurt by you. Again."

"Thanks for the advice, but I'm good. Chloe and I talked things out," Rico said defiantly.

"And now you both think everything is going to go back to normal? Chloe has been my best friend for ten years, I'm not going to stand by and watch as you ruin her life. Either end things with her or I'm showing her the picture," Sheila demanded.

"Hey, what are you guys talking about?" Chloe asked, returning and spinning the lock on her locker.

"Uh, nothing," Rico said hastily. "Sheila was just telling me how happy she is we worked things out."

Chloe looked at Sheila and raised her eyebrows. Rico knew Sheila had spent much of the past week dragging his name through the mud.

"That's sweet," Chloe said, and focused her attention on switching out binders and books. She slammed the metal door shut and replaced the lock.

"I've got to go." Sheila shouldered into Rico. Chloe watched, and Rico shrugged his response.

"My next class is in B Hall," Chloe said. "I'll see you later." She kissed him on the cheek and faded into the swarm of students.

13. RICO

After

Wake up, this is all a dream. You're having a bad trip, but when you open your eyes you'll be in your own bed and none of this will have happened. Rico opens his eyes, but to his dismay, he is still wearing the baggy board shorts and Day-Glo shirt, now covered in urine and blood splatter. And he is alone. He picks up the shotgun from the ground and walks around the side of the gas pump.

He's just scared and hiding behind the pump. But there is no one on the other side either. Rico approaches one of the abandoned cars and pulls the handle. The door creaks open, releasing the smell of stale cigarettes. He checks the floor and backseat, but there is no sign of Jayden. He gets out of the car, dropping down to the ground and looking underneath. Nothing.

"Jayden," he whispers, "it's okay. You can come out." There are no signs of movement. Rico raises his voice. "Jayden."

He knows Jayden could not have gone far. He walks over to the burnt-out building, assuming it's the most likely location after searching the cars. The front windows are completely shattered, most likely from an early raid, allowing Rico to see past the scorched walls and into the building. Nothing inside appears salvageable—what wasn't stolen by looters has been lost to the fire, resulting in a large pile of ash and disheveled metal displays. Rico climbs onto the burnt hood of the car and slides down into the store, his feet sending up a cloud of soot as they land on the ground.

He doesn't see any distinguishable footprints in the ash, and although he knows Jayden couldn't have run through the store without leaving a trail, Rico decides to at least have a look around to be safe. His rubber swim shoes slip and slide over the surfaces as he walks around and steps on the broken shelves, the metal preventing him from gaining traction. Three of the glass drink cooler doors are intact, but the others have been destroyed.

"Jayden? Are you in here?" Rico calls out. The space behind the drink cooler shelves appears black, but a shape darts from one section to another. Rico inches his way forward, squinting to make out what is moving. "Jayden?"

Rico reaches into the duffel bag, pushing aside the wet clothes and candy bars, until his fingers slide along a cool metal cylinder. He powers on the flashlight and illuminates a darkened corner he had not noticed before. A blackened human skeleton lies twisted on the ground; several of the ribs, broken off, are scattered around it. He stumbles backward, crashing into a shelving structure.

Rico turns the light onto the drink coolers. The dispensers are empty, but stacks of boxes are piled up beyond the shelves. He hears scratching and swivels the light, illuminating the bright eyes of a raccoon. The animal turns and bolts into the darkness of the space beyond the cooler. Rico's heart sinks with the diminishing expectation of finding Jayden. He returns the flashlight to the bag. His skin and clothes are smeared black from climbing through the gas station, and when he wipes sweat from his brow, he leaves behind a dark streak as if marked for war. His remaining threads of hope begin to sever as he takes in the sight beyond the burnt-out car. Seven of the infected are drifting around the parking lot and four more are in the street heading his direction, drawn by the shotgun discharge and the crashing shelf.

Rico spots a door behind the counter connecting to the drink coolers—it's labeled Stockroom with a nailed-on plaque—and he boosts himself up and onto the surface of the counter.

The top of the register is smashed to pieces and the drawer hangs wide open, empty. On the ground a handful of coins in the ash reflect the small amount of light filtering through the shattered window frame. A second scorched skeleton lies on the ground, but this one is missing half a skull as if someone shot the man or woman in the head before the body burned. The infected meander through the parking lot, unfocused. Quietly slipping off the counter and onto the ground, he grabs the flashlight once more and turns it back on, keeping it pointed at the floor.

He turns the handle on the door, but when he attempts to pull the door open, he encounters resistance. Rico places one foot against the wall next to the door frame, using his body weight to leverage the door by pushing against the wall. The door slowly begins to give and then, with a loud creak of the hinges, flings open, nearly throwing him off balance. The three closest threats hear the noise and reorient themselves, drawn to the building. Rico steadies the shotgun against his shoulder with one hand, the flashlight in the other.

He shines the flashlight into the black doorway, cutting through the darkness, and is greeted once more by the cinderblock walls and boxes he saw through the cooler shelves. There is no sign of the raccoon. Rico slips into the room, pulling the door mostly shut. Looking through the coolers from the inside now, he watches one of the infected women reach the car and hears her grunt when she is unable to enter the station. A man's face appears, peeking over the wall through a windowpane. Knowing he is safe enough from them, Rico turns his back to the storefront to investigate the remaining boxes.

The stockroom suffered minimal damage from the fire; it looks to Rico as if the flames burned out as they reached the drink coolers, and he's able to walk around without slipping and sliding. The majority of the untouched boxes are full of generic knickknacks, sunglasses, and Daytona Beach shot glasses, with a few boxes containing sunscreen and tanning lotion. Behind one stack of boxes he finds another box with a shredded bottom corner. The hole is no doubt from the raccoon or other vermin. Rico rips the top of the box open, discovering a treasure trove of jerky within. The bags near the hole are torn and he leaves them inside the box but salvages enough jerky to last several days. Cases of water are piled up along the wall and Rico shoves a box away to reach them.

A rattling sound from behind catches his attention. The woman has found a way to clamber onto the hood of the car and slides face forward into the station, rolling off the end of the vehicle and into the broken shelves. Not wanting to underestimate the threat, and knowing that with each passing second Jayden slips further away from him, Rico refocuses on finding an exit and searches along the walls for a door. He rounds a stack of beer boxes but is stopped by a hiss near the floor.

The raccoon has its back arched, its lips pulled back, and it swats a claw at him. It launches forward, and Rico swings the flashlight in impulsive defense. The raccoon sails across the room, crashes into a pile of empty cardboard boxes, falls into an open box, and disappears. Next to the beer boxes, he sees a large metal door with several dead-bolt locks and a panic bar latch—it had been blocked from view when he first inspected the room.

The sunlight momentarily blinds him as he pushes through the back door and out of the building. Rico shields his eyes and gets his bearings. The door clicks shut. There is no handle to open it from the outside, only the three keyholes for the deadbolts and a brick on the ground that was used to prop the door open. The back of the gas station is home to two dumpsters; the rotting odor they emit is nearly overwhelming, and Rico buries his nose in the crook of his elbow. No infected are in sight; those who had been loitering around back were drawn to the front.

The end of the flashlight is covered in a sticky mixture of blood and fur from the raccoon. Rico wrinkles his face in disgust and crouches to the weeds sprouting from a crack in the pavement; he rips them from the ground and uses the leaves to wipe the gore away. After readjusting the strap on the duffel bag, he checks around the side of the building. There is one infected woman ten feet away, but her back is turned to him.

If I were a terrified six-year-old boy, where would I run? Rico wonders, his eyes moving from building to building. None of the buildings look appealing or safe. Most of the windows are smashed in, blood splatter tarnishes several storefronts, and others, like with the gas station, are burnt out from fires. The roof has collapsed on one building. There is no sure place to start; he cannot even be certain Jayden is still alive.

Throwing caution to the wind, Rico pumps the shotgun, steadies it with the stock against his shoulder, and pulls the trigger. The woman's body crumples to the ground as her head bursts in a spray of blood and brains. Rico continues around the side of the building without lowering the gun. Pumping the gun again he aims at a man in the street and pulls the trigger. Three more pumps and three more shots. Three infected men and one woman remain in front of the gas station, plus the woman that found her way inside.

There's no time to find ammunition in the duffel bag. Rico whips the shotgun around, slamming the stock into the temple of the closest man. The man stumbles and falls, but crawls forward. Rico brings the shotgun down with a resounding crack. The woman growls and reaches out. Rico swings the shotgun on her hand, hearing the impact of gun on bone. She snarls and jerks backward, cradling her arm against her chest. One of the men overtakes the woman and lunges at Rico before he has a chance to protect himself. He knocks Rico to the ground and lands on top of him.

Rico tightens his grip on the shotgun, using it as a lever to shove the man off. Flecks of spit drip from the man's mouth and land on Rico's face. Rico brings his leg up, jamming his knee into the man's groin with as much force as he can muster, and catches the man off guard enough to twist sideways and slip out from under the body. He kicks and connects with the man's throat and smashes his windpipe. A gasping replaces the snarls but he continues to move forward.

Rico races toward the car that smells of stale cigarettes—the driver's door remains open. He reaches the vehicle, dodging the other man, and dives inside, slamming the door on the second man's fingers. Rico pushes the door slightly ajar, allowing the infected man to pull back just enough, and then slams the door fully shut. The man scrapes his broken fingers along the window in a vain attempt to get ahold of Rico.

While Rico tries to catch his breath, the woman and the man with the crushed windpipe arrive at the car and bash their fists against the windows in frenzy. Rico reloads the shotgun. After climbing across the armrest to the passenger seat, he sets his back against the door and watches the three infected in pursuit. He aims the gun at the driver's side window and pulls the trigger. The man vanishes from view with the explosion of glass, leaving only a circle of red on the pump behind him. The woman fills the empty window, reaching through with her broken hand and then her face. Rico pumps and pulls, and the woman collapses forward, covering his bare legs with blood and hair. He pulls his knees to his chest, flailing his feet at the woman's body to shove her away. Crushed Windpipe moves in behind her, unable to fit more than an arm through the shattered window because the woman's body is taking up most of the space. Rico finds the latch on the passenger door and pulls it. His body weight pushes the door open and he tumbles out. He looks across the top of the car and locks eyes with Crushed Windpipe. He pumps the shotgun and aims it. With a soft thud, Crushed Windpipe's remains fall to the ground on top of the other man.

A pounding sound on the pavement catches Rico's attention. He watches in anguish as the horde of infected he and Jayden encountered earlier stomp or drag their feet, grumbling as they edge nearer to the gas station.

14. ASHER

Before

Asher unlocked his front door and stepped inside to the familiar sounds of explosions and gunfire. He set a box of cupcakes on the kitchen counter and filled a glass with water. His phone vibrated with a text from Ellis.

> E: Sorry I had to bail so suddenly, but I'm glad we got lunch! Let me know what you think of the cupcakes.

Asher put the phone away. He was still trying to wrap his head around what had happened. One minute everything seemed to be going great, and then Ellis checked his phone and his mood shifted. He mumbled a transparent lie about needing to pick up an assignment from a professor. He paid for the cupcakes they had picked out, but handed the entire box over to Asher and left the bakery alone. The text he sent implied nothing weird happened. Asher opened the box and stared at the four cupcakes inside. He lifted out the one with the raspberry jam filling and bit into it. The moist cake and jam mixed in his mouth, and he gave in and texted back.

A: You were right. I've only tried one so far, but I'm pretty sure this is what Heaven feels like.

He hit Send and took another bite. He was so focused on the cupcake he missed Mark walking into the kitchen.

"Geez, take it to your room, why don't you," Mark said, reaching into the fridge to grab a beer. Asher coughed to clear his throat.

"What?" he asked.

"It looked like you were about to make love to that cupcake," Mark teased.

Asher offered the box to Mark, who contemplated taking one for a moment before shaking his head.

"Nah, I'm going to stick to beer, thanks, though. Renee's here, she might want one." He yelled her name on his way out of the kitchen. A minute later Renee appeared.

"What's up?" she asked.

Asher held the box out to her, unwilling to eat all four alone, and she grabbed the red velvet. His phone vibrated again, another text from Ellis.

E: Which one did you try? The red velvet is my favorite.

"Uh, can I try that one? I'll trade you the last bite of the raspberry jam." Renee held her untouched cupcake out, and Asher sank his teeth through the smooth cream cheese frosting. He swallowed and responded to Ellis.

A: I tried the raspberry one first, but I just had a bite of the red velvet.
You're right it's delicious. But I think I might have to give the win to raspberry.

"Who're you texting?" Renee asked, covering her mouth as she chewed.

"Just this guy I met the other day; he's friends with this girl I went on a date with," Asher answered.

"Oh really?" Renee said.

"What? Why are you looking at me like that?" Asher asked.

"No reason, just didn't know you went on a date." Renee threw out the cupcake wrapper and asked about the date. Asher told her about the party, meeting Stacey's friends, and having to carry her up two flights of stairs. He left out the entire incident at the pool. When Renee asked about a second date, he shrugged and said he hadn't talked to her lately. Renee found it weird that he was in contact with Stacey's friends.

"Friend," Asher corrected. Renee said it would make it easier if Stacey's friends approved of him from the beginning.

"If we didn't approve of you, would you still hang around here all the time?"

"Probably. I said it's good if they approve, not that approval is necessary. Plus, you guys love having me around."

"Yeah, whatever. You're not the worst," Asher answered. "What are you guys up to tonight?"

"I don't know, they've been playing games and drinking all day. I'm getting kind of hungry, though, so I might head out and pick something up. Do you want to join?"

"I already ate, but I'm not doing anything, so I can ride along."

"Cool, I'll grab my keys."

***

Renee pulled into a parking space in front of the burrito bar. The place was crowded as she and Asher pushed their way through the front doors.

"Asher!" He looked around until he saw Stacey sitting in a booth with one of her friends and waving him over.

"Who is that?" Renee asked.

"Stacey," he answered.

"Don't be weird, go talk to her while I order." Renee prodded him in the ribs, leaving to get in line. Asher returned Stacey's wave and twisted and turned through the crowd. As he approached the booth she scooted in, leaving a space open for him.

"Hey," he said, smiling.

"You remember Michelle, don't you?" Stacey asked.

"Hi." Michelle's voice was flat.

"Of course. What's up?" Asher asked, trying to seem casual although the look he received from Michelle made him slightly uncomfortable.

"Just taking a break from studying to gorge our faces. Is she getting you food?" Stacey motioned toward Renee ordering at the counter, her eyes hard as she glared at Renee's back.

"Nah, I ate already. I just wasn't doing anything so I offered to ride along," Asher answered.

"That was nice of you, that's your . . ." Stacey's voice trailed off, leaving the territorial question lingering in the air.

"She's my roommate's girlfriend, Renee," Asher answered.

"Sorry, I didn't mean to imply anything," Stacey said, the fight leaving her voice. "I don't know where my mind is right now; I've been cramming it with economics."

"It's cool, don't worry about it." Renee approached the table carrying a plastic bag. "But it looks like I've got to go. Good luck with your exams, and let me know if you're free after. Maybe we can finally schedule in that second date." Asher stood from the table and noticed the grin spreading on Stacey's face. She readily agreed to a post-exam celebratory meal. He waved and followed Renee out to her car.

As Renee reversed out of the parking space, she jumped in like a concerned mom asking how her son's date went.

"It went well. I don't know—she was being kind of weird. We're going to dinner soon," Asher answered. She asked him why he was lacking enthusiasm when talking about Stacey. Asher was rarely the gushing type about anything, but he was always open with Renee when she prodded him about a topic.

"I guess I don't really know her; we just met. But back there she was possessive and jealous. She seemed angry that I was with you, and she doesn't even know you," Asher answered. Renee parked and turned off the engine before answering.

"Then why did you ask her out on a second date?" Renee watched Asher as he stared out the windshield, but even being physically present, he was mentally absent. Renee grabbed her bag of food with a huff and threw open the door.

"I guess I'm just tired of being the only person not in a relationship. Is it terrible if I like someone wanting to pay attention to me for a change?" he answered before storming off.

***

Three hours later Asher sat at his desk browsing the Internet when there was a knock on his door. He glanced over his shoulder as the door opened.

"Can I come in?" Renee asked, peeking her head into the room. Asher turned back to his laptop and invited her in. She sat on the edge of his bed and apologized for pushing him too hard in the car.

"Thanks, but don't worry about it. It's fine." Asher dismissed the apology. "You didn't do anything wrong."

"I want you to be happy, but you shouldn't think you have to date anyone that comes along, if it doesn't make you happy. You'll find someone else. Look at Mark, he can be a complete douche bag, but he's my douche bag," Renee reassured him.

"So what you're saying is that I need to find my own douche bag?" Asher joked.

"Yes, that's exactly what I'm saying." Renee laughed. "I convinced them to play a four-player game instead of those war games, so you should stop feeling sorry for yourself and come hang out with us." She left his room. The last part of her comment stung, but Asher knew it was the truth, and she meant it to motivate him. He checked his phone as he followed her and saw three unread texts. The first was from Stacey:

S: Cn't wait 4 our date! Perfect incentive 4 studying!!! :D

The other two were from Ellis and sent forty-seven minutes apart, saying that he would have to try the raspberry cupcake the next time they went to the bakery together and then asking what Asher was doing.

Asher slid the phone across the dining room table, deciding to spend a distraction- free evening with his friends. Renee watched him and held out a controller.

**

Hours later when Asher climbed into bed, he answered the texts by wishing Stacey luck and texting Ellis.

A: Heading to bed, see you in class tomorrow.

E: Goodnight, sleep tight.

A: You too, don't let the bedbugs bite.

E: And if they do, bite them too!

Asher fell into a deep sleep.

15. WENDY

After

The last bit of sun slips away, replaced by a full moon. Wendy settles her back against the cooler metal of the siding, keeping watch over Asher. He is curled up on the seat across from her. His chest moves as he breathes, his sleep calm and mostly free of the night terrors that often keep Wendy up. She runs her fingers down the wood grain of the baseball bat Tonya returned to them.

"Hey." Tonya's voice stirs her and Wendy twists around. Tonya's head is fully outlined and the moonlight through the window illuminates the side of her face, highlighting her defined cheekbones. Her braids hang over one shoulder, and even in the poor lighting Wendy can tell how beautiful the woman is.

"Hi," Wendy answers, wrapping her fingers around the handle of the bat.

"I wanted to apologize for earlier. I didn't mean to pepper spray your friend. Well, I did mean to pepper spray him, but only out of fear," Tonya says.

"I understand. I'm sorry we scared you," Wendy says.

"It's hard to know what's going on in the world anymore. You couldn't trust strangers enough before all of this, and now . . ." Tonya shrugs.

"Why are you letting us stay on the bus, then?" Wendy asks.

"You're just kids. And Todd is a good judge of character; if he was willing to offer I'm not going to doubt him. If I can't trust my own husband, then how do I survive?"

"Fair point, we appreciate it all the same."

"You didn't have to accept. I can't imagine what your parents have to be going through right now, so far away from their children. If the tables were turned I would hope someone would make sure my daughter wasn't alone."

"Marie?" Wendy repeats the name she heard both Tonya and Todd say, though she has yet to see or meet anyone else on the bus besides the two of them.

"Yes, Marie."

"She's here, isn't she? I heard you and your husband mention her, but I didn't want to push my luck asking about her."

"She's asleep right now, but you can meet her in the morning."

"Was she asleep earlier?"

"No. She was awake and very scared. She's deaf so she didn't know what was going on until I told her after everything had settled."

Wendy is shocked. She wonders how they have managed to survive this long while protecting a deaf child—the ability to hear the smallest sounds have proven vital in keeping her and Asher alive. Tonya asks where Wendy and Asher are going next, and Wendy purses her lips before lying. "I don't know."

But she does know; at least, she has an idea, even though she dreads admitting it. Images flash through her mind: the castle, the oversized flowers, and the lake. She looks over to Asher's sleeping body, her chest burning with the secret she's harbored. If nothing, no one, is waiting at her destination, then everything will be for naught. Asher will have given up being with the person who meant the most to him so he could blindly follow Wendy on a wild goose chase. She believes she doesn't deserve his companionship, and that he would never be capable of what she'd done. He is too kind. And she is going to break him.

The silence stretches between Tonya and Wendy—neither woman knowing what to say. Feeling herself starting to nod off, Wendy reaches down and pinches her wrist, twisting flesh between her thumb and index finger until the pain makes her alert. She tries to imagine losing one of her senses and attempting to make it through this mess, and doubts whether she could have even lasted the first couple of days, much less the last few weeks. Gruesome images of their encounters return as she drifts off. Her chin starts drooping down to her chest, and without the energy to fight it, the fogginess takes over her thoughts.

***

Wendy watched as the blood dripped onto the floor, staining the carpet; her hand clenched around the knife.

"Please, I don't want to die anymore."

BANG. BANG. Wendy looked at the door; cracks appeared in the wooden slats where it started to give.

"I'm sorry. Please, Wendy."

The slats splintered and chunks of wood fell to the floor. A hand appeared through the hole, swinging wildly and feeling for its target. There was so much blood. It was already too late.

"I'm sorry too, but it'll be fast. You won't hurt anymore; that's what you want, isn't it?" Wendy asked. The hand found what it was searching for, the fingers wrapping around hair and pulling. A scream filled the air.

***

"Wake up. Wendy, wake up." Asher gently shakes her shoulder. Wendy's screams stop as her eyes pop open and she gasps. She kicks, catching Asher in the gut and propelling him backward into a seat. Asher holds his hands up in surrender. The skin around his eyes is still red and raw, and his eyes are bloodshot, but he keeps them open and watches her. The sky beyond the windows is blue with thin streaks of pink. Wendy realizes she had passed out for several hours.

She gets to her knees, apologizing profusely to Asher, and looks over the seats. The top of Tonya's head protrudes from one of the back seats. Todd is sitting up in the last seat, gazing out through the emergency exit door. Asher brushes off the apology, as he always does with Wendy. Embarrassment floods Wendy.

"I was supposed to be keeping watch," Wendy whispers, her eyes darting toward the back of the bus.

"In case we changed our minds about you staying here?" Todd asks without facing them. Wendy's eyes widen, but when Todd looks at them he has a reassuring grin. "I'm messing with you."

"I didn't mean—"

"You can never be too safe. It's the same reason Tonya stayed awake while I slept. It would have been stupid for you to blindly accept our offer and not keep watch. You haven't survived this long by being stupid." Todd looks into the seat across from him, and his hands form a variety of shapes and movements. A little girl's head peeks up from the back seat. Her eyes, a stunning shade of light brown, move from Wendy to Asher.

Wendy lifts her hand in a wave, and the girl drops out of view again.

"She's shy," Todd says.

"I bet. Your wife told me about her last night," Wendy tells him.

"What about her?" Asher asks.

"Marie's deaf," Todd answers, and his hands begin moving again. The girl's face reappears and she gives both Asher and Wendy a tentative wave. Asher searches his bag, and when he steps away from his seat, he's holding three cans in his hands.

"I don't know what she likes, but here are some options." He tests the waters by stepping down the aisle and holding out the food in offering. Todd signs words to his daughter, and she tiptoes forward to see what Asher is holding. Her clothes are dirty, as to be expected, but cleaner than what both Wendy and Asher are clad in. Her hair is done up in braids with elastic hair ties at the end. She accepts a can of pineapple in her left hand, using her right hand to tap her chin and pull her hand forward and down.

"That's 'thank you' in sign language," Todd explains.

"How do I say 'you're welcome'?" Asher asks. Todd cups his right hand out in front of his chest and makes a downward scooping motion toward his stomach. Asher repeats this to Marie and she smiles before running to the back and handing her dad the can. Todd pulls the lid off and Marie disappears again, the only sign of her presence a slurping sound as she drinks the juice. Asher offers a can to Todd, but Todd declines. Asher turns to Wendy with baked beans and chicken noodle soup.

While they eat, Asher and Todd converse. Todd explains that his family has been living on the bus for three days, taking advantage of the security it provides while he scavenges for supplies each day. Asher and Wendy avoided the highway for as long as possible, scared off by the idea that it was overcome by infected people who flooded the interstate at the onslaught of the outbreak. Todd relays a similar thought process, but he and Tonya eventually needed the highway to reach a mall where a refugee camp was being set up when things first became serious. He says they're unaware of whether the camp is thriving or abandoned, but hoping for medical supplies and food either way. They're doing what all survivors are doing: searching for sanctuary, for shelter, and a purpose.

"Was the pile of bodies in front of the bus when you guys got here?" Wendy asks.

"Yeah. The seat covers were all removed too. Someone used this bus for shelter before we did. I would guess that those bodies were those *things*, and whoever it was cleared them out and destroyed the seat covers that were covered in blood just to be safe. It doesn't work that way, though, the blood. I've gotten it on myself accidentally. You'd only get sick if it lands in an open wound. They did us a favor, though, I know that."

Asher rubs a hand over the small cuts along his arm from landing on the glass shards yesterday. They need to decide soon what their next course of action is going to be, but Wendy doesn't want to bring it up in front of a man that is still a stranger to them. Thankfully, before she can come up with an excuse to talk to Asher in private, Todd stands and announces he needs to stretch his legs, leaving them on the bus with Tonya, who is still asleep, and Marie.

Once Todd is out of immediate earshot, Wendy turns to Asher and asks what they should do. The sun has climbed higher, the streaks of pink completely gone. The day is only going to get hotter. She feels uneasy sitting around, especially when she and Asher are outnumbered and could be overpowered. When Asher seems wary about hitting the road so soon, she points out that the invitation was only for a night and they need to avoid creating issues by overstaying their welcome.

"I know, it's just"—Asher pauses to check whether Todd is on his way back yet—"wasn't it nice to actually get some sleep last night? Both of us got a full night of sleep instead of trading off after a couple of hours."

"Which we shouldn't have done, because we don't even know them. I should have fought to stay awake longer," Wendy argues. She's getting frustrated with his resistance. Asher's ability to search for the best in everyone can be a blessing or a curse.

"But you didn't, and we're fine. Where are we even going if we leave?"

Todd reappears at the top of the steps. Their conversation ends, but she feels relief at not having to provide Asher with an answer. She sees a benefit in his argument for staying, another day or two could be useful in deciding how to broach the topic with him. If they were to leave now, they'd cover the remaining ground and make it to the park before lunch. She looks up and smiles as Todd passes her on his way back to his family.

"I'm going to toss this." Wendy holds up the soup can. She grabs the empty can of baked beans from Asher as well and heads outside. Although it is early morning, the heat and humidity have already started to set in. She inches closer to the pile of bodies. Her eyes well with tears for all of the lost lives in front of her. Laughter spills through the open windows of the bus, sending a chill down her spine. Wendy places the empty cans next to the pile, an offering to the dead.

She knows now where she has to go and what she has to do.

16. ASHER

Before

"Well, this is awkward," Ellis said.

Asher looked up and was consumed with déjà vu; Ellis loomed above him holding two smoothies. This time, however, Asher was sitting on the floor with two smoothies as well, instead of a book.

"You got the smoothies on Monday, so I figured it was my turn." Asher stood with the cups in hand.

"But you treated me to a tea," Ellis argued.

"Yes, but I didn't actually pay for the tea, so it doesn't count," Asher countered. "What'd you get?"

"I decided to switch it up. This one is honey, apple, and cinnamon." He raised one hand. Raising the other cup, he continued, "And here we have chocolate, banana, and *almond* butter. I remembered you don't like peanut butter."

"How very thoughtful of you. Both of those sound tastier than what I got. Kale, pineapple, and Granny Smith apples, or mixed berry." Asher offered the green smoothie and then the purple one. "I'd be willing to trade you for the chocolate and banana smoothie?"

"Here ya go. I think I'm going to stick with the honey-apple. No offense, I just hate kale. Now what to do with these other two smoothies?" Ellis contemplated as they entered the classroom and took seats toward the back.

"It'd be a shame to just toss them," Asher answered.

"How much of a suck-up do you feel like being? We could tell Mr. Bernstein we got them for him as thanks for being such an entertaining professor." Ellis faked a large cheesy grin.

"Charming. Is that what happened Monday? Why you had an extra smoothie for me?" Asher teased. "Someone turn you down before you got here?"

"I don't get turned down," Ellis quipped, and his grin turned real. "What's it feel like?"

"You're hilarious." Asher punched Ellis on the arm.

"What are you up to tonight?" Ellis asked, sucking on the straw.

"Stacey is supposed to text me when she gets done with an exam today. We made plans to go to dinner," Asher answered.

"Oh. That'll be fun." Ellis's smile faltered and he turned in his seat to face the front.

"You okay?"

"Yeah, of course. Bernstein is here; I'll take the smoothies to him." Ellis picked up the cups and approached the front of the class.

**

Asher knocked on Stacey's door. She quickly answered, as if she was standing nearby waiting for his arrival.

"Hey," she greeted him, the excitement rising behind her voice.

"Hi. You ready?" Asher asked, rocking back and forth on his feet, his hands shoved in his pockets.

"Yeah, let me lock up."

Asher heard a noise behind them and looked over his shoulder to see Ellis's front door open. Brandon, Ellis's boyfriend, stepped out, followed by Ellis. The two were laughing as Ellis pulled the door shut.

"Okay, let's go," Stacey said. Ellis turned around and pretended to be surprised to see Asher by placing his hand on his chest and dropping his jaw. His lips curled in exaggeration, revealing his large white teeth and making him look almost devilish.

"Asher?" Stacey said hesitantly, noticing Asher and Ellis watching each other.

"Hey, you two, what are you up to tonight?" Ellis asked. He stared at Asher in defiance, daring Asher to call him out.

"We're heading out to dinner, you?" Stacey answered. All of her previous enthusiasm was slipping away.

"What a coincidence, we were leaving to get something to eat as well. Not sure where we're going yet, though," Ellis responded. "Oh! I'm being rude, you two haven't met. Brandon, this is Asher—we have a class together, and he's Stacey's boyfriend. Asher, Brandon."

"He's not my boyfriend," Stacey sputtered, and looked down.

"Nice to meet you." Asher forced an attempt to be friendly, and extended his hand. Brandon returned the gesture, mumbling. Ellis continued to ignore how uncomfortable he was making the encounter, instead asking where Asher and Stacey were going for dinner and inviting himself and Brandon along. When Asher tried to protest, Ellis cut him off by announcing he would drive and then marching away. Brandon stared at Asher before following his boyfriend.

"I'm sorry, do you want to go somewhere else? This isn't how I planned on tonight going," Asher said to Stacey.

"No, it's fine. We had already settled on the place anyway; it'll be cool. It's not like our first date was just the two of us. One day it'll happen." Stacey stood up on her tiptoes and kissed Asher on the cheek before descending the stairs as well. Asher admired how she managed to make the best of the situation. Halfway down the staircase he heard a car horn blast, evaporating his admiration and replacing it with additional annoyance. At the bottom of the stairs he watched Stacey get into the back seat of the car, Brandon in the front passenger seat, and Ellis in the driver's seat hitting the horn. While sliding in next to Stacey, Asher caught Ellis watching him in the rearview mirror and furrowed his brow.

"What took you so long?" Ellis asked and started the car. Asher glared silently in response. Conversation was limited until they reached the restaurant.

"So how'd your exam go?" Asher asked Stacey, putting his menu down.

"It was all right; Michelle and I spent the entire night studying and my brain was fried. But I had good motivation for making it through." Stacey squeezed Asher's hand. He smiled, but in his peripheral vision he caught Ellis rolling his eyes across the table.

"What are you majoring in, Brandon?" Asher faced Brandon, changing the subject to something more neutral and bringing him into the fold. Brandon glanced up from his menu as if he forgot Asher was even there.

"Computer Science," he answered, looking to his menu again.

"Is that like, building computers or making websites?" Asher asked, trying to prevent Ellis from having an opportunity to pipe up.

"A combination of both. Some of the classes teach the hardware side and others teach software and coding. If you want to work with computers you need to know everything," Brandon explained. He droned on about technology, and Asher was pleased to see how bored Ellis was becoming. Ellis's attempt to crash the date was successful, but Asher refused to give him additional power, and every time he tried to interrupt, Asher was ready with another irrelevant question for Brandon. It wasn't until Brandon said he wanted to work in search engine optimization, and Asher admitted he didn't understand what that meant, that Ellis perked up with glee.

"There are a lot of things you don't understand," Ellis jibed. Before Asher could respond, the waitress arrived to take their orders. Once she walked away, Brandon continued as if nothing had happened.

"I'm sure a lot of people don't understand what it is, or at least think they don't," Brandon began, "but it's pretty easy to understand. You use the Internet to search for information and find the answer to a question sometimes, right?" Stacey and Asher nodded. "When you use a search engine, the results appear as a list. I would work to optimize a website's priority level in the results and therefore move it higher up the list. For example, you wonder what spices to use when cooking a steak. A spice company would hire me to code their web page so their business appears at the top of the list." Brandon finished, pleased with the opportunity to brag about his own abilities and understanding. Asher admitted to himself that the topic was incredibly dull. The evening was crashing and burning for everyone.

"What about you? What are you majoring in?" Brandon asked Asher.

"Creative writing, much to the disappointment of my parents," he answered, rethinking his initial impression of Brandon being moody and silent.

"Well, I can understand that; it's not a very lucrative career choice, is it?" Asher's opinion of Brandon dropped again.

"I think writing can be highly lucrative," Stacey jumped in. "Most of us read books, watch movies and TV. We need creative people to come up with the stories. Plus, I think there's something romantic about the idea of being a writer and spending time in coffee shops and bookstores observing people." Ellis snorted, shooting his water all over himself.

"Sorry, don't mind me. Is that why you got the job at Cup o' Joe? So you can observe people for your stories?" he asked, wiping water from his face and attempting to keep a straight face.

"Isn't that *your* job? Like the other day when you came and watched me work for an hour?" Asher snapped. Ellis turned stark white, and anger flashed across Brandon's face. Asher abruptly stood and excused himself to go to the restroom without waiting for a response.

He shoved the men's room door open and was relieved to see it was empty before kicking the garbage can out of frustration. Leaning against the wall, he took a deep breath and closed his eyes. He counted to thirty and opened his eyes as the door swung inward and Ellis entered. Asher glared at Ellis and tried to stride past him and out of the restroom, but Ellis grabbed his upper arm, holding him back. "Let go of me."

"Wait. I wanted to apologize," Ellis said, his voice thick with remorse.

"What is your deal?" Asher asked.

"I don't know, it's just—" Ellis began.

"You're being an ass." Asher cut him off.

"You're right, that's fair. But what you're doing is just as bad," Ellis retorted.

"What *I'm* doing? I haven't been rude to you yet. You're the one that ran off yesterday, and then stopped talking to me in class today before inviting yourself out with us tonight. You don't have the right to call me an ass." Asher jerked his arm out of Ellis's grasp and continued to the door.

"You're leading her on," Ellis stated, "you're being an ass to Stacey."

"No, I'm not." Asher faced Ellis again.

"Then why did you ask her out on a second date?" Ellis asked.

"Because I like her."

"Yeah, well, I like her too, but you don't see me asking her out."

"That's because you're gay." Asher raised his voice. Neither of them spoke, instead staring at each other in seething silence. With one last insult, Asher said, "You're no different than my brother and his friends," and shoved the door and walked out, leaving Ellis behind. He returned to the table, picking up that neither Brandon nor Stacey spoke much while he and Ellis were gone.

Shortly after, Ellis returned and calmly reclaimed his seat. The tension was thick enough to slice, and the ruined evening slowly and silently slipped by until the foursome was once more in Ellis's car.

Asher and Stacey were the first to get out of the car, with Asher mumbling, "Thanks for the ride," to Ellis without looking at him. He and Stacey wordlessly climbed the stairs to her apartment, and she hesitated with her keys in front of the door. Not wanting to be standing in front of the door when Ellis and Brandon eventually reached the top of the stairs, Asher could not take it anymore and spoke up. "Look, I really like you. You're fun and sweet, but—"

"There's always a but," Stacey interjected.

"I just don't think this is going to work out, and I'd rather end it now before you get hurt." Asher was sincere in his delivery but couldn't avoid letting Stacey down. He knew it wasn't going to work and chose to rip the bandage off all at once rather than slowly peeling it away.

"Who says I'm the one that's going to get hurt? I'm a tough girl, maybe I'd have hurt you." Stacey looked up at Asher, and he caught the light reflecting off of the tears building in her eyes.

"I don't want you to think this is about you, because it's not. It's about me, and tonight—"

"But tonight being horrible wasn't because of you or me," Stacey pleaded.

"I'm sorry. I'm really, really, sorry." Asher walked away before anything else could be said. He descended the stairs on the opposite end of the hall from which they came up, still wanting to avoid Ellis and Brandon.

At home, he opened the front door to the familiar sounds of war. The gunfire and explosions only served to fuel his sour mood. While brushing his teeth he heard his phone ding from the nightstand. He avoided opening the text, but unable to sleep, curiosity got the best of him.

E: Sorry for being an ass tonight.

Asher placed the phone on the nightstand without responding. Ten minutes later he wrote back.

A: Heading to bed, forgetting today happened. G'night.

Ellis's text arrived within seconds.

E: Sleep tight.

A: Don't let the bedbugs bite.

E: If they do, bite them too.

17. RICO

Before

Rico stood in front of the large gate surrounding the imposing house. Building up his courage, he pushed the call button on the panel next to the gate. A female voice echoed from the intercom system.

"Hello?"

"It's Rico," he said, and a buzz sounded as the gate swung inward. The garage housing the cars stood off to the side with the doors down, so he could not see his imprisoned SUV. He reached the front door and it opened before he could grasp the handle. The doorway framed a tall, slender dark-haired beauty, Theresa, who would have been a model in a different life.

"Rico, I didn't realize you were stopping by," she said, remaining in the entrance to block him from entering the house.

"It was a last-minute decision. I had my mom drop me off on her way to work," Rico responded, trying to take a step forward.

"You should have called first, your father isn't even home yet." Theresa's lips pressed together in a hard line, her face devoid of emotion. She reached out and firmly grasped the door as if to swing it shut in Rico's face, even as he watched her.

"Am I no longer allowed or welcome in my father's house?" he asked, tilting his head to the side in forced confusion. Theresa opened her mouth to answer, but appeared to weigh her options for responses before sighing and stepping to the side. Rico stepped over the threshold and into the foyer. "Would you like me to wait in the living room or the office for him?"

"The living room is fine. I'm sure he wouldn't want you going through his things while he's out," Theresa said in a condescending tone. Accustomed to her attacks, Rico theatrically scoffed at the suggestion he'd have any interest in his father's belongings. "I'll take you there."

"It's cool. I wouldn't want to interrupt whatever riveting task you were up to. I'm sure I remember the way; this was my home my entire life until you moved in." Rico left Theresa frozen in the marble foyer. He passed through the familiar halls, his family portraits long gone and replaced with new photos, and reached the living room. The large TV that occupied most of one wall was filled with vibrant colors as cartoons flashed on the screen. Looking down, he found his stepbrother lying on his stomach playing with toy cars. Jayden jerked his head up and saw Rico standing behind the couch.

"Rico!" he exclaimed, dropping the cars and running across the room. He threw himself at Rico, who, catching him, spun him around in the air.

"What's up, buddy?" Rico asked the giggling child, setting him back down on his feet.

"Do you want to play cars with me?" Jayden asked.

"Of course," Rico answered. Jayden grabbed Rico's hand, pulling him around the couch and over to the toys where they spent the next hour racing around and crashing into each other.

"I'm home."

Rico heard Antonio's voice carrying down the hall from the front door and he automatically stiffened. Antonio entered the living room and was startled to see Rico on the floor with Jayden. "Rico, what a surprise."

"How was work, babe?" Theresa appeared through a different doorway and kissed him on the cheek.

"It was fine; working on a case for a basketball player that got a DUI the other night. How long have you been here?" Antonio asked, steering the conversation back to his son.

"Wasn't it nice of him to visit? Will you be staying for dinner?" Theresa's voice exuded the pleasantness she put on around Antonio, but her eyes were cold and unwelcoming. The last thing she wanted was to spend another minute around Rico.

"I think it'd be nice if you ate with us, as a *family*," Antonio said. The emphasis stung Rico more than any look Theresa could give him. But watching the developing unease in Theresa's face caused Rico's response to be genuine, even if only out of spite.

"I'd love to. What are we having?"

"Arroz con pollo," Theresa answered. "I better get back to it." She turned and left the room.

Antonio patted Jayden on the shoulder, instructing him to go wash up. The kid groaned but did as told. Once Antonio and Rico had the room to themselves, apprehension about coming over began to creep into Rico. He stood, not wanting to give his father the benefit of towering over him. Antonio loosened his tie and undid the top button on his shirt. "To what do I owe the pleasure of your company tonight?"

"Just wanted to come see my pops, y'know?" Rico said, shrugging, but his comment was laughed off.

"I can count the number of times you've been in this house in the past year on one hand, none of which were by your choice. It's about your car, isn't it?" Antonio saw through his son and took the direct approach. Antonio relished making people uncomfortable; it was part of what made him so successful as a lawyer.

"I'm doing some community service hours tomorrow," Rico said, avoiding his father's question.

"You skipped your afternoon classes on Monday," Antonio countered, shutting down Rico's implied behavioral improvement. Rico should have known his father would keep tabs on him, but he'd doubted Antonio cared enough to follow up with the school.

"I wasn't feeling well," Rico claimed.

"Empty your pockets."

Rico withheld his frustration, instead obliging by reaching into his pockets and extracting his phone and wallet. He dropped them onto the coffee table and pulled his pockets inside out. Antonio's face remained expressionless while he fingered through the pockets of the wallet. Finding nothing of note, he returned it to the coffee table with a flippant toss. He asked how Rico was getting to the community service site, and Rico's throat tightened. Here came the moment of truth, his one play to get his keys back.

"Uhh." Rico hesitated and looked down at the ground in performance mode. "Chloe is doing community service as well. I was probably going to get a ride with her."

"Probably? Probably get a ride from the girl you got arrested with?" Rico had hoped the idea would force Antonio to provide the vehicle as an alternate solution, but the idea backfired. "That's why you're choosing to volunteer? Not because you want to contribute to society, but because your little friend is going to be there. Are you actually going to get any work done or just smoke dope behind the bleachers?"

"No," Rico said, "that's not what's going to happen. It's a roadside cleanup, picking up trash—"

"That's something you're good at, picking up trash, you've done enough of it!" Antonio cut him off.

"Like father like son, I guess," Rico screamed. He lost control, only stopping when he saw Theresa.

"Dinner is ready," Theresa said, her voice barely above a whisper. Antonio looked from his wife to his son, red in the face. Rico swiped his wallet and phone off the table and marched toward the hallway.

"You will get back in here and apologize to my wife," Antonio yelled at the back of Rico's head. "Enrico Javier Martinez, do you hear me?"

"Where are you going?" Jayden stood by the staircase, looking at Rico as he stormed past. Without answering him, Rico reached the front door and flung it open. The stained-glass pane shook from the force. He raced down the driveway to the gate and, without waiting for it to open, climbed up to the top and dropped down on the other side. He stormed away from the house.

After ten minutes of jogging he was covered in sweat; he stopped to catch his breath. He shot Doug a text asking what he was doing.

Rico slipped his fingers into the elastic band of his boxers and grabbed the baggie with only one pill remaining. Gathering enough spit in his mouth, he popped the pill into the back of his throat and swallowed. He discarded the baggie and continued to put as much distance as he could between himself and his father.

***

Doug found Rico sitting on the beach, his feet buried in the sand, staring out at the horizon. Kicking off his own shoes, Doug crashed next to Rico.

"What it do, Rico Suave?" Doug reached up and grabbed a spliff from behind his ear. He lit it and handed the spliff to Rico, who accepted and took a long drag before speaking.

"I want in," Rico said, blowing the smoke from his lungs.

"You want in what?"

"What you do. Selling." Rico motioned to Doug's pockets.

"You want in?" Doug asked. Doug inhaled again, passed the spliff back, and said "No, thanks."

"Come on," Rico pleaded.

"I take my business seriously. I don't need to entertain some bored rich kid. No offense."

"I'm not some bored rich kid," Rico said.

"It's not a secret who your dad is."

"From this point on I'm not accepting another dime from him. I'm making my own money. He's dead to me."

Doug shook his head, already regretting what he was about to say, and exhaled. "All right. If you're serious, I guess it's game on."

Doug held out his hand and Rico firmly grasped and shook it.

18. RICO

After

Rico searches the crowd of the infected for a break. There are too many of them and they're too closely packed for him to make it safely through. With his return path to the boat blocked, and every passing second diminishing the likelihood of finding Jayden, he racks his brain for a new plan.

The first wave of the horde steps into the street and is quickly followed by the line behind them. The stench of their bodies is awful, and it gives Rico an idea. He runs to the dumpsters at the back of the gas station. The rancid smell of decay is overwhelming and his stomach churns as he's hit with a punch of odor by lifting the lid; bile burns his throat as it shoots upward into his mouth. A swarm of flies surge upward and he has to swat them away from his face, the buzzing ringing in his ears.

Rico throws open the lid of the second dumpster. The first wave of infected have reached the corner of the gas station when Rico peers around the side; they catch sight of him, snarling and growling as they reach toward him. Rico levels the shotgun at the leader and pulls the trigger, blasting him in the chest. Those directly behind him trip, creating a domino effect, but it doesn't stop the herd. Rico bangs the shotgun along the front of the dumpster, creating more of a ruckus and inciting them.

With a silent prayer, Rico taps his forehead, chest, and shoulder to shoulder before slipping around the opposite side of the gas station, hoping the smell of the rotting garbage will mask his scent and confuse the monsters. With any luck, he has created enough of a distraction to give Jayden a fighting chance, wherever he is.

A loud slam against the dumpster resonates; they've reached the back and search for their prey. Rico edges to the front, ducking down next to an old ice cooler to avoid the attention of the handful of stragglers still filtering through the pumps. The dumpster distraction won't hold up long—once they realize he's nowhere in sight they could come searching around front. Rico takes his chances with more infected in front of him than behind him, and he bolts from the building and across the parking lot. He doesn't risk a glance behind him until he reaches the opposite street corner. His sprinting has caught the attention of two, but they're thinner and weaker than the frontrunners. They abandon the swarm and change course toward him, but they're unimposing.

Rico drops to a jog and after a couple of blocks to a walk. His hair is plastered to his face with sweat and he can feel a drop trickling down his spine. His throat is dry and scratchy from dehydration, and his temple is throbbing. One of the infected from the gas station followed him longer than the others, but now appears to have lost interest. Rico feels the relief of safety and stops to catch his breath. His legs feel ready to give, and he sits on the sidewalk against a building and opens a bottle of water.

He chugs the entire thing, gasping for air at the end, and fights the urge to open a second. His muscles ache and exhaustion starts to set in. Riding off of the remaining adrenaline, he forces himself to stand and continue moving. The best chance to find Jayden is to return to the boat, and he prays the kid will have done the same. The sun sinks lower as Rico wanders through the town, and he periodically calls Jayden's name in a loud whisper, but hears nothing. He laughs when he realizes that if anyone is watching, they could easily mistake him for the infected with his lumbering movements. A blister pops on his left foot, and his stomach starts to ache in hunger. He forces his shaking hands to rip open a packet of jerky, shoving the dry strips of meat into his drier mouth.

The surf shop looms ahead. Rico is almost to the stretch of beach they arrived on. He drops the empty packet in the street and hobbles across the road to the sand. His stomach drops when he looks across the beach, one of his threads of hope snipped.

"No, no, no, no, no, no," he repeats, collapsing. The shotgun slides out of his hand and he lifts the strap from the duffel bag over his head, tossing everything aside. He crawls forward, too weak to muster the strength to regain his footing, and falls face-first into the sand. A dam in his chest bursts and everything he had bottled up begins to pour out. His body shakes as hot tears drip out of his eyes, maniacal laughter escaping his mouth. He rolls onto his back, the gritty grains clinging to him and falling into his mouth.

The beach is empty; no sign of Jayden or the life raft. The boat is nowhere to be seen. His head lolls to the side and he sees the window from earlier with the flapping curtain, but now it's closed. His eyes hadn't deceived him in the morning. Ready to believe that everyone was dead or infected, he'd accepted the idea that it had only been the breeze and the curtain. But he *had* been watched, and they closed the window, wanting him to know. After he and Jayden left the beach, someone stole the raft, and with a source of gasoline, sped off with his father's yacht, robbing Rico of his last prospect for survival and protecting the kid. *A kid with no chance of being alive hours after disappearing*, the voice in Rico's mind says, and he is too weak to ignore the truth any longer. He'd wasted his last bit of strength returning to a beach that had nothing to offer him.

"What do you want from me?" he screams into the darkening sky, his lungs burning. "You've already won! You've taken everything!"

Rico pushes himself up onto his elbows, rolls onto his stomach, and drags himself toward the shotgun. He stretches out his arm as far as he can, feeling around until his fingers touch the metal of the shotgun barrel. His fingertips wrap around the barrel, and he pulls the gun close. He uses it as support to push himself up onto his knees. He pumps the shotgun one more time, placing the stock in the sand

and his forehead firmly against the hole of the barrel, closing his eyes tight. With his left hand wrapped around the barrel, holding the gun in place, his right hand travels down the length of the gun in search of the trigger.

"Rico?"

He accepts what's to come, and smiles knowing chemicals have flooded his brain allowing death to come easier. He hears the soft sound of Jayden's voice and whispers, "It's okay, kid. We're going home."

"Rico!"

The voice is louder this time, calling his name from a distance. He opens his eyes and lifts his head, looking down the stretch of sand past the lifeguard stands. Jayden comes charging toward him as fast as his little legs can carry him, his arms outstretched. Rico releases the shotgun. Jayden throws himself forward, knocking Rico back, his arms wrapping around Rico's neck.

"I'm sorry I ran." Jayden's voice quivers, his mouth near Rico's ears. Rico grabs the boy in a tight hug, unable to believe he is really there. "I shouldn't have run."

"It's okay, it's okay." Rico pulls Jayden off him and looks the boy over. His face is streaked with tears, and ash has transferred from Rico's body and clothes to the boy, but otherwise he appears unharmed. "You're okay."

"I was so scared, and I ran. I didn't mean to, I didn't want to leave you. But then I was all alone," Jayden begins, panic emerging in his voice. "And I couldn't remember how to get back to the gas station, so I found the beach and I walked and walked looking for the boat, and then I heard you yelling and you were here."

Rico gets a second wind. "C'mon, we're going back to the surf shop." He grabs the shotgun and takes Jayden's hand.

"What about the boat?" Jayden looks around the beach for the first time and out over the water. "Where is the boat?"

"Don't you worry your little head about that." Rico hooks the strap of the duffel bag with the shotgun, sliding the bag down the gun, over his arm, and onto his shoulder. The strap digs into his sore muscles, but he ignores the throbbing to lead Jayden away from the water. They return to the surf shop as the sun fully vanishes. After leaning a surfboard against the broken door, and a clothing rack against the surf-board, Rico and Jayden gather what remains of the beach towels and clothing options to create a nest behind the register. They make a small meal out of trail mix and jerky, enjoying a bottle of water each, without speaking. They're too burnt-out to form cohesive thoughts and words, and simply thankful to be reunited.

Before long, Rico can hear Jayden suckling on his thumb. He clicks off the flashlight, allowing a creeping darkness to settle over them. Without the security of the boat and the ocean, Rico fights to stay awake and keep watch, doubting the makeshift barricade he created at the door will stand against even a strong gust of wind, but the exertion of the day tugs at him. He feels his body slumping, and the world slides away from him.

19. ASHER

Before

Texts were awkward and tentative between Ellis and Asher in the days following the double date, but as the week continued, they moved past it. Ellis left town for the weekend with his family and Brandon, and on Monday, Ellis and Asher sat together in class. Ellis showed up on Tuesday while Asher was working. He claimed to be studying in the coffee shop again, and his face did stay buried in a textbook. They were unable to hang out afterward because Ellis had a presentation.

It wasn't until the following Friday afternoon that they were both available. Asher was getting out of the shower after a long opening shift when he heard his phone. He toweled off and read the message from Ellis, the only person he texted nowadays aside from Renee.

E: I'm starving and bored.

A: Sounds like a First World problem.

E: Waaaaaaaaah. Help me.

E: Please?

E: What are you doing?

A: I just got out of the shower, about to get dressed. I am kinda hungry.

E: My savior! What are you in the mood for?

A: Hmm. I'm not picky, are you or Brandon craving something in particular?

E: Brandon is back home for the weekend, so it's just you and me.

Asher had wondered why Ellis was hungry and bored when he could've had Brandon come over. But while he was glad to have somewhere to go instead of spending another Friday night in, he was annoyed that the only reason Ellis wanted to spend time with him was because he had nothing better to do. Asher shoved the thought from his mind.

A: I have some salmon I need to cook before it goes bad. Do you like asparagus?

E: Asparagus is disgusting! Salmon does sound delicious though.

A: Green beans? Bacon?

E: Does anyone NOT like bacon? And yes to the green beans.

A: Perfect. I know just what to make. I'd invite you over, but as per usual the roommates are blowing each other up again.

E: If it weren't for the added "up" I'd be on my way ;)

Asher rolled his eyes when he read that, but smiled at the same time.

A: Perv.

Ellis invited Asher over to cook at his apartment. Asher gathered the food items.

"Where you off to tonight?" The voice startled him and he jumped, bumping the back of his head on the freezer. He stood, rubbing the sore spot. Renee leaned against the wall, a beer in hand.

"Oh, hey. Just heading over to a friend's place to cook dinner," Asher answered, putting everything into a bag.

"The girl you went on the dates with? From last week?" Renee asked.

"Uh, no. I ended up breaking that off after our second date. Have you seen the soy sauce?"

"It's in the cabinet above the microwave. Why'd you break it off? The whole jealousy thing?"

"It just didn't feel right. And I thought about what you said the other day about not being in a relationship just to be in a relationship." Asher pulled the soy sauce from the cabinet and searched a bit longer before finding a bag of brown sugar.

"You seem to be in a better mood at least, so I guess you should be happy you're alone?" Renee laughed.

"Thanks, good to know I'm happier when single." Asher leaned against the counter. "I don't know if it's that I'm happier, but I feel like I'm at least okay with it. For now, that is. I've come to terms with it."

"That's a good outlook on it, like the glass is half full," Renee said.

"Exactly. And one day the glass is going to be entirely full, but I'll get there when I get there. For now, I have to go before this fish is out too long." Asher grabbed the bag, messing up Renee's hair as he passed.

"Have fun, jerk! I'll see you when you get back," Renee called.

***

"Hello there," Ellis greeted Asher. "It occurred to me that we're taking another step in our friendship by you coming into the sanctuary that is my home."

"It looks pretty nice," Asher answered, walking into the kitchen area and placing the bag of food on the center island. "A lot nicer than my place." He looked around the apartment; it was an open layout with the kitchen, dining area, and living room as one large space. It was decorated simplistically but with nice subtle touches throughout. Instead of the standard college-student posters plastered all over the walls, there was a piece of framed artwork hanging behind the dining room table, and a framed picture of New York City above the couch in the living room. A large bowl of fresh fruit rested on the coffee table, and potted plants lined the windowsill.

"Would you like something to drink?" Ellis asked. "I have water, soda, and wine, both red and white."

"Just water for now, thanks," Asher answered, taking the food out of the carrying bag.

"You sure? I figured if we were having a fancy dinner, we might as well go all out with some fancy wine. I raided my parents' wine collection last time I was home, and now it's not even going to be put to use," Ellis said, moping.

"Are you trying to get me to succumb to peer pressure?" Asher asked. "Water while cooking, wine while eating. Sound good?"

"Deal. Now what can I do to help? Although I have to warn you that I'm not a great cook." Ellis grabbed two glasses and filled them with water.

"I'm using a recipe my grandma taught me—if I told you the generations-old family recipe, I'd have to kill you," Asher said with a straight face but started laughing when Ellis looked at him like he was crazy. "Cut the bacon strips in half, wrap them around five to six green beans, and place them on a baking sheet." Ellis turned on music and jumped in, following Asher's directions slowly and methodically. Asher seasoned the fish and placed both baking sheets in the oven. "And now we wait."

"About that wine?" Ellis asked. Asher made a show of giving in as Ellis grabbed a bottle and extracted the cork. With glasses in hand, Ellis sat on one end of the couch, and Asher followed him, sitting on the opposite end. Asher wondered whether to address the previous week or to let it go, and settled on taking a drink and waiting for Ellis's lead. Ellis remained equally quiet, so while the smells of dinner cooking wafted through the apartment, Asher looked around the living room and noticed framed pictures on the entertainment center. One showcased Ellis with a pretty blonde girl and two older adults. Directly next to it was a picture of Ellis and Brandon with their arms linked around the other's shoulders.

"Is that your family?" Asher asked.

"Yeah, that's my older sister, Ivy, and our parents," Ellis answered.

"When was it taken? You look young. Well, younger," Asher said.

"About three years ago, on one of our family vacations," Ellis answered.

"You guys look happy." Asher took another sip of his wine, trying to mask his envy.

"We are. Happy. Most of the time," Ellis said. "But each family has their issues."

"Sorry, I didn't mean to offend you. I think it's awesome that your family is close."

"No, you didn't. I think I take it for granted how close my family is, and I just assumed that all families were that close until you told me about your brother."

"It's not that I'm not close to them—I try to be. I just don't have as much in common with them; we don't see eye to eye on a lot. My mom and I get along better than I get along with anyone else, though." Asher took another drink, allowing the wine to build up his confidence, and asked, "Did any of your family have issues with you being gay?"

"Yes and no." Ellis paused. Asher wondered if he was pushing a boundary line by asking, but Ellis continued. "In my mind it made all the difference in the world. I was different, and society says there is something wrong and abnormal with me. I felt disgusted with myself, and I was afraid of what would happen when they found out. So I acted out—I did things to get in trouble so that when my parents got mad at me, I could feel justified in my anger with them. I never did anything major, just stuff like throwing parties when they were out of town, missing my curfew. I just knew that when they found out they wouldn't love me anymore, so I needed to give them a different reason." Ellis stopped and wiped a tear away.

Asher looked down at his cup and swirled the wine around. He felt guilty, like he was intruding on a private moment, a voyeur to Ellis's past anguish. He regretted asking something so personal, but at the same time, he felt their friendship strengthening.

"Eventually, they sat me down and asked me what was going on, what made me start acting out. I broke down and started crying, and then I cried more, because 'boys don't cry.' Before I even knew what I was saying, I told them I was gay. And they just looked at me and finally my dad was like, 'Being gay just means you like the same sex, not that you break the rules.' I spent years destroying myself on the inside, terrified, and listing all of the things I didn't deserve. And it didn't even faze them. And that's when I knew it was going to be okay. I just had to promise not to throw any more house parties and to let them know if I was going to miss curfew."

The oven beeped, disrupting their conversation.

Asher shot off of the couch. He pulled the baking sheets out of the oven while Ellis grabbed plates.

"Oh my God, this smells delicious." Ellis leaned over the food, smelling everything, and moaned while his stomach grumbled. "Told you I was starving."

They loaded up their plates and sat at the table eating. Ellis was halfway through his green beans when he said, "These are literally the best green beans I've ever had. I'll never be able to eat them any other way. I'm going to tell my mom to start making them at our family dinners."

"If you do that I'm going to have to kill your mom so it doesn't get out," Asher whispered.

"You already taught me how to make them—does that mean you think of me as family now?" Ellis asked.

"You've earned my trust." Asher finished off his wine. Ellis replenished both glasses without asking.

"I saw Stacey the other day," Ellis said between bites.

"Oh yeah? How'd that go?" Asher felt wrong about how he'd handled Stacey, but he tried to sound nonchalant with his inquiry.

"She glared at me and walked off without responding after I said hello," Ellis said. "You must have done a number on her."

"It was only two dates; we didn't even know anything about each other. She was probably pissed at you for causing the world's worst double date," Asher answered.

"Sure, sure, it was all my fault." Ellis laughed and downed his second glass of wine. "I guess it actually was."

"Don't worry, you did me a favor. Or, well, you did both of us a favor," Asher said.

"How did I do both of us a favor?" Ellis asked.

"Not you-and-me both of us, Stacey-and-me both of us. It wouldn't have worked out; you were right about that," Asher said. He found himself wishing he had drunk many more glasses of wine. His voice shook from his nerves and discomfort. "I'm gay."

Neither Ellis nor Asher said anything while the declaration lingered between them, the admission soaking into their minds. Ellis looked up at Asher, the fear he once felt was etched into Asher's face. He moved forward and wrapped his arms around Asher in a hug, squeezing tight. Asher could feel Ellis's heart beating against his own racing heart as he returned the hug.

"I know," Ellis said. "It's okay." Asher released the hug and pulled back, letting out the air he'd been holding in his lungs. "And I really am sorry about the other night. I thought you were gay, but that didn't give me the right to act the way I did, or to force you out like this."

"If it weren't for you, I'd have continued going out with Stacey and just made things worse. I haven't told anyone since I came to school here, and it's been eating me alive. I just couldn't hold it in anymore," Asher said. He agreed that Ellis shouldn't have pushed him, but spending time around Ellis and seeing the life he led inspired Asher.

"And look, the world didn't end," Ellis said, squeezing Asher's arm. "I know it's hard to deal with everything alone, but you're not on your own anymore. I'll always be here for you. And at least you can start moving forward now. Trust me, it does get easier."

"Thanks, I'm going to really need a friend through this. Not that I think I'm going to lose any friends, but still," Asher said, starting to feel like himself again.

"Do you want to talk about it?" asked Ellis.

"I will. Eventually. But for tonight I think just saying it is enough," Asher answered. "Sorry, I keep steering the conversation to downer subjects."

"Stop. From now on you don't get to think of you being gay as a downer subject," Ellis interjected. "It's a part of you, but it doesn't define you. We're all more than our sexuality. And there is nothing wrong with you, understand?"

"Yes, sir," Asher laughed. "I don't think there's anything wrong with me. At least, not anymore."

"Good. But we don't have to talk about it anymore tonight if you're not ready. How about a movie?" Ellis carried the dishes to the sink while Asher picked out a DVD. As the movie started, Asher felt a flutter in his stomach. For the first time in as long as he could remember, he allowed himself to feel happy.

***

Hours later, when Asher opened his eyes, everything was darker and he was confused, unable to recognize his surroundings. He sat up and a blanket fell off him. He was still on Ellis's couch; he'd fallen asleep during the movie. His mind started to reawaken, and he realized he didn't remember much of anything from the film. Ellis had placed a pillow under his head and draped a blanket on top of him. Asher slipped his phone out of his pocket to check the time: 4:37 a.m. Laying his head back down on the pillow, he wrapped the blanket tighter around his body and closed his eyes.

***

"Good morning, sleepyhead." This time when Asher opened his eyes the sun was pouring into the living room, the blinds were pulled open, and Ellis stood in pajamas over him, a steaming mug in each hand. "Did you sleep well?"

"Actually, yeah, I did. Sorry for passing out during the movie," Asher said, sitting up to make room for Ellis and accepting one of the mugs. "I thought you didn't like coffee?"

"I have it for when Brandon stays here. And don't worry about it. You're cute when you sleep. It's just a shame you didn't make it to the end of the movie to learn who the actual killer was." Ellis sat on the couch and put his feet up on the coffee table while stirring the tea bag in his mug.

"I guess we'll have to find another time to watch it again," Asher answered.

"What do you have planned for today?"

"You don't want to rewatch the movie, do you?"

"No, no, no. I enjoy it, but not enough to watch it twice in twenty-four hours. I just meant I don't have any plans for the day. There isn't much here to eat, but we could start by grabbing breakfast? I'm starving."

"You're always starving. We'll have to stop by my place first, though—I need to shower and change out of yesterday's clothes."

"Awesome, I'll go jump in the shower now." Ellis got up from the couch and disappeared down the hall. The shower started, and Asher surfed the Internet on his phone while sipping his coffee. Ellis eventually reemerged in shorts and a T-shirt, his hair still damp from the shower. He was locking the door when Stacey's door opened and she stepped out, stopping in her tracks when she saw Ellis and Asher together.

"Hey," Asher said, blood rushing to his cheeks as he tried to maintain eye contact. He could only imagine the thoughts running through Stacey's head. His hair was sticking up and his clothes were disheveled. For all intents and purposes, he was doing a walk of shame. She stepped back inside her apartment and shut the door.

"That wasn't awkward." Ellis took the stairs two at a time to the parking lot. He followed Asher in his own car, and when they arrived, Asher unlocked the front door to silence for a change. He was guiding Ellis to his bedroom when Renee stepped out of the kitchen in exercise shorts and a tank top, holding a bowl of cereal.

"And where have you been all night, mister?" Renee asked, placing a hand on her hip.

"Good morning to you too." Asher introduced them, avoiding Renee's question. Renee extended her hand to shake Ellis's with a knowing smile.

"So this is the friend that has stolen you away from us," Renee teased, her face lighting up. Asher pushed his bedroom door open, hoping to end the conversation.

"Yeah, I guess so," Ellis answered, noticing how red Asher had turned. "Although if Asher weren't rude and had invited me over sooner, we could've been sharing him."

"So much for manners." Renee said. Asher butted in that he needed to shower so they could leave for breakfast. Ellis extended an invitation to Renee, but she had finished half the bowl of cereal already and said she needed to run to the mall.

"Do you guys want to go with me?" Renee asked.

"Fine by me. Ellis, you can hang out in my room if you want," Asher said.

"Nope, I'll keep him company." Renee reached out and grabbed Ellis's hand and pulled him behind her to the living room. Asher saw the mess of beer bottles and cans covering the coffee table, but instead of fighting the situation, he hurried to get into the shower.

He released everything into the blast of hot water. All of his fears circled the drain with the dirt of yesterday. He had never felt so alive, so clean, as he did in that moment. Asher knew that everything wouldn't change with a snap of his fingers, but admitting his secret to himself and to another soul released him, and now he would get a fresh start. Ellis's words about not loving himself came back to him and he vowed to never shelter his emotions from himself again. If coming out could be this freeing and satisfying, then he could only imagine where things could go from here. The water began to cool and he realized how long he had been standing in the stream without actually washing. He grabbed his sponge and scrubbed until his skin was a light pink and the water was too cold to tolerate. Laughter carried through the walls as he toweled off. He dressed and stepped out.

"What's going on out here?" he asked.

"We're becoming fast friends," Renee said with a pat on Ellis's leg. "You guys go get breakfast, and I'll be ready when you get back." Renee returned her empty bowl to the kitchen before slowly opening the door to Mark's room and slipping inside.

"I like her—she's cool," Ellis said.

"Yeah, she is. Mark's pretty lucky," Asher answered.

20. ASHER

After

Asher watches Wendy closely; she hasn't said a word since returning to the bus. Instead, she seems to be deep in thought, almost meditative, and he doesn't know how receptive she will be toward his breaking her concentration. Nobody wants to make the first move, and the tension mounts as the heat sets in. The unasked question of "what happens now" hangs in the air. It's difficult for Todd and Tonya to discuss their stance with Asher and Wendy right there. Asher knows Wendy wanted to keep moving, but she hasn't been forthcoming as to where. As much as Asher wants to remain supportive of her, it starts to grate against him to feel left out.

"I'm going to stretch my legs," Asher announces to no one in particular. He leaves his pack on the seat as a show of trust, but grabs the bat as a precaution. Wendy turns her face to his as he steps into the aisle, locking onto his eyes. Asher gives her a subtle nod and breaks eye contact.

"I'll go with you; I could use a walk," Wendy says. "We'll be back in a few."

They move beyond the burnt bodies, passing empty cars that had been raided by Todd or the bus's previous occupants. They continue walking until they're confidently out of earshot, but still visible.

"I figured it was best to give Tonya and Todd a chance to talk without us overhearing them. Besides, I really do need a walk—it was getting stuffy on that bus."

"Yeah," Wendy mutters.

Asher drops the tailgate on a truck with a loud thud.

"Sorry," he says, crinkling his face. He hops up onto the tailgate and climbs onto the top of the cab to survey the road. He doesn't spot anything out of the ordinary and returns to the tailgate. He swings his legs back and forth, watching Wendy step onto the hood of the car behind the truck.

"I'm leaving," she says while gazing off to the side.

"What?" Asher asks, stunned by the abruptness of her declaration.

"When we get back to the bus, I'm getting my stuff and going."

"What about Todd and Tonya and Marie?"

"What about them? I don't owe them anything; I don't even know them." Wendy shrugs her shoulders. Her behavior strikes Asher as odd. He's become used to her not sharing information with him, but she's never been flippant.

"I just can't sit around on a bus until we die; I need to keep moving."

"You've not even been on the bus for a day! Don't you feel safer with more people than just the two of us?"

"Asher, you don't even know that they want us hanging around. It's their bus, and I need to go on," Wendy argues.

"What about me? And what I need?"

Wendy twists her body away from him. "If they say it's cool to stay, then stay."

"I'm going with you," Asher says.

"You don't have to do that."

"So that's that? We've had each other's back for weeks, but overnight it's just done. You're going to go at it alone? You don't need me anymore?"

"You said it yourself—you feel safer with more people. Besides, they'll need all the help they can get protecting that little girl."

"Marie."

"What?"

"She has a name—it's Marie, not 'that little girl.'"

Wendy sighs and throws her hands up into the air. "I didn't mean it as a slight, you know that."

"Are you uncomfortable because they're black?"

"Excuse me?" Wendy snaps, taken aback. "I'm not racist, I don't care that they're black. Look, Asher, you don't understand—"

"You're right." Asher cuts her off. "I don't understand, because for whatever reason you refuse to tell me anything. You let me follow you along, expect me to just do whatever you need, and now you're done with me and I can stay behind while you go off on your own. How are you going to sleep? What about yesterday in the woods? If I hadn't been there, you'd be dead right now. And I would have been dead if it weren't for you. Is that what you want? Are you on some suicide mission?"

Wendy cringes, and realizing what he said, Asher's jaw drops. He remembers the call, the drive to the hospital, and the days that followed.

"Wendy, I'm sorry, I didn't mean—"

"It's okay." Wendy waves him off. "I know you didn't."

"You can't keep feeling guilty; it wasn't your fault."

"That's why I'm doing this, why I have to go. I'm not ready to talk about it, but I just need you to understand that. I don't know what I'm expecting, or what the point is really, but I need to do it."

"Do what?"

"There's somewhere I have to go. And you'd think I was foolish if I told you where, but I've made up my mind. And you know what, maybe it is a suicide mission, not intentionally, but that's why I can't ask you to go with me."

Asher nods. He knows there's nothing he can say to dissuade Wendy from leaving.

"Look, everything since this all started has been a huge risk," he explains. "Even if I stayed behind, there's no guarantee that I make it to tomorrow morning. But I won't wonder every day where you are and if you're okay; I'm already doing that with enough people. You don't have to ask me, because no matter where we're headed, I'll follow you. You're all I have left of—" Asher stops, his stomach clenching and his heart skipping a beat. Their friendship has been built on a cracked foundation of heartbreak and longing for someone else. Regardless of how much Asher cares about Wendy now, he won't let her go alone, because he's not ready to release the past yet.

"Yeah, well, I could say the same." Wendy breaks eye contact, running her hands through her hair. "You know, I used to wonder how people that smelled bad didn't realize it, and now I think I'm slowly understanding."

Asher laughs, thankful for Wendy's ability to tactfully let him off the hook. The tightness in his chest begins to release. His anger toward her for wanting to run off, even at his expense, subsides. She wears her scars differently than he does, keeping them covered up, too proud to let anyone see her hurt. "If we're hitting the road again we should probably hurry up and gather our stuff."

"You know the huge park up the road? You can just barely see the tip of the tallest castle spire over the trees from the highway?" Wendy asks. Asher nods and mentions the Ferris wheel and roller coasters. Without further explanation, she slides off the hood of the car and approaches him, wrapping Asher tightly in her arms. "Thank you for doing this for me."

"You're right—your hair does smell disgusting." Asher crinkles his nose, angling his face to the side with exaggerated disgust. Wendy shoves him away and starts walking to the bus. He finds her mention of the theme park curious, as she'd never brought it up before now. He hadn't realized how close they'd come to it, and he's afraid to ask if that *is* where they're heading. A memory tweaks a sore spot in his heart, but he doesn't say anything. He doesn't argue or call it foolish like she'd expected. When they reach the open door, Wendy gives a courtesy knock before climbing the steps.

Marie is sitting on the aisle floor near the back exit, a book open in her lap. Tonya is in shorts and a bra, her spine and ribs protruding under her skin, a large overnight bag open on a seat, and she pulls a T-shirt over her head before noticing Asher and Wendy. They apologize for intruding, but she tells them there's no need for modesty anymore. Todd sits on the edge of the seat in front of his wife, cleaning his pistol, but he sets it down and stands.

"Tonya and I talked about it, and we want to invite both of you to stay with us for however long you'd like," Todd begins.

"Thank you, sir," Asher says, using his manners for the first time in weeks, "but I think we're going to hit the road again."

"It's not that we don't appreciate it," Wendy says.

"You two can't just go off on your own." Tonya steps up next to her husband. "It's not safe out there."

"I understand that—" Wendy starts.

"There's a better chance of surviving in a group," Todd interrupts.

"If you're worried about Marie being a liability, she's not, I swear," Tonya interjects, trying and failing to hide the pleading in her voice.

Asher reassures the couple that he and Wendy don't think of Marie as a burden. They're grateful for the offer, he continues, but they've set out on a task and can't stop until they see it through. Tonya tries to counter, but Todd rests his hand on her forearm to silence her rebuttal.

"I'm sorry you two don't want to stay." Todd's voice is tired and defeated. He gathers his wife to his chest, nods his head to Asher and Wendy, and kisses Tonya on the forehead. She looks at Asher and Wendy with tears in her eyes, but they don't spill out. Asher glances down at Marie, focused on her book, and grasps what the appearance of Wendy and him could have meant for the family. There are no words to soothe them, so he focuses on gathering up his bag in silence.

Cans clang together as Asher slides his arms through the straps of his backpack and hoists it onto his shoulders. Wendy stands nearer to the door, her own bag ready to go.

"Here," Todd says, holding out a gun to Asher.

"That's not Wendy's gun," Asher responds.

"It's one of ours, and I've got some extra ammo for you as well. That one gun isn't going to last the two of you much longer."

"No, I couldn't. You guys were generous enough already, I can't take something that would help keep your family safe." Asher holds up his hands, turning down the gun.

"The only thing that will help us feel better about you two leaving is the hope that you have a chance," Todd insists before turning to Wendy. "Your gun is still under the front seat; don't forget to grab it."

"Thank you." Asher accepts the gun and shakes Todd's hand.

Marie steps up behind her dad and tugs on his arm. Todd turns his attention to her, forming gestures foreign to Asher. Marie signs back to him and points out the emergency door window. Asher's eyes follow her finger and Todd's gaze to what has caught her attention.

A hundred yards away, rounding a bend in the road and rapidly gaining, is an entire herd of infected. They maneuver through the cars and toward the bus at a steady pace. The air begins to hum with growls and moans as they close in.

"Where did they come from?" Asher asks, stunned by the sea of bodies.

"It doesn't matter, there are too many of them. We'll never be able to fight them off. Once they reach this bus we're done for," Todd answers, his voice empty and dry.

21. ASHER

Before

Asher sat on the balcony, staring out into the near-empty parking lot. He passed a beer back and forth between his hands and periodically checked his phone. Tonight was Brandon and Ellis's one-year anniversary, but Asher was unable to convince himself to feel happy for them. After Asher came out to Ellis, he began to realize just how much Ellis meant to him; the deep connection between them continued to grow. But it didn't affect Ellis's relationship status, and when Asher would catch himself hoping otherwise, he felt a pang in his heart. He knew it was selfish and arrogant to expect Ellis to throw Brandon to the wayside.

But, Asher thought, *if Ellis is truly happy and in love with Brandon, then why does he spend so much time with me? Why do we text nonstop until one or the other finally grows too drowsy to continue? And each night the texts end with the same exchange about the bedbugs. Because we're friends, and that's what friends do.*

However, there was also the fact that Ellis had been texting Asher all through dinner on his anniversary and up until the previews started before a movie he and Brandon were seeing. Asher put the phone back in his pocket and took another drink from his beer, which had started to warm. The past week and a half had been as close to perfect as Asher could ask for. After going to breakfast, they'd picked up Renee and spent hours hanging out at the mall, all three forcing each other to try on awful clothes for laughs. Asher did buy Ellis a button-up shirt covered in embroidered birds as a thank-you gift for helping him accept himself. They passed signs for one of Orlando's famous theme parks on the drive back from the mall, and Ellis promised to take them both one day. Having grown up in the area, he had a pass but hadn't been there in months.

Ellis had even come back to the apartment and had met Mark and Derrick, and the five hung out for dinner. Sunday they both had homework to catch up on, and Brandon returned to town, so Ellis was occupied. The week went as usual, or the new usual, as well. Ellis brought smoothies to class, did homework in the coffee shop while Asher was working, and they grabbed meals together. The occasions when Asher would begin to feel guilty were generally flushed away by Ellis initiating contact and making plans.

"Hey." Renee stepped out with a beer in her hand, allowing the sounds of music and talking to escape until she slid the balcony door shut again. Asher raised his drink in greeting. "You okay?"

"I'm fine," he answered. Renee sat in the chair next to his, and he could feel her eyes on him. He didn't feel like playing games, so he gave in, hoping to get whatever was coming done and over with.

"You don't seem fine; everyone keeps asking where you are," Renee said.

"Sorry, the music was giving me a bit of a headache." Asher pulled his phone out and checked it again. Still nothing.

"Is there anything you want to talk about?" Renee released him from her gaze, turning her attention beyond the railing, allowing him to look away and feel less pressure. But it didn't work.

"Why are you always so pushy?" Asher snapped, more hostile than he intended.

"I'm not trying to be pushy. I guess I was just actually concerned about my friend who seemed off today. Sorry for asking." Renee stood, but before she opened the door Asher stopped her.

"Wait, I'm sorry, I didn't mean to rip your head off—you can sit back down." Renee sat and took another swig of her beer. "Sorry,"

Asher apologized again. "It's been a weird day, and I *have* been pouting around. I just didn't think anyone was going to care enough to actually say anything. And the music really was giving me a headache, but I don't want to be alone out here either."

The sliding door opened again and Mark stepped out with a cigarette, lighter in hand. He closed the door and lit the cigarette.

"What are you two talking about?" he asked, exhaling smoke.

"Nothing, just taking a break from the music," Renee half lied.

"Where's your boyfriend at?" Mark asked Asher.

"My what?" Asher choked on his beer, froth spilling down his front.

"Your boyfriend, Ellis. You guys are dating, aren't you? Why isn't he over?" Mark took another drag from his cigarette and stared at Asher.

"He's not my . . . we're not . . . I'm—" Asher struggled to speak but couldn't get the words out.

"You're not dating? My mistake. You both seemed so happy and flirty, we thought you were." Mark put out his cigarette and went back into the party. Asher watched him leave without knowing what to say. He turned to Renee and saw amusement.

"He's not wrong," Renee said.

"But I've never even—"

"Said you were gay? You didn't have to; we all figured it out a long time ago. None of us care. We figured you bringing Ellis here was your way of telling us. And Mark has a point. I've never seen you as happy as you were the day I hung out with you two. And he's drawn to you."

"We're just friends; he has a boyfriend." Asher dismissed Renee's comments, but, as if on cue, his phone vibrated.

E: Movie is over! It was hilarious! What are you up to?

"Who's that?" Renee asked, leaning forward.

"Who do you think it is?" Asher said.

A: Hanging out with Renee and the roommates. Mark has friends over.

"Did you not invite him?" Renee asked.

"No, I didn't. He already had plans tonight, with his boyfriend. It's their anniversary. I told you, we're just friends," Asher said.

"You really don't get it do you?" Renee shook her head in disbelief. "Oh my God!"

"It's not like that."

Renee opened her mouth but noticed the look of despair on Asher's face and closed it. Without pushing the topic any further, she instead sat back in her chair and gazed at her now-empty bottle. Asher told her he'd be okay—she could return to the party. She hugged him and then Asher was alone on the balcony.

E: Sounds like a blast! Just got home, and I'm exhausted. See you tomorrow?

Asher confirmed their plans, and after the brief text exchange, and bedbugs shtick, he slid the balcony door open. As the blast of music hit him, he slipped unnoticed through the party and to his room.

22. RICO

Before

Electronica pulsed through the room and multicolored lasers darted above the sea of heads. A haze of smoke and fog settled around the occupants. Rico resisted an urge to join the crowd. Tonight he was working and had to scope out clients. The cargo shorts felt foreign on him and the pockets were weighed down as he merged into the mass of bodies. Rico spotted a girl with dreadlocks dancing and slowly approached her. He stepped in front of her and waited until she finally acknowledged his presence.

"You buying?" he asked, leaning in so she could hear him over the music. He signaled down, opening his hand to show her the pills.

"No, thanks," she yelled back, and returned to dancing. Rico closed his hand around the pills, feeling a twist in his stomach. He'd anticipated selling to be easy money, and was surprised after approaching several people and being turned down by each. An anxious sweat rolled down his forehead as he looked for someone else to approach. He was trying to maneuver his way through a group of kids he recognized from his school when he felt a hand on his arm. He turned in the midst of the students, and was face-to-face with the unknown girl who'd kissed him at the party. Her mouth moved but he was unable to hear her words.

"What?" Rico screamed out, turning an ear to her.

"I heard you're selling?" she repeated. She didn't give off any signs of recognition, either she didn't remember kissing him or didn't care. He smiled and nodded his head in response.

"You interested?" he asked. The girl nudged a couple of her friends, and they started pulling out money. Rico ensured nobody was watching too closely and shoved his hand down into his cargo pocket.

***

"How'd it go?" Doug asked, leaning against the warehouse and smoking. Rico used one hand to pull his drenched shirt away from his skin and the other to grab a wad of cash from his pocket and hand it over. Doug counted it bill by bill. He started to grin, recounted a number of bills, and extracted them from the wad for Rico. Rico graciously received his payment and began counting but was interrupted by Doug. "Never count your pay in front of me—it's insulting."

"What?" Rico asked. "You counted the money in front of me. I was just curious as to how much I made."

"You made as much as you earned. No more, no less. I counted the money because I'm in charge. Rule number one: never question me. Rule number two: do what I say, when I say, without talking back."

"Sorry, I didn't mean anything by it." Rico slipped the money away.

"I know you didn't. There are just some things you need to know, proper etiquette." Doug's hard exterior dissipated. "You ready to celebrate your first night?"

Doug opened the warehouse door and stepped inside, waiting for Rico. Although he had just left the rave, it felt like an entirely different place now. The weight and expectation of selling was gone from Rico's pocket and shoulders.

"This one's on me," Doug said, holding out a round, unfamiliar white pill in the center of his palm. Rico reached over and tossed it into his mouth without question. The lasers illuminated his face, and he knew he was home.

***

Rico grabbed a textbook from his locker and tossed it into his bag. He jumped when he noticed Chloe leaning against the locker next to his, hidden by the door.

"You didn't show up Saturday," she said, her face failing to mask her anger.

"Sorry," Rico said, slinging his bag onto his shoulder.

"Really, that's it? Just sorry?" Chloe asked.

"I don't know what else you want me to say." Rico shrugged and walked off with Chloe at his heels.

"I must be an idiot. You got me arrested, I forgive you, and then you don't even follow through with your promise to do community service with me."

Rico stopped and turned to face Chloe.

"*I* did not get you arrested. *We* got arrested. *We* were both blitzed. We were *both* in our underwear. I'm sorry I wasn't there Saturday, but you haven't even asked me why."

Chloe, taken aback, ogled him, openmouthed. "You're right. So why weren't you there Saturday?"

"Because Friday night when I went to my dad's to get my car back, he threw me out and told me not to come back again," Rico lied. "I'm sorry if I didn't want to pick up trash for a couple of hours, but I just couldn't."

"I didn't realize—"

"I know you didn't, but maybe next time you should stop for a second and think about the fact that I'm not actually a terrible person before you get up on your high horse."

"I don't think you're a terrible person."

"It sure seems like it. Besides, everyone else thinks I am, so I guess you might as well join them."

"I'm not everyone else."

"I've got to get to class; I'll see you later."

Rico left Chloe in the crowd and sulked his way to math class. A pop quiz only served to make him feel even more abysmal. He frequently skipped math and couldn't remember the last time he'd bothered with the practice questions. The numbers and letters seemed to swirl around the page as a migraine formed in the front of his brain. He strained to focus on the paper, but it intensified the pressure and soon he felt a sweat break across his forehead. Rico jotted down answers he knew were wrong, attempting to use equations he did understand, before flipping the page over and raising his hand.

Mrs. Young called on him but declined his request to visit the nurse until the quizzes were collected. When he persisted, she tilted her head, noticing the sheen on Rico's face and the lack of color in his skin, and obliged.

Rico grabbed his bag and rushed for the door. Striding down the hall as quickly as possible, he felt his stomach flip and his throat became warm and full. He barely made it to an open stall in the restroom before bile shot out of his mouth. He slumped sideways against the partition and wiped his mouth with the back of his hand. The wall was cool against his forehead, giving him the slightest relief, but he felt his body start to sweat in other places as well.

He heard heavy footsteps on the tile, and seconds later Doug was standing over him in his usual school attire of camo and combat boots.

"Not feeling so good, buddy?" Rico could hear the smirk in Doug's voice.

"I feel like death warmed over," Rico grunted.

"Yeah, well, you look like it too," Doug said.

"Shouldn't you be in class?"

Doug held up a wooden paddle—a bathroom pass, and said he'd watched Rico rush past. He came to check on his new salesman before their evening run. Rico threw up a second time, getting more in the toilet, and warned Doug that he was too sick to work. Doug reached into his bag and pulled out another of the white pills Rico took at the rave. "Your body is flushing the remains from this weekend; it's going through withdrawals. Thirty bucks."

"I don't have any cash on me right now," Rico said.

"It's cool, I'll deduct it from your pay tonight."

"I told you, I don't think I'm going to be able to go tonight."

"Trust me, take this, and you'll feel supreme by the time school lets out."

After swallowing the pill, Rico climbed to his feet and staggered to the sink. He swished a mouthful of water around and gargled before spitting it out, but the sour taste remained on his tongue. He splashed several handfuls of cold water on his face.

"Attaboy," Doug said, patting him on the back. Rico picked his bag up and they left the bathroom together. Doug returned to class, but Rico wandered off to the library and into his usual corner. Making sure he would not be disturbed, he placed his headphones on his ears and turned on his electronica as the pill took over.

23. RICO

After

Rico's temple throbs with a migraine. He wipes sweat from his forehead and focuses on the road. The bicycle he found that morning hits a small bump and Jayden's arms tighten around his waist, squeezing the shotgun into Rico's chest. It's been two hours since he started pedaling alongside the highway, the ride uneventful, and his body aches with the strain of the activity. He squeezes the brake and stops.

Jayden releases his grip and hops down to stretch his legs. Rico, shotgun in hand, pushes the kickstand down, and relaxes in the grassy median with a bottle of water.

"You should drink some too," he says, holding it out to the kid. Jayden grabs the bottle and finishes it off. He drops it to the ground and kicks his makeshift toy around.

"Where are we going?" Jayden asks, speaking for the first time all day.

"We're going to go see your grandparents," Rico answers. Without the boat, he had been forced to come up with an alternate strategy. Rico had promised Theresa to not bring Jayden back to Miami, and with nothing there for them anyway, there was no reason to return to the place they fought so hard to escape. The only options were heading further north or inland. Although he had never been to Jayden's grandparents' house, he knew they lived in Orlando and figured they were old enough to still be listed in a phone book. It would only be a matter of finding a phone book once they reached the city; he'd already pocketed a map of Florida he found in the surf shop. Best-case scenario is that they'll find the grandparents alive; worst-case scenario, they will be in the same predicament they are now.

Rico hands Jayden a packet of trail mix. "Eat."

"I hate raisins." Jayden plucks one of the dried and wrinkled fruits out and flicks it away into the grass.

"Hey, don't waste food. Even if you don't like them they're good for you." Rico grabs Jayden's hand before he can flick another raisin.

"Then you eat them. Can't I have a candy bar?"

"I tell you what, if you eat all of the trail mix, including the raisins, I'll give you a candy bar. Deal?"

Jayden thinks before holding out his hand with his pinky sticking up. He chews with exaggerated disgust, feigning puking after each mouthful. Rico laughs, shakes his head, and tosses back a handful of his own. Rico washes down the salty crumbs with a mouthful of water, but a loud thump catches his attention.

A boy about Jayden's age appears from around the back of a car on the opposite side of the median. He's still too far away to distinguish his features, but Rico feels Jayden stiffen next to him, and the kid's eyes widen in fear.

"Come on, let's go." Rico gets to his feet, pulling Jayden up with him. The boy notices the two of them and changes course toward them. Rico swings a leg over the bike but Jayden hasn't moved. "Jayden, come on."

The boy is halfway across the median when Rico cocks the shotgun and levels it at him. His skin is blistered and peeling from deep sunburn, and all of his baby fat has melted off from starvation. When he opens his mouth, Rico realizes he's missing all of his front teeth and has been incapable of feeding off of anything other than scraps without being able to bite. His small fingers, the only tools left to him, are covered in dried blood.

"Jayden, move."

Jayden remains stationary as the boy reaches a spot five feet away from him. Rico hurries forward and pulls the trigger. The boy's body jerks backward and blood sprays from his chest. Jayden snaps out of his trance and turns to Rico, his face and shirt splattered with blood. Rico reaches into the bag and pulls out his jeans, crusted from the salt water, and uses them to wipe the blood from Jayden's cheeks.

"That was a little boy, like me," Jayden whispers. "Is that going to happen to me too?"

"No, kiddo. I'm going to protect you, I promise." Rico squeezes Jayden's shoulder. When Rico returns to the bike, Jayden follows him, the half-full packet of trail mix dangling from his hand. Rico offers Jayden a candy bar, but the kid shakes his head.

***

The highway becomes less crowded in the rural miles between Daytona Beach and Rico and Jayden. There are small stretches without cars, although wrecks and multicar pileups block many sections. Rico speeds past the remains of a family lying in a circle in one of the empty stretches, the sun reflecting off the gun in the father's withered hand. Heat and humidity become unbearable and Rico's headache and muscle pain intensify. Eventually, they pass a highway sign welcoming them into Orange County, and Rico pushes hard on the pedals to climb a steep incline.

At the top of the hill, Rico swerves the bike to the left, slamming into the side of a car. The bike topples over, sending Rico and Jayden crashing to the ground. A wall of infected have their backs to Rico and Jayden; they're pushing and shoving each other down the highway. Three of the stragglers turn around at the sound of the bike skittering. Rico pushes himself to his feet, wincing at the pain. Scrapes and fresh spots of blood cover his left arm and leg, and his shoulder is sore from taking the brunt of the impact. Jayden is in a similar state, and his eyes are filled with tears. Rico drops the duffel bag and helps Jayden up.

Rico directs Jayden to a yellow car ten feet away. Jayden shuffles his feet, glancing back at Rico. Firmly grasping the shotgun, Rico rushes to meet the closest man, shoving the stock into his chest and knocking him back several paces. Swinging to his right, he slams the shotgun into the woman's temple with a loud crunch, causing her to topple to the ground. One of the men reaches out, clawing at Rico, and receives a gun smash to the face. A stream of blood flows from the man's nose and dribbles down his shirt, his yelp of pain causing a handful of others to turn their attention toward the commotion. The man he rammed in the chest springs forward, knocking Rico off balance. He releases the shotgun, throwing his hands out to catch his fall. He looks over his shoulder and catches sight of the man's teeth near his calf. Rico kicks, connecting with the man's jaw, but he is quickly being overcome.

The shotgun lands out of reach, under a nearby car. Rico pushes up onto his hands and knees, ready to bolt for the car, but is obstructed by two women. Changing course, he grabs the nearest car handle. The door swings open and he throws himself inside, pulling the door shut behind him. Two pairs of hands slam against the window. Rico kicks around the trash on the floor and looks through the glove compartment, searching for something to use as a weapon. He comes up empty-handed. The banging on the windows increases as another three join in. Rico scrambles out the backseat door and runs to the SUV parked behind the vehicle. The driver's door hangs open. He watches through the windshield as the infected continue pounding on the windows, distracted by their own noises, but one notices his escape and abandons the car in pursuit. The SUV is clean, aside from a layer of dust that settled on the dashboard.

Rico hops into the back and opens a side compartment panel. A car jack and a tire iron are nestled inside. He grabs the tire iron as the man reaches the hood of the SUV, and then he slips out of the vehicle. A stench of rot drifts from the man's hot breath, his teeth yellowed and his lips cracked and bleeding. Rico jabs the tire iron through the man's eye socket, and he drops.

Rico crouches down and darts from car to car until he's in front of the yellow car. A hand grabs Rico's ankle from under the car. He stifles a yell and jerks his leg away, falling backward onto his butt. Jayden crawls out from under the car and wraps his arms around Rico's neck.

"You scared the crap out of me," Rico says, returning the hug.

"I didn't run away this time," Jayden responds.

"No, you didn't. I'm proud of you."

"I didn't know if you were going to come back, but I didn't run."

"You did good, kid, you were so brave."

"We aren't going to my granny and gramps anymore, are we?" Jayden's chin wobbles.

"We are, don't worry. We just aren't going to get there today." The path to the SUV is clear and Rico slowly leads Jayden to the safety of its interior. The infected that had been trying to get to Rico in the car have dispersed, drifting back toward the throng twenty yards ahead. Jayden nestles into the floor of the backseat, keeping his head down to avoid seeing or being seen through the window.

Rico is tense and he turns the tire iron in his hands while glancing from window to window. Even though they avoided detection, making their way to a temporary sanctuary, the fear bears down on him. Rain falls, landing slowly but picking up a steady pace. Within minutes, there's a downpour and a storm begins. Rico's skin begins to crawl and he's itching for a fix. He can't recall the last time he'd been sober for this long, but when he glances down at Jayden, he quells the storm. The kid has his knees pulled into his chest, back against the door, head resting on the edge of the seat. His eyelids flutter periodically but otherwise he is peaceful. The rhythmic beating of the rain is reassuring and tranquil. Rico's shoulders slump as the tension leaves his body.

24. ASHER

Before

"Oh my God, I'm so full." Ellis leaned back in his chair and slapped his hands on his stomach. "I'm going to need to unbutton my shorts after that."

Asher finished his sesame chicken and pushed the plate away. "I think that was the best Chinese food I've ever had. I didn't even know this place existed."

"It's a family favorite—sometimes my mom orders takeout from here for our dinners. Plus they give you so much that we always have leftovers, and Chinese food is always better the next day." Ellis signaled the waitress. Asher glanced down at his own empty plate.

"Would you two like anything else?" the waitress asked.

"No, thank you, just the check," Ellis answered.

"Together or separate?"

"Separate." "Together." Asher and Ellis answered at the same time.

"Together; my treat." Ellis smiled and the waitress left to grab the check. Asher reached for his wallet but Ellis insisted. "Dinner was my idea."

The waitress placed the check and two fortune cookies on the table and walked away. Ellis handed a cookie to Asher and opened the other.

"'Plan for many adventures ahead,'" Asher read aloud and placed the strip in his wallet. "What about yours?"

"'Money does not make the soul rich.' That's not even a fortune! That's just a statement. I want yours; adventures sound much more appealing. Trade me." Ellis held the paper out to Asher.

"Too late. Besides, you're the one that chose who got which cookie," Asher said, laughing. Ellis, looking resigned, put the fortune in his pocket and tossed cash onto the table. The waitress waved to them as they exited out into the warm night.

***

When Ellis opened his front door, a whiff of food drifted through to them. Brandon was cooking at the stove and glanced over his shoulder as Ellis and Asher entered.

"Oh, hey, Asher. Ellis didn't tell me you were coming over. I'm only cooking enough food for two people," Brandon said, turning back to the stove.

"It's cool, we just finished eating dinner anyway," Asher replied. Ellis hadn't told Asher that Brandon would be over either.

"He also didn't tell me you guys were eating dinner," Brandon said, cutting his eyes at Ellis.

"You didn't tell me you planned on cooking or would get out of class early." Ellis dismissed Brandon's remarks and collapsed onto the couch. "Did you pick up a movie?"

"Yeah, it's on the table."

Ellis lifted his head from the cushion, but before he could regain his feet, Asher stepped forward and grabbed the case. Ellis took the disk from Asher and pressed the power button on the DVD player.

"You're starting it already?" Brandon asked.

"I'm going to wait for you to finish cooking. I'm just getting it set up—calm down." Ellis rolled his eyes to Asher, who tried to make himself as small as possible on the couch. Ellis sat next to him with his phone in hand.

"You're seriously on your phone again?" Brandon made no attempt to hide his frustration. He turned to Asher before grumpily adding, "He spent our entire anniversary on his phone."

Asher sank farther still into the couch, not knowing how to respond, raising one shoulder and hoping he was showing compassion and solidarity. Brandon fixed his attention back on the stove, and when Asher looked over, he saw Ellis mimicking Brandon.

"I'm texting my dad," Ellis said, and dropped his phone into his lap. Asher felt his own phone vibrate.

E: Sorry SOMEONE is in a pissy mood.

He glanced back up, but Ellis was staring at the flashing DVD menu. Brandon pulled a plate from the cabinet, let it clatter against the counter, and dumped his dinner onto it. He sat down at the table without saying anything else.

"Why don't you come sit on the couch?" Ellis asked.

"Because I'm eating," Brandon answered without looking up.

"Is there a new rule against eating on the couch?" Ellis shot back.

"Can we not do this in front of your friend?" Brandon asked. "I can see the TV from here, just hit Play."

The movie was a comedy, but the air was too thick and the tension too high for anyone to dare to laugh. Brandon refused to abandon the table until halfway through the movie, but he sat on the floor on the far side of the living room rather than on the couch. Asher sprung to his feet the moment the screen faded to black and the credits scrolled. He said his good-byes without a response from Brandon. The shouting began before the door was fully shut. He resisted the urge to eavesdrop and hightailed it to his car.

Asher could see the living room light spilling through the balcony door when he parked, but nobody was playing video games when he entered his apartment. Mark or Derrick had presumably forgotten to flip the switch before abandoning the common area.

"You're so stupid," Asher mumbled, dropping fully clothed onto his bed. *But,* he thought, *I haven't done anything wrong. I made a friend;*

that's all Ellis and I are. Friends. There had not been any sort of physical action initiated by either of them, even if a part of Asher longed for it. To just touch Ellis, hold his hand. He thought about what it would be like to kiss, even if just for a second. *Stop it*, he thought, *you can't think about things like that; it isn't going to happen.* There was a knock on his door, and he looked up to see Renee standing in the doorway.

"Hey, I thought I heard you come home," she said. "Can I come in?"

"Yeah," he replied, and laid his head back down on the pillow. Renee stretched out on the bed next to him.

"Where've you been?"

Asher recounted the entire night, cringing at the worst parts as he relived each moment, finishing with the screaming as he left.

"And they had this entire fight in front of you?"

"No, they probably thought the door was shut before they started."

"That's good, I guess."

Asher rolled over onto his side, supporting his head on his hand so he could watch Renee's reaction to what he said next.

"I think I'm Ellis's emotional paramour."

Renee burst out laughing. "Emotional paramour?"

"I'm being serious, stop laughing. And yeah, I think he's having an emotional affair with me. There hasn't been any kind of physical contact. But you and Mark both said that you could tell there was something more than a friendship going on."

"Well, yeah, there is. He's protective of you; he's always standing near you as if to step in if something is going to happen. And when you move, he moves too."

"And there are the other things too. He visits me at work, saying he's only there to study, but I catch him looking at me a lot. And he skips classes to spend time together. We fall asleep each night texting each other, starting again the next day as soon as one of us wakes up."

"He's focusing his time with you, so as not to focus on his actual relationship."

"Exactly. We haven't had any issues or fights, other than the double-date night, but by hanging out with me, he gets to pretend everything is fine before going home to his boyfriend."

"I guess you really are a, what did you call it? An emotional paramour?"

Asher's phone vibrated and he groaned.

"Is that him?"

"Yep."

E: So sorry about tonight. Are you okay?

Asher held the phone up to Renee.

"If you're okay? Nothing about the fight? What are you saying back?" Renee scooted closer to read as Asher typed.

A: I'm fine. Is everything all right with you?

"I was the one able to just get up and walk out, so he doesn't need to be worrying about me."

"That's the thing, though, Asher—he *is* able to get up and walk out as well. Nothing is forcing him to stay with Brandon."

Asher's phone vibrated again but he ignored it, focusing on what Renee said. Asher realized how his wishful thinking had been playing with his mind and his interpretation of his and Ellis's relationship. His stomach sank like an anchor.

"Are you okay?" Renee asked, sitting up.

"No, I just realized how much of an idiot I am," Asher answered, and buried his head under the pillow. Renee rubbed his back but granted him the silence he wanted.

25. WENDY

After

"Do you have a lighter?" Wendy asks Todd, keeping calm.

Tonya grabs one of their bags and brings out a red candle lighter that she offers to Wendy.

"What are you going to do with that?" Todd asks.

"Some of these cars have gas. I can use them to create a distraction," Wendy responds. She removes a tank top from her bag and throws it over her shoulder.

"Wait, you can't go out there by yourself," Asher protests.

"I'll have a gun, and we don't have time to argue," Wendy asserts. Asher reaches out and grabs her bag, swinging it up onto his own shoulder.

"You'll move faster without it."

"I'm going with you—I can cover your back," Todd says.

"This is insane, neither of you should be going out there," Tonya interjects.

"Take Marie and go with Asher; we need to slow them down and this might be our only option." Todd kisses Tonya, then bends down to Marie, kissing her forehead and signing a message.

"If you continue west there's an exit two miles away that's elevated. Get to the top of the ramp and we can meet you there," Wendy says.

"You three go out the front; we'll go out the back. Don't slow down; we'll be right behind you," Todd says, checking Marie's shoelaces.

Tonya grasps Marie's hand and leads her away, Asher close behind them. With a final look back, the three descend the steps. Wendy gets down on the ground, reaching for her gun and switching the safety off. She reconvenes with Todd at the emergency exit.

"You ready?" he asks, his hand resting on the handle, a large hiking pack on his back.

"No," Wendy answers. "Let's do this."

Todd throws the door open and they jump out, hitting the ground running. The infected have gotten closer. Wendy spots a large pickup truck and charges for it, Todd directly behind her. Todd gets down on one knee between Wendy and the herd with his rifle up and aimed. Wendy grabs the shirt in both hands and rips it into long strips to tie together for a rope. She checks the progress of the infected. They are twenty yards away, but the pair remains unseen.

Wendy stuffs one end of the makeshift rope into the gas tank, leaving enough slack to light and give them time to escape. She holds the tip of the lighter to the shirt rope and pulls the trigger. Nothing happens. She tries again with the same result.

"Dammit," she mumbles.

"What is it?"

Wendy shakes the lighter and pulls the trigger once more, but still no flame. She shoves it toward Todd. "Can you try?"

Todd lowers his rifle and takes the lighter. They switch places, and Wendy trains her pistol on the approaching herd. Todd tries the lighter but is also unsuccessful.

"This isn't working; we need to go." He stands up, abandoning any further attempts to ignite the cloth. The front leaders of the herd have closed the gap enough to spot Todd, and they quicken their pace. Todd grabs his rifle and gazes through the scope, targeting a young man who has broken away from the group and burst into a run. He looks healthy, and if it weren't for his travel companions and the long scratches down his face, Todd wouldn't know any better. He pulls the trigger. The young man jerks backward but remains standing. Todd fires again. The gunshots rile up those who hadn't yet caught wind of the duo, and the herd surges forward, their howls and gnashing ripping through the air. Todd lowers his rifle and grips Wendy's shoulder. "We've got to move."

"No, this is going to work." Wendy pulls the trigger on the lighter again and again in desperation and finally the smallest flame, barely visible in the bright sunlight, springs from the tip. Screaming out in triumph, she places the fledgling blaze next to the bottom of the rope, waiting as it smokes and catches. A solid fire takes hold and Wendy scrambles to her feet, shoving the lighter into her back pocket. Todd fires off five additional shots into the crowd before running alongside Wendy. They cover fifty feet of asphalt before the truck explodes behind them, sending a blast of heat and propelling them unsteadily forward. Wendy peeks back; the infected are flocking toward the flaming truck like moths to a bug zapper.

They run for half a mile before slowing to a walk. They've established enough distance, and they don't want to exhaust their limited energy.

"Thank you," Todd says to Wendy.

"For what?" she asks.

"Thinking on your feet; coming up with a plan that saved the lives of my family. For following through with it when I was going to abandon ship," Todd says.

"You're welcome. But I did it for all of us, myself included. If it hadn't worked, I could have killed us both. Besides, it bought us some time, but some of them, maybe even most of them, are going to continue in this direction."

"Yes, but you've stopped the front line. Don't diminish your intelligence. It's gotten you far."

Pride floods Wendy and she looks away from Todd. "I can't take all of the credit; Asher's pretty smart too. And it wasn't always just the two of us. Plus, your family has made it this far, and you've had a tougher go of it than we have—I'm sorry, I didn't mean it like that."

"It's okay. You're right; it hasn't been easy. Before, we faced our share of difficulties having a disabled child. Don't get me wrong, we love our daughter with our entire hearts, I would never take back a single moment. No parent wants their child to face hardships in the world or have things harder than others. This new world isn't deaf friendly, but being deaf doesn't stop Marie. Her sense of smell is elevated. She smells them before we do, sometimes before we can hear them. She notices movements we don't see; our eyes are lazy and hers are strong."

Wendy has new respect for Todd and his family. She had been too self-absorbed to grasp the risk they were taking in allowing Asher and her to stay in the bus. They've, like Asher, retained an element of humanity and compassion, which she's allowed to slip away since the outbreak. *Since before the outbreak,* she thinks.

"Thank you," she manages to say.

"For what?" Todd asks.

She thanks him for providing shelter, for watching over her and covering her back today, for having a nature that allows him to help those he doesn't know. She apologizes for not listening when he said to abandon the lighter and risking his life.

"I was a cop before all of this. I had to put my neck on the line every day, and if I made one wrong step, judged someone inaccurately even for a second, it could have cost me everything. I can get a good read on people. You and your friend are good people. And I don't know how many of those are left."

"That's why you have so many guns?" Wendy asks.

"Yeah. Just because I'm black doesn't mean I stole them," Todd responds. Wendy's eyes go wide and her jaw drops. Todd laughs. "I'm just teasing you, don't worry."

Wendy forces a chuckle before changing the subject. "Do you mind me asking why she got so emotional when we said we were leaving?"

Todd hesitates before answering. "I'd be lying if I said we weren't being hopeful or selfish. Comfort in numbers is the practical part. If you and Asher stayed, we'd feel more secure. Someone else would be watching our backs, Marie's back, relieving some of the stress. But it's more than that. About a week after this all reached Orlando, our little boy came home from school and wasn't feeling well. One of the other preschoolers bit him, and we would have thought it was just a run-of-the-mill biter, but the stories on the news and what I was encountering with work made me paranoid. We rushed him to the hospital and waited for hours in the emergency room. It was packed and people were just getting angrier and angrier." A tear slides down Todd's cheek.

"You don't have to go on," Wendy says, knowing what comes next.

"We were so scared. He wasn't our little boy anymore. He wasn't our Chad. And Marie, we had to think of Marie," Todd continues talking but stops walking. When he looks at Wendy, his eyes, glazed with tears, are pleading for forgiveness. Not from her, but from someone who can make the deep pain go away. "We didn't want to take a chance that something would happen to either of you if you were alone. No more parents should lose their babies."

Wendy knows his guilt too well, more than she's willing to admit. Her eyes burn and she tries to blink the tears away. She approaches Todd, holding out her arms. He pulls her tight against his chest as the sobs break forth. The raw emotion escaping the large man rips through Wendy, and unable to hold back any more, she feels her resolve weaken as the tears pour from her eyes. She weeps for Chad, whom she never met; for Todd and Tonya, who lost their son and welcomed her and Asher in; for Marie without her brother and surrounded by silence; for Asher who lost everyone, and for—

Wendy's walls shoot back up as she forces the name back down, her throat clenching and her body stiffening. Todd disengages from the hug, feeling Wendy's rigid stance, and takes a step back to wipe his eyes.

"Sorry, I didn't mean to break down," Todd mutters.

"Don't worry about it; sometimes it's best to let it all out," Wendy responds, drying her face on her shoulders. "Why don't you give me your pack and let me carry it for a bit, let your back have a break."

"Nah, I've got it. Let's just keep moving."

They continue and keep an eye out for any sign of the others. They pass a male body leaning against a car with his head bashed in, but the clothing is unfamiliar, and they keep walking without getting close enough to inspect any further. The path is blocked a mile out from the exit by a massive pileup. Cars have been blackened as a result of an accident; corpses can be spotted through multiple windows. Wendy reaches the line of cars first and climbs onto a trunk, and then the roof, with Todd at her heels. She surveys the other side of the accident; a flipped car blocks two of the lanes on the highway, the catalyst of the wreck. The highway beyond the flipped car is wide open for fifty yards.

There are the familiar dark stains of old blood covering the pavement, along with shattered glass and tread marks from tires, but it is otherwise clear.

"If the burning truck doesn't slow them down, this barricade will," Wendy says.

"Either way, we've put some good distance between us and them."

It takes several minutes of careful maneuvering through the wreckage. Some of the cars are unsteady, and the additional weight causes them to shift and creak under pressure.

"Do you mind if I ask you something?" Todd asks once they reach stable ground.

"It's only fair," Wendy replies.

"You were so determined to leave earlier, why?"

After Todd's admission she knows she has to be equally honest and show the same respect. "This is going to sound stupid, but there's a theme park just a couple of miles from here. Someone that meant a lot to me and I once joked that if the world ended and we were left standing, that's where we'd go so we'd have the entire place to ourselves. And now that the world has ended, and I don't have anywhere else to go, it seems like as good an option as anything else."

"I don't think that's stupid," Todd responds. "It's given you motivation, kept you alive."

"I know you're trekking to the mall, but if you're serious about having comfort in numbers, you're welcome to join us. I don't know what's going to be waiting for us. I mean, everything was shut down when the outbreak reached its peak, so I don't think it will be swarmed with those things. But you never know. Everyone was told to go to the mall, and if even one of those things slipped in, it could all be compromised."

"So we get close enough to find out, and if it's not safe, we leave and try the mall next. No harm, no foul. But it means enough to you that you must check. Do you think this person that meant something to you is going to be there as well? If the idea stuck in your head . . ." Todd's voice trails off as he sees the look that flits across Wendy's face and she hangs her head.

"Wendy! Todd!"

Before Wendy can answer, they spot Asher running toward them from under the exit sign. They burst into a sprint to meet him. Wendy and Asher grab each other in a bear hug, but Todd runs past them and up the exit ramp where Tonya and Marie are waiting.

"You guys made it! Did it work? We heard an explosion."

"Yeah, it did," Wendy answers. Asher pulls away, giving her a head-to-toe and checking for any signs of injury.

"You're okay? You look okay. When we hit that pileup, we were regretting letting you guys stay behind. That would have provided enough of a wall to stop them; we almost turned back to find you."

"There was no way of knowing something like that would be there," Wendy says. "Better safe than sorry. You guys made it here without any trouble? We didn't encounter anything after the mob."

"Yeah, well enough. We ran into one of them, but I took it out with the bat. Didn't want to use the gun and draw more of them toward us."

"Smart. Look, there's something you should know."

"What? Did one of them get you? You look fine. Is it Todd, did one get him?"

"No." Wendy shakes her head. She explains to him the conversation she had with Todd and confirms where she wants to go as they walk toward the exit ramp. Wendy watches Asher purse his lips but nod his head. "Are you okay with that?"

"I will be. I was supposed to go there with someone else; not like this. But at least now I can get closure."

It hadn't occurred to Wendy that they'd both have a connection to the park. They climb the ramp, and when they reach the top, Tonya steps away from her family. "Thank you, for everything. You risked yourself for us, and I don't know how to pay that back. Todd told me where you want to go. Of course we'll go with you."

"If we're all on board we should get close enough to scout it out today while we have light," Todd declares.

"You're right—it's a couple of miles off the exit," Wendy responds, leading the charge.

26. RICO

After

The humidity from the rain, paired with the heat, warms up the interior of the SUV until Rico feels as if he's being roasted. Jayden has become restless in his sleep and periodically cries out. The rain has cleared up, and the herd's moved on, uninhibited by the storm. Rico slips into the front seat and opens both doors to create airflow and allow the stagnant heat to escape.

Jayden screams, his body flailing, and Rico grabs him to try and soothe him. The little boy snaps awake, his eyes wide with fear until they lock on to Rico's face and he steadies his breathing.

"You okay?" Rico asks.

"Do we have any water?" Jayden asks, climbing from the floor onto the seat.

"There's some in the duffel bag." As Rico answers, he remembers dropping the bag to the ground after they fell off the bike.

"Where's the bag?" Jayden looks around and into the trunk.

"We need to go get it," Rico says.

"You lost it."

"I didn't lose it; it's just outside, wise guy. Get up here; we'll go get it." Rico pats the center console. Jayden hops up and follows Rico.

Rico swings the tire iron aimlessly at his side, watching as Jayden jumps and splashes in puddles along the highway. The duffel bag looks a little worse for wear, having been trampled by the infected and pummeled by rain, but is still holding together. Rico extracts a dented bottled of water for Jayden, who guzzles it. The candy bars are smashed but still in their wrappers. He peels one open and the kid greedily accepts, biting and licking the chocolate and caramel from the foil. Rico drops the tire iron into the bag and shoulders the bag again. He gets down on the ground and searches for the shotgun. He finds it, but it is wet from the storm. He checks it out, tilting it side to side with the barrel pointing away from them.

"Will it still work?" Jayden asks.

Rico looks at the little kid and grins; there's chocolate all over his mouth and cheeks. "I'm not sure. It's just a little wet, so I think it will."

"Are you going to test it?"

"No, not yet. It's too loud."

Jayden looks around the road and turns back to Rico. "I don't see any of those people."

"Better not chance it," Rico explains. He lifts the bike up onto its wheels and tries his best to wipe the water off the seat.

"Are we going to my granny and gramps now?" Jayden asks him.

The sky is a brilliant blue, and it's early enough to make more progress and at least try to locate a phone book. A flash streaks across the sky. Rico shields his eyes and searches for the cause but the sky is empty. It must have been a trick of light.

"Yeah, hop on the pegs," Rico answers. Jayden wraps his arms around Rico's waist and secures the shotgun against his chest.

They take the first exit, wanting to get off the highway before running into the back of the mob again. Rico counts three different gas stations at the traffic light and pedals to the nearest one. The parking lot is full of cars, but unlike the gas station in Daytona Beach, the building is not burnt-out with a car driven through the front. Two pay phones are attached to the side of the building; one with the phone dangling toward the ground and the other without a phone at all. The phone book holders on both pay phones are empty.

"Of course there's nothing here; you didn't think it was going to be that easy, did you, Rico?" he mutters to himself. He takes Jayden by the hand and they walk around to the front. A chain is wrapped around the door handles with a large padlock hanging from it.

"It's locked," Jayden says.

"I see," Rico responds. He looks through the window but quickly pulls Jayden away. He sees blood covering the walls and at least four infected wandering through the store.

"What is it?" Jayden asks, straining to look through the door.

"Nothing, we'll check the next one," Rico says. They get back on the bike and pedal across the street to the next gas station. There are no pay phones on the outside of the station, but someone spray painted "We R Payin 4 UR Sins" on the brick wall.

There's no chain on the door and it freely swings open. Rico takes the tire iron out of the bag and hands it to Jayden. "Stay behind me, and keep a tight grip on this. And if you need to use it, swing it like a baseball bat. Can you do that for me?"

Jayden nods and squeezes his hands so tightly around the tire iron that his knuckles turn white. The inside of the station is quiet. The shelves are completely devoid of all food items, and other merchandise is strewn about and broken on the floors. Rico looks behind the counter but the space is empty. Moving aisle to aisle, he finds no movement or bodies: alive, dead, or infected.

Having cleared the store of any threats, Rico walks around the counter, rooting through the shelves under the register, searching for a phone book. He rifles through the papers in a cabinet but finds nothing. They search the entire store but come up empty-handed.

"Why are we looking for a phone book?" Jayden asks.

"Because I need to look up your grandparents' address so we can find their house," Rico explains.

"But I know where they live."

"Yeah, in Orlando, that's where we are." Rico nods, playing along with Jayden. "But I need to know more specific than that so we can get to their actual house."

"But I know where they live," Jayden repeats.

The thought never occurred to Rico that a six-year-old boy, who lived hours away from his grandparents, would know their actual address. Rico didn't know the address of his own grandparents' house.

"What do you mean you know where they live?" Rico asks him.

"Granny sends me letters and cards, and I write her back. She's my pen pal. And I write the address on the envelopes too," Jayden says.

"You know where they live," Rico repeats in awe.

"That's what I just said. You can see the fireworks every night from their house too."

"What fireworks?" Rico asks.

"From the park. Granny sent me a picture of them, she took it from the porch."

It hits Rico that Jayden is talking about the fireworks from a theme park. He snatches the map from the duffel bag. The paper is damp from the rain, but he is able to slowly peel the pages apart and spread them on the floor. He locates the nearest theme park, twenty miles away, and asks Jayden what street his grandparents live on. His eyes sweep in a circle around the perimeter of the park, until they land on the right street.

Pink streaks slip into the sky outside. Rico decides that it's too late to set out tonight. He retrieves the bike and wheels it inside as a barricade against the door, refusing to lose another mode of transportation.

"Aren't we going?"

"Not yet, it's getting dark." Rico finds that the locks are still intact on the door and makes sure they are secure. He moves their belongings behind the counter and sits on the ground studying the map while Jayden flips through magazines. There are several routes to their destination, and Rico works on memorizing them. Darkness sets in and he returns the map to the bag.

He lies down on the hard floor, continuing to repeat the directions over and over, until he feels Jayden lie down next to him, resting his head on Rico's stomach.

"Rico? Are you asleep?"

"No, kid, I'm still awake."

"Can I ask you something?"

Rico is wary, from the kid's tone, but says, "Of course."

"Is my mom going to be at my granny and gramps?"

Rico's chest tightens and he hesitates before answering. "No, she won't be there."

"They got her, didn't they? I had a nightmare that she was like that little boy."

Rico is unable to see Jayden, but he knows tears have wet the kid's face by the cracking in his voice. He reaches down and squeezes Jayden's shoulder.

"No, they didn't get her," Rico tells him, and it's the truth. Rico's sleep has been filled with the same nightmares, often seeing his own mother like the creatures roaming the world now.

"If they didn't get her, then how do you know she won't be there?"

Incapable of telling Jayden the truth, Rico fumbles for an answer. Finally, he says, "You remember what I told you when we left on the boat?"

"Yeah," Jayden answers.

"That's how I know." Rico feels his eyes flood with tears as he thinks about not only the motherless boy next to him, but also his own mom. He's unable to explain to Jayden that he's an orphan because he's unwilling to admit the same thing about himself. Everything he put his mom through, every problem he caused because of his addictions, plays out before him. He was supposed to make things right, show her he could change and be the son she deserved, and it's too late. She'll never see the man he's trying to be. The first tear slides down his cheek and he quickly wipes it away. *Men don't cry*, he hears his dad's voice in his head say, *especially not Martinez men*.

Screw you, Dad, he thinks to himself, arguing with the competing voice in his head and crying at a gas station for the second time in as many days.

***

A soft shaking brings Rico out of his sleep. It's early, but the first crack of light has broken through the dark sky and slips into the windows. Jayden kneels next to him, shaking him gently so as not to startle him, but Rico sits and surveys the area.

"I need to pee," Jayden says.

Rubbing the sleep from his eyes, Rico yawns and nods his head. He grabs the shotgun and stands up. The store is undisturbed and the doors closed and locked. He escorts Jayden down the hallway marked Restrooms, and stops in front of the door with the faded men's sign. Rico carefully pushes against it with the gun. The door swings on its hinges and the room beyond is shrouded in thick blackness. The putrid odor of old urine and feces seeps out.

"I don't want to go in there," Jayden says, his shirt pulled up over his nose.

"I don't blame you." Rico releases the door. They return to the front of the store, and after checking through the glass doors, Rico turns the lock and steps outside with Jayden. Jayden steps away and pees on the wall. He finishes up and they switch places.

They eat the remaining trail mix and share a bottle of water while Rico surveys the map once again. The fastest route is the highway, and the herd should be well beyond them. Rico follows the exit ramp and pedals along the shoulder, weaving occasionally back onto the road to avoid cars. A flock of vultures circle overhead, and Rico wonders if they know something he doesn't.

They periodically spot stragglers from the group, but Rico pedals faster and easily escapes. He breezes past the exit four miles before the one they need to take, and feels an inkling their luck might actually be turning around. Just as he allows himself to entertain the idea that things are going to be smooth sailing, the wind shifts direction, bringing with it the smell of the infected.

Rico slows to a stop. Gazing out as far as his eyes can see, he discerns the back of the group shifting and moving in a wave. They're between him and the next exit. Road names, rights and lefts, and intersections flash before his eyes.

The sun is bright at their backs; they can turn around and return to the previous exit and find another way to the right neighborhood.

"What's wrong?" Jayden asks.

"Nothing, I was just thinking," Rico responds. He resumes pedaling and turns the handlebars to return east, passing all of the cars facing west like a salmon swimming upstream, and taking the last exit they'd passed instead.

Rico feels as if he's traveling through a lucid dream, his path simultaneously familiar and unknown. Defunct traffic lights hang above an intersection, a pair of sneakers looped around the wire between two of the yellow traffic signal boxes. Rico takes a right, pedaling down the center of the road. There is no risk of an accident, but he finds himself slowing down and even stopping to go through intersections, anticipating a car speeding through. What was once a thriving tourist area has become a ghost town. Windows are shattered, the wooden planks used to board them up ripped free. Neon lights are out, and every surface is covered in dirt, dust, or mold. The once-bright paint on the buildings is faded and dull. Someone has tagged another building, different handwriting than the gas station but the same sentiment: "God Abandoned Us." Rico wonders if the people leaving these messages truly believed them or painted them as a mockery, having seen them in a movie or TV show.

They roll into the intersection across from the park and stop at the welcome sign, taking in the ironic smiling faces painted on the sides in greeting. The warm grins have transformed into predatory sneers rather than friendly embraces. Rico pushes forward and continues to the right, leaving the sign behind without a second glance.

The lawns in Jayden's grandparents' neighborhood are overgrown, the grass knee-high with weeds poking through. A cat scurries across the street and disappears in a yard. One of the front houses has become nothing more than a pile of ash and blackened framing. Several other houses are covered in spray paint, more of the same messages as well as phallic images. Vandals raided and ransacked the neighborhood at some point—windows are busted, and broken furniture clutters lawns and driveways. Farther down, Rico spots a person standing in a yard, back turned to them; he cannot tell if they've turned but he is unwilling to find out. Rico tells Jayden to close his eyes as he turns down another street and spots a woman hanging from a second-floor window. A noose is tied around her neck, her business suit is covered in blood, and one shoe is missing.

"Do you know what their house number is?" Rico asks as they reach the proper street.

"Twenty-six eighty-nine," Jayden recites.

The numbers are attached to a crooked mailbox in front of the fifth house on the left. The paint is a pale pink with a once-white garage door, but the driveway is empty. Rico faces the bike toward the street for a quick getaway and leaves the duffel bag hanging from the handlebars. They approach the front door and Rico instructs Jayden to stay behind him. The screen door emits a piercing shriek when Rico pulls the handle, and a cobweb stretches across the door frame. The front door is locked. Rico lifts the doormat and a large, dead potted plant, but there isn't a hidden key.

He looks through the thin window next to the door and knocks softly on the glass. The house is dark but seemingly unoccupied. He knocks again before giving up.

"They're not here, are they?" Jayden asks, crestfallen.

"I don't know. They could be scared and hiding," Rico responds. He carefully closes the screen door and leads Jayden around the house in search of another entrance. Rico pushes swaths of long grass away with the gun, combing for unseen surprises. The sliding glass door in the screened-in back patio is also locked and the blinds are closed. On the last side of the house, a small window is set high in the wall and open an inch. Rico stabs through the screen with the tire iron and rips it out.

He lifts Jayden up onto his shoulders and has him push the glass up and survey the interior.

"It's a laundry room," Jayden calls down to him.

"Is it clear?"

"What do you mean?"

"Is there anyone in there?"

"No, it's empty."

"How far into the house can you see?"

"Just the laundry room. The door is closed."

"Okay. I want you to be very careful, but do you think you're able to get through the window and drop down onto the other side without getting hurt?"

"I'll fall on my head."

"I'll hold you up and help you go in feetfirst. Can you go in feetfirst and hang on by your hands until you drop down?"

"Yeah, I think so."

Rico holds the kid up so he can get both of his legs through. Then Rico sees only Jayden's arms, shoulders, and head before he slips out of sight.

"You okay, kid?" he asks after hearing a soft thump.

"Yeah," Jayden says.

Rico drops the tire iron through the window but sets the gun against the side of the house. He jumps up and grabs the ledge, hefting his body upward. He puts an arm through the window, helping to steady his body, and continues pulling himself through. The frame is tight around his shoulder, just barely granting enough room for him to carefully scrape through. His torso is in the laundry room, his legs up in the air outside, and he teeters forward, losing his balance. The washer and dryer are across from the window, and there is nothing to grasp as he slides forward. His outstretched hands hit the floor and send a jolt up his arms. His right arm buckles underneath him as he twists his body and lands on his shoulder. He rolls onto his back and his legs slam into the dryer.

He holds his finger up to his lips; he and Jayden remain silent. Not a single sound comes from anywhere else in the house. Rico inches to the laundry room door and cracks it open. It takes a second for his eyes to adjust to the low lighting and allow him to make out shapes. He steps out of the room and onto the tile of the kitchen. The air around him is stuffy but lacks the smell of decay that permeates the outside air. Closed floral curtains fill the kitchen window space, the sunlight nearly blinding him when he pulls the stiff fabric apart.

"Look," Jayden says. The kid is pointing to a picture on the fridge of himself when he was three and in the arms of his mom. Rico, still amazed that a six-year-old was accurately able to recall the address to get them here, removes the magnet holding the picture up and hands the five-by-seven to Jayden.

"Here, why don't you put this in your pocket so you can see her whenever you'd like?"

"But it'll get bent!"

"Do you want to put it back on the fridge?"

"No!" Jayden lifts up his shirt to reach his shorts pocket and slips the picture in as carefully as he can.

Rico moves to the living room and opens the blinds to the sliding glass door, letting in more light. When he returns from retrieving the shotgun and locks the door, he finds Jayden sitting on the couch looking at the picture.

The interior of the house has been untouched; all of the pictures hang on the walls, the kitchen cabinets are shut, and the napkins are folded at each seat at the dinner table. Rico and Jayden are the first people to set foot in the house since the couple abandoned it. When looters and vandals destroyed other houses in the neighborhood, this was one of the few that remained untouched.

There is a pantry door in the kitchen next to the refrigerator. It is small, but Rico lightly taps against the wood before opening it. Hiding behind the door is a jackpot of canned goods. Rico calls Jayden into the kitchen, and they carry the cans to the table. He digs through the drawers for a can opener and silverware. They inhale a feast of beans, soup, corn, and pineapple until their stomachs are bloated.

"I never thought I'd be this full again," Jayden says, rubbing his belly and slouching in the chair.

"We can't eat this much every meal, just on special occasions," Rico says, gathering up the empty cans and carrying them to the garbage.

The sun is starting to set when Rico steps out the front door. He basks in the warmth and what little light remains for a moment before grabbing the bike. Three houses down he spots a red wagon turned on its side in the tall grass. Parents should be standing in doorways, calling their kids in for the night, as children race up and down the streets on their own bikes. A boy should be pulling his laughing sister around in the wagon.

Rico's eyes land on the garage door. He forgot about the garage. He wheels the bike past the threshold and leans it against the hallway wall, and extracts the flashlight from the duffel bag.

"What are you doing?" Jayden asks.

"Do me a favor and sit on the couch for a minute, please," Rico answers without looking at him. He grabs the tire iron and tiptoes down the hallway. A sturdy door with a deadbolt stands alone on the long wall. Rico tests the door, and as expected, it is locked. He can't hear anything on the other side. He clumsily unlocks the door while trying to maintain a grip on the flashlight and tire iron and shoves the door open.

Exhaust fumes pour out of the pitch-black doorway. He covers his nose and mouth with his shirt and shines the flashlight into the dark hole. The light reflects off the windshield and hood of a silver car. An older man sits in the driver's seat, his head slumped down to his chest, and a woman sits in the passenger seat with her head drooped off to the side. Rico drops the flashlight onto the hard cement floor and slams the door to the garage shut.

He backs away until he bumps against the opposite hallway wall, frightening himself. He tries and fails to gather his composure before retreating to the living room, but the smell of the exhaust fumes stays with him as if permanently burnt into his nose. Jayden is sitting on the couch, as he was told, confused and scared.

"We need to go," Rico says more to himself than to Jayden.

"Why can't we stay here?"

Rico grabs the duffel bag and crams canned foods in at random. By the time the bag is full, it's so heavy that the strap strains away from the material and Rico can barely carry it.

"Why can't we stay here?" Jayden asks again, jumping off the couch and confronting Rico.

"It's not safe," Rico answers. He fears passing out at any moment, not sure if the fumes dissipated, leaving behind only an odor, or if he doomed Jayden and himself by bringing them into the house. The smell fuels his paranoia, and his skin begins to itch. He knows they cannot stay in the house any longer than necessary. He doesn't hear Jayden asking where they're going or pointing out that it's nearly dark. Rico pulls open drawers in searching of anything useful, ripping open the junk drawer so forcibly it drops to the floor and breaks. The kid whines about being ignored and Rico spins.

"It's not safe here!"

"It's not safe anywhere!" Jayden screams.

Rico freezes and looks at Jayden. The boy's terror has melted away, replaced with an anger Rico has never seen in him.

"I want to go home," Jayden seethes.

"We can't go home," Rico says.

"Then I want to stay here," Jayden replies. "I don't want to sleep in another car or gas station."

Rico chews on his lip, debating. "Okay. I know what we can do."

27. RICO

Before

Rico pressed his finger on his computer's mute button when he heard the loud bang against his bedroom door. The handle shook but the locked door remained shut until he jumped up and stuck his head out.

"First thing, your music is way too loud. I've been calling your name from the living room," Melissa said, pushing the door further open.

"I didn't hear you," Rico said.

"That's my point. And second of all, why are you still here? Do you need a ride to your dad's?"

Rico hopped back onto his bed and unmuted the music. Melissa slammed the laptop shut. "You don't get to ignore me. Get up and get ready."

"I don't want to go," Rico stated.

"Clearly you don't want to go. But you're also under the age of eighteen, so you don't have much choice in how you spend your free time. I'm going to put on my shoes, and when I walk past here again you better be ready."

Annoyed, Rico stomped around his room, stepping over old dishes and on dirty clothes. He slid open a dresser drawer and grabbed a clean shirt. After pulling the shirt over his head, he froze to listen for his mom's whereabouts. He heard her bedroom door open across the hall as he reached into his sock drawer and felt around the bottom for the plastic bag.

"Ready?" Melissa leaned against the door frame, her arms crossed.

"No." Rico slipped his hand into his pocket and passed his mom, headed for the bathroom.

***

The radio played as they rode through town. Rico had his feet up on the dashboard against Melissa's protestations, drumming his fingers on his knee while staring out the window.

"Look, I know you don't want to go, and I understand that and don't blame you. But it's not fair to that little boy. You're his hero, and he's caught in the middle of this just like you are. Don't punish him," Melissa said.

"I'm going, aren't I?"

"Only because I forced you. It's just for a couple of hours. Do you want me to stay?"

"Mom, I'm not a kid; I don't need you to hold my hand." Rico rolled his eyes. "I can take care of myself."

"You're still my kid. I don't care how old you get. I just don't want him to say something to you and cause an issue."

"All of their friends are going to be there, so he'll want to front for them and seem like a good guy."

When they drove up to Antonio's house, the gate was open, the driveway packed with cars. Melissa pulled off to the side of the road and stopped.

"You're sure you don't want me there?"

"Mom, you're being embarrassing, I've got it. Besides, it's not fair to put you in a situation where you're stuck around them. I'll behave."

"Promise?"

"Promise."

"All right. I'll be back in a couple of hours."

Walking up the driveway, Rico fought, and lost, the urge to look over at the garage. All of the doors were down, caging in his car. He pushed the front door open—music and laughter intensified, making him cringe. A group of children ran past, screaming and chasing each other. Rico sauntered along to the living room but found it abandoned other than the cartoons occupying the television screen. Beyond the living room, through the large opened French doors, groups of adults socialized, glasses of wine and cocktails in hand, while more kids played in the pool or ran around the yard with water guns.

Rico stepped back outside into the sunlight, and was immediately blasted in the face with a stream of water followed by high-pitched laughing. Wiping his eyes, he saw Jayden in front of him wearing swim shorts and a huge grin, a water gun angled upward at Rico.

"Why I oughta—" Rico smirked and lunged, grabbing Jayden and slinging him over his shoulder. Jayden squealed and dropped the water gun. Rico started tickling him before he spotted Antonio standing across the pool. Antonio had been deep in conversation, but his face turned to stone as he watched his sons interact. Rico stopped tickling Jayden and placed him back on his feet, messing his hair. He bent down and returned the gun to Jayden. "Happy birthday, kid."

"You made it," Theresa said, holding a tray of finger foods. Rico straightened and forced a smile.

"Yeah, wouldn't miss it," he answered. "Here, let me help you."

Rico grabbed the tray from her and looked around until he spotted a table with similar trays and plates, a large inflated number six attached by ribbon.

"Just over there," Theresa said, pointing to an empty spot before scurrying away as if close contact would spread Rico's delinquency.

"I'd be lying if I said I wasn't surprised to see you here," Antonio said, coming up behind his son. Rico grabbed a sandwich and stuffed it in his mouth. He pointed to his bulging cheeks while chewing. Antonio watched until Rico had chewed twice as long as needed and swallowed.

"Wouldn't miss it," Rico mustered, repeating the line he'd used on Theresa.

"It means a lot to us that you're here, and a lot to Jayden," Antonio said.

"No use punishing the kid." Rico grabbed another sandwich and bit into it.

"He really looks up to you, idolizes you."

"I'm surprised I got an invitation, then. Don't want him looking up to me too much, he might start acting like me." Rico smiled and watched the color rise in Antonio's face.

"Rico—"

"Don't 'Rico' me. I know you didn't want me here. I didn't want to be here, but as much as you and I don't care about each other, we both care about Jayden. So let's cut the crap." Rico walked away from the table and his father, and found an empty bathroom to lock himself in. Rico slipped his fingers into his pocket and pulled out a single pill, rolling it between his fingers. He counted to ten, telling himself he didn't need it. "Screw it." He tossed the pill into the back of his throat and swallowed.

The kitchen counter was lined with enough bottles of wine to put an elephant to sleep. A large cake from some uppity bakery was displayed on the island, covered with images of race cars and a cartoon drawing of Jayden. Rico pushed his finger into the back of the cake, tasting the icing. It was good, but not worth the price he knew Antonio paid. *Not that anything he has is worth the price he paid*, Rico thought.

He grabbed an open bottle of wine and washed the taste of the pill from his mouth, but then he kept drinking. After downing a third of the bottle, he heard footsteps coming from the hall and dashed into the pantry.

Theresa stepped into the kitchen, color rising in her neck and cheeks, Antonio directly behind her. He grabbed her by the arm, and when she pulled away, he snatched a fistful of her hair and jerked her head back. She gasped in pain and he tugged harder, whispering in her ear, then shoved her into the counter and stalked off. She grabbed a bottle of wine and a glass, filled it to the rim, and gulped it down in one go. A single tear slid down her cheek. She refilled the glass but hesitated before bringing it to her lips, instead pouring it down the drain. Theresa ran her fingers through the back of her hair, walked over to the cake, slid it off the counter, and carried it away.

Rico's fingers loosened around the neck of the wine bottle and it nearly slipped from his hand. He scrunched up his eyes, shaking his head. The pill and alcohol had already taken hold of his brain, and he was too impaired to trust his own views on what had transpired. Chanting started in the yard as everyone sang "Happy Birthday." Rico slid to the ground and finished off the bottle.

28. ASHER

Before

Three weeks had passed since movie night with Ellis and Brandon. Asher continued to spend time texting Ellis, and they hung out, but they had scaled back from that day. Ellis rarely made it to the coffee shop anymore, and smoothies were a thing of the past. Asher knew he was partially responsible because they were close to crossing a line and he hadn't tried to stop it. Brandon was an ever-present and never-mentioned topic, looming over Asher's head and in Ellis's apartment.

But today they were going to the beach with Renee, Mark, and Derrick.

"Can you help me carry this out to the car?" Derrick asked, tugging a packed and heavy cooler out of the kitchen. Asher grabbed the opposite handle and together they lifted it.

"Holy crap, is there a body in here?" Asher asked.

"Just about. We've got a bunch of beer, Renee's stuff for margaritas, and stuff for sandwiches or whatever," Derrick answered. They carried the cooler out and placed it in the trunk of Derrick's car, which already contained a couple of beach chairs. Ellis's car drove past, honking its horn, then he parked and stepped out, carrying a beach bag.

"I stopped and grabbed some junk food, figured what's a beach day without snacks," Ellis said, and tossed the bag next to the cooler.

"I'll go get Mark and Renee," Derrick said, leaving them by the car.

"Brandon doesn't mind you being gone all day?" Asher asked.

"Nah, he has to work today," Ellis answered and shrugged. "And I can make my own decisions. I'm not just going to stay inside on a day like this."

"I didn't mean anything like that—I just didn't know if he had plans with you today," Asher said.

"We've been doing a lot together recently, ever since, well, you know. But it's important to take time out to spend with friends too. Or in Brandon's case, work." Before Asher had the chance to respond, they spotted Derrick, Mark, and Renee.

"Shotgun!" Mark yelled, claiming the front seat. They rode with the windows down and the music up, Asher's knees knocking against Ellis's and Renee's in the cramped backseat. Ten minutes into the ride, Mark shouted, "Kentucky," and punched Derrick in the arm.

"You can't punch the driver, asshole," Derrick exclaimed. "I'm going to crash and kill everyone."

"Stop being a wuss, you're just mad you didn't see it first," Mark said.

"What's going on?" Ellis leaned over and asked Asher.

"It's a game. When you're on the road, if you see an out-of-state license plate you call it and punch someone," Asher explained right before Mark called out, "Ohio," and punched Derrick again.

"What did I just say? I will drive this car into a telephone pole to kill you," Derrick said.

"Lighten up, dude," Mark said.

"Texas," Derrick yelled and punched Mark as hard as he could in the arm. The game continued for another fifteen minutes with first Renee and then Ellis joining in, and lastly Asher, before the novelty wore off and Mark started flipping through radio stations.

The beach parking lots were packed, and long lines of honking cars crowded the roads looking for space. Tourist season had officially ended weeks ago with Labor Day, and the Floridians were reclaiming what was rightfully theirs. Ellis and Asher carried the cooler and followed Mark's lead, searching for a large enough patch of empty sand to stake. Drinks were flowing before towels and chairs were set up. Mark and Derrick grabbed beers and Renee pulled out red cups.

"Anyone want a margarita?" she asked.

"Sure," Ellis said.

"Yeah, why not?" Asher agreed. He turned to sit, but Ellis was standing between him and a chair with a tube of sunblock lotion.

"Would you mind getting my back?" he asked, offering the lotion to Asher.

"Uhh, okay." Asher hesitantly opened the lid and squeezed a glob into his palm before rubbing both hands together. Ellis turned his back to Asher, who started at Ellis's defined shoulders, massaging the lotion into his skin before working his way down to the small of his back. Goose bumps shot up his arms and a shiver ran down his spine while touching Ellis, and even though it was such a mundane task, he imagined a degree of intimacy from feeling Ellis's muscles under his skin. He noticed a scattering of freckles across Ellis's shoulders and the top of his back, evidence of countless days spent out in the Florida sun.

"Get a room already," Mark said with a belch. Asher dropped the lotion and winced when it landed on his foot.

"Thanks," Ellis said, turning to face Asher. "Do you want me to do you?"

"W-what?" Asher stammered.

"Your back. Do you want me to put sunblock on your back?" Ellis clarified.

"Oh! Oh, no, I'm good, thanks."

Renee straightened up from the cooler and handed the boys their cups. Asher brought the plastic to his lips, and the refreshing, cool lime mixed with tequila was the perfect counter to the heat bearing down from the sun. He relaxed as he swallowed. Ellis sat in the chair on Asher's right and tipped his cup forward, touching Asher's.

"Cheers," Ellis said.

"Cheers."

Mark and Derrick, having consumed a multitude of beers each, disappeared to play Frisbee farther down the beach. Renee flipped over on her towel to even out her tan. Asher drained the last of his margarita, which had turned lukewarm, and stood.

"I'm going down to the water to cool down," Asher said to Ellis.

"That sounds like a genius idea." Ellis pushed himself up from the chair, taking off his sunglasses and dropping them onto the seat. "Renee?"

"Not yet, thanks, though," Renee answered.

The two walked around other sunbathers, chairs, and umbrellas until they reached the wet sand. A wave crashed to shore and ran up the beach and around Asher's feet. Asher inhaled, allowing the scent of the salt water to fill his nose. The water pulled back, and Asher started moving forward. Ellis was slightly ahead when Asher reached the waist-high depths. He stopped, only moving to jump upward into an approaching wave, keeping his head above the peak. Ellis dove headfirst into the wave and submerged. When he surfaced, he glanced around for Asher.

"What are you doing back there, come on!" Ellis gestured Asher closer to him.

"Hold on a second," Asher said, remaining stationary. Ellis waded toward Asher and the beach, but a yard away, Asher called, "Wait, stay there."

"Is something wrong?" Ellis surveyed the surface of the ocean but nothing was amiss. "Are you peeing?"

Asher's face flushed in response.

"You are!" Ellis exclaimed and started laughing.

"Whatever, urine is sterile; everyone pees in the ocean," Asher said, and finally started walking again.

"Don't get too close to me, I don't want to stand in your pee water," Ellis joked, still laughing and walking backward. Ellis wasn't paying attention and a wave crashed down on his head and pulled him under. Asher dove into the wave and swam further out, allowing the tide to pull him along. When he surfaced, the water was up to his chest. Ellis joined him. "I think the wave pulled me directly into your pee."

Asher would have laughed had it not been for the fin cutting through the water three feet away.

"Shark."

They ran as fast as they could to the shore, a difficult feat with the tide pulling against them as another wave formed behind them.

Asher looked over his shoulder and saw the fin shrinking in size as the wave grew around it. Ellis was in front and Asher stretched his arm out to give Ellis a boost forward. The wave crashed around them, but the water only came up to their knees, and neither was able to spot the fin anymore. They jogged up the beach.

"You two okay?" Renee asked.

"There was just a shark like two feet away from us," Asher said.

"Shut up. Are you serious?" Renee asked.

"Dead serious. We almost died," Ellis replied.

"Screw that, I'm not going in the water. Looks like I'm having margarita numero dos to cool down. You guys want another one?"

"Uh, no, thanks, I'm going to stick with water from now on," Asher said, eyeballing the pile of beer cans Mark and Derrick had created.

"I'm good too, thanks, though." Ellis lay on his towel and closed his eyes. Asher joined him, finding it easy to doze off under the warm sun, the salt water drying on his skin. He was unaware of how much time had passed when he was awoken by the sound of Mark's voice.

"Who wants to hook up with my friend?" Mark slurred as he stumbled down the beach with his arm around Derrick's shoulders.

"Is this really happening?" Renee asked. "Oh my God."

The three of them watched the train wreck in awe. Mark and Derrick were four yards down the beach when a girl stepped in front of them, blocking their path. After two minutes, Mark turned around and walked back to their spot and sat in one of the chairs.

"Who is that girl?" Renee asked.

"She came forward and said she'd probably hook up with Derrick as long as he bought her dinner first," Mark answered.

"I can't believe you did that," Renee remarked.

"It started off as a joke, but if it helps the guy out, then good for him," Mark said, opening another beer and gulping down half the can in one go.

As the sun drooped, the beach cleared out. Mark gathered all of the beer cans in a garbage bag while Renee shook the sand off the towels and folded them up. Asher collapsed the beach chairs, and once Derrick saw the group preparing to leave, he broke away from his conversation with the girl and helped Ellis carry the cooler back to the car.

"Keys," Asher said, holding out his hand. Derrick tossed them over, and Asher sank into the driver's seat with Ellis claiming the front seat and the other three climbing into the back.

"How'd it go?" Mark asked Derrick.

"Good, her name's Courtney, and she gave me her number. We're going to grab dinner tomorrow night; she lives in Orlando as well," Derrick said.

"I'm the best wingman." Mark smiled.

"No, you're embarrassing, but I guess it worked today," Derrick answered.

29. ASHER

After

"It's the happiest place in the universe," Asher says, mimicking the painted-on smiles. "It says so right there on the sign." The theme park's motto is painted in a cursive font under the three-foot-tall glass letters of the name.

"Let's go; these faces are giving me the heebie-jeebies." Todd takes charge, walking through the large archway and onto the park's property. Unlike the highway, and the surrounding streets, the road leading to the park is completely devoid of cars except for a large white van with darkened windows pulled up onto a curb. Asher tugs the driver's side door open, but all that spills out are empty water bottles labeled "Archon" within a half circle. The symbol looks familiar to Asher, but he can't place it. They continue.

Wendy twists her long, sweat-drenched hair into a ponytail and holds it off her neck. Asher watches Marie tap on Wendy's waist, and when Wendy looks down, she sees Marie smiling and holding out her hand in offering, a hair tie in the middle of her palm. One of Marie's twists is coming undone, but the little girl is unconcerned. Wendy looks toward Tonya and asks, "How do I tell her thank you?"

Tonya shows her the gesture and Wendy repeats it to Marie. She accepts the hair tie, fastening her hair in a messy bun. When they reach the toll plaza, all of the barricade arms are down, but they slip around them, or under, in Marie's case, and pass the booths. There is a steep ramp into the parking garage, and Asher can feel his calves burn as they climb.

The structure is deserted when they emerge onto level ground. The shade and cement surroundings provide a refreshing and cooler environment, a welcome reprieve after the excitement of the morning. The air smells fresher; the only odor is wafting from their bodies.

"What now?" Asher asks.

"We go up to the top of the garage. It will give us a vantage point to assess our surroundings," Todd says, uncapping a bottle of water.

From the roof, they observe a section of the highway; it is clear of the herd of infected. Off in the distance a tendril of black smoke slowly rises from the truck Wendy blew up. The park is full of roller coasters, a Ferris wheel, and numerous buildings surrounding a large lake, with a castle standing as the tallest and farthest point. Most of the ground is blocked from view by trees and the various structures, but from what they can see, everything is just as deserted as the parking garage.

"My God, Wendy, I think you might have just brought us to the safest place in the universe," Asher says, giving her a pat on the back.

"I knew they shut down when everything started happening, but I was skeptical that it would be this empty," Wendy says.

"Think about how many people these parks used to feed a day, and most of the food probably comes from cans or dry goods. This is it; this is better than the bus," Tonya says.

"We can't get ahead of ourselves," Todd interjects, but the corners of his mouth twitch into a smile.

"There's nothing left to do now but get in there," Wendy says, adjusting the pack on her back.

The group descends the parking garage stairs, losing restraint and skipping steps, to reach the walkway leading into the park. The giddiness of their discovery begins to overtake any fears, and the adults have to keep reminding themselves to slow down to a speed Marie can maintain. Finally, Asher hands his backpack to Tonya, and Tonya instructs Marie to climb onto his back. They speed up their pace, smiling at each other whenever their eyes meet.

Behind the empty ticket booths stands a large fence blocking the entrance into the park. The gates are chained shut, but when Asher pushes against one and Todd pulls against the other, they are able to create enough of an opening for the girls to slip through. After passing all of the supplies through the gap, Asher and Todd release the gates and begin their climb over the top. Asher reaches the peak first and pauses to look around.

Bright and colorful storefronts and façades line the sides of the street. Off to the right, a large building labeled City Hall displays an American flag waving on the corner. Ten feet beyond the gate, in the center of the street, a raised flowerbed stands full of wilted and dead flowers. The path leads away from the flowerbed and between the buildings down to the large lake, where it splits in both directions. The castle looms large and regal on the opposite shore, flocked by trees.

Todd reaches the top of the fence and cups Asher's shoulder with his hand before hopping down to the other side.

"Are you going to stay up there all day?" Wendy asks. He swings his leg over the top and jumps down. Wendy grabs his pack and tosses it to him with a smile. Then he senses something is off. The hairs on the back of his neck stand, but before he can fully register the feeling, he hears a click, and he tenses.

"Get down!"

Asher searches for the source of the deep voice.

"Down! Now!"

Todd grabs Asher's bicep and shoves him to the ground.

"What in the—" Asher mumbles. He raises his head and looks around. Tonya is lying a few feet away, using her body to shield a terrified Marie. Wendy's hand slowly moves to her back where her pistol is tucked.

"Hands where we can see them!"

Asher raises his hands in surrender. Wendy hesitates before she relents and holds both hands up. Todd and Tonya raise their hands, but Marie, unable to hear or understand the orders, keeps her hands out of sight.

"The girl as well."

Tonya lowers her hands to sign the instructions to Marie.

"Put your hands back up!"

"She's deaf," Todd yells. "She's terrified and can't hear you!"

Tonya returns her hands to the air and this time Marie follows suit. Asher catches movement on the roof of one of the storefronts. The end of a gun pokes out over the edge of the building. The door of the same building opens and a man steps out. He is tall and thin with light-brown hair and freckle-covered skin. Todd could easily take him on, if the man wasn't carrying a rifle.

"Are you armed?" the man asks, his voice deep and raspy but different from the voice that had been calling out the orders.

"Yes," Todd responds.

"Are you in charge?" he asks. To the outside observer it would appear that Todd is in charge, though leadership had not yet been established.

"Yes, I'm in charge," Todd answers.

"Get to your feet."

Todd slowly stands, keeping his hands raised above his head. The man with the rifle looks him over, the gun trained on Todd.

"Have any of you been bitten or scratched?"

"No," Todd says.

"Remove her gun." The man nods at Wendy. "Slide it toward me."

Todd apologizes and takes the gun out of her waistline. It rattles as it skips across the cobblestones, stopping when it hits the man's boot.

"Do you have any more weapons?"

Todd removes the hunting knife from Wendy's calf sheath and slides it across the ground as well. Next, he steps over to Asher, gathering the gun he gave Asher on the bus along with the bat. Once all of their concealed weapons have been taken, the man whistles and a young woman with short, spiked auburn hair and a soft face steps out from City Hall. She is also armed with a large rifle strapped around her torso. She is wearing a pair of baggy camouflage pants. She lets the rifle hang by her side while patting Todd down for weapons. Todd is cleared and instructed to get back down on the ground, and Wendy stands for a pat down next. This continues uncontested with Asher and Tonya, but when Marie is made to stand, she is shaking and crying. The young woman quickly searches Marie and steps away, allowing Tonya to shield her daughter. The young woman steps aside.

"Leave your bags and get up slowly," the man orders, and waves them forward. They follow him down the street toward the lake, the woman close behind them, and take a right when they reach the split. Just minutes before, the buildings seemed to promise safety, but now Asher can see how the colors have faded and the walls are covered with dirt. One building is stained with a dark-brown splatter that Asher is confident was once red. *Nothing is as pretty up close,* he thinks. His stomach churns, and he forces himself to look straight ahead instead of at the buildings. The man leads them to a fence at the edge of the park with an Employees Only sign.

On the other side of the fence, the buildings lose their coloring altogether—everything is the drab gray of concrete. They stop in front of a large solid-metal door, and the man lowers his rifle as he retrieves a key ring with a dangling blue keychain. He inserts the key and turns it, opening the door to a dark room.

"I'm not taking my family in there," Todd says forcibly.

"Relax," the man says. He reaches his hand into the room and lights flicker to life. The man enters and everyone else follows. One side of the room is filled with cardboard boxes. The other side is a row of large metal cages. Tonya squeezes Marie tightly against her side and Todd stands as tall and intimidating as possible.

"What is going on?" Todd asks.

"Standard procedure; we can't take any risks," the man answers, holding the door to the nearest cage open. The group hesitates until the man lifts his rifle and levels it at Todd's chest. They enter the cage and the man locks them in.

Before leaving, the young woman faces them with genuine sympathy and says, "I'm sorry, but you have to understand." She steps out, and the door clicks shut behind her. They watch the lock turn as the man twists the key.

The walls of the room are too thick to call out, and there is no one to call out to. They're left with the sounds of their breathing and Wendy's footsteps as she paces. Asher tells her she's making them all more nervous. Marie is huddled between her parents, her cheeks streaked from tears. The overhead fluorescent lights flicker, adding to the ominous feeling. Asher leans back against one side of the cage, the metal digging into his back, finding it hard to believe that moments earlier sanctuary felt like a possibility, and now they are prisoners awaiting an unknown fate. His stomach growls in heaviness and hunger.

Time drags on until a click grabs their attention and Wendy, Todd, and Asher jump to their feet. The door opens and the man with the freckles steps back into the room followed by a woman with graying hair and deep-set eyes. The skin around her lips is wrinkled. Asher recognizes his and Wendy's packs in her hands, and when the young woman with the auburn hair follows them into the room, she's carrying Todd's pack. Asher looks beyond the shutting door at the darkening sky. They've been detained for hours.

"Against the back wall," the man says. The keys jingle in his hand; he holds them poised to unlock the cage. They obey his command, pressing as far back as they can against the cement. The graying woman and the young woman with the auburn hair slide the packs across the floor. The man quickly shuts and locks the cage again, and with a look between him and the graying woman, she dismisses him and the younger woman.

"What's going to happen to us?" Todd asks.

"I can't fully answer that just yet. I was told you claim that none of you have been bitten or scratched." Her eyes drift to Asher's cut-up arm. "We've made the mistake of blindly trusting people's word on that matter before. Until we know for sure, you stay in here. We're not unreasonable, though; we've brought you your belongings to make matters more comfortable."

"And once you realize we are telling the truth?" Todd asks.

"Then we go from there. We see if you're a good fit for us," she responds. The woman nods and leaves.

"Every weapon is gone," Todd announces, searching his pack.

"The spare ammo for my gun is missing too," Wendy says.

The cans of food and bottles of water seem to be accounted for in Asher's pack. His small yellow notebook is shoved down under the cans, toward the bottom, and no longer closed by the elastic band; whoever searched his pack must have opened it and flipped through, or more likely read a few pages. His gut clenches at the thought of some unknown person reading his private thoughts. He pushes the notebook to the side and sees the navy-blue hoodie with the yellow stitching around the sleeves.

"Everything is here," Asher says, breathing a sigh of relief.

"Do you trust her?" Wendy asks Todd.

"I couldn't get much of a read on her," Todd answers.

"But what does your initial instinct say?" Tonya asks, speaking up for the first time since imprisoned.

"She's smart. She has a plan, and she knows how to execute it," Todd explains. "As much as I'm not happy being trapped in here, I can't blame her. Neither her nor that girl with her seems thrilled about locking people up, but they're not unhappy about it either."

"A necessary evil," Tonya interjects. Todd nods.

"They've been here a while," Wendy says. "They have a system, and it's working for them. They've learned from their mistakes."

"It's not even been three months. They've adapted quickly," Asher thinks out loud.

"So have we; we're still alive," Wendy says.

Asher takes the hoodie out of his bag and slips his arms through the sleeves. It was marginally large for him before the outbreak, but now it hangs off him even more. They spend the rest of the evening making small talk and creating a makeshift dinner, attempting to pass the time and keep spirits high. Asher is exhausted but his mind continues reeling, preventing him from falling asleep.

"I need to pee," Asher says, unable to hold his bladder any longer. Everyone, Asher included, exchanges awkward looks as they glance around the room. Wendy picks up the bottle Asher had been drinking from, and after finishing off the last inch and a half of water, she hands him the empty container.

"We won't look, promise," she says.

There is a moment of hesitation as he stands on the opposite side of the cage, and attempts to block out everyone, trying to get his body flowing. Thankful that he finishes before the bottle overflows, he screws the lid on and sets it down in the corner.

"Sorry," he says, blushing and rejoining the group.

"It's just nature; we're all going to have to do it," Tonya says.

Marie, nestled between Todd and Tonya, is the first to fall asleep, and Asher feels himself giving in. Pulling the hood up over his head to block the harsh light, Asher curls up with his head on his pack.

***

The heavy metal door slams into the wall. The man with the freckles is breathing heavily, his face red and contorted in rage. Asher wonders how long he's been asleep, confusing the man's aggression with the infection. But then the man speaks and Asher realizes he hasn't turned, but something big has happened.

"How many more of you are there?" The man seethes, spit flying from his mouth.

"What are you talking about?" Todd asks.

"How many more are in your group? You five come in first—if you aren't heard from by morning, they send in reinforcements?" The man holds the rifle up, his hands bloody and bruised, aiming it directly at Todd.

"Something's wrong," Wendy whispers at Asher's side.

"What did you say?" The man turns the rifle on Wendy. Asher moves in front of her.

"We don't know what you're talking about," Todd says, holding his hands up in surrender.

"Bring him in!" the man calls out the open door. "If you're lying to us, not a single one of you will live to see the outside of this cage again."

30. ASHER

Before

Asher heard a buzzing, but his phone was inactive. It was Ellis's phone, lying on Asher's bed. He gave in to the temptation, picked it up, and saw Brandon's name. The shower turned off and Asher tossed the phone away, scurrying to the computer chair. Ellis opened the bathroom door, letting steam filter out. Asher half turned his head to look over his shoulder as Ellis emerged with a towel wrapped around his waist. His wet hair clung to his face and drops of water ran from his shoulders down his chest.

"I forgot my bag," Ellis said, grabbing the bag with his clothes from next to Asher's bed.

"No worries." Asher looked away, his heart racing. "Your phone rang."

While Ellis read the screen, Asher glanced over at him again; the corners of Ellis's mouth turned down.

"You okay?" he asked.

"Yeah. Sorry, I was just reading a text. But I'm done in the bathroom. I can get changed in here if you want to jump in the shower."

Asher left Ellis to his phone and clothes, slipping past him to the bathroom. He took his time, allowing the water to wash over his face and body before scrubbing off the salt from the ocean. Asher kept the water on long after he was fully cleaned and rinsed, only turning it off before the time he was spending in the shower became weird. He stepped out and toweled off, wrapping the towel around his waist the same as Ellis had.

"I'm coming out; are you fully dressed?" Asher asked.

"You came out to me a while ago, but what does that have to do with being dressed?" Ellis joked. Ellis was lying on the bed, his legs hanging off the edge and his shirt riding up, exposing two inches of stomach, messing with his phone. He looked up when Asher walked out and was met with a sneer.

"You're so funny," Asher said, opening a drawer and pulling out a pair of underwear. He stepped into them and slid them up under his towel. He repeated the motion with a pair of shorts and dropped the towel on the floor. "Is everything all right with whoever called you?"

"I don't know. Brandon's being all pissy," Ellis answered. "He texted me when I didn't answer." Ellis held his phone out. Asher looked at the screen and saw the text from Brandon without a response from Ellis: I hope you had fun on your date today.

"Oh." Asher handed the phone back.

"I called him to tell him that I was in the shower when he called, but I guess he was at my apartment and knew I wasn't there, so he got even more pissed," Ellis said.

"I'm really sorry; I didn't mean for anything like this to happen." Asher moved to sit on the edge of the bed with Ellis, but changed directions at the last second and sat in the computer chair instead.

"It's not your fault—it's been a long time coming. I think we both finally reached our boiling points," Ellis said. He lay back on the bed staring at the ceiling. "If you could be anywhere in the world right now, where would it be?"

Asher was caught off guard by the sudden change of subject. He knew what he wanted to answer, but instead of speaking, his tongue caught in his throat. His mind reeled to a day from his childhood. Asher and his brother had been racing through the large field between his house and a lake, chasing fireflies and smearing them against their skin, leaving behind glowing streaks. "It's kind of sadistic now when I think about it. But we didn't know any better; we were just carefree and wrapped up in the idea of shining through the dark. It was back when Brady actually cared about me."

"That's sweet," Ellis said. Asher took a deep breath and tried to concentrate on anything other than Ellis being on his bed. Ellis continued, "If I could be anywhere it'd be the Maldives, staying in one of the cabanas. No cares—just the water and the sun."

"That sounds nice. As nice as the beach was today, I don't think it could even compare," Asher said. He watched Ellis's chest rise and fall with each intake and exhalation of air. Asher looked down at the floor to divert his eyes.

"Can I hug you?" Ellis asked, sitting up again. Asher's heart skipped a beat and his stomach flipped. Their eyes met and they stared at each other.

"I don't think that'd be a very good idea," Asher said, angry with himself even as the words slipped through his lips.

"Nor do I," Ellis responded. "But no matter how many times I tell myself that, I still feel this compulsion to touch you."

Asher blushed and his heart pounded. He didn't know if he should smile or puke.

"I lied." Ellis said. "When I said if I could be anywhere it'd be the Maldives, that wasn't true. I wanted to say 'lying next to you.'"

"You have a boyfriend," Asher said, unsure if he was saying it to remind Ellis or himself. It required all of his restraint to not jump out of his chair and embrace Ellis, but Asher knew that if he made a move he wouldn't be able to stop at a hug. Ellis sighed loudly and rubbed his hands over his own face.

"I should go; I'm sorry. This wasn't fair of me. I'm being crazy." Ellis stood from the bed, and Asher rose as well.

"Wait. You're not crazy. When you asked me where I wanted to be, I lied too. When I'm around you my entire mood brightens. I've felt physical heartbreak when I've thought about not getting to be with you, and the days you don't visit me at work. Because talking to you gets me through the day—it makes a bad day good. Seeing you makes being at work worth it." Asher paused for another deep breath to try and stop the word-vomit. "But you have a boyfriend. And I can't do anything about that. And I won't do anything about that because I'm not that person. I can't hug you, because if I do I'm afraid I won't let go. It scares me, but it's the truth." Tears formed in Asher's eyes, and when he stopped, Ellis wore a somber smile.

"I don't want to make you be that person. There isn't anything you did to make me feel like this; it started that night at the party. I got a feeling that I couldn't shake, and it just grew and grew. I met my parents for drinks and told them everything I was feeling, everything about you. They told me my face glowed when I talked about you, more than ever before. But you're right—I do have a boyfriend, and I have a responsibility to Brandon. My dad told me my first love didn't have to be my only love, and although that's what I was already feeling in my heart, I couldn't abandon him. I've tried so hard in the time since that day to make it work, but I can't and it doesn't. I don't know what this is"—Ellis motioned between himself and Asher—"but I do know what Brandon and I are, and because of that I have to go."

Asher stepped out of Ellis's path to the door. Ellis grabbed the handle and stopped. He turned and looked at Asher before leaving the bedroom. Asher listened to the front door open and close. He wanted to chase after Ellis and throw caution to the wind. Instead, he dropped face-first onto his bed and into his pillow. The emotion that had been building up escaped. He wasn't sure whether to be happy about finally expressing his feelings and learning Ellis felt the same, angry at letting Ellis walk out the door, or a combination of both as he allowed their friendship to end.

31. RICO

Before

"Where the hell were you this weekend?" Doug asked. Rico opened the passenger door and slid in.

"It was my stepbrother's birthday," Rico answered, buckling his seat belt.

"You ditched everything for some little brat's sleepover?" Doug took a drag from his cigarette and blew the smoke out the window, pulling away from the house.

"He's not a brat; he's just a kid. And it wasn't supposed to be a sleepover, but it doesn't go over well when the neighbor kid finds you passed out in the pantry with an empty wine bottle when looking for a place to hide during hide-and-seek," Rico lied. He hadn't been able to get the confrontation between his dad and Theresa out of his head. Each time he replayed it, the details became hazier, and he questioned whether his memory was accurate or an effect of the drugs and alcohol. He'd snagged cash from a hidden jar under the sink, called a cab, and slipped out of the house unnoticed.

"Damn, that sucks. But it doesn't excuse you from not showing up. I worked the party alone, thanks to you. You're lucky I was able to move everything; but this won't happen again or you're out."

"Sorry, I promise it won't happen again." Rico shrugged. Doug pulled into the school parking lot, swerving around a stopped car, and punching the horn to get to his assigned spot.

"You're skipping third period," Doug told Rico.

"What? Why?" Rico asked. He wasn't opposed to skipping class, but the adrenaline came from the impulsive decision and not from following orders.

"It's your shift." Doug grabbed a large bag full of smaller bags of marijuana and tossed it to Rico.

"What am I doing with this?"

"Shoving it up your ass. Selling it, what do you think you're doing with it? You know the place; I'll collect the money after school." Doug climbed out of the car and slammed the door. Rico glanced around the parking lot and stuffed the drugs into the bottom of his bag underneath his books.

***

The morning passed at glacial speed, each minute drawn out and intensified. When Rico passed a school guard in the hallway, he felt the weight of his bag triple, convinced the guard knew what he was carrying. The bell rang after second period, and he gathered his belongings and rushed from the classroom.

"Sorry," Rico exclaimed, slamming into another body. He stumbled backward and then reached down to help the girl he had bumped. "Here let me."

"Hi," Chloe said, clutching a folder to her chest.

"Hey. Sorry." Rico looked at Chloe. Expecting anger, he was surprised by the amount of pain staring at him. "How've you been?"

"I've got to go." Chloe joined the crowd shuffling down the hall. Rico chased after her, the drugs in his bag forgotten.

"I'm sorry about everything. I can make it up to you for real this time," Rico persisted. "Can we start again?"

Chloe sighed in exasperation; they'd started over too many times to count. Rico brushed a strand of hair behind her ear, and she conceded, "Five o'clock at Brew House."

Rico stepped to the side with a smile. The warning bell rang and everyone sped up. He put his head down and entered the bathroom, hanging his bag from the hook on the door in the stall for the disabled. He pushed the latch closed and waited. It was well after the final bell before there was a knock. Someone put cash through the space between the partition and the wall. He grabbed the money and dangled the drugs over the top of the door. A beat passed and the baggie remained hanging from his hand. Rico faked a cough and felt a slight tug. Shoes squeaked on tile as the unknown customer fled the bathroom.

Nobody else knocked on the door, but on two occasions, Rico froze up as other students used the facilities. When the bell rang again, he snatched his bag off the hook and rejoined the students spilling into the halls.

"How'd it go?" Rico stopped at the sound of Doug's voice behind him.

"It was fine," he answered.

"Any sales?"

"Yeah." Rico dug the cash out of his pocket and handed it over. "Do you want . . ." He motioned to his backpack.

"No. Keep them on you, I'm going to send you on a run after school."

"I have plans after school today."

Doug's nostrils flared. "You signed up for this."

"I know," Rico started defensively, "but I really can't reschedule this. I wouldn't have made plans if I knew you needed me after school, but today isn't good for me."

"Then I guess it's in your best interest to handle the run as fast as possible. This is nonnegotiable." Doug shouldered by and disappeared down the hall.

***

The second half of the day slipped away, and when school was dismissed, everyone grabbed their bags and swarmed the doors. The weight in Rico's stomach grew heavier when he was called to his teacher's desk.

Ms. Stark was focused on her computer screen but looked up when he acknowledged her.

"Yes, ma'am?"

"Mr. Flynn has sent me an e-mail asking to have you stop by his classroom before you leave for the day."

"For what?"

"He doesn't say, I'm sorry." Ms. Stark returned to typing.

The hallways were deserted. Rico reached Mr. Flynn's classroom. He knocked on the open door before entering. Mr. Flynn looked up.

"We missed you in class today," he said.

"Sorry, I wasn't feeling well," Rico lied, beads of sweat popping out on his forehead. He resisted the urge to look at a clock.

"I checked your attendance; it seems my class is the only one you missed."

"Like I said, I wasn't feeling well. I needed to rest." Rico fought the urge to bolt—time was wasting while he stood in the doorway.

"I assume the nurse would verify that you were lying in her office until she cleared you?"

"I didn't go to the nurse's office; the smell makes me feel worse." Rico's phone vibrated in his pocket.

"So you'll excuse me if, given your track record for attendance, I don't believe you?" Mr. Flynn's expression was stone. Rico could feel bile rising in the back of his throat and a sense of anxiety overtaking him. His hands shook and the room swayed. Mr. Flynn noticed Rico's condition, and his expression changed. "Are you okay?"

"I really need to go, sir."

"You missed a quiz. If you can sit down—"

"I think I'm going to pass out." Rico left the classroom, gripped the wall, and staggered down the hall as quickly as possible. Half an hour had passed since the final bell rang, leaving an hour and a half until Rico was scheduled to meet with Chloe. He had two texts and a missed call from Doug. Rico found a bench outside, emptied his stomach, and dialed Doug's number.

"Where the hell have you been?" Doug shouted.

Rico wiped sweat from his forehead and explained. Doug told him an address to drop off the remaining drugs.

"How am I supposed to get there? I don't have a car; you're my ride everywhere."

"Next time you'll remember that before you decide to go off the grid for a weekend."

The line went dead. He keyed the address into a map application on his phone. It was a thirty-five minute walk. He would be cutting it close to reaching the meeting with Chloe on time. Rico's stomach lurched and he leaned to the side, releasing a second mouthful of bile. He hitched the backpack up onto his shoulder and wiped his mouth as he started the trek.

***

Car after car sped through the busy intersection in front of a large apartment complex. Rico leaned against a pole for support, waiting for the red light to stop traffic. He checked the time on his phone for the umpteenth time in the past three minutes. The walk took six minutes longer than expected. He had to wait at multiple intersections and his body continued to shut down. The chance of making it to Chloe on time was becoming slim.

At last, traffic stopped. On the opposite side of the street, the light changed to a walk symbol and Rico jogged across. The large apartment complex was in shambles. The buildings hadn't been washed or repainted in years and half of the windows were missing shutters. There were seedier areas of Miami, but Rico had the feeling that illegal activity was more common than not here. The complex was fenced, but the lock on the footpath gate was broken. Rico walked along a cracked sidewalk, looking for the apartment.

When he found it, he knocked on the door. He heard someone stirring inside, but another minute passed before the door opened. Standing before him was a large man with a goatee and beer gut. He sized Rico up. "Doug?" He had the voice of a longtime smoker.

"Uh, no. Rico. Doug sent me," he answered. Rico tried to glance around at the interior of the apartment, but the man's body blocked most of the doorway.

"I was told Doug was coming. I don't deal with street kids." The man began to close the door. Rico's pride was stung, but he was also annoyed with having gone through the trouble to get to this apartment. He wasn't leaving until the job was done. Rico quickly jumped forward, placing his foot in the path of the closing door. The man looked down, then at Rico's face.

"I have it. Doug wouldn't send just anyone." Rico put on his best poker face, attempting to look professional. He almost faltered and removed his foot, but the man relented and stepped back.

"Make it fast," he said. Rico followed him down the dimly lit hallway and into a shabby living room. The air was stale, and the faux leather of the couch was cracked. Tufts of stuffing were sticking out. Coffee cups covered the end tables and a bong rested on the floor in front of the beat-up couch. Rico did not know if he should sit or wait for some sort of cue.

"Is it in that bag of yours?" The man dropped onto the couch—it squeaked under the strain of his weight.

"Yeah, hold on." Rico extracted the large bag and held it out.

The man leaned forward and swiped the bag, turning it over. He opened the seal and sniffed the contents. Rico wasn't sure where it came from, but suddenly there was a scale on the edge of the coffee table and the buyer weighed the bag.

"There's more here than I was expecting."

"I'm not sure what Doug told you—"

"I don't appreciate being lied to."

"Sir, I'm not lying—"

"Sir. Ha. No need to call me sir. I believe you; you really don't know what I was told. But this is more than I agreed to, and your boss is well aware of what he's doing. I have half a mind to turn you out completely, but I'm guessing that's why he sent you instead of coming himself. Doug's a coward—you can tell him I said that—and I deal with men. For your sake, I'll accept this today; I can move it around easily enough. But if this happens again, neither of us is going to be happy."

"Got it," Rico said, timid from the threat. The man left the bag on the scale and vanished into another room. Rico's nerves began to fray as he waited. If anything were left in his stomach, it would have come up. He was going to be late to his meeting with Chloe. Finally, the man reemerged from the room with a roll of cash.

"Don't forget to relay that message. Let's call today a show of good faith, an honest mistake forgiven. Once."

"Trust me, I'll make sure it doesn't happen again." Rico grabbed the cash and dropped it into the bottom of his bag. He rocked back and forth on his feet, a cold sweat running down the back of his neck. "Should I—?"

"Go? Yeah," he answered, reaching into a smaller plastic bag and pinching out a portion of the marijuana. Rico turned and darted down the hall.

Outside in the hot sun, he let out a scream of frustration as he pressed the Call button for Chloe. After several rings, it clicked over to voice mail.

"Dammit. Hey, Chloe, it's me. I'm going to be late, but I will be there, I promise. Please wait for me." He ended the call and dialed Doug's number, but it also rang through to voice mail. He didn't bother to leave a message.

***

Out of breath, Rico reached the front of Brew House and peered through the large front window. Many of the tables were occupied with customers, some his own age, most older college students. There was a long line standing in front of the counter, but he couldn't pick out Chloe's blonde hair. Dialing her number again, he moved around to look inside from different angles. The call went to voice mail again.

He crouched, his back against the wall, running through ideas of what to do next. He could go in and wait, hoping that Chloe was late as well. Or he could leave with the assumption that she left when he didn't show up on time. Rico hadn't committed to either option yet when his phone vibrated.

"About time," he said, seeing the alert with Chloe's name. The screen filled with a picture. He felt the air pulled from his lungs; the image was of himself at a party kissing the unknown girl.

32. RICO

After

A wheezing breath fills the air. Rico rolls onto his back and listens, trying to place the source. The night before, Rico pulled the cushions from the couch and stuffed them in the laundry room next to the washing machine. Jayden sleeps deeply, curled up with his thumb in his mouth.

The wheezing continues, carrying through the laundry room window Rico left open while they slept. He'd been paranoid about the fumes and sought out the room with the high window for safety. He grasps the window ledge and lifts himself so he can peer out. An old woman is hunched over directly under the window. Because the woman has her back to the house, Rico is only able to see her ratty hair and messy clothes. Her back rises as she takes another deep breath, and Rico realizes she could be a friend of Jayden's grandparents who, having seen movement in their house, is seeking them out.

"Ma'am?" Rico whispers. The woman tenses at the sound of his voice and her head gently tilts from side to side. "I'm up here, behind you," Rico says a little louder.

He slams the top of his head against the frame of the window when she turns. The entire left side of her face has been ravaged. Her cheek is missing; she has few remaining teeth. What was once her left eye is a dark and bloody socket. Her right eye catches sight of him, and her breath gurgles in her throat as she opens her mouth, spilling out a stream of red-tinted drool. She hobbles against the wall of the house, stretching her arms upward toward him.

Rico drops back in from the window and slams it shut. Jayden sits up yawning, his hair sticking up all over the place.

"I'm hungry," Jayden says.

"Come on, I'll get you something to eat." Rico moves the chair propped against the laundry room door. Cans are still scattered across the dining room table. Rico grabs the can opener and opens three cans at random while Jayden climbs up onto a chair.

Rico slips out of the house with the tire iron. He sneaks around to the side. The old woman is under the window, clawing at the house and leaving bloody streaks. Rico approaches her from behind and shoves the tire iron through the base of her skull.

With a can of soup in hand, Rico decides to explore the house. The first room he enters appears to be a guest bedroom. There are generic pictures of the beach along the walls and a vase of dried flowers on top of a small dresser. A thick layer of dust covers everything, and Rico's nose tingles. He shuts the door before sneezing. At the end of the hall, he opens a door leading to a much larger room, the master bedroom. The bed is made, and there are lines in the carpet from its being vacuumed. There is a dust coating in here, but it is much thinner than in the guest bedroom. Several pictures of Jayden, and Jayden with Theresa, hang on one wall. The largest of them all, however, is an older picture of the grandparents' wedding day.

Next to the closet is an open door leading into a bathroom. His-and-hers sinks are across from a large tub with massage jets and a standing shower. The counter is clean and clear of anything except a drinking cup, soap dispenser, and a toothbrush holder with two toothbrushes, one green and one yellow. Rico checks the cabinets under the sinks, finding normal toiletries such as shaving cream, razors, hairspray, soap, and toothpaste. He opens the medicine cabinet and his heart races.

The small shelves are lined with orange pill bottles in various sizes. He hesitates, his hand stretched halfway out, deciding whether or not to take a closer look. *It can't hurt just to read the labels*, he thinks.

Rico grabs the biggest bottle first. The pills rattle inside as he twists the container and reads the label. Painkillers. He sets the bottle down on the counter and grabs another at random. Bottle by bottle he discovers the cabinet is full of painkillers, muscle relaxers, and antidepressants. Within moments, he has transferred every bottle onto the counter and stares at them like a kid in a candy shop. He picks up a bottle at random, unscrews the top, and pours three small blue tablets into his hand. He watches them roll around his palm.

"Rico?"

Jayden's voice causes him to jump, and the pills fly from his palm, landing and disappearing in the long threads of the bathroom rug.

"Shit," Rico whispers to himself, setting the bottle on the counter as he drops to his hands and knees to recover the pills. By the time Jayden steps through the bathroom door, Rico has reclaimed two pills and closes his hand into a fist to hide them.

"What're you doing?" Jayden asks, looking from Rico's face to the several pill bottles and back.

"I was just checking to see if there was anything around here we could use," Rico answers.

"I need to go to the bathroom," Jayden says. "Should I go outside?"

"Sure. I'll go with you."

Rico drops the two pills back into the bottle and screws the lid on.

"Are we still leaving?" Jayden asks, pulling up his board shorts.

"What was that?" Rico asks, still focused on the bottles.

"Last night you wanted to leave. Are we still leaving?"

On one hand, they don't have anywhere to go. On the other, Rico fears both what is hidden in the garage and behind the bathroom door.

"Yeah, we're going to leave," Rico finally says. Yesterday he was craving a fix, and if they remain in the house, he might relapse. The downward spiral could get the kid killed.

Rico gathers their supplies and pushes the bike out onto the patio as the sun rises. He slides the door shut, saying a silent prayer and thank-you for the temporary shelter and restocking of supplies. Before they lost the boat, he was guiding them north. With Orlando being a bust and without any other destination, he steers the bike through the neighborhood, returning to the main road to find the highway and revert to the original plan.

Looking to his left, he can spot the top of a Ferris wheel peeking out above the tree line. Jayden's story about the nightly fireworks returns to him, and he has an idea. Without knowing if the highway is clear, it would be idiotic to take their chances blindly. But if he can get to the top of the Ferris wheel, he could scope out a clear path. He pushes down on the pedals, taking them in the direction of the park.

They reach a traffic light, and Rico realizes the perpendicular road leads to a fence, barricading a service area behind the park. The gate is chained shut in front of a large abandoned guard shack. The top of the fence is lined with barbed wire. All that remains in the deserted area behind the buildings are three parked golf carts and a large van. Rico jams the end of the tire iron into the wire securing the fence to the bottom bar. With some effort, he is able to pry off wires and lift the bottom of the fence high enough for them both to crawl underneath.

"Here, you know the drill." Rico hands the tire iron to Jayden and takes the lead with the shotgun.

The service road stretches in both directions, curving around the park and out of sight. From here the Ferris wheel isn't visible, but the quickest route will be cutting through the park. They pass the golf carts and vans, angling toward a break between two buildings. The sound of slow footsteps approaching catches Rico's ear as they reach the building's corner. He pushes Jayden behind him and against the wall, pressing his side to a closed door and bracing himself with the shotgun. A young woman steps around the corner and Rico reacts on autopilot, plunging the shotgun forward and smashing the butt of the gun against her temple.

The young woman collapses, dropping a rifle, the sound of metal on concrete ringing through the silence.

"What the—" a raspy voice says, and the corner of the building explodes in a cloud of dust and debris, the air filling with gunfire. Rico crouches, pulling Jayden to his knees. He steadies the shotgun and cocks it defensively. The gunfire ceases and the voice calls out, "Show yourself, now."

Rico looks at the young woman, lying on her side and angled away from him, her short auburn hair swept across her forehead. Other than the trickle of blood, she appears peaceful, as if she were resting.

"I didn't mean to hurt her," Rico tries to explain, "I was caught off guard."

"Step out where I can see you," the voice says.

"I have a small child with me."

"Both of you put your hands in the air and step out."

Rico remains frozen in fear. He and Jayden can't make it back to the fence in time without the man firing at, and potentially killing, one or both of them. But he has no guarantee that if he steps out with his hands raised they will not meet the same end. The person with the raspy voice tries to creep forward, but his shoe scuffs the ground.

"Don't come any closer," Rico calls out.

"Let's resolve this like civilized adults," the voice answers.

Rico hears a click and the door next to him flies open, hitting him in the side, and knocking him off balance. Everything happens in slow motion. He straightens out his arm to break his fall while toppling over, but also loosens his hold on the shotgun. His right shoulder collides with the pavement and the momentum spins him onto his back. A thickset man stands in the open doorway, lifting Jayden off the ground by the front of his shirt as the kid screams.

"Let go of him!"

Jayden swings his arm up, hitting the man in the head with the tire iron. The man yowls in pain, shoving the kid outward and releasing him. Jayden's small body flies backward. He slams against the service road back-first; his head snaps against the pavement with a resounding crack.

A weight lands on top of Rico before he can move. He looks up into the freckle-covered face of a second man. Freckles wrenches the shotgun from Rico and tosses it away, then pulls his fist back and punches Rico in the face. Rico feels his nose crunch, and instantly his face is wet. His vision blurs and he becomes dizzy. He receives another punch and his head ricochets between flesh and pavement. After the third punch, everything goes in and out of focus. Suddenly, the weight is gone from his chest and he rolls over on his stomach. He attempts to push himself up onto his hands and knees, but pain shoots through his entire body.

Rico can hear yelling from behind, but individual words are indecipherable as he focuses on crawling away. The ground swirls under his hands, and black spots swim in front of his eyes. Everything tilts forward and he collapses again. The screaming continues, and he picks out a single word: "kids."

"The kid," Rico mumbles to himself. He tries to lift his head to look for him, but everything goes black.

33. ASHER

Before

It was dark in the room and the clock read 8:37 p.m. when the phone started ringing. Asher rubbed the sleep from his eyes and looked around for the phone. He hit the Answer key and held it up to his ear.

"Hello?"

"Hey," Ellis responded. "Were you sleeping?"

"Uh, no. Well, yes, but not for the night. Just snoozing."

"I can let you go, then—sorry for waking you up."

"No, no. I'm awake. Are you okay?"

"Yeah. Brandon just left."

The words hit Asher like a ton of bricks. He sat up in the bed, suddenly alert. All he could muster was, "Oh."

He didn't know how appropriate it was to ask if he should come over, but he didn't care. Asher slipped his shoes on and left the bedroom. The entire apartment was dark and silent. He was not the only one to take a nap after the long day at the beach, and he was thankful he didn't have to face anyone on his way out.

The jaunt to his car and the drive to Ellis's apartment were surreal, and he wondered if he was having a lucid dream. Everything was a haze, and when he parked and pulled the key out of the ignition, he realized he hadn't even turned on the radio. Asher felt queasy climbing the stairs to Ellis's front door. No matter what transpired, Asher knew that once he knocked there was no turning back. He took a deep breath and steadied his shaking hands.

Ellis answered at once. He'd been standing at the door and waiting since they hung up. His eyes were red and his pallid face was still wet from tears. But he smiled when he saw Asher. Asher noticed a cardboard box on the counter in the kitchen; it was overflowing with items, and a keychain with a single key rested next to it.

"Hey," Asher said, shoving his hands in his pockets and leaning against the counter.

"Hey yourself," Ellis responded. He observed Asher's posture and apologized.

"It's okay, rough day."

"That's my stuff, and the key to my apartment," Ellis answered, pointing at the box. "I called Brandon when I left your place; I asked him to meet me here so we could talk. Shortly after I got home, he knocked on my front door instead of letting himself in. He said he already knew what was going to happen and that we should just call a spade a spade. Then he dropped the box on the counter and started gathering the things here that were his."

"I'm sorry," Asher said, but the words were insincere. As much as he wanted to feel sorry, he couldn't.

"It's for the best. And it wasn't as easy as it sounds. Once he got all of his stuff, we started fighting. But it's done now." Ellis shrugged.

"I didn't mean to come between you two," Asher said, and he meant it.

"You didn't. Neither of us had been happy before I even met you. We had a talk months ago when I told him I wasn't happy, but we stayed together. We promised each other things were going to improve, and they didn't. You didn't cause this. You just gave me the strength to do what needed to be done. You gave me courage when I was a coward."

Ellis took a step forward in Asher's direction. Asher tried to think of an excuse to deny what he wanted for himself, but for the first time his mind was clear and he didn't feel ashamed. Instead, he felt elated and smiled, even if it was selfish.

"Could you still use that hug?" he asked Ellis, pulling his hands out of his pockets. Ellis beamed, his own smile reaching from ear to ear. He extended his arms outward, and a second later the two were embracing, their arms wrapped tightly around each other. Asher squeezed Ellis against him so forcibly he worried he was going to crack Ellis's ribs, but he refused to loosen his grip. He buried his face deeply into Ellis's neck and inhaled, picking up on a slight musky undertone mixed with his own soap from Ellis's shower hours earlier. Asher continued to breathe in and out, feeling Ellis's racing heart beat against his own.

Ellis lifted his head from Asher's shoulder and pulled back. Neither released the hug, but they were able to look each other in the face. Ellis's eyes began to close as he moved his face forward. Asher closed his eyes in response, and when their lips touched, he felt goose bumps. A shiver shot down his arms and legs. He grinned, breaking the kiss. He pressed his forehead against Ellis's.

"I've been wanting to do that for a really long time," Ellis said.

"Me too," Asher answered.

"Your lips smell like baby powder," Ellis remarked, causing Asher to burst out laughing.

"It must be my lip balm," Asher answered.

"I should double-check, just to make sure." Ellis leaned forward again and their lips reconnected.

34. ASHER

After

A thickset man steps through the doorway, supporting a teenage Hispanic boy with a blood-soaked and swollen face. The boy's arm is around the larger man's shoulders as he is part carried and part dragged into the room. Asher has never seen him before, and by the puzzled looks on the others' faces, they have no idea who he is either.

"How many more of you are there?" the man with freckles asks again.

"We don't know him," Todd says.

"Don't play stupid with me," he sneers, taking a step closer to the cage. "He attacked one of ours. He's lucky to still be alive. Someone better start speaking."

"Enough."

They turn in unison to the door, where the woman with graying hair has reappeared. Her arms are crossed firmly in front of her chest and her lips are pressed tightly together. The man lowers the rifle, taking a step back.

"But you know what they did," he says.

"No. We know nothing of the sort. We know what this boy did"—her eyes dart to the blood-soaked Hispanic boy—"arguably in self-defense."

"He attacked Ellie," he sneers.

"And she's awake and speaking," the woman replies. "This is a discussion for outside these walls. Now unlock the other cage."

The man looks ready to protest and opens his mouth, but he wordlessly closes it and obeys the command. The thickset man sets the teen against the opposite cage wall, trying to prop his body up. The teen raises his head and mumbles something, but it is too quiet and too far away for Asher to hear.

"What did he say?" the man asks.

"J?" The thickset man answers.

"J? The letter?"

"Or J-a-y. A name, perhaps the little boy," the woman says.

"How is he?" the thickset man asks, genuinely worried.

"Breathing. He hasn't come around yet," the woman answers. The thickset man nods and steps out of the cage. Asher watches silently as the cage is locked, the five of them forgotten. The thickset man leaves the room but the woman whispers something into the ear of the freckled man and he hands her the key ring. She approaches the door to Asher's cage and unlocks it. Her eyes focus on Asher and she points a long thin finger at his chest, saying, "You. With me."

Asher looks from the woman to the man, his rifle at the ready, to Wendy and then Todd, Tonya, and Marie huddled together.

"Hurry up," the woman says.

"Where are you taking him?" Wendy asks.

"Never you mind," the woman answers, never taking her eyes off Asher. "You can bring your bag."

Asher's heart jumps. He grabs the bag, letting it hang by his side rather than sliding his arms through the straps, and hesitantly takes one step forward, followed by a second. He glances back before stepping out of the cage. The four faces staring back at him are etched with fear; this could be the final time they see each other. He notices that Tonya has reached out and grabbed Wendy's hand. As soon as Asher clears the cage door, the woman shuts and locks it, returning the keys to the man.

Asher walks outside, blinking, into the sunlight. The lights had been on in the cage, but the natural sunlight is glaringly brighter.

Sweat droplets form immediately on his skin from the Florida heat, the hoodie, and anxiety for what is about to happen. Asher ignores the warmth, not wanting to cause any aggravation by stopping to take off the hoodie. The woman leads him back into the park and down the street to a rustic saloon with picnic tables out front, the man with the rifle only half a pace behind them. Asher glances around, but the thick-set man has vanished.

The woman sits on a bench and motions for Asher to sit across from her. He takes his seat, using the opportunity to strip the hoodie off and lay it on his bag.

"I should introduce myself. My name is Mag," she says, holding out a hand.

"Asher." He returns the shake.

"As you've obviously surmised, there was a bit of an incident this morning. Daniel," she says, nodding at the man with the rifle, "Ellie, and Aubrey were on their way to check up on your group and they were attacked. Daniel is under the impression it was an ambush, but I don't think that's conclusive from what we know. There are a few similarities, or coincidences, in a time where it's hard to take anything at face value."

"Why are you telling me this?" Asher asks.

"I want to sort things out as quickly and easily as possible," Mag answers.

"I get that, but why me? I'm not the leader of the group," Asher says.

Mag's eyes flit in the direction of Asher's bag before returning to his face. "I get the impression I can trust you."

"You read my journal."

"Yes," Mag answers. She reaches into her shirt pocket for a pack of cigarettes. She places one between her pursed lips and holds the pack out in offering, but Asher shakes his head. She returns the pack to the pocket and pulls a lighter from her pants. Mag takes a long drag on the cigarette and turns her head away from Asher to blow out the smoke. "It's my job to screen anyone that comes through here. To discover whatever I can about them and decide if they pose a threat."

"And because you know from my journal that I'm gay, you see me as weak and nonthreatening," Asher says.

"No. Because I read your journal and saw an unguarded side of you, and know you're still alive after months out there. I know you're strong," Mag says, taking another deep drag.

Caught off guard by her response, Asher relaxes.

"I see you as nonthreatening," Mag continues, "because you want to find the good in others and to be accepted. You don't come across as murderous in your words."

"Thank you," Asher says.

"Do you know that boy they brought in?" Mag is abrupt and direct in her approach.

"No."

"You've never seen him before?"

"Never."

"Are there any more people in your group besides the five of you?"

"No."

"How long have you been traveling together?"

Asher hesitates before answering. In the less than forty-eight hours since he met Todd, Tonya, and Marie, he already feels protective of them. And with how Todd has stepped up to keep Wendy and him safe, he knows the protective feeling goes both ways. However, anyone on the outside looking in would find it peculiar that two groups of strangers would have already formed such a loyal bond. Asher begins explaining, "Wendy and I have known each other since before whatever happened, happened."

"And the family you're with now?"

"We met them on the highway . . . two days ago."

"Two days?" Mag seems surprised, as Asher expected.

"Yes."

"So you can't speak for whether they know who that boy is?"

"They don't. They were completely alone when we met them, and they never mentioned him to us," Asher answers.

"But he could have been someone they knew, and perhaps thought they lost, before you and Wendy joined up with them?"

Asher tries to answer, but realizes he knows almost nothing about his new companions. His gut tells him he can trust them, but he can't give a definitive answer in case they *did* know the boy and state otherwise. "I guess so."

"But you were not privy to a backup plan in case you five fell into a trap?"

"No. It was Wendy's suggestion to come here; none of us had any intention of being here. We just followed her," Asher explains.

"You followed Wendy? But I thought Todd was the leader?" Mag taps the ash from her cigarette, watching Asher closely for a reaction.

Asher's lips part and his eyes grow large, having revealed something contrary to the role Todd had been portraying, and potentially marked Wendy as a threat. Mag easily gained his trust, and smoothly turned it against him to take advantage of the situation. He scowls and says, "Todd said you were smart."

"Did he?" Mag asks. The corners of her mouth twitch as she tries not to smile. She snubs her cigarette out on the top of the picnic table. Asher notices several small dark spots from this repeated action.

"You've been here a while, haven't you?" he asks. Mag's eyes turn up to him but she doesn't speak. "There are marks all over the table where you've interviewed others. There are even a couple on my side where people have taken you up on the offer to smoke."

"Yes, I arrived days after the park closed its gates."

"You don't even know what the outside world is like anymore, what we've had to go through to survive," Asher says.

"Make no mistake, Asher, it has been far from easy to live even within these boundaries. We've struggled—nobody that lives here hasn't lost somebody dear to them."

"Did I pass?" Asher asks, unable to find sympathy for the woman that manipulated him.

"What would you do if I decide all five of you are not welcome to stay?"

"It's all five or none," Asher answers.

"And the boy?" Mag asks.

"I don't know him. I don't know why he attacked Ellie. Is she the girl with the short hair?" Asher asks, and Mag nods her head. "But you said earlier he had a small child with him. So if he felt threatened, or felt the child was threatened, then I'm sure he was acting defensively. If you're going to turn someone protecting a child away, then I don't think we're going to fit in with you, and we'll leave with him."

"You pass," Mag answers.

35. ASHER

Before

"How does this look?" Asher asked. He was wearing a blue button-up shirt tucked into khaki shorts.

"Untuck your shirt," Ellis said, "I'm wearing shorts and a T-shirt."

"I don't want your parents to think I'm a slob," Asher said, pulling his shirt out of his shorts.

"It's dinner, not the opera," Ellis answered. He had relayed his parents' invitation to dinner that morning. Asher had agreed but spent the rest of the day wondering if it was a good idea.

"I know, I'm sorry. I just never expected to have a boyfriend, or to be going to dinner with his family."

"You deserve both of those things. I'm sorry that you spent so long thinking there was something wrong with you, but now you get to start being happy. Don't apologize, embrace it."

"Thank you."

"You're welcome."

"Let's do this."

***

Ellis squeezed Asher's hand. They unbuckled their seat belts and got out of the car. The house looked like it belonged in a magazine. The lawn was bright green, the grass and bushes perfectly manicured, and a cobbled walkway led up to a large wraparound porch.

They climbed the steps to the front door. In the entryway, Asher knew the time to jump ship had passed. Everything was pristinely clean and the large, open first floor made Asher feel dwarfed in comparison. A flight of stairs stood directly across from the front door, with the living room to the left, and the kitchen and dining room to the right. Ellis's parents worked together to prepare dinner in the kitchen, their backs to the front door.

"We're here," Ellis called out. His dad set down a pan he had just pulled from the oven, and greeted his son with a hug; his mom followed with a kiss on the cheek. Ellis's dad noticed Asher standing by the door and waved him over.

"Come in, come in!"

"Hi," Asher said.

"You must be Asher." Ellis's dad extended a hand. "We've been asking Ellis to bring you by for over a month."

"Nice to meet you, Mr. Williams," Asher responded, shaking his hand.

"Call me Ben," he said.

"Laurel." Ellis's mom introduced herself, her tone stiff, unlike her husband's. "I'm glad you were able to make it tonight."

"Is Ivy here yet?" Ellis asked.

"Not yet; she texted me, something about her sorority taking longer than she expected it to. In the meantime, we have wine!" Ben exclaimed. He grabbed glasses from the cabinet. "Asher do you have a wine preference?"

"No, sir. Anything is fine."

"I told you, call me Ben; none of this 'sir' stuff. I get called that enough at work," Ben said.

"And he's lying, Dad, he prefers white. He's just trying to be polite," Ellis interjected.

"It's a good thing I didn't open a red, then. You aren't doing me any favors by being polite. We live for wine in this house, but if you're going to drink, we want you to at least enjoy it." He pulled a bottle of white from a wine cooler and poured everyone a glass. "I would say cheers, but we might as well wait for Ivy."

Asher accepted a glass and thanked Ben before taking a sip. As Laurel finished making a salad, Asher and Ellis set the table. The front door opened, and a girl with long blonde hair pulled back into a ponytail appeared, wearing a yellow button-up shirt and bright pink shorts. Asher recognized her from the picture in Ellis's living room.

"Sorry I'm late! Chapter ran over. I stopped and grabbed a bottle of wine to make up for it," she said, missing Ellis and Asher by the table as she headed straight to the kitchen.

"You seem flustered," Laurel said, eyeing her daughter. "Your shirt isn't even properly buttoned."

"Dammit," she answered. She unbuttoned her shirt with her back turned to her parents, but facing Asher and Ellis.

"Ivy, your brother and Asher are here," Ben said. She looked up and saw the two guys with their heads turned away while her shirt was half unbuttoned.

"Sorry." She pulled her shirt together, blushing, and rapidly remedied the issue. "I'm Ivy. As you can tell I don't give the best first impressions."

Asher introduced himself with a chuckle, excusing her.

"Dinner's ready," Laurel interrupted, handing the salad bowl to Ivy and grabbing a plate of fish.

***

"And now for that toast." Ben stood at the end of the table, holding up his glass of wine. "To a wondrous meal made by my lovely wife, having the family together, and getting to finally meet Asher, whom we have heard so much about."

"Cheers." Everyone held up their glasses, clinking the rims together. The air was filled with sounds of silverware against the plates.

"So, Asher, what are you studying?" Laurel asked.

"English and creative writing," he responded after swallowing a bite.

"What do you plan on doing with that?" she prompted.

"Mom," Ellis warned.

"What? I'm just trying to get to know him." Laurel frowned.

"Ultimately, I'd like to write for a living. Books, poetry, something," Asher answered, and resumed eating.

"What kind of books would you like to write?" Laurel continued.

"Probably fiction—give people an escape. I want to write books people can get lost in."

"I think that's nice," Ben said. "People get so inundated with everything going on, it's important to rest and relax the mind as well. Not to mention I'm envious of anyone with a creative mind."

"Has Ellis told you what our parents teach?" Ivy asked.

"No, actually, he hasn't," Asher answered.

"That's because it's boring," Ellis said.

"Mom teaches upper-level government courses, and Dad teaches economics," Ivy said.

"When you say it like that, it makes us sound like dull drones," Ben said, "but we can appreciate culture and art."

"We simply put an emphasis on thinking practically and critically," Laurel said, spearing a stalk of asparagus on her fork and raising it to her lips.

Asher pushed the food around on his plate, his appetite lost as he became uncomfortable with the topic of conversation.

"This tilapia is great, Mrs. Williams," Asher said, hoping a compliment could sway her in his favor.

"Thank you," she answered. She didn't request that Asher call her by her first name. Ellis reached down and squeezed Asher's knee.

***

"Sorry about that," Ellis said to Asher while scraping scraps into the garbage bin. They'd volunteered to clean up while everyone else retired to the living room.

"About what?" Asher asked.

"My mom. She was a lot more intense than I expected her to be," Ellis said.

"It's fine."

"No, it's not. I feel like I set you up in front of a firing squad."

"And I survived," Asher reassured Ellis.

"Come with me." Ellis pulled Asher over to the staircase, and they slipped up to the second floor and into a bedroom. Asher strolled around the space, taking in the belongings of a younger Ellis. There was a desk in the corner with framed photos filling the top shelf, documenting Ellis at all ages in soccer team photos, choir performances, and hanging out with friends. A blue hoodie with yellow stitching hung off the back of the desk chair. The top of the dresser held relics including action figures and an old gaming system. A twin bed was shoved up against a wall. The walls were covered in posters of different cities from around the world. A large map of the world took up an entire wall with red and blue tacks pushed into various locations.

"What do these mean?" Asher asked.

"The red thumbtacks are places I want to go; the blue ones are places I've been," Ellis answered, reaching over and lacing his fingers through Asher's. "So what do you think of my old room?"

"It's nice. I don't know what I would have expected, but I like it," Asher answered. "I think most of us had posters of celebrities and bands or whatever as kids, so this is refreshing."

"I told you I was a rebel when I was younger."

"Yeah, but that made me think you'd have all kinds of emo bands, y'know? Teen angst."

"I focused my angst into escaping. Escaping this house, Orlando, everything. That's why I covered everything in pictures of cities as far from here as possible. But I'm glad I stayed—if I weren't here anymore I wouldn't have met you."

"I'm glad you didn't leave as well." Asher kissed Ellis. Ellis stepped backward without releasing Asher, pulling him onto the bed. His cool hands moved under Asher's shirt and gripped his sides. Asher slipped a hand into the waistband of Ellis's shorts and the passion and fervor of their kissing swelled. They heard a knock on the door and Asher bolted upright and off of Ellis, as if Ellis had turned into an electric wire. He fell against the chair, knocking the hoodie onto the floor. Ellis jumped off the bed, helping Asher up. The door creaked open and Ivy stuck her head in.

"What are you two doing in here?" she asked with a sly grin.

"Nothing, nosey," Ellis said.

"I'm not being nosey; Mom sent me up to check on you guys," Ivy said. She sat on the desk with her feet in the chair.

"I was just showing Asher around the house," Ellis said.

"Yeah, it's a really nice house." Asher flushed.

"It sounded like you were getting quite the tour." Ivy winked at Asher.

"Shut up," Ellis said, pushing Ivy off his desk.

"Come downstairs. Mom's drunk and wound up—I don't want to deal with her on my own." Ivy left the room and Ellis faced Asher and sighed.

"C'mon," he said, and they followed Ivy out of the room.

36. RICO

Before

Tap. Tap. Rico lifted his head from the pillow, dazed and looking around the pitch-black room. Nothing was out of place. He thought his mom might be moving around the house, but there was no light shining under his door. He had tried several times to call and text Chloe to no avail after leaving Brew House. At home, he felt so nauseous that he turned down the dinner his mom had cooked and went straight to bed, climbing under the covers fully dressed.

Tap. Tap. He could make out a shadow coming from the other side of the closed blinds. He threw the blankets off and inched closer. He stuck his pointer and middle fingers between two of the blinds and slowly pulled them apart. A pair of eyes stared back at him. His heart skipped a beat and he fumbled backward. The back of his knees hit the bed and he collapsed back onto the mattress. Total panic was setting in, soothed only by the laughter coming from the window.

"Dude, hurry up," Doug whispered. Rico recovered enough to open the blinds. Doug's silhouette filled the frame, barely illuminated in the moonlight. "What are you waiting for? Let me in."

"Jesus, what is wrong with you?"

"You should have seen the terror in your eyes when you glanced through the blinds," Doug whispered, trying to hold in his laughter while Rico removed the screen from the window.

"What are you doing here; what time is it?" Rico asked, letting out his annoyance once Doug was in his room.

"It's only a little after midnight. And I need my money," Doug answered.

"You couldn't wait until tomorrow? You're lucky my mom hasn't woken up." Rico walked over to the discarded bag in the corner of his room and extracted the wad of cash. Doug counted it out in front of him, as usual, and handed over Rico's cut.

"Perfect, he bought the excess. I was counting on that," Doug said with giddiness as he pocketed the money.

"Yeah, I'd like to thank you for setting me up with that maneuver of yours. He was pissed." Rico shoved the money into his sock drawer.

"Calm down, princess. That's why I sent you, because he'd know you weren't lying when you told him you didn't know what was going on. Had I gone, he would've probably beat my ass for trying to pull one over on him."

"He would have. And he said if you try doing it again, no matter who you send, you're going to pay for it."

"So you're *his* messenger now, is that it?"

"I'm just letting you know what went down."

"He didn't hurt a hair on your pretty little head. No harm, no foul. Tell you what"—Doug grabbed another twenty—"take this as my appreciation for your overtime on this one."

Rico accepted the money, but balled his hand into a fist around it.

"Is that all you need? I was sleeping."

"Damn, you really are a cranky little bitch tonight, aren't you? I was kidding when I called you a princess earlier, but I guess Sleeping Beauty should only be woken up by true love's kiss." Doug puckered his lips. "What crawled up your ass and died?"

Rico tossed the additional twenty dollars onto the dresser and ran his hand through his hair, explaining his missed meeting and the picture from the party.

"Dude, you are such a girl. Look, I'm sorry I made you late to your make-up session, but I told you before you needed to be sure this is what you want to do. Now this is going to be your last opportunity to decide: do you want to stick with me and do what I tell you first and foremost, or do you want to lay in bed with your tissues and ice cream moping because some girl doesn't like you? There are plenty of other bitches; get over this one or I'm dropping you."

All pretense of friendship evaporated. The moment passed and the fight left Rico's body. "You're right. What's done is done, but this is what I need to do. Sorry. You can still count on me."

"You bailed on me this weekend; I messed your day up and could have gotten your ass kicked. We're even. Are you down for a little joyride?" Doug pushed his fingers into his pocket again, but instead of money, he held two little pills. "My treat?"

Doug's right, Rico thought, *if this is how Chloe wants to act, then that's on her. I tried to explain, and she wouldn't let me. It's time to move on. I can't be a moping little boy anymore.*

"Follow me." Doug climbed out the window.

"Where are we going?" Rico asked.

Doug looked over his shoulder with a smirk. "Off to Neverland."

***

Neverland was an average-looking house on the outskirts of town. Nobody was giving it much upkeep, but it didn't look like anyone would contract a disease from stepping inside. The lawn was overdue to be mowed; the grass reached past Rico's ankles as they walked up the driveway. He thought he spotted mushrooms in the yard, but they might have been an effect of the pill he'd taken before leaving home.

Doug bounced up the steps and threw the front door open. Light and music spilled out as he vanished inside, leaving the door wide open. Rico stepped into the square of light and tilted his head, enamored by the kaleidoscope of color streaming out the door.

"Hey, buddy, are you coming in?" A body stepped into the hall, blocking most of the light. Rico grabbed the handrail and boosted himself up the steps. The guy laughed, raising a beer bottle to his lips. "You're tripping balls, dude."

Rico continued down the hall, passing a small kitchen, the counter covered in empty beer bottles and an overflowing garbage can in the corner. The next doorway opened into a dining room cast in half-light; several bulbs were burnt out in the chandelier. A shirtless guy was stretched out across the table whispering to a thin red-haired girl sitting in a chair next to him and giggling.

"Are you looking for someone, buddy?" Rico faced the same guy from the front door again. His nerves were tweaked by being called "buddy" once again. "Take it easy, I'm just trying to help you out."

"Doug."

"Douggie Fresh? Living room." He pointed down the hall and stepped into the kitchen. Clanking glass could be heard over the music. Rico walked to the end of the hallway and into the largest room. Thumping speakers vibrated in each corner and a large TV against one wall was host to a racing video game.

"Where've you been?" Doug screamed over the music, waving Rico over to a couch. Rico ducked while walking in front of the television. His attention was drawn to the colorful screen as he sank onto the couch next to Doug. Several minutes passed while he watched race after race, mesmerized without realizing what was happening around him. Doug shook him by the shoulder and laughed.

"What is he on?" one of the racers asked.

"I gave him a sample of the new stuff you gave me," Doug shouted back.

"Only half a pill, yeah?"

"Whole. He's seasoned, he can handle it." Doug laughed again.

"Dammit, Doug, I told you it's strong." The racer popped a beer can open and downed the entire drink.

"You're good, yeah?" Doug looked into Rico's eyes.

"Yeah, yeah," Rico answered, enraptured once more by the screen. Doug pushed himself up and entered the hall as the girl from the dining room emerged. The skirt around her waist was twisted and her red hair was messier than earlier. She leaned down to talk to the racer, but her words were muted to the room. Rico noticed a flash of green between their hands before she straightened up and slipped away. Doug returned holding two beers and pushed one into Rico's hand.

"I'm okay," Rico said, trying to hand the beer back.

"You're not a quitter are you?" Doug scoffed.

Rico looked down at the bottle before leaning back and downing half of it.

"Attaboy." Doug patted Rico on the back.

***

Everything was dark, and there was a kink in Rico's neck. He sat up, realizing he was bent over the arm of the couch, sleeping. The house was silent. He could distinguish the dark shapes of the furniture, but he didn't see anyone. His head felt heavy as he tried to rub the pain out of his neck; his throat was dry and scratchy. Rico attempted to stand, but his foot hit a bottle and sent it clattering across the floor. He froze, hovering above his seat, and listened for any other disturbance, but the quiet set back in. Having better adjusted to the dark, Rico slowly tip-toed his way to a couple of doors leading off the living room in search of a bathroom. One door was slightly ajar. It was a poorly furnished bed-room with a mattress in the corner and clothes strewn about the floor. The window was missing curtains and blinds, allowing the moonlight to filter through and illuminate two bodies on the mattress.

Squinting, he recognized the body closest to him. Doug slept on his stomach, barely covered with a sheet, leaving the top of his bare butt exposed. Rico started to retreat, but the person next to Doug stirred and rolled over. Her blonde hair, reflecting the moonlight, fell away from her face. Chloe.

Rico's legs gave out from under him and his vision blurred as the room spun in front of him. His stomach flipped and liquid rushed up his throat as he dropped onto his knees and passed out for the second time.

37. RICO

After

The gentle rocking back and forth lures Rico from his sleep. The first thing he sees is water sloshing up against the small port window. He's alone in the bed. He flips the light switch on in the minuscule bathroom and relieves his bladder. The hot water hits his hands as he lathers the soap, and it strikes him finally that Jayden is gone from the bed.

"Jayden!" he yells out, abandoning the running water in the sink and darting toward the deck. "Jayden!"

There is no answer as Rico climbs the stairs two at a time. The deck is barren. He looks overboard into the deep-red ocean water. The rhythm of the current picks up, tossing the boat forcibly back and forth. Rico drops to his knees and holds the railing tightly to stabilize his balance. A large wave crashes over the top of the boat, and the red water spills across the white deck. A second wave crashes over the side, soaking Rico. Expecting salt water, Rico gags and coughs out warm blood, his mouth filled with a coppery taste.

Rico pulls himself to his feet as the boat continues rocking back and forth. He shoves away from the railing, but the deck drops out from under him and a huge wave rises from below. He falls forward, slamming into the deck. His hands slide along the blood-soaked surface as he slips toward the ocean. The railing slams against the small of Rico's back and he flips backward, plunging headfirst into the thick rolling blood. Rico kicks and flails his arms, trying to reach the surface, but the current pulls him around until he is unable to distinguish which direction is up.

His lungs burn from the lack of oxygen. Rico can't hold his breath any longer and opens his mouth. Bubbles flow out while the blood pours in. His head breaks the surface, and he chokes and spits, using the opportunity to suck in a mouthful of air before being pulled under again. Kicking as hard as possible, he surfaces more easily this time.

The boat is gone and the sea has calmed down. Rico finds himself in the center of a ring of face-down bodies. Paddling in a circle, he fails to discover a gap in the corpses as they slowly drift closer, trapping him. The nearest body bumps against his shoulder and he shoves it away, dipping back under the blood. Another body bumps into him, but before he can push it away, its hand latches on to his forearm. Rico panics and struggles to break its hold, but another hand grabs him by his hair, pulling his head back and causing him to yelp. Another hand grabs Rico by the ankle, refusing to release when he kicks, twists, and turns his leg trying to get free. Theresa's voice croaks in his ear: "You promised."

Rico seizes up when one of the bodies raises its head. Staring back at him is his father, Antonio, with the right side of his face in shreds. Antonio's hand grabs Rico by the throat, squeezing tightly and pulling his body closer through the blood. Rico shoves his free leg through the thick ocean, trying to connect with Antonio and push him away, but nothing lands. Opening his mouth, Antonio reveals a row of razor-sharp teeth. Antonio stretches forward, his hot breath on Rico's face, and a small wave breaches between them, splashing Rico in the face.

**

Rico twitches awake on the hard floor. He can feel fluid running down his tender face and only manages to get his eyes halfway open. He lifts his head, wincing. The fluorescent lighting hurts his eyes, and when he distinguishes the concrete floor and the caged walls, he fights off a laugh.

"Hey, are you okay?"

A deep voice startles him, and when he looks for the source of it, he sees a large black man watching him through the wall that divides the cells. The man has a half-empty bottle of water in his hand—the other half of the water is on Rico's face and clothes.

"Are you a cop?" Rico croaks.

"Yes."

"That's good. I just dreamed it all. What are you serving us in here?"

"Serving you?"

Rico's mind clears away the fog clouding his thoughts. The black man is in a cell as well, or a cage, but they are not in a prison. Bits and pieces of the assault behind the park start to return.

"We couldn't tell if you were still breathing or not, and you weren't responding to noise," the man continues.

"Where's Jayden?" Rico asks, his throat dry and cracking.

"I don't know. I don't know who that is."

"My brother. Who are you?"

"Todd," the man says.

"And them?" Rico looks at the woman and child huddled together in a corner. Todd introduces them. Rico grabs on to the side of the cage and uses it to get to his feet.

"I don't know if you should be standing just yet," Todd says. Rico asks for water and slowly crosses to Todd.

Todd places the top of the bottle through the cage and tilts it above Rico's open mouth, allowing the water to slowly flow out in a thin stream. The water is lukewarm but refreshing. He keeps swallowing until the bottle is empty, but when Todd offers a second bottle he shakes his head, wanting to reserve it for later.

The water Todd splashed him with has loosened the dried blood plastered to Rico's face and Rico gently wipes some of the flakes off, only wincing twice from pressing too hard against his tender skin.

"So what did you guys do to get locked up?" Rico asks.

"Showed up," Tonya answers.

Todd explains how they arrived, why they're being contained, and brings Rico up to speed on the last status update on Jayden. He tells

Rico that their companions, Asher and Wendy, have been taken away one at a time.

"How long has it been since they brought me in here?" Rico asks.

"I'm not sure exactly, a few hours. Maybe four or five," Todd answers.

Two more hours pass before the main door opens. Rico watches as Freckles walks in, followed by two women. One woman has graying hair and the other has straight black hair and carries a white box. Freckles unlocks Rico's cage and the woman with the black hair enters. Shying away from her, Rico presses his back against the wall.

"It's okay, I'm a doctor. I just want to take a look at you and make sure there's no lasting damage," she says. She crouches and opens the white box, which contains bandages, bottles, and tubes. Patting the ground next to her, she asks, "Can you come sit here, please?"

She snaps on a pair of latex gloves and pulls a small light out of her pocket. She shines it in each of Rico's eyes. She has him follow the light without moving his head. Next she presses against his nose, causing him to flinch. Ripping open a small square foil package, she hands him a wet napkin and allows him to wipe away more of the dried blood.

"Rico, right?" she asks. "You've had a mild concussion, so I'll need to keep an eye on you, but it's not too serious. Your nose isn't broken, but your face is going to be bruised, swollen, and sore for a few days. Other than that everything should clear up nicely with time."

"What about Jayden? Have you looked at him too?"

"I have; that's how I know your name. He's asked for you."

"Is he okay?"

"He's awake. His concussion was worse than yours; he hit the ground hard. He's in a lot of pain, but I have him under close observation. He'll need more time than you to fully recover, but he will be fine."

"I need to see him—I promised I would protect him." Rico attempts to stand and make it to the cage door, but Freckles blocks it with his rifle. Their eyes meet and mutual hatred passes between them.

"Thank you, Alexandria," the graying woman says. Alexandria takes her first aid box and walks around Freckles and out of the room. Freckles relocks the cage door.

"What about Jayden? I need to see him," Rico pleads.

"That's not an option right now," the woman says.

"Where are Asher and Wendy?" Todd asks.

"Get to the back," Freckles says, standing in front of Todd's cage.

Todd relents and steps away, powerless to do anything. Freckles opens the cage and aims his rifle at Todd's chest.

"Tonya and Marie, with me," the woman says.

"Absolutely not." Todd blocks his wife and daughter.

"I don't think you're in a position to bargain," Freckles says.

"Daniel." The woman's voice is commanding.

"Where are Asher and Wendy?" Todd repeats.

"They're safe, and if you want your wife and child to be safe as well, you will allow them to come with me," the woman answers.

"How can we believe you?" Tonya asks.

"What choice do you have?" the woman asks. "If my intentions were to have you killed, there would be no point in having kept you alive thus far. I wouldn't have returned your belongings."

Rico watches as Todd gathers his family in his arms and kisses them. Tonya leads Marie by the hand from the cage and they go with the woman.

"Lights out," Daniel says. He flips the light switch off and slams the large metal door behind him.

38. ASHER

Before

"I love you too, Mom. I promise to call more often." Asher paced around his room. "Yeah, I'm going to look at flights tonight. I could just drive too. Yes, I promise, love you too. Bye."

Asher hung up and placed the phone on his desk. He walked over to the bed and laid down, not bothering to get under the covers.

"How'd it go?" Ellis asked, putting his own phone on the nightstand.

Asher's mom was babysitting Brady's two kids for the weekend, but seized an opportunity to call him while they napped. She chastised him about not calling home enough and wanted to make sure he was *certain* he didn't want to come home for Thanksgiving. But he was going to go home for Christmas and said he needed to study before finals. She wanted him to check flight prices. She didn't want Asher on the road in case of a snowstorm. Standard mom worries.

"What are you thinking about?" Asher asked.

"It's nothing," Ellis said, rubbing his face into the pillow.

"Is everything okay?" Asher propped himself up on an elbow.

"The whole time you were on the phone with your mom I had to make sure to remain as quiet as possible. And it was hard to hear your conversation and know that I wouldn't be a part of it. It's stupid,

I know. I'm just not used to it." Ellis shrugged and played with a loose thread on the comforter.

"It's not stupid. You're right; it isn't fair to you." Asher reached forward, running his fingers through Ellis's hair. "I don't want you to think I'm ashamed of you."

"I know you're not, and I know you're taking steps forward. I don't want to pressure you at all. But you asked and I'm not going to lie to you."

"I appreciate that. I want to come out to my family, not because you pressure me, but I'm tired of hiding everything. But I'm afraid. It scares me to think about what will happen. My family isn't like yours; they won't accept this." Asher's eyes burned, the weight of the realization crushing him. His throat constricted and he had to take short shallow breaths. Ellis pulled Asher over, cradling his head against his chest.

"There is nothing wrong with you—you realize that, don't you?" Ellis asked. Asher nodded, but he wasn't sure if he believed it. He'd spent his entire life being told homosexuality was wrong, and a few months and friends weren't enough to counter a lifetime of hatred.

"Don't let what your family thinks change that either. You didn't choose to be gay—the only thing you get to choose is when to tell them."

"And what happens when I lose them?"

"You'll have me. You'll always have me, every single day. No matter what happens, I'm not going anywhere. And my family will be there for you too." Ellis rubbed the space between Asher's shoulder blades.

"Thank you." Asher counted his blessings. "I never thought I'd have any of this—a boyfriend, dinners with his family, happiness. I couldn't even let myself dream about it, because I refused to admit I wanted it."

"You deserve to be happy."

"So do you. And you deserve better than having to remain a secret part of my life."

"We'll get there when we get there," Ellis responded to calm Asher. "I had a long talk with my sister about you last night."

"You did?" Asher asked, perplexed.

"I needed advice. I have something I need to talk to you about, but I didn't know how to say it until Ivy and I talked."

Asher felt the room tilt. Immediately his mind began playing games with him, and he grew anxious about what was coming. He sat up, separating himself from Ellis, ready to move quickly when the other shoe dropped and Ellis broke up with him. His thoughts became overwhelming: *You should have known,* and *Did you really think some-one like Ellis could truly care about you?* But it had only been a minute since Ellis had said he would always be there. Though he'd clarified, "no matter what happens."

Ellis quietly watched the range of confusion and emotions pass over Asher, and when he cleared his throat, Asher watched his lips to focus on the words.

"First, I want to say sorry. I owe you an apology, because when you met me I was broken. My relationship with Brandon turned me sour, and when you came into my life, I used you as a crutch. I thrust the responsibility of fixing me onto your shoulders when I felt I wasn't capable of doing it myself. I stayed with Brandon out of fear, but I refused to let you go once I got to know you. I'm glad I did, even if that's selfish. Because being around you gave me strength and showed me that it was okay to leave. I didn't love him anymore, not romantically anyway. A part of me still cares about him; I always will because I'm the person I am today because of him. But I let him go because you started occupying my heart." Ellis stopped and inhaled.

Asher, still confused by what was happening, did not know whether he should reach down to grab Ellis's hand or move off the bed alto-gether and sit in his desk chair. He did neither, remaining still as Ellis continued. "You fixed me and brought me so much joy. Every day you continue to make me happy. Ivy told me she noticed a change in me almost immediately after I met you. She had started getting worried before because I was moping around and morose. But the more time I spent talking to you, the more I smiled, the more I laughed. I don't know how to thank you enough for that. I don't know how you saw me through the wall I had built around myself to keep everyone out. How you saw the cracks and ignored them. Now all I can think about is how I'm falling in love with you and for the first time I feel completely safe."

A huge smile spread across Asher's face. Fearing the worst, he received words exuberantly better than he could have imagined. He leaned in and kissed Ellis. "I'm glad I make you feel safe, because you make me feel the same way. And you've given me a confidence I never had before—you've shown me I'm good enough, and that I'm worth it."

"You're more than worth it."

***

Asher reached the top of the stairs, balancing a box of cupcakes between his chest and one hand, using the other hand to flip through the keys on his key ring until he found the freshly cut piece of metal Ellis surprised him with two days earlier. He pushed the key into the lock and twisted.

"I got you a treat." Asher stepped into the kitchen and stopped, nearly dropping the cupcakes on the ground. Ellis sat on the edge of the counter, a smile fading from his face. Brandon stood three feet away, coyly smirking at the shock on Asher's face.

"Hey," Ellis said, walking over to Asher. He lifted the box out of Asher's hands and pecked his cheek. A surge of spiteful pride rushed through Asher's chest as he watched the smirk on Brandon's face disappear, replaced by a flash of anger. "These look great, thank you," Ellis said.

"Hi, Brandon, what are you doing here?" Asher attempted nonchalance, but the hostility was obvious.

"He just showed up a few minutes before you," Ellis said. "I was about to text you to let you know but my phone is charging in the bedroom."

"Yeah, I was just stopping by. The other day I found a book that belongs to Ellis," Brandon said. "But I've returned it, so I should probably go." Asher stepped to the side, not wanting to hinder the path to the door, but Ellis had another idea.

"Nah, we were about to order pizza. If you're hungry, you might as well stay and eat a slice. We don't mind, do we, Ash?" Ellis asked.

"No. Not at all," Asher lied, wanting to be respectful in a home that was not his. He tried to remember his southern hospitality.

"Great!" Brandon exclaimed with too much enthusiasm. After Ellis placed an order for delivery, the three continued to stand around the kitchen, trying to make small talk.

"Brandon was telling me he landed an internship with some tech development company next semester," Ellis explained to Asher.

"Well, it's a new start-up company, so there wasn't a lot of competition for the spot, but it'll look great on a resume." Brandon reveled in the praise, turning to Asher. "How's the coffee shop gig going?"

Brandon was trying to push his buttons, but Asher smiled and said, "It's been going really well, actually. I love it. I ride my bike to and from work every day, which helps me stay in excellent shape, y'know?" Asher ran his hand down his flat stomach, his eyes darting to Brandon's softer center and back up to his face. Asher knew he was being petty, but he couldn't stop himself from feeding into Brandon's goading.

"Anything else new going on in your life?" Ellis hesitantly asked, trying to steer the group to a friendly common ground.

"In fact, there is. I met someone online," Brandon replied, straightening his posture and puffing out his chest.

"Great, that's great," Ellis said. If Asher hadn't known any better, he would almost think Ellis was upset.

"He really gets me, understands me as a person, in a way I never thought anyone would be able to. And he respects me," Brandon continued, cutting his eyes at Ellis.

"I think you should go," Asher said, stepping in front of Ellis.

"It's fine," Ellis said, putting his hand on Asher's arm.

"No, it's not," Asher replied to Ellis before facing Brandon again. "You're being rude, and you should leave."

"This isn't your apartment. Ellis says I can stay." Brandon crossed his arms in front of his chest, pleased at having struck a nerve in Asher.

"Then I'll leave." Asher snatched his keys off the counter, but Ellis grabbed his arm.

"Please don't leave," he pleaded. Asher's eyes moved from Ellis's face to Brandon's, who was no longer attempting to conceal a smile. Asher flushed with anger, and he focused on his breathing. Ellis released his arm and turned away. "Brandon, I think it's best if you do leave. Thank you for returning my book."

Asher readjusted his stance and held Ellis's hand. He gave it a squeeze, but it went unreturned. Brandon quietly brushed past and slammed the door as he left. Ellis released Asher's hand and walked over to the sink, keeping his back to Asher. His back and shoulders rose and fell as the silent seconds ticked by. No longer willing to bear the tension, Asher opened his mouth.

"I'm sorry if I upset you, but I wasn't just going to stand by while he took jabs at you," Asher said.

"Why? Why couldn't you just let him say whatever he needed to say?" Ellis spun around.

"Because he was being an ass! It wasn't right!" Asher fired back.

"And why wasn't it? He's angry and he has every right to be! We were together for over a year and then I walked away from him. Of course he isn't thinking about what's right." Ellis's voice quaked.

"So what, I'm just supposed to remain quiet when he tries to make me feel this big for my job." Asher held up his hand, his thumb and pointer finger an inch apart.

"This isn't about you! Stop thinking about yourself for a minute, and ignore him so he can say what he needs to in order to be happy!" Ellis threw his hands in the air. "He's hurt, he's angry, he's going to take whatever he can and throw it at us. It's a defense. You're not the only person with feelings!"

Asher stared at Ellis, overcome with defeat and emptiness, the tension overbearing. Ellis's words stung deeper than anything Brandon had said, but they hurt because they were true. Asher hadn't thought of anyone but himself since the night he met Ellis. As Asher was about to speak, Ellis beat him to it.

"I'm sorry he insulted you about your job. And I'm sorry I didn't stop him. I might think it's fair for him to attack me, because I broke up with him. But that still doesn't give him the right to attack you," Ellis apologized, hanging his head.

"I'm sorry too. I need to know when to step in and when to let you fight your own battles. Brandon has just always made me uneasy." Asher tried to rationalize the confrontation, but he knew he was doing it for his own benefit.

"I'm sorry he was just sprung on you today. I should have just gotten the book back from him and sent him on his way, but I was trying to be the friendly, good guy. I don't know what I'm doing; this is all new to me."

"You are the friendly, good guy—that's what drew me to you. This is new to both of us and neither of us knows what to do. We just need to be on the same side, as a team."

There was a loud knock on the door. Ellis answered, collecting pizza from the delivery boy and handing him cash. While placing slices on the plates, Asher grinned.

"Why are you smiling?"

"We just had our first fight."

"And that's something to be happy about?"

"We've got it out of the way now. It's inevitable—every couple fights, and now instead of dreading what our first fight is going to be about, it's over and resolved. And we have cupcakes and pizza to make up over," Asher explained.

"Make up, or make out?" Ellis asked playfully, smiling as well.

"Both."

39. ASHER

After

Asher sits on the edge of the cot, the paper crinkling under him with every slight movement. The curtain around the cot is pulled back and a woman with straight black hair steps through with a stethoscope around her neck.

"Hello, Asher. I'm Alexandria," she says, extending her hand. "Sorry it took so long; I've been with another patient."

"It's okay," Asher says. Alexandria runs a series of tests on him, from listening to his heartbeat and breathing to checking for lice to testing his reflexes. She inspects the cuts on his arm, then has him strip down to his underwear so she can check for any bite marks or scratches.

"You can put your clothes back on," Alexandria says, after completing a full physical on Asher.

"How come we were all locked up if you were going to check us over for bites anyway?" Asher asks, zipping his pants up.

"When the virus first broke out, there was a gestation period of generally three to four days. It varied based on the person. Now, signs of being infected show up within the first twelve hours, and the person you once were is completely gone within twenty-four. We lock you up to be safe. I examine you for scratches or bites because we take every precaution. You never know when someone's body will still fight it off for those three to four days," Alexandria explains.

"You know a lot about this."

She tells him that she'd been working at a nearby hospital when the infection started to gain traction. She was able to observe its effects on people and look for the signs of how it spread. Those who contracted it always retained their strength initially; anyone coming in was immediately put in restraints to prevent an attack. Then fatigue and starvation set in, and the longer an infected victim goes without eating, the more sluggish he or she becomes. But there's no recovering from it. Once infected, the mind dies; all semblance of humanity dies too, replaced by a ravenous hunger as long as the body remains alive. She tells Asher at first it was slow, and doctors felt it could easily be isolated, but every hospital was quickly overrun and panic caused it to spread faster. She was forced to abandon her position; there was nothing left she could do for anyone. The park was only five miles from her house, and she knew there would be an on-site medical facility with supplies few people would think of, so she packed a bag and migrated.

"How do you guys still have power?"

"Theme parks have backup generators, just in case. We use them as minimally as possible because they're loud, and if we lit up the entire park, we would draw too much attention. Plus we don't have the resources anymore to keep them going long-term. The Health Services building and the holding cells are important enough to have the generators turned on when necessary. Most of the other buildings are not."

"What happens to me now?"

"Mag is waiting out front for you; she'll explain. I just do the tests," she says. Asher slips his feet back into his shoes, picks up his bag, and they leave the room.

Mag's back is turned to them when they enter the waiting area; she's talking to the thickset man who carried the battered teen into the cage. Asher remembers her referring to him as Aubrey. Aubrey chews on a fingernail until he sees Alexandria.

"How is the boy?" Aubrey asks.

"He needs some rest, but he'll recover," Alexandria answers.

"It was an accident, you have to know that, I didn't—" Aubrey begins.

"We know it was an accident." Mag cuts him off. "I think it was all a misunderstanding, and we're going to get to the bottom of it."

"You need to take some deep breaths and relax before I'm tending to you as well," Alexandria says.

"She's right. Go home and get some sleep, Aubrey. You're no use to anyone like this," Mag says, placing a reassuring hand on his bicep. Aubrey nods and slouches his shoulders as he leaves the waiting area. Mag turns to Alexandria and says, "The girl?"

"That's where I'm going now." Alexandria disappears through a different door than she and Asher came through.

"So what happens now?" Asher asks.

"We sit, and we wait." Mag reclines into one of the chairs and Asher follows her lead, but chooses a chair three spaces down from her.

After fifteen minutes of silence, the door opens and Wendy appears. Asher jumps from his chair and darts across the waiting room, relieved to see her.

"You're okay," Asher says.

"Yeah, Mag came and got me about an hour after they took you. We were freaking out in there, didn't know what to believe."

"Where are Todd and Tonya and Marie?" Asher asks, turning to Mag.

"They're still locked up, for the time being," Mag answers, getting to her feet.

"Why?" Asher asks.

"We're just taking things slow," Mag answers.

"But you let us go," Wendy points out.

"Yes," Mag says. Asher and Wendy wait for her to elaborate but she doesn't. Mag reaches the front door and holds it open.

Wendy laces her fingers into Asher's. He squeezes her hand, but otherwise they remain unmoving. Mag sighs at the two of them refusing to budge.

"You two need to get cleaned up. If you walk, I'll talk," Mag says. Hefting their packs onto their backs, they give in and exit Health Services.

Mag leads them through the back route behind the buildings, a maze of monotone colors that starkly contrast the vibrant and lively atmosphere sold in the park. Weeds poke up through the cracked sidewalks, and there are more dark spots on the asphalt and ground from earlier bloodshed.

"We're walking," Wendy says, "I thought you were going to start talking?"

Mag chuckles. "Feisty. To get straight to the point—"

"Please do," Wendy says.

"To get straight to the point," Mag continues, "your stories checked out with each other and what I found and read in your bags. I don't think either of you pose a threat, and you're being extended a probation period to see if you fit in with us."

"And the others?" Asher asks.

"I haven't spoken to them yet," Mag answers.

"And why not?" Asher asks.

"I will speak to them when the time is right," Mag says.

Wendy raises her voice. "The time is right now."

Mag spins. When she speaks, her voice is quiet and level but seething. "You two need to get something through your heads right now. You are not in charge; you do not make the decisions around here. I understand you survived out there, but we survived in here and it was not easy. I make the calls in here; I decide who gets interviewed and when. I choose who to bring into our camp, because if I make the wrong choice, people die. You get ten seconds to decide if you want to follow me or if you want to be led to the front gates. That's the decision you get to make."

"We'll stay," Wendy says.

"But—" Asher opens his mouth to speak, and is stopped when Wendy squeezes his hand.

"We'll stay," Wendy repeats. She is unwilling to meet Asher's gaze, instead diverting her eyes to the ground and chewing on her bottom lip.

They follow a pace behind Mag in silence. Each time Asher wants to speak up, one glance at Wendy stops him. Finally, Mag turns at the corner of a building and they step through a large privacy fence into the park. The small-town appearance at the front of the park is replaced by a whimsical vibe. There are unnatural plants of various sizes and colors along the buildings and walkways. There are no straight lines anywhere—all of the buildings are oddly shaped and curved and twisted. They pass a large roller coaster that towers over the buildings, each wooden plank used in its construction painted a different vibrant color.

"Are we going to be offered a cookie that says 'eat me'?" Asher whispers to Wendy, eliciting a small smile. His heart cracks at the same time. This is what Ellis wanted to show him and never got the chance to.

The air is haunted. What should be bustling is desolate, yet it still feels like they have to squeeze through to avoid bumping shoulders with phantoms. Unintelligible noises reach Asher's ears, and for a moment he believes that ghosts really are drifting around him, whispering. But when they round a bend in the street, he can see a camp set up at the base of the castle.

People mill about, and Asher catches a glimpse of children chasing each other. There are tents and makeshift shelters that house the approximately twenty people standing around. They tend to fires, talk in small groups, or hang clothing to dry. Asher takes in their clean appearances; many are wearing outfits that include park shirts. Those standing closest to them break from their chores and turn to watch.

"Isn't it kind of hot out for fires?" Asher asks Mag.

"They're boiling water to purify it," Mag answers. She continues through the center of camp, Asher and Wendy at her heels. Most of the observers turn back to their tasks, already bored with the newcomers, but the back of Asher's neck prickles from being watched. Mag holds up a hand for them to stop and approaches a woman, speaking to her out of earshot.

"This is insane," Asher says to Wendy. She doesn't hear him; she is busy looking around the camp.

"Here, this is for you to get cleaned up." Mag holds out a large tin full of steaming water. Asher grabs the container, taking the weight out of her hands. It is heavier than he would have expected Mag to be able to carry, and he is surprised she handled it with such ease. "I'll take you somewhere more private."

"How come everyone stays outside in tents and stuff?" Wendy asks. "With the rain and everything aren't there enough shops and whatnot to stay in?"

"People stay in the stores as well, but it gets stuffy in the heat. Some prefer to sleep outside, and it helps us stay alert," Mag answers.

"So there are more people we didn't see?" Wendy asks, perking up. Asher looks at her questioningly, but she's focused on Mag.

"A few," Mag says. She points out a restroom area to them. "This is where we generally do the washing up. The family restroom is the cleanest; there's a doorstop to prop the door open so you can still see once inside. We've moved a shelving unit in there as well and it's stocked with clothes in a variety of sizes. As I'm sure you saw, it's going to be various souvenir shirts and the like. We can get what you're wearing as clean as possible once you've changed."

"Ladies first," Asher says.

"No, you have the water. It's fine, go ahead, I'll sit here with Mag," Wendy says, still not meeting Asher's gaze.

Asher carries the large tin, hot water sloshing over the sides, to the bathroom. The door is propped ajar enough for him to squeeze the toe of his shoe into the crack and kick it open. Hefting the tin up onto the sink, he strips his clothes off for the second time in an hour. A stack of washrags sits on one of the shelves, and he grabs one.

The lack of lighting casts foreign shadows across his face, but not enough to mask the streaks of dirt and splatters of dried blood. His face is gaunt, his jawline and cheekbones more pronounced than ever from his weight loss. It's been over two months since his last real meal. Asher's eyes trail down to his collar and shoulder bones. Although he'd been nearly nude during his physical, he has not processed how drastically his physique has changed until now. Bringing the rag up to his face, he scrubs his forehead first. Scrub, plunge, wring. Scrub, plunge, wring.

His skin is pink and raw to the touch when he stops. He dips his matted hair into the filthy water, running his hands through the tangles to dislodge as much dirt as he can. When he finishes, there is still dirt caked under his nails, but the water is already lukewarm and brown.

He grabs a pair of swimming shorts and a T-shirt with an action hero posing on the front and slips them on before stepping into a pair of rubber sandals. He balls up his old clothes and carries them out of the bathroom under his arm, his muddied shoes hanging from his hand.

Mag is standing ten feet away talking to a balding man around her age, or a few years older, leaving Wendy alone on the bench.

"Hey," Asher says, dropping down next to Wendy.

"Hey yourself," Wendy answers.

"The bathroom is all yours. Sorry the water isn't hot or clean anymore."

"It's okay," Wendy says, ambling away.

Asher turns his attention to Mag in time to see the man lean forward and kiss her before walking away.

"Your husband?" Asher asks.

"No, he's dead," Mag answers.

"Oh, sorry."

"Not recently, ten years ago. A drunk driver hit him. George and I have been together for four years, but neither of us felt up to getting remarried. Now, more than ever, we realize just how important the people we love are."

Asher picks at the dirt in his fingernails, thinking about everyone in his life he will never see again. Every connection he had from before the outbreak has been lost. Even though he knew Wendy before, they weren't friends until they had nothing left.

"I'm not a monster, you know," Mag says.

"I didn't say you were," Asher says.

"You didn't say as much, but I could see the look in your eyes earlier when I told you two to decide on the spot what to do."

"I told you I wouldn't stay here if all five of us weren't welcome."

"And it hasn't been decided that they aren't welcome."

"But you're not in any rush to interview them. There is a little girl who is terrified enough because she's locked up, but even more so because none of them have a clue what is going on, and she's had to go through all of this without being able to hear. Your priority is letting Wendy and I bathe and not letting Marie know that she's safe."

"I'm all done," Wendy says, reappearing behind them. "I didn't know what to do with the water so I've left it in there, but I can go get it or pour it out."

"No, no. I'll have someone come by later and take care of it," Mag says, jumping up and straightening her clothes.

Mag leaves them in a pair of metal chairs on the outskirts of the camp. A woman brings them each a disposable container of food before quickly retreating.

"They're afraid of us," Asher says.

"Who can blame them? Apparently we've missed a lot of action that's gone down here," Wendy says. She pushes her food around with her fork.

"What's going on with you?" Asher asks, closing his food and setting it down.

"Nothing, I'm just not that hungry."

"Who are you looking for?"

"What?" Wendy turns to Asher, finally meeting his eyes.

"You told me yesterday that you wanted to come here but wouldn't explain why, and I didn't press it. But you've been avoiding looking at me since Mag forced us to decide what we wanted to do, which you were quick to answer for the both of us. I saw you searching around when we first got here too, and you asked if there were others that just weren't at the camp. I'm not stupid, and I've earned the right for answers. Who are you looking for?"

"You're right; you're not stupid. I am," Wendy says. She takes a deep breath and runs her fingers through her freshly rinsed hair before continuing. "I lied to you. Not just about why I wanted to come here, but I've been keeping a really big secret from you."

"I don't understand," Asher says, furrowing his brow.

A tear slides down Wendy's cheek and she ignores it, letting it dangle from her chin.

"I've been here before, once, with Ivy. It was so hot and crowded. We kept bumping into sweaty people, feeling their wet skin rubbing against us. And I swear nobody was wearing deodorant—it reeked. Ivy made a joke about needing a plague to wipe out everyone because there were too many people on the planet. I laughed and told her that was the only way I would ever want to come back here, if we could just have the place to ourselves." More tears stream down Wendy's face and fall freely into her lap.

"You thought that if you remembered that day and could make it here, she could too," Asher says.

"Hoped so, yeah. But she's not here. And I was stupid to think she would be," Wendy says.

"No, that doesn't make you stupid. She's your best friend—of course you would want to hold on to hope of seeing her again," Asher says, rubbing her back.

"No, I was stupid because I risked everything to get here knowing she wouldn't be here. You could have died; Tonya or Marie or Todd could have died. And the whole time I knew she wouldn't be here. But I was lying to myself, trying to say there was a chance I was wrong and it hadn't happened. You know how your brain will alter horrors to help you cope? I tried to force mine to do that so that I would keep moving forward."

Wendy's chin quivers as a sob escapes her throat.

"There's no way you could have known she wouldn't be here. Look at me, Wendy, look at me." Asher pleads with her until she looks at him. "You couldn't have known."

"I could," Wendy says, "because I watched the blood drain from her body as she died. I killed her."

40. RICO

Before

"Get up, c'mon," a voice yelled. Rico felt a sharp pain in his head. His leg was jostled, causing the nausea to return, his cheek pressed into a cold and wet substance. He cracked his eyes open and moaned. "Up. Now."

He rolled onto his back and stared up at the yellowed ceiling for a minute before lifting his head, bringing on another wave of pain. He looked toward his feet and the doorway to the living room to see the video game racer from the night before watching him with a bowl of cereal in his hands, talking with his mouth full.

"I think you pissed yourself. I told Doug he should've only given you half a pill." He shoved another spoonful of cereal into his mouth. "I've got to go, so clean this up and get out."

Sitting upright, and trying to ignore the migraine, he realized that the crotch of his pants *was* wet. He saw the puddle of vomit he'd passed out in and wiped his covered cheek with the back of his hand. The memory of seeing Chloe in the bed returned and blood rushed to his head in rage. The blankets were gathered in a messy pile toward the foot of the bed, but the mattress was empty. Rico extracted his phone from his pocket to check the time, a different wave of sickness filling his stomach when he realized it was almost noon. At least he didn't have any missed texts or calls. His mom either woke up too early to wake him before leaving for work, or too late and assumed he had already left for school.

He found a wadded towel in the corner and used it to wipe up as much of the puke as possible, before wandering out into the living room holding it away from his body. The racer reemerged from one of the closed doors, shaking his head.

"Do you have a laundry room?" Rico asked.

"Through the kitchen, just drop it in. I'll get to it later," he answered. After tossing the towel in the washer, Rico found the racer waiting outside on the front steps with a cigarette in his mouth. "Do you need a ride somewhere?"

"Yeah, thanks. Doug drove me here," Rico answered.

"What's your name, kid?"

Rico smiled at being called "kid"; the racer looked to be about four years older than him at most.

"Rico, you?"

"Eric. A bit of advice? Be careful with Doug. He thinks he's bigger and better than he is. I give him a lot of leeway because he's my cousin and he doesn't really have anyone else, but he's going to get in a lot of trouble one day. He'll bring you down too." Eric stubbed out his cigarette and locked the front door. He jumped down the stairs and Rico followed him around the side of the house to an old pickup truck. "Hop in the back. No offense, but you're not riding up front in those piss pants."

***

Rico had thrown up two more times before he was able to peel his dirty clothes off and get in the shower. He felt chilled to the bone, even with the scalding water. He scrubbed vomit and urine off his body until a layer of skin was missing as well. The steam from the shower did little to warm him and relieve his migraine. He bent over halfway through brushing his teeth and emptied what was left in his stomach into the sink.

He collapsed onto the bed the second he had sweatpants pulled up and a hoodie over his head, his entire body aching and shivering. His phone chimed but the sound was too distant to reach. His mind swam in and out of consciousness and the room slowly faded. He never heard his mom return home, but eventually there was a knock on his door and the lights came on.

"Hey, what do you want for—" Melissa's voice faltered. "Enrico! What's wrong?"

Melissa dropped to the bed, slipping her arm under his shoulder and back, trying to support him into an upright position. Sweat streamed off his forehead—his pillow was drenched, and warmth radiated from his skin.

"It's just a cold, I'm okay," Rico insisted, trying to push her away.

"This isn't a cold—we need to get you to the hospital." Melissa tried to lift him further up and out of bed, but he weakly fought back.

"No, no. I just need to lie down, no hospitals."

"I'll be right back." Melissa disappeared for several minutes before returning with a glass of water and pills. Rico tried again to push his mother's hand away, but finally relented. "When was the last time you ate?"

"I dunno. Yesterday."

"We need to get something into you. I'm going to run to the store and get some soup or broth or something."

"I don't want anything, I just want to be left alone."

"You're going to eat. Stay here; not that you're really going anywhere."

Rico's phone rang again and he groaned. Melissa searched around the floor for the source of the sound, picking up the pants he discarded earlier. She crinkled her nose at the smell and held them slightly closer.

"Rico, did you pee your pants?"

"What? No, no, no." Rico was reeling, trying to think of an excuse, having forgotten about urinating in his pants.

"It smells like pee—I'm around it enough every day, I know what pee smells like."

"Chloe got a new puppy. She dropped me off at home after school, but we swung by to pick up the puppy and he peed in my lap." Rico rolled onto his other side, away from her accusatory look. Melissa allowed him to protect his pride rather than push the subject, and placed the phone on his nightstand. She carried the pants out of the room as she left.

Rico forced himself up and reached for the phone. Seven missed calls, one from his mom, six from Doug, and thirteen texts from Doug.

He read through the texts ranging from R U Alive? to Eric told me he droppd U off n U lookd like shit to I called U 5 times RU ALIVE???????

Rico texted back a simple yes and almost passed out again from the effort. The phone started ringing again. Rico hit Answer and held it to his ear.

"What?"

"Dude, what the hell? I've been trying to check on you all day!" Doug screamed.

"Yeah? Well, I'm alive, so thank you for your concern and fuck off." Rico pulled the phone away to hit End, but he heard Doug's muffled voice and cut him off. "I'm done, I'm out."

"Hey, man, look, I'm sorry I just left you on the floor this morning, but there was no way you were getting up for class and I figured Eric would just let you stay. But at least he gave you a ride. You didn't need me there," Doug argued.

"I'm not talking about that. I'm talking about who was in your bed."

"Wh-Who was in my bed?"

"I saw her, when I walked into that room, before I passed out. I saw her."

"Why do you care about some girl being in my bed? Wait, you're not like, a gay, are you? You're not in love with me, right?"

"Chloe. I saw Chloe in your bed."

"Chloe?"

"Yeah, Chloe. So you can fuck. Right. Off."

"I don't even know what you're talking about! Why the hell would Chloe have even been at Neverland, much less in my bed?"

"I saw her, and I saw her blonde hair."

"That was Holly, you jackass. That wasn't Chloe. You saw her blonde hair and you're all hung up on Chloe, and your blasted-ass mind made you think you saw Chloe. What is wrong with you? You couldn't even talk by the time I went to bed, and you're going to trust what you saw when you were in outer space? Geez."

Rico thought over Doug's words. Before he could respond, he heard the front door open again.

"I've got to go."

41. RICO

After

"Where's Jayden?" Rico asks when the lights return along with Daniel. Daniel ignores him, dragging his rifle along the cages, filling the room with rattling. "When do I get to see my brother?"

"Why are you in here?" Todd asks, stepping up to the front of his own cage.

"What are we going to do with the two of you?" Daniel switches his focus between them, his lips pulled back showing yellowing teeth.

"Where are my wife and daughter?" Todd demands.

"You two sure do have a lot of questions," Daniel says. "It doesn't seem like you're in the position to ask them, though."

"We just want to know where our families are," Todd says.

"You're like scared little animals shaking in their crates." Daniel laughs.

"I swear to you, if any harm has come to them, I will destroy you," Todd says, pressing his body against the cage.

Before Daniel has an opportunity to react, the door opens.

"Mag, I didn't know you were coming back tonight." Daniel steps back as the woman walks in.

"I was wondering where you were. It's getting late, but there's no need in keeping a father away from his wife and daughter longer than necessary. Unlock him," Mag says.

"You can't be serious. It's dark out; what if he jumps you?" Daniel protests.

"That's what you're for," Mag answers.

"And if I can't see?" Daniel asks.

"Then let's go get Aubrey and see if he's up to it, and tomorrow morning I will find someone with better eyesight to take over your duties," Mag says.

"I've got it," Daniel says. He pulls the key ring out of his pocket, slowly flipping the keys to find the correct one.

"Wait," Todd interrupts. "What happens to Rico when you take me?"

"He'll have to stay here until it's time for me to come for him in the morning," Mag says.

"In the dark?" Todd asks.

"Of course not, the lights are on aren't they?" Mag answers.

Daniel freezes, raising his head to stare threateningly at Todd. Rico feels his mouth dry out.

"Now, yes. But from the time you left with my wife and daughter, we've sat in the pitch black," Todd explains.

"That's enough." Daniel raises his raspy voice.

"Daniel," Mag says.

"You don't really believe this stranger do you?"

"Why would I lie? What do I have to lose? For all I know my wife and daughter are gone, and you're leading me to the same end. But if that's not the case, and if they are okay and I can be reunited with them, I'm not going to risk that for a lie. Either way, I can't look past the further mistreatment this teenage boy will receive. I will wait, and I will be reunited with my family when he can be reunited with his brother," Todd says, maintaining a calm and collected voice.

"Maybe the generators went out." Daniel looks Todd dead in the eyes.

"I stood by when I had to; I kept my mouth shut and my head down before all of this happened. But I became a police officer so my daughter didn't have to be raised in a world where she didn't feel safe, and I won't stand by anymore and keep quiet. And I won't allow my wife, my daughter, this boy, or myself to be called animals. We are people, and there aren't a whole lot of people left anymore."

"Daniel, please wait outside," Mag says, but it's an order, not a request.

"Mag—"

"Now."

Daniel shoves the keys back into his pocket, and glaring at Rico and Todd, he stomps from the room and slams the door. Rico jumps at the loud bang. His head begins to throb with more intensity and he grabs on to the side of the cage to steady himself.

"Your families are fine; they're safe," Mag says to both of them.

"I think you'd understand why we can't fully believe you, especially after the way he treated us," Todd replies.

"I understand your hesitation, and I make no excuses for Daniel leaving you both in the dark. But he's on edge. Someone close to him was attacked." Mag focuses on Rico. "It's not right, and I'll talk to him and have him cool down."

Rico scoffs at being told to understand Daniel's behavior because someone he cares about was hurt. He rolls his eyes, but when Todd places his own hand over Rico's fingers, which are looped through the wall, he keeps quiet.

"Now, generally I conduct my interviews one-on-one, but, to show you I can be reasonable, I won't separate the two of you," Mag continues. She proceeds to ask them both a series of questions about who they are and where they came from. Rico answers as honestly as he can, with the least amount of words, wanting her to leave.

"When will I get to see my brother?" Rico asks when Mag places her hand on the doorknob after the interview.

"If all goes well through the night, I see no reason why you can't see him at some point tomorrow," she says, and is gone. They hear the key enter the lock from the outside and a click from the bolt moving into place.

"This is bullshit," Rico says, sliding down to the ground.

"I know, but right now there isn't anything we can do but play along," Todd says. "She holds all of the cards."

"She wants us to give that asshole a pass because I knocked out his friend, but he can at least see her. I was trying to defend Jayden—I promised I would look out for him." Rico buries his face in his hands.

"I learned a long time ago that I couldn't expect things to play out as fair. Some people are just now learning how to survive; I've had to learn from the day I was born."

"But you were a cop," Rico says, lifting his head.

"That was part of surviving for me. If I became a police officer I could provide my family with an extra protection," Todd answers.

"You don't seem like a cop. I mean, you're big and intimidating and all, but you care," Rico says.

"We're not all bad. Some of us truly wanted the world to be a better place."

"Yeah, well, in my world all cops cared about was power and influence."

"You've had some run-ins with officers?"

"A time or two," Rico understates, feeling somewhat self-conscious.

"You seem like a good kid to me."

"Thanks." Rico half smiles before grimacing in pain.

"It would take a good kid to make it this far. All the way from Miami? With a child too?"

"We used my dad's boat for most of the journey. I didn't really have to do much."

Rico's stomach growls and he retrieves chicken noodle soup from his stash. Most of the flavor is overpowered by an abundance of sodium, but it sates his hunger. As the night progresses, both he and Todd attempt to sleep, but neither is very successful. Rico drifts off periodically, but wakes often from the anxiety of having another nightmare about drowning in blood. Finally, his body gives out for a couple of dreamless hours, but when he wakes up, he is still exhausted and his body is sore from the hard floor.

He rolls over and sees Todd crouching in a corner with his head between his knees. He isn't sure if Todd is asleep, so he rolls over quietly. The confinement is getting to him. He wants to know everything will be fine, but deep down all he feels is hopelessness.

42. WENDY

After

Tonya and Marie run up to Wendy and Asher before Wendy can explain to him what happened, but she knows Asher doesn't believe her. She jumps from her seat, elated to see the mother-daughter pair, and joins Asher in a group hug. Wendy and Asher push their neglected food toward the two, but a young man approaches with additional offerings.

"Craig," he says, holding out his hand. They introduce themselves, all still timid around the other refugees. "I won't bite," Craig jokes, "and neither will anyone else once they get to know you. Newcomers and all that jazz."

Wendy resumes eating, needing something to occupy herself. But the spoonful of rice can't wipe away the image of Ivy lying on the closet floor, blood soaking into her shirt and down to the carpet from her head, as her eyes fill with tears and she looks up at Wendy, begging for help and forgiveness. The sound of Ivy's screaming rings in the back of Wendy's mind, cutting off as abruptly now, when Tonya puts a hand on Wendy's arm, as it did that night.

"—missed the churros, we ran out of those pretty early on." Craig continues talking. "But we have popcorn kernels, so we make that about once a week. There's a candy store toward the front. Nobody really wants to venture too far from camp, but the runners have brought the kids some treats before—"

Wendy gives Tonya what she hopes is a believable smile. She knows the woman has her own worries and doesn't want Tonya to waste energy being concerned about her as well. Both women turn their attention back to Craig, smiling and nodding at all the right times and places.

***

As the evening winds down, people retire to their tents until only two middle-aged women and an older man are left tending the fires. Wendy looks up at the castle; Craig had told them that two of the turrets and one of the spires are manned by gunmen at all times, but she's unable to see anyone in the dark. The sky beyond is dotted with brilliant stars, able to shine brighter without the pollution of city lights. Marie curls up, her head in Tonya's lap, her eyes drooping.

"So, do we just stay out here all night?" Asher asks, voicing everyone's concern. Mag never reappeared, or explained the next order of business or where they would sleep. All four are used to sleeping on hard and uncomfortable surfaces, but before they can nestle in together, one of the women steps away from the fires.

"Do y'all have anywhere to sleep tonight?" she asks, her southern accent thick.

"No, ma'am," Asher says, "Mag didn't really leave us with a welcoming committee."

The woman introduces herself, Marsha, and perks up at the hint of Asher's North Carolina accent. Her nails are long, although two are broken, and she must have a bottle of nail polish on reserve, because they appear freshly painted. Her hair is wrapped in a headscarf with the knot on the top of her head. Wendy stifles a laugh at the idea of being able to care about appearance anymore. But like Craig, Marsha is willing to treat them as people and ushers them to one of the old stores neighboring the camp. She explains that all of the tents are occupied, but if the store is too stuffy they can try and create a makeshift tent in the daylight. Marsha pulls a keychain flashlight out of her back pocket, slapping it against the open palm of her hand twice to try to keep it on, and shines the dim light into the building.

Many of the clothing racks have already been stripped of their offerings, moved to the bathroom for easier access after washing up, and pushed off to the side to open the floor space. Marsha lights a path around the sleeping bodies, gingerly stepping around outstretched limbs. They reach a corner at the back of the store that's unoccupied. Marsha says it's to give them privacy, but Wendy wonders if it's to keep them separated still. They thank her for her hospitality, and she retreats to the outdoors.

"I'll keep watch," Wendy says out of habit. Nobody argues. The firelight spills through the windows, but not enough to reach the group as they feel around the ground for space. Asher finds a stuffed bear on a shelf and places it in Marie's hand. Wendy sits with her back against a sharp corner, relying on the stiffness to keep her awake.

In the darkness her mind returns to Ivy, her screams ending, and Wendy crawling away. She could hear him on the other side of the closet door, fighting to get to her, but she retreated into the attic until she couldn't hear anything.

Sweat beads appear on Wendy's skin and she starts to have difficulty breathing. The panic attack sets in, just like when she saw the stack of burnt children. Only then she had Asher to pull her from it, and now he's asleep. Asher, her only connection to Ivy. She focuses her attention on the sound of his breathing and her body relaxes.

She had pitied Asher initially, and his inability to let Ellis go. But then she felt comfort in their relation. She'd always thought that he sensed she was searching for Ivy, and he was along for the ride in search of his own answer. She'd lied about what she did, to protect him, but more to protect herself. *You did it so you could survive,* she thought. That had been her motivating thought since that night—to survive. Survival was why her brain allowed her to think Ivy could have lived, because Wendy needed that thread of hope to drive her and allow her to do what was necessary without hesitation.

Exhaustion sets in, and she gives up, waking Asher and switching watch. She's too worn out to dream, trading in the darkness of the store for the darkness of sleep. Laughter wakes her in the morning, and she watches two kids play a game of speed involving one trying to slap the other's hands.

Wendy sits up, the last of her group to stir, and watches Tonya redo Marie's hair after having the chance to wash up. Wendy pulls the elastic band from her wrist and offers it back to the little girl, but she signs a message to Wendy.

"She's saying it's yours now, a present," Tonya explains. Wendy repeats the sign for "thank you" that Todd taught Asher.

"What do we do now?" Wendy asks.

"I'm hopeful Todd will rejoin us today, and then I guess we just learn to live again."

***

Wendy finds Mag talking with a woman holding a young girl's hand. She doesn't want to interrupt, but she stands on her toes and gives a small wave to catch Mag's attention nonetheless.

"Wendy!" Mag calls out to her, waving her over. "This is Ashley, and her little girl, Charlotte."

Charlotte steps behind her mom, grabbing a handful of Ashley's skirt and pulling it over her face. Ashley takes a protective step backward, placing a hand on her daughter's head. "She's shy."

"Wendy was a student at a nearby university. I think she's going to be a great asset around here," Mag says. Ashley gives a curt nod, pretending to agree, while she appraises Wendy as if she's a feral animal. *Not that that's a poor assessment*, Wendy thinks. Mag says good-bye and leads Wendy away. Mag explains, "Some people just take a little longer."

"I get it. We've seen the bloodstains. Several people have said you haven't had an easy go at it."

"You have to understand, we were ambushed only a month ago and our numbers were greatly affected—"

"I do," Wendy says, cutting Mag off. "That's not why I wanted to find you, though. I just had a few questions—"

"I'm on my way to go release Todd and Rico—"

"Awesome. But that's not all—"

This time it's Mag who cuts in, visibly annoyed at being interrupted twice. "I would have thought you learned yesterday that I don't take too kindly to being interrupted. I've been running this park with respect. I respect the residents, and they respect me. But I will be stern, and I will put my foot down when I need to. If we're going to rebuild civilization,"—Wendy bites her tongue to keep quiet—"then we cannot devolve into those creatures roaming the world. Manners."

"I'm sorry. I guess I haven't had to think about something as trivial as manners when I was starving and being stalked by 'those creatures' that tried to kill and eat me at any chance they got."

Mag places a cigarette between her thin lips and allows Wendy to continue.

"I just wanted to know what I could do to be of use around here, idle hands and all that."

"Use the day to relax, just breathe. Enjoy the fact that nobody here is trying to kill and eat you. Now I've got things to do to keep my people safe." Mag stalked off, leaving Wendy behind in a cloud of nicotine.

43. ASHER

Before

Ellis was missing. The bedroom door was shut, which was odd. Asher extracted himself from the bed, plucking a sweater from the dresser as he walked to the door. Light filtered into the hall from a table lamp in the living room. Ellis was sitting on the couch, gazing off into space, a piece of paper in his hand and the book Brandon returned lying next to him.

"Hey," Asher said. Ellis was startled by the sound of his voice, and his hand instinctively balled around the paper.

"Hey," Ellis repeated. Asher leaned against the wall, tugging at the bottom of the sweater, waiting for a cue from Ellis. Ellis flattened the paper and folded it in half, placed it inside the cover of the book, and moved both items to the floor. He patted the spot on the couch next to him and Asher joined him, wrapping his arms around his knees.

"You okay? It's four in the morning," Asher asked.

"Yeah, I couldn't sleep well, so I got up and came out here so I wouldn't wake you up," Ellis explained. "But when I decided to clean up to pass the time, something fell out of the book Brandon returned. Here."

Ellis kicked the book over toward Asher. Asher didn't recognize the handwriting but the bottom was signed "Brandon." The handwriting was cramped and hard to read at first but after rereading a couple of words, Asher could make it out.

> Ellis,
>
> I don't fully know what to say or how to say it so please bear with me. I guess I should start by saying that even if it felt like it, I never stopped loving you. I know things haven't been great between us and I've pushed you away and have been angry and hurtful. I don't know why and I can't say sorry enough, but it wasn't because of you. You didn't do anything to deserve being treated that way and I don't know how to forgive myself for hurting you. I can only ask that you try and find a way to forgive me even if I haven't earned it. You're the better person, you always have been. I should also tell you that I intended on proposing to you this Christmas. I know it sounds cliché, Christmas, but I wanted to make your favorite holiday even more memorable. I understand why you can't be with me anymore, but I want you to know that you have my heart always, and I will never stop fighting to win you back.
>
> Love, Brandon

Asher finished reading the letter and folded it back in half.

"So what happens now?" Asher fought the tightening of his chest, the physical torment of a breaking heart, and the urge to flee. His question was met with a look of revulsion from Ellis.

"We go back to bed and then in a few hours we shower, eat breakfast, and go on with our day." Ellis ripped the letter in half, then in quarters. He stomped his way into the kitchen and to the garbage can. He tore the letter into smaller pieces before making a show of dumping the shreds into the can and slamming the lid down. He turned to Asher. "What did you think would happen now? I would suddenly change my mind and scurry back to Brandon? Am I supposed to just ignore how unhappy I was or how happy I am now because of a few words, and a ring?"

"I just didn't know—"

"What? If this changed anything?"

"Well, yeah. I guess."

"Maybe if you stopped doubting yourself, then you wouldn't have to wonder things like that," Ellis said.

"You're right. I'm sorry. I shouldn't have doubted you."

"Remember what you said last night? We're on the same team, you and me. We have to take it one day at a time, but together." Ellis rejoined Asher on the couch, placing his hand on Asher's knee and squeezing.

***

Asher was brushing his teeth, fresh from the shower, when Ellis poked his head into the bathroom. Ivy had invited the boys to brunch with her and her roommate. Asher leaned over the sink and spat out the frothy toothpaste, agreed to go, and Ellis disappeared.

"Crap, I didn't pack an extra shirt." Asher rooted through his bag, pulling out underwear and a pair of shorts.

"Just grab one of mine from the closet. The perks of dating a dude," Ellis said, tapping on his phone.

Ellis rolled the windows down, enjoying the warm breeze, and turned up the music as they rode. Asher quietly sang along, and soon Ellis joined him. Their angst from earlier faded the longer they spent on the road, and with the music blasting, both boys threw out their inhibitions and sang at the top of their lungs. Asher finally swiveled the volume down as Ellis turned the car into the restaurant parking lot.

Asher held the door open for Ellis and a family of three. Before the hostess could acknowledge them, they saw Ivy standing from her seat and waving. She occupied a booth, sitting across from another blonde, and as they neared, Ivy rushed to greet them, hugging first her brother and then Asher.

"Hi!" she said cheerfully, switching sides and sitting next to her roommate. "Asher, this is Wendy. Wendy, Asher."

Asher reached over the table to shake Wendy's hand.

"How've you been, Wendy?" Ellis asked.

"I've been good, super busy between school, work, and the sorority. This semester has been crazy; I haven't even been able to make it to your parents for dinner yet," Wendy said in exaggerated exasperation.

"And whenever all of her other commitments aren't consuming her, she's off gallivanting with Glenn. We're lucky to have snagged her away today," Ivy teased, but Asher caught a hard, almost resentful flash in Ivy's eyes.

"Glenn is Ivy's boyfriend; he's a doctor," Ellis explained, leaning into Asher.

"He's not a doctor," Wendy said.

"Yet," Ivy said.

"He's in med school," Wendy told Asher. "He'll be a doctor soon."

"And then our princess gets to ride off into the sunset with her prince," Ellis teased.

"Funny, you're funny." Wendy rolled her eyes at Ellis.

"I tease Wendy all the time about being my little princess and living a fairy-tale life. She's the vice president of their sorority, dating a doctor, soon-to-be doctor"—Ellis corrected himself with a wink to Wendy—"and landed an internship with one of the best advertising agencies downtown."

"And I worked hard for every bit of it," Wendy said. The waitress arrived and conversation died when everyone realized they hadn't yet checked the menu. Halfway through the meal, Wendy's phone interrupted them and she excused herself. Asher did the same and joined the end of the line for the restroom. He pulled his own phone out of his pocket to pass the time and he noticed a text from Mark.

M: Having ppl over 2nite. That cool?

A: Yeah, not sure if I'll be there or not.

M: Thx. C U maybe.

The line slowly moved along, and when Asher was next up, the door opened and the emerging man gave a sheepish apology as he passed. Asher tried to be as quick as possible to escape the smell.

Wendy had yet to return to the table, and Ellis and Ivy were leaning toward each other in whispered conversation. Ellis looked over
his sister's shoulder, and he noticed Asher midsentence. He stopped
talking and straightened up. Ivy tossed her blonde locks behind her
and twisted in her seat, smiling warmly at Asher before occupying her
mouth with a forkful of her omelet.

"Feel better?" Ellis asked.

"Yeah, I need to slow it down on the coffee." Asher pushed his mug
into the center of the table. A looked passed between Ivy and Ellis, but
recalling Ellis's comment about Asher's self-doubt, Asher ignored it.

"Sorry, that was my mom, asking about Thanksgiving," Wendy
said, returning to the table.

"Are you going home for Thanksgiving?" Ellis asked.

"Actually, no. Not this year. Glenn's parents invited me up to their
place so that we can formally meet." Wendy blushed. Asher noticed the
fleeting hard look from earlier pass over Ivy's eyes again.

"That's exciting! I didn't realize you hadn't met before," Ellis said.

"Yeah, between Glenn's schedule and mine it's hard enough for us
to get any time together, so it never worked out." Wendy stabbed her
fork into a potato.

"I'm sure it's going to be fine; they're going to love our little princess as much as we all do." Ellis jumped, bumping into the table. "Did
you just kick me?"

"No," Ivy said, and stuffed her mouth with a piece of toast.

"What about you, Asher?" Wendy asked between chewing and
swallowing, covering her mouth.

"My family lives in North Carolina. I go home for Christmas, so we
don't see much of a point in me flying up when I'll be home in a couple
of weeks anyway," he answered. "I generally just go home with one of
my roommates."

"But this year you'll go over to my parents," Ellis said.

"Yeah, of course," Asher agreed.

"You sound unsure," Ivy said. Ellis glared at her.

"No, not at all. We just hadn't talked about it and I didn't want to
invite myself," Asher said. Between the shifty conversation he'd cut in
on from the bathroom and Ivy's reactions to Wendy, Asher noticed

glimmers of Laurel's personality coming through in her daughter. He had to fight the urge to pass judgment.

"To be honest it hadn't even crossed my mind—I don't think I realized it was next week," Ellis said. And with the recent disturbances, Asher found it hard to blame him. Ellis snagged the check before anyone else had a chance to look at it and waved off their attempts to contribute. He admitted that he was using the family credit card to pay, having cleared it with his dad. They said their good-byes in the parking lot and exchanged hugs. Ellis and Asher wished Wendy good luck with meeting Glenn's parents and told Ivy they would see her soon.

Asher buckled his seat belt and rested his hand on Ellis's knee. Even after Ellis turned out of the parking lot and onto the road, he didn't place his hand on top of Asher's as he usually did. Asher slowly retracted his hand at the second traffic light, playing it off by turning the music up. Neither of them spoke, or sang, until they were through the front door and Ellis held out his phone to Asher.

"What's this for?"

"Check the texts."

"No." Asher pushed the phone toward Ellis. "I don't need to."

"Please," Ellis begged, placing the phone against Asher's chest.

"What's this about?"

"Just look," Ellis answered. There was no other option than to grant Ellis's request, so Asher opened the messages folder. There was a thread from an unsaved number.

Hey.

Sorry about last night.

Hello?

Okay, I get it, you're mad. I'm sorry, again.

I don't know if you found it or not, but I wrote you a letter, it's in the book. It's the real reason I dropped the book off. Just let me know when you read it, please.

Asher read the texts and the timestamps. Each text arrived sporadically throughout the morning, with the most recent received while they were at brunch, around the time he went to the restroom. They all went unanswered, and when Asher returned the phone, Ellis deleted the entire text thread.

"I deleted his number. You probably realized that from the texts. I just needed you to know I'm serious about this. I don't want to talk to him, I don't want to think about him, I don't want anything to do with him."

44. RICO

After

"Today's the day, kid," Rico says, squeezing Jayden's hand. The boy had been under Alexandria's watchful eye for a week, but she cleared him to leave the infirmary. Rico stayed by his side, sleeping on the floor each night to maintain closeness with his brother. Todd and Aubrey switched off bringing them their meals and sat with Rico to keep him company when the kid was asleep. Aubrey sneaked Jayden a small bag of gummy candies one day, telling the boys, with a wink, it was their little secret. Rico knew the man was trying to make amends for putting Jayden in the infirmary in the first place. Jayden is incapable of holding a grudge, and Rico followed the kid's lead, happy that Jayden is okay.

There's a knock while Rico slips the water shoes onto Jayden's feet. Todd leans against the wall, a rifle slung across his back.

"Your escort is here. You boys ready to see your new home?"

"They gave you your guns back?" Rico asks. Todd and Wendy had been trying to get their weapons back for days, but Daniel was using every ounce of persuasion he had with Mag to hold them off.

"Just this morning. Aubrey is on fence patrol so he couldn't walk you two to the castle. I gave Mag my old badge, and after days of inspection, she believed that it wasn't counterfeit. She needs the extra muscle on patrols anyway."

Jayden hops off the bed and grabs Rico's hand. Todd guides them through the backlot and toward the park, but tells the boys to crouch down and wait next to an overturned golf cart. Two infected emerge from the tree line and press against the barbed-wire fence lining the perimeter. Rico watches as Todd pulls a walkie-talkie from his belt and calls to the camp.

"We're in a blind spot," Todd explains. "There are a few sections the tower sentries can't see."

Todd leaves the boys hiding, and with a knife in hand he approaches the fence. The cries of the infected get louder as Todd gets closer. He shoves the knife through the fence and the bodies crumple, joining the other rotting bodies littering the ground.

"Do they ever get in?" Jayden asks, squeezing Rico's hand.

"No, we're going to be safe in here," Rico says, but he's feeling uneasy.

Todd returns and they continue through the fence and into the land of strange flowers. Jayden's eyes grow large as he takes in all of the colors. Rico ruffles the kid's hair. "Come on, you'll have time to explore later."

***

"And push!"

Rico shoves his shoulder against the back of the van, digging his feet against the ground and heaving forward. The van rolls several yards forward. Rico stands to catch his breath and repositions himself.

"There's no way to jump the battery?" Rob asks, wiping his brow in the crook of his elbow, sweat glistening on his balding head.

"The heat killed it; nothing we can do about it now," George says. "On my count, we're going again . . . one . . . two . . . three!"

They repeat the process until the van reaches the perimeter fence. One of the patrol members had noticed a support pole leaning inward during his round behind the castle and gathered enough people to push the van against it for reinforcement. Rico readily volunteered, itching for something to do other than stir rice over a fire.

Rico reenters the park, and the smell of roasting fish makes his stomach grumble. A thin Asian girl, the only other refugee close to his own age, spears several fish with sticks and places them into the flames to cook.

"Where did you get these?" Rico asks, stepping up to help. Since his arrival in the park, he has yet to eat anything that isn't out of a can.

"The lake," she answers, her voice just louder than a whisper. A small net is bundled up next to her, and it appears to be made from torn strips of fabric.

"Yuki, right?" He had heard her name before, but has never spoken to her. She stays mostly to herself. She nods. The space around the fire slowly fills as the smell carries into the tents and stores. The fish finish cooking, and Rico and Yuki skin them and divide servings among the hungry. Rico sets aside a larger chunk, waiting until everyone else has their piece, and hands it off to Yuki, following her to the lake to eat. "That was really smart to build that net."

"Everyone does something. I catch fish."

Rico finishes his last bite and sticks his fingers in his mouth, licking the juices. "How come you never talk to anyone?"

"My English not very good."

"What are you talking about? Your English is great. I can understand you."

"I listen, I learn."

"Well, you're doing a great job."

Rico wants to ask her about her parents, and how she ended up in Florida, but he doesn't. Few people mention their lives before the park. He wonders if it's out of shame, sorrow, or both, like himself.

"Rico!"

He turns and Jayden runs to him, holding a sheet of paper in the air. The kid collides into him, and Rico pulls him down into his lap.

"Rico! Look, I got an A on my math test!" Jayden spends the mornings in school. One of the refugees, Mr. Nichols, is a former elementary teacher and embraces the opportunity to continue educating the children. Rico takes the paper from the boy—it's a page torn from a notebook on which Mr. Nichols wrote out a series of equations. Jayden got all but one correct.

"You know how we're going to celebrate, don't you?"

Jayden's face lights up, and Rico turns to invite Yuki with them, but she is gone. Rico looks around but doesn't see her anywhere.

Every few hundred yards the entire appearance of the park changes into different worlds. On one side of the castle stands the multicolored and whimsical flower land, but on the other side, the land they walk into looks like a small Germanic village with timber-framed buildings and long sloping roofs. They pass the entrance to a multitiered carousel full of carved horses and carriages. The faces of the rearing horses look warped and twisted in the absence of children on their backs. Behind the carousel is a row of carnival games.

Jayden wasn't the only child to perform well on the test. Asher stands at a game with Marie, using the little amount of sign language Tonya and Todd have taught them to instruct her to throw a baseball at wooden blocks shaped like milk bottles.

"Frankie!" Jayden yells, running off to a basketball game with another boy.

"Babysitting?" Rico asks Asher. He doesn't know much about Asher, other than how he came into the park, but they share a living space, and Asher and Wendy are both good to his brother.

"Yeah, Todd's on patrol, and Tonya and Wendy are helping clean up the store across from ours. Want some?" Asher holds out a small bowl of popcorn. Rico reaches in, watching Marie throw the ball and knock down four of the six bottles. She throws a second ball and the remaining two spill off the table. Asher hops over the counter and resets them.

"So this is what our lives are now, huh? We're turning into carnies?" Rico jokes.

"It's a far cry better than what we faced out there. And you came all the way from Miami? Whew."

"Do you ever wonder why this happened?"

"Every day. Who doesn't?"

"But why did we get to survive? Why do we deserve to live?" Rico reaches up and scratches his neck. He's lost count of how many days it's been since his last fix, but in moments of downtime he craves a pill, a blunt, anything. His mind trails to Jayden's grandparents' house, and he wonders if the bike is still on the other side of the fence. *Would anyone know if I slipped away? It's just down the street,* he thinks.

"You okay? You look a little twitchy," Asher says.

"Yeah, sorry. I was just thinking. It all seems so mundane now. We're in here. They're out there. The kids had a math test today, as if that even matters. We survived so they can learn multiplication?"

"Well, when you put it that way . . ."

A scream rips through the air and the boys jump, their bodies automatically switching into defensive mode. But it's only Jayden at the other end of the row of games, jumping up and down with his fists in the air, celebrating making a basket. Rico shakes his head and laughs, the tension releasing. He nods to Asher and walks away, picking up speed, and he lifts Jayden into the air and spins him in a wide circle.

He notices a shape in the shadows of the carousel, and sets the kid down. The shape shifts, stepping out into the light. It's Daniel, his rifle held across his chest, and he takes one final look at Rico before turning and walking off toward the castle. Jayden tugs on Rico's arm, begging him to take a shot. Rico obliges but misses, his thoughts far away and a shiver running through him.

45. ASHER

Before

"I don't know who is more stuffed, the turkey or me." Ben Williams pushed his chair back from the table and grabbed his stomach with both hands.

"That was a delicious meal, thank you, Mr. and Mrs. Williams," Asher said, wiping his mouth with a napkin and crumpling it onto his plate.

"You're very welcome." Ben raised his wineglass to his mouth. "We still have dessert."

Laurel collected her and Ben's plates, then returned to the table with the half-full bottle of wine, topping off her glass.

"Can you pass me the bottle, please, Dad?" Ivy asked, holding out her hand. She refilled her own glass, and, noticing Ellis's and Asher's glasses, split the remainder between both of them. Asher felt guilty for his judgment of her at brunch the previous week and blushed while thanking her.

"You kids looking forward to the semester ending?" Ben asked.

"I don't know about them, but I am. Only one semester to go after this," Ivy said.

"Well, one semester until grad school," Laurel remarked.

"I just meant of undergrad."

"What about you two? Looking forward to grading all of those finals?" Ellis asked with a smirk.

"It's not too bad; just running Scantrons through a machine for me. And that's what I have a teaching assistant for," Ben said.

"Have you started studying yet?" Laurel asked, looking at Ellis.

"Mom, c'mon. You know better than to ask that; I'll start this weekend. When do I ever start studying before Thanksgiving?" Ellis rolled his eyes.

"I'm ready to take a nap in front of the TV, what do you guys say?" Ben plopped on the couch, propping his feet on the coffee table. Laurel followed his lead, lounging against him, and turned the television on.

"I'll be there in a minute." Ivy picked up her glass of wine and climbed the stairs to the second floor. Ellis reached his fork over to Asher's plate, spearing a chunk of sweet potato.

"What are you thinking about?" Ellis asked Asher.

"How thankful I am to be here with your family. And how relaxing today's been."

"Relaxing up until school was brought up," Ellis scoffed, "and school always gets brought up with those two."

"Nah, it wasn't too bad. Nothing outside of general concern."

"I need some air; come with me." Ellis stood from the table, beckoning Asher through the house to the back door. The backyard was smaller than what Asher would have expected for a house this size, but as nicely manicured as the front yard. The porch was lined with bushes and brightly colored flowers. The breeze sent a chill up Asher's spine. Ellis led him to a hammock suspended between two trees. Between Thanksgiving dinner, the rocking hammock, and the glasses of wine, they were out within minutes.

***

"Boys. Boys!" Ben called into the backyard. Asher sat up in the hammock, almost flipping it over. He looked groggily toward the porch where Ellis's dad leaned out of the doorway. "We're about to cut the pies, figured you'd want to be awake for some dessert."

"Yeah, we'll be right there," Asher said. The sky was a mix of colors, and the temperature had dropped several degrees. Asher reached back and shook Ellis's shoulder to wake him up. Ellis groaned and rolled over, the shift in his weight capsizing the hammock and spilling them onto the ground.

"What's going on?" Ellis asked, rubbing his head.

"Pie," Asher said as they carefully extricated their limbs and fixed the hammock.

Two pies were on the counter with a stack of small plates between them. Laurel and Ben debated how large to slice the pieces, but Ivy was off to the side, against the furthermost counter, looking pale and chewing one of her thumbnails. She obsessively checked her cell phone instead of paying attention to anyone. With a huff, Ben picked up the knife and sliced each pie into eight equal-sized slices.

"Pumpkin or pecan?" he asked Asher, pronouncing it "pee-can."

"Pumpkin, please," Asher replied, accepting a plate and loading the slice with whipped cream.

"Which would you prefer, Ivy?" Ben asked. She continued watching her phone like it was a bomb waiting to detonate.

"Ivy," Laurel said, her voice snapping. Ivy looked up, as if she just realized others were in the room.

"I'm fine," she responded. "I don't feel well, I'm going to skip out on pie."

"Skip out on pie? Are you like a Thanksgiving scrooge?" Ellis asked. Ivy waited until their parents' backs were turned and gave Ellis the middle finger, receiving a blown kiss in return. She excused herself, and a door slammed shut upstairs. "Geesh, someone is dramatic."

Ivy didn't reappear, and the sun was replaced by the moon. Everyone was resisting sleep on the couches, so Ellis took the initiative to say good-bye and call it a night. Christmas music was already playing on the radio, but Asher kept it turned low while Ellis dozed off in the passenger seat. Asher pulled into his complex and parked in the nearly deserted parking lot. The apartment was dark and empty—Mark and Derrick had both gone home for the holiday.

"Good night, sleep tight," Ellis said, his voice heavy with sleep.

"Don't let the bedbugs bite," Asher responded, closing his eyelids.

"And if they do, bite them too," Ellis said.

46. ASHER

After

The sun sinks behind the castle and the crowd around the fires builds. Aubrey and Ellie had found a supply of beer hidden in a kitchen, previously overlooked until they were scrounging for anything left of use. The cans are warm to the touch, but spirits rise as the adults indulge in a lost pleasure. Asher and Wendy snag a can each, and she grabs another for Rico.

"What? Who's going to check his ID?" Wendy says when Asher looks at her questioningly. They find Rico playing cards with Jayden, Marie, and Tonya. Wendy holds out the can, and Rico reaches halfway for it before pausing and retracting his hand. "Come on, it's one drink. Don't tell me you've never drank before?"

"Don't pressure him," Tonya says, placing a card down on the ground and lifting her own can to her lips.

"I'll just save it for Todd," Wendy says.

As if on cue, Todd cuts through the crowd, sidestepping Marsha as she dances with one of the men, and plops onto the ground next to his wife. Wendy tosses him the extra beer.

"I wondered what all of the excitement was about; I could hear it from the back." Todd pops the tab. "To being a family."

Asher and Wendy lean in and tap their drinks to Todd's. Asher smiles, ignoring the abysmal taste of the cheap warm beer, and feels Wendy squeeze his hand.

The sun is nearly gone and the party continues. Ashley climbs up onto a chair and sings for everyone, and Todd pulls Tonya away from the card game to join him in a dance. Wendy gets to her feet, trying to pull Asher up with her, but he laughs and shakes his head. She moves on to Rico.

"This isn't my kind of music."

"Oh, come on! Just let loose!"

Rico gives up and follows her into the mix. Asher empties the rest of his beer, feeling lightheaded after only one drink, and already needing to pee.

"Stay here," he says to Jayden, also signing the message to Marie.

He walks toward the border of the flowered land, rounding the corner so he's out of sight. As he's finishing, he hears footsteps, but glancing around he doesn't see anyone. The footsteps stop, but he sees a shadow move against a side wall between him and the camp. He steps out from behind the large planter and the shadow shifts. If he tries to break for the camp, he'll be cut off, but if he walks further away, he can slip through to the backlot and loop back around behind the castle.

He starts walking again, keeping his head facing forward while he listens to the footsteps that fall in line behind him. Asher speeds up, and the footsteps behind him speed up to match. The fence to the backlot is ten yards away. Asher breaks into a run and the footsteps become heavy and fast. He rounds the fence and slams into another body, screaming out.

"Shh! Shh!"

Arms wrap around his torso, and Asher lifts his legs off the ground and shoves his feet against the fence. The body holding him stumbles and falls, releasing its hold on Asher. Asher rolls away, getting to his hands and knees, ready to take off running.

"Geez, Asher, what is wrong with you?" Craig says, sitting up and rubbing the back of his head.

"Why were you following me?"

"Following you? I was helping with patrol and was heading back to camp. You slammed into me when I tried to round the fence into the park." Craig helps Asher regain his footing.

"Someone was following me, I saw them, well, I heard them, but I saw their shadow, and I started running and they started running behind me—"

"Have you been drinking? Where did you get alcohol?"

The smell of beer carries from Asher's breath as he talks. "That's not important! You're not listening, someone was trying to get me."

"In the park?" Craig grabs his gun off the ground, having dropped it when Asher slammed into him, and peers around the fence. Craig disappears and Asher waits, his heart beating out of his chest.

"There's nobody in here, come look."

Asher surveys the empty backlot before following Craig back into the park. The bright colors are dimmed as the last vestige of sunlight slips away; the street is completely empty. Asher wonders if he's losing his mind. It's been two weeks since they arrived at the park—is the lack of danger bringing him to the point where he's imagining threats?

"I'll walk you back."

"No, I can't be around everyone right now. It's too loud; they're too happy. I need to let them be."

"I know the perfect place, c'mon."

Craig leads Asher to the entry of the multicolored roller coaster and hops the turnstiles.

"What are we doing here? There's no power."

"I know. But there's a service staircase along the first hill, you should see the sunset from there."

They walk up the exit and onto the load platform. A ride vehicle sits waiting for passengers, and a giant cobweb stretches across the first seat. At the end of the platform, Craig starts climbing a steep staircase and Asher follows. They're both out of breath once they reach the peak. They can see the glow of camp but can't hear the sounds of the partyers. Only a sliver of sun remains on the horizon, and the sky is mostly dark blue except for a few pink hues. They can see beyond the barbed wire fence, but it's too dark to make out anything beyond the treetops.

Asher notices movement along the fence and freezes, his mind jumping to whoever was chasing him. A body presses against the fence from the outside, but from the way it lurches he can tell it's an infected. He can hear a whisper of its grumble.

"Give me your gun."

"Are you crazy? No."

"Look, right there, at the fence."

Craig strains his eyes but doesn't see what Asher is talking about. He sighs and hands the gun over. There's a scope attached and Asher is able to get the infected in the crosshairs before pulling the trigger. He nails it through the chest and it falls over backward. The gun was quieter than he was expecting, but the radio on Craig's hip still squawks.

"It's Craig, one of the nasties on the fence. Sorry 'bout that."

Asher returns the gun and Craig searches through the scope.

"How did you do that?"

"Years of hunting back home with my dad and brother."

"Does Mag know?"

"She never asked."

"I'm going to tell her in the morning. We could use you up in the towers. We're stretched thin enough after . . ."

Craig stops talking, looking back out over the trees. Asher knows there was an incident about a month before he arrived, however, nobody will talk about it. But he's seen the bloodstains, and he's all too familiar with the look of horror that's permanently fixed in the eyes of the survivors.

"Why does everyone report to Mag?"

"She's a good leader. She carried us through."

"Through the ambush?"

"Yeah. When they attacked, she was able to hide those unable to fight, kept them safe in the tunnels."

"The tunnels?"

"No one's mentioned the tunnels running under the park to you?" Craig asks. "They create direct routes between the lands, the stores, and the attractions. Some of the tunnels lead to the backlot. When the park was open, they allowed workers to avoid swarms of tourists, and during the ambush, they provided safety. A group rammed a section of the fence down and tried to seize the park for themselves, killing anyone in their way. Mag hid people and used the tunnels to surprise and take out the group. They retreated to the City Hall building when they realized they were losing, but Mag found a supply of fireworks and shot them off into the sky. What was left of the ambush took off, thinking they were being blown up. But a lot of people died by the time it was over."

"Wow," Asher says.

"Mag is a great woman, smarter than people want to give her credit for. Although the fireworks bit gave us days of infected showing up."

"But how did she know about the tunnels? Did you know about them?"

"I did. But that's because I worked here before the outbreak. It's why I came here, didn't have anywhere else to go and thought some of my coworkers might come back too."

"And did they?"

"Can you keep a secret?"

"I don't like secrets anymore."

"Secrets build trust."

"Secrets destroy people."

"They do that too. I'll tell you, but this stays between us. How else would someone know about the tunnels? And know them so well?"

"Mag worked here?"

"Not many people trust and respect minimum-wage workers; they wouldn't let Mag lead if they knew she was just a ride attendant before this. Why do you think Daniel hates her so much? He hates how she runs things, but he hates her more because he doesn't think she deserves to be in charge."

"But he listens to her."

"He knows he'll never have the respect of anyone here if he doesn't. But he's smarter than people realize as well. He tries to hide it, hoping people won't pay him half a mind, but there are flickers of it if you're watching."

Asher dangles his legs over the side of the incline, swinging his feet back and forth. The sun is long gone, the only light coming from the camp. Even beyond the park limits, everything is dark.

"Be smart about who you tell things around here, Asher. Not everyone will have your best interest at heart."

47. RICO

After

Rico, Asher, and Wendy stand at the top of the metal stairs, looking down into the black tunnel. Asher's flashlight does little to illuminate anything other than additional stairs. It took them a few days after Asher told them about the tunnels, but they found a door behind a set of metal lockers in a former break room. Someone had tried to hide the entrance, or keep someone or something from getting out.

"Should we go down?" Asher asks.

"What are you afraid of, the bogeyman?" Rico teases. Wendy elbows him in the ribs and he drops his smile.

"No, some of them might be down there," Wendy says.

"I doubt it. Craig said people hid down here, but he didn't mention any infected," Asher says.

"Better safe than sorry, at least we know it's here now. I don't like everyone else knowing stuff we don't."

Rico agrees with Wendy. They close the door and replace the locker. Asher checks his watch, he'd found one lying around in the store, and says he needs to get to the tower for his shift. Rico and Wendy split at the camp and Rico wanders down to the lake. He sees a figure at the end of the paddleboat dock. Yuki is casting out her net.

A scuzzy film floats atop the water, but the fish break the surface for the grains of rice Yuki tosses. She ignores Rico as he steps up beside her. Once enough fish swim into her trap, she pulls the ropes and closes the net. Rico helps her heave them onto the dock.

"Fish for dinner again, huh?" Rico asks. It's the fourth night in a row.

"Yes."

Yuki drags her net away, and Rico realizes how ungrateful he sounds. He chases after her to apologize. She gives him a small smile. The novelty of eating fish has worn off on everyone, and unlike the first day, only a few people immediately come forth as the food cooks.

"How long have you been here?" Rico asks.

"Since the beginning. I was on holiday when airports closed," Yuki answers.

"Is it rude if I ask where you're from?"

"Tokyo. It's funny. We have the monster movies, but the monsters are in America."

"Ain't that the truth." Rico laughs.

***

Rico waits for everyone to fall asleep before he slips the flashlight from Asher's bag. He shoved the tire iron down the side of his pants earlier when nobody was around. He knows the store well enough to navigate his path in the dark, staying along the walls until he reaches the front and the firelight spills through the doorway. Marsha tends the fire with her usual overnight crowd. Rico ducks behind a tent, taking care to go unseen, and slips through the camp until he's on the far side of the castle.

He turns the flashlight on once he's safely inside the break room and the door is closed. The room is empty as he expected. The lockers are heavy, and when he tries to push them alone, they screech across the floor. He freezes and listens, but it's hard to tell if anyone has heard the noise. He tries to grab the locker and lift from the bottom. It's slow work; the lockers falter and almost tip at one point, but inch by inch, he moves them until he can open the tunnel door enough to squeeze through onto the top step.

The flashlight cuts through the dark, still only revealing the stairs. The stairs groan and the noise echoes against the walls as Rico slowly descends to the floor, the tire iron in his other hand. He hears a click and stops, moving the flashlight from wall to wall, but only sees long stretches of cement. Pipes and fluorescent bulbs line the ceiling, useless without electricity, and names of stores, restaurants, and rides are painted on the walls with arrows. Halfway down the tunnel he feels movement on the top of his shoe and jumps, sweeping the light downward as a rat takes off.

The tunnel ends in a fork, offering two separate paths. Rico hasn't seen a park map, so the names on the wall are meaningless to him. He tries to calculate his position from what he knows of the layout above ground and guesses that he's under the carousel. He takes the path to the right, hoping it will lead him to a building near the guard shack so he can check for the bicycle.

There's a crinkling under his foot and Rico crouches down to pick up a wrapper. It's old and the rats have nibbled the foil away where residue from a protein bar remained. Rico turns it over in his hand, reading the Archon label, and tosses it aside. The floor slopes downward as he continues, and he starts to distinguish a constant dripping through the quiet. He rounds a corner, focusing on the pipes, as the dripping gets louder. The light hits a section of the pipe, and he sees water forming and then a drop falls. But it doesn't hit the floor. A second later there's a splash and Rico hears heavy breathing. He lowers the light, landing on the pale and gaunt face of an infected. Her hand, where the water landed, is stretched outward and her feet slide forward through the puddle on the ground. Her breathing shifts into a growl and she takes a slow step forward.

Rico tightens his grip on the tire iron. He hasn't been this close to one of them in weeks, and his heart starts pounding. She's starved, all of her fat and muscle stores depleted by her own body, but the look of rage on her face is more aggressive than any Rico has seen. She's desperate for anything. She moves her leg forward and it slips in the puddle, bringing her to her knees. She looks up and cries out as Rico brings the tire iron down on her head the first time. He hits her until she is still.

The sports watch on his wrist beeps and he checks the time.

"Shit."

He only has forty-five minutes until Asher will wake up for his tower shift, and if he isn't back and the flashlight isn't in Asher's bag, they'll know he's up to something. His foray into the tunnels has already taken longer than he'd anticipated. He turns on his heel and races back toward the break room. When he rounds the corner at the fork, he's blasted in the face by a bright light and throws up his hands to shield his eyes.

Todd lowers the light, allowing Rico to see his face.

"We need to get you out of here, now."

Rico's shoulders drop, but he nods and follows Todd up the stairs and into the break room. They push the lockers back against the wall together, but Todd asks Rico to sit before they leave.

"What were you doing down there?"

"You know about the tunnels?"

"Everyone that works patrols knows about the tunnels. We have to check to make sure the entrances are still sealed. And if someone had come by here, you would have been locked down there."

Rico hadn't thought of the patrol checking the room; he'd never noticed anyone coming or going.

"Are you using?" Todd asks.

"What? No, I don't—"

"Save it. I'm a cop; I know an addict when I see one."

Todd's face is soft and kind as he speaks, and the effect isn't lost on Rico. He doesn't argue being an addict, but he tells Todd he's not using. Todd asks if he was trying to find the Health Services building.

"No. I was trying to slip out to the guard shack where I came in. I figured my best bet for going unnoticed was to find a way through the tunnel. Nobody would see me from the castle, and I didn't think any of those things would be down there."

Todd asks why he needed to reach the guard shack, and if he was planning on slipping away in the night, leaving Jayden behind.

"I wanted to see if the bike was still there. If I brought it back to camp, it could just give us something to do around here."

"Why didn't you just say that? We could check in the morning."

Rico shifts uneasily, but seeing the genuine concern in Todd, he says, "Part of me thought about maybe riding back to Jayden's grandparents' house. There were a bunch of pills there. But part of me just really wanted to do something wrong, against the order of this place. I'm so bored, there's nothing new here. And when I get bored I do stupid things."

"Then we find a way to keep you occupied so you can stay safe."

Rico's watch beeps again, the five-minute warning.

"Can we get back before Asher wakes up and realizes I stole his flashlight?"

Todd pulls the teen into a tight bear hug, messing his hair the way he's seen Rico mess Jayden's hair.

The weather changed while they were down in the tunnels. Flashes of lightning streak across the sky and a downpour quickly soaks them. The campfires have been doused and the tents deserted. Todd and Rico splash through the empty camp and squeeze through those crowding around in the store, everyone looking like drowned rats. Lights dance across the ceiling, those with flashlights have turned them on to illuminate the room.

"Where have you two been?" Tonya says, detangling herself from her daughter and rushing to her husband.

"Is that my flashlight? I was looking for it," Asher says.

"Yeah, sorry, I borrowed it to go to the restroom."

Tonya opens her mouth, but Todd gives her a subtle shake of his head. The storm started thirty minutes earlier, too early for Rico's excuse to be valid. But nobody pushes it.

Mag approaches, telling Asher not to worry about his guard shift until the storm subsides. The watchmen have abandoned their posts, unable to see anything through the rain, and are waiting it out in the castle. As Mag walks away, Aubrey replaces her.

"I just wanted to see how you guys were handling the storm, with the little ones and all. I know thunder can scare some; it's so loud," Aubrey says.

"Marie can't really hear it, can she?" Todd says, but he maintains a hint of a smile.

"Oh right. Yeah, I guess I didn't think of that." Aubrey looks embarrassed by his folly.

"I don't mind the storm," Jayden says, "at least we're not still on the boat."

"Either way, I figured these might help you through." Aubrey hands each child a lollipop. "Anyone else need anything?"

"I think we're good," Wendy says.

Aubrey nods and excuses himself. Asher and Rico exchange a look and turn away so Wendy doesn't see their grins. Rico couldn't tell if Wendy was intentionally denying Aubrey's advance or not. Aubrey had tried to dance with Wendy at the party, an opportunity Rico was ready to seize as his escape, but she had turned him down. He couldn't fault the man for trying.

48. ASHER

Before

Dale and Asher closed up the coffee shop and waved to the girl working the front desk as they pushed through the front doors of the library.

"Have a good Christmas," Dale called out, departing for the parking lot.

"You too," Asher replied. He pulled his headphones from his bag and selected a cheerful holiday playlist to celebrate the end of the semester. The ride across campus was quick that evening, as most students had already abandoned the school for the winter break; Asher didn't encounter a soul.

At his complex, unlike campus, almost half of the parking spaces were occupied and music resonated from each building as students celebrated another completed semester. He was startled by a noise from behind while chaining his bike. Ellis stood waiting under a streetlamp.

"Hey," Asher greeted him. "I didn't expect to see you here. I thought I was meeting you at yours?"

"Yeah, that was the plan, but I figured it'd be easier if I just came over here," Ellis said, fiddling with the zipper on his jacket.

"What would be easier? Your parents live closer to your place—aren't we still having dinner with them?" Asher asked.

"Can we go for a walk?" Ellis asked. The elation Asher had felt earlier from completing a semester's work evaporated and was replaced with a burgeoning sense of dread.

"Yeah, sure," he said. Asher waited for Ellis to say something, not knowing how to start the conversation himself. They ended up at the deserted pool behind Asher's building. Ellis unlatched the gate, allowing them to step through.

"I saw Brandon today," Ellis said, after sitting in one of the chairs. He turned his head and saw Asher watching him. "I was leaving the psychology building after my last exam, and he was walking across the courtyard with some girl. I don't think he noticed me; he was smiling and laughing with her."

"You were bound to cross paths with him at some point; we go to the same school. I'm surprised it took this long. I'm surprised *I* haven't run into him yet." Asher brushed the incident away.

"I know, but I didn't think I'd feel the way I did when I saw him," Ellis continued.

"What do you mean?"

Ellis finally looked directly at Asher.

"I've been telling myself for months that I feel nothing for him, that he doesn't exist, and that I've moved on. But when I saw him today I felt something snap inside me. It was like a crack in the wall I've put up around me, and suddenly all of these emotions poured out."

"Like anger or frustration?" Asher asked. He could help Ellis through those emotions.

"A bit, but not like you're wanting or I thought before. The strongest emotion was heartbreak. For the first time I honestly felt heartbroken over what happened with Brandon." Tears formed in Ellis's eyes. "And it made me acknowledge that I still love him."

The physical pain created by Ellis's words was crushing, forming thoughts in Asher's mind that he didn't know how to decipher. He fought to steady his breath and asked, "So what does this mean for us?"

"I don't want to hurt you," Ellis said, his voice shaking. "I care about you, and I dragged you into this. It's not fair to you, and I wish I could erase all of the pain and hurt I've created."

"But . . ." Asher interjected and waited for Ellis to continue.

"But I can't drag you along while I figure things out. Because right now I don't understand how I'm feeling, and I can't expect you to understand or sit and watch while I sort everything out. This is something I have to do for myself, by myself."

"And Brandon?"

"He doesn't know anything about what is going on right now—he didn't even see me. But I'm not going to lie to you either; I am going to have to talk to him about this. I need to, and I want to."

"Just like that."

"Just like what?"

"It all ends, just like that."

"It hasn't all ended. Our relationship, romantically, yes. But I don't want to lose you. I still need and want you as a friend. I know I'm not allowed to ask that, but it's the truth."

Asher wiped a tear away and focused on a crack in the cement.

"If you two get back together are you going to be happy?" Asher asked.

"I don't know. I honestly don't know anything at this point. But I have to explore it and see what happens—I owe myself that."

"I want you to be happy, that's what I care about. And I thought you were, but I'm not going to hold you down because that wouldn't make either one of us happy." Asher looked up. All this time, he'd been the selfish one, caring only about his own happiness and too wrapped up to see the truth in front of him. The pool lights reflected off Ellis's wet cheeks.

"I don't deserve you, you know that, don't you?" Ellis asked, reaching forward and grabbing Asher's hand.

"Please don't," Asher said, pulling his hand away and tucking it under himself. "I know you're trying to make me feel better and I appreciate that. But hearing that doesn't do anything. It just muddles everything for me. If you're letting me go, just let me go."

"Okay," Ellis said. Asher got up and suddenly their arms were wrapped around each other. Asher buried his head into Ellis's neck one final time. Ellis squeezed him, and they released each other. Asher wiped his eyes and turned away. He followed the sidewalk back to his apartment, but when he reached his front door, he faced the parking lot. Ellis stood next to his car. Neither of them had anything left to say, so Asher went inside and left Ellis alone in the night.

49. ASHER

After

Asher sits on one of the wooden horses, looking out toward the end of the village. Nobody has explicitly told him not to go beyond the border, but other than the patrol and runners, nobody else strays too far from camp and never beyond the village. Not that he is too eager to leave the camp after the incident in the flowered land, and he has yet to set foot in that area again.

He pays closer attention to everyone since that night, hoping to catch someone gazing at him just a second too long, or waiting to see if someone watches his movements more than others. Still, he doesn't know who would have chased him like that. There's an answer, right out of reach, but he can't see the dots through the haze to make them connect. He runs his hand along the carved mane of his horse, the paint chipping, and hops down. He closes his yellow notebook and tucks it into his back pocket.

***

A group gathers near the center of the camp, the fire rekindled after the storm, and Tonya, Rico, and Wendy stand around the outer rim.

"What's going on?"

"Gotta do something about the smell," Rico says.

The weather is only getting hotter as summer approaches, the sun scorching, and the humidity thick. The smell of the rotting bodies building up around the fences has gotten into the park, and Asher crinkles his nose as the breeze brings on a fresh wave of dead, as if on cue. The more bodies piling against the fence, the weaker the defense becomes as well. Mag stands on an overturned milk crate, commandeering respect as everyone dutifully awaits her instructions.

"We're going to take a small group beyond the fence. Volunteers only—if you're not entirely comfortable, do *not* put yourself in a position to be at risk or risk the livelihood of another."

Mag explains the plan: gather the bodies into a pile and set them ablaze, and those unwilling to volunteer trickle away. Asher shakes his head in annoyance. Everyone wants safety, but few are willing to step forward and protect the park. By the time Mag finishes, only Asher, Tonya, Rico, Wendy, Rob, Daniel, and George are left.

"Not much of a group, huh?" Asher says.

They gear up with hand weapons, Wendy and Daniel packing guns for good measure, and trek across the backlot to the guard shack gate. Rico shifts uneasily around Daniel, but Asher places himself between them. They reach the gate, and the smell is overpowering. George passes around a box of latex gloves and face masks from the Health Services building while Daniel unlocks the chain.

"You and you"—Daniel points to Wendy and Tonya—"stay here. Swing the gate shut and lock it if any of them approach."

"Why can't you? We were out there last; we can handle our own," Wendy says.

"We don't have time for your lip service," Daniel says.

"I'll do it," Rob interjects.

Rico peeks around the group, mumbling about a missing bike. Asher raises his eyebrow, but Rico just shakes his head. They pair off, stepping off the asphalt road and into the trees. Asher and Rico approach the first body, the corpse bloated, and when Asher grabs ahold of an arm and lifts, it separates from the body with a loud rip. He stumbles backward, the arm still in his hand, as maggots pour out from the shoulder joint. Asher barely has time to drop his bat and raise his mask before throwing up. Rico is ashen, and they realize they might have made a mistake by volunteering.

"Come on, boys, hold it together," Tonya says, as she and Wendy pass, carrying a body between themselves.

Nature has not treated the bodies well; even the most recently killed are further decayed than expected, sped along in the process by the heat and the air. Bugs crawl on and in the bodies, and animals have scavenged meals off some. The oldest bodies have decomposed to the point of appearing as nothing more than leathered skin and bones. A pile of a dozen corpses slowly builds, two of which are fresh kills by Asher and Tonya. George douses one side of the pile with gasoline and tosses a match onto it, letting it burn as they continue their work. Asher and Rico dump another body onto the pile, sending a flurry of ashes and embers spiraling upward, and Asher catches a flash of blonde hair at the end of the road, near the intersection.

"Why are Wendy and Tonya all the way out there? I thought we were just gathering them from the fence?"

"What are you talking about? They're right there," Rico says, pointing to the women as they step onto the road with a small body that has rotted beyond the point of recognition.

"But I could have sworn—" Asher starts, craning his neck to try to see around a tree and blinking the sweat out of his eyes. Another infected steps out from the trees, her long and stringy hair having possibly been blonde months earlier, with three more moving in on her heels. "Dammit."

They notice the burning pile, and Asher and Rico standing nearby, and increase their speed. The boys ready their weapons and rush forward, meeting the infected halfway down the road, and split up in an attempt to divert their attention. Asher swings the bat, cracking it against the temple of the girl in front, and she falls to the ground tripping the man directly behind her. He attempts to push upward, but one of his arms has been amputated and he's unable to stabilize. Asher brings the bat down on the crown of his skull. Rico plunges the tire iron through the chest of one, rips it out, and shoves it into the throat of the other. The encounter is over in a matter of minutes.

"Get back! Now!"

They hear Rob calling from the gate, waving everyone in. Asher's heart stops. The intersection is filling with another dozen infected. It's not a complete horde, but it's more than the small group is willing to handle on their own. The boys turn and run. Wendy and Tonya are already back inside the perimeter, restrained by Daniel and George, as Rob pushes the gate shut before Asher and Rico can reach them. The women scream out, trying to fight off the men, begging for Rob to wait. He clicks the lock on the chain as Rico and Asher slam against the fence.

"Unlock it!"

"Let us in!"

Asher loops his gloved fingers through the chain link fence and pulls, metal clanging against metal, but Rob backs away, watching in terror. Asher looks along the top, but there's no gap in the barbed wire that would allow them to climb over. Rico drops down, grabs the bottom of the fence, and pulls up.

"Asher, crawl under."

The infected have reached the fire and are approaching fast. Asher grabs the fence.

"You first."

Rico tries to argue, but Asher shakes his head—there's no time. The metal of the fence digs into the latex gloves and his skin as he pulls it as high as possible to allow Rico through. A gunshot goes off and the closest infected drops. Wendy, in her struggle to free herself from Daniel, has pulled out her gun. She fires off another shot before Daniel wrestles the gun away from her. Although she downed two of the infected, the gunshots rile up the remaining crowd, provoking their aggression.

"Hurry up," Rico says. He's cleared the bottom of the fence and pushes out on it for Asher. Asher releases his hold, and the opening becomes smaller. He's able to get his head and one arm through, but the fence snags on the neck of his shirt, choking him, and preventing him from squeezing in. He releases the bat and retreats to detangle his shirt, but as he frees the fabric from the fence, an infected grabs at his shoe. Asher kicks at the hand, but a second infected reaches for his exposed calf, forcing him to twist away and miss his chance to get through the fence. One of them knocks into the burning pile, sending a body tumbling to the ground, and its ragged clothes catch fire. It screams out, stumbling wildly and flailing. The others close in on Asher from the front and side.

Asher darts into the trees.

He can hear the others calling out for him, watching as he runs along the perimeter, but he doesn't stop or look back. He's unsure of how many infected split off to follow him, but he can hear their footfalls and growls as they fight to maintain their chase. Additional corpses, fallen branches, and rocks impede Asher's path. He has to dart around trees, and it's hard to breathe with the medical mask on. He rips it off and tosses it aside. His lungs and legs burn. It's been weeks since he's had any form of exercise; the park has made him lazy. He's focused on breathing and maintaining speed and doesn't see the gnarled tree root, and then he's on the ground. His face slams against the dirt and pain shoots through his ankle. He tries to stand but can't put weight on his injured leg. He climbs to his knees and uses the side of a tree for support, hobbling from trunk to trunk.

Asher keeps an ear on the sounds behind him while searching along the fence for an opening or a sign of a patrol member. He doesn't understand how they were ambushed by so many infected at once. It's not unusual for one or two to wander to the park from time to time, but not over a dozen at once. He hears a branch break and one of the infected steps into view. Asher can't outrun it any longer as it picks up speed, reinvigorated by catching up to him. He hobbles to a thick branch, lifting it into his hands as the infected reaches forward. Asher brings the branch across its arms and hears a crack, but he's unsure if it's a bone or the wood. He loses his balance and falls on his hip. The infected leans forward and Asher whacks it in the head, this time splintering the branch in his hands, and the body topples to the ground next to him. There's a thick stone next to its head and Asher bashes stone against skull until nothing is left but a bloody pulp.

He continues along the curve of the fence, the snarls and growls of the infected dropping away, pulling himself along hand over hand as he hops on his good leg. Movement catches his attention from inside the perimeter and he picks up the pace.

"Todd! Thank God," he pants.

"What are you doing out there? Are you okay?" Todd asks, approaching the fence.

Asher explains what happened, casting furtive glances over his shoulder, and asking how he can get back in. Todd stays with him, guiding him to the section of the leaning fence supported by the van. Todd climbs onto the roof of the van as Asher works his way up the fence, his good foot slipping out from under him twice.

"You can do it; I'll help you over the barbed wire, just give me your hand," Todd says, keeping his tone even for Asher's sake. Todd grabs hold of Asher's arm with both of his hands, his grip firm, and lifts him up and over the top of the fence.

As Asher catches his breath on top of the van, he notices the stream of blood running down Todd's forearm and dripping from his hand. There's a laceration a couple of inches long from one of the barbs. Todd rips the bottom of his shirt off and Asher helps him tie it around his arm.

"Something's off, Todd," Asher warns. "I don't know what it is, but there's something going on out there. There were too many of them all at once."

"Hordes aren't unusual—we encountered way more on the road."

"I know. Call it intuition, but I can't help worrying that something big is going to happen." Asher contemplates telling Todd about being chased as Todd helps him back to camp, but he keeps it to himself, worried he'll sound too crazy. *And maybe you are losing your mind a little,* he thinks, *you're getting stir-crazy.*

They can hear the raised voices before they round the corner of the castle. Tonya sees Asher first and stops arguing. Within seconds, three bodies bombard him and squeeze tightly.

"I'm okay," he whispers, exhausted.

Mag informs them that Alexandria will come to inspect Asher's ankle and stitch Todd's arm, and they retire to their section of the store. They pass Rob along the way and Asher hears Wendy call him a coward. Rob averts his gaze without offering an apology.

50. ASHER

Before

The water continued to pelt Asher's skin, turning cold; the soap had long since washed down the drain. It had been three days since Ellis broke up with him, but Asher replayed the conversation over and over in his head. Immediately following the confrontation, Asher had to face a group of Mark's friends celebrating the end of finals in the living room with beer pong and shots. Asher wasn't up for putting on a fake face for anyone and locked himself in his room, pretending to be asleep when Renee knocked on his door.

He had crawled into bed to force himself to fall asleep, but was assaulted by Ellis's scent infiltrating his nostrils. Ellis's pillow, brought over from his own apartment, was still resting at the top of the bed. He fought the urge to throw it out and instead stuffed the pillow into the closet. But on the morning of the third day since the breakup, he had woken up facedown in it, inhaling the fading scent. The water became too cold to tolerate anymore, and Asher shut it off.

Wrapped in a towel, Asher walked down the hall and through the living room to knock on Derrick's door. A muffled grunt greeted him in response.

"You awake?" Asher asked, and received a response that did not qualify as English. "I'm out of the shower. We should probably head out soon if you want to stop and grab something to eat."

He had gotten Derrick to agree to drop him off at the airport in exchange for breakfast on the way. Asher finished getting ready and pulled a coat from his closet, tossing it on top of his suitcase. He left his room again to make sure Derrick had gotten up, and found him with a bad case of bed head watching TV in the living room.

"You ready?" Derrick asked.

"Yeah, you?"

"Yep."

"You're not showering or getting dressed or anything?"

"Nah, I'm heading straight home from dropping you off, so why bother when I'm going to be in the car for four hours?"

Only a handful of cars remained in the parking lot. They stuffed their luggage into the trunk and got in the car. Halfway to the airport, Asher felt his phone vibrate. He expected a checkup from his mom, but saw Ellis's name instead. Over the past three days, Asher had received scattered texts here and there from Ellis, initially asking how he was doing and then a few poor attempts at having a casual conversation, which pathetically died off after two or three responses. There'd been no mention of Brandon, and Asher had zero desire to initiate that conversation. Asher opened the text.

E: Just remembered your flight is today. Do you need a ride to the airport?

Thankful that he not only booked an early flight, but that Derrick agreed to take him, Asher typed a hurried answer to Ellis.

A: Thanks, but I'm on my way to the airport right now. Derrick is driving me.

E: Oh, ok, cool. Have a safe flight then!

"Everything all right?" Derrick asked.

"Yeah, it was just my mom making sure I was on my way to the airport," Asher lied. He stared out the window the rest of the ride.

When Derrick pulled up to passenger drop-off, Asher solemnly thanked him for the ride and wished him a merry Christmas. The actual holiday was still a week and a half away, and holiday travelers had yet to swarm the airport. The ticketing and security lines were short and quick, composed mostly of other college students flying home, and Asher found himself sitting at his gate with an hour and a half to spare before boarding. He put his headphones in to drown out his somber thoughts. After thirty minutes of shuffling through songs and finding nothing appealing, he abandoned the distraction and walked to the newsstand. The lackluster paperback selection was unappealing, but on a smaller rack, a pocket-sized yellow notebook caught his attention. Asher picked it up and approached the register with a pack of candy.

Asher tapped a pen to the page over and over again, racking his brain for something to write, to release everything pent up inside, but the words refused to flow. He threw the notebook and pen into his bag and slumped into his seat. Against his better judgment, and influenced by his anger, Asher gave in and opened a new message to Ellis.

A: Have you talked to Brandon?

The minutes ticked by without a response and Asher regretted sending the text. Given that Ellis almost always had his phone on him, and had already texted Asher today, Asher knew that he read the text and was choosing not to respond. Not that Asher blamed him. He realized how the text came off, demanding and crazed. But then his phone vibrated.

E: Yeah. We met up for coffee the other day.

Ellis's response was honest and concise, but left something to be desired. They met up for coffee, but were they just leaving it at that? Did Ellis get the closure he needed and figure out what he was feeling? But Asher remembered the letter that Brandon had written Ellis, saying that he was never going to stop fighting to get him back. Nothing

was as simple as meeting for coffee and clearing the air. Asher decided
he might as well plunge all the way in, having already tested the waters.

A: How'd it go?

E: I don't know. Honestly I wish I knew what I wanted, but meeting up
with Brandon just made things even more confusing.

A: How so?

E: I guess I thought I would talk to him and we'd be able to just jump
back into everything as if nothing had changed. But everything has
changed, and when I actually saw and talked to him I didn't get the
same feeling as the day I saw him on campus. Suddenly I didn't want
to be there anymore once he sat down at the table.

Asher felt the blood surge to his head, a flutter in his stomach,
and a sense of hope spread through his chest. If Ellis already had
doubts about fixing things with Brandon, then there was a chance that
he'd misinterpreted his feelings in a moment of weakness. His phone
vibrated again.

E: I talked to my parents about it all, and they think I need to use
winter break to be by myself and figure things out. You're flying home
today and Brandon drives home tomorrow, so that gives me a couple
of weeks to deal with everything.

A: That's good. I just want you to be happy.

E: Thanks. I want the same for you too. I just wish I knew how to
make everyone happy. No matter what, I'm hurting someone.

Asher switched gears, deciding it was in his best interest to be
friendly with Ellis, not to push him away and make things worse.
He acknowledged to Ellis that he did feel hurt, but not to focus on
that. Asher agreed to Ellis's request from the night they broke up, to

continue being there for him, that being friends was better than nothing. Asher understood that if Brandon and Ellis repaired their relationship, remaining friends would be impossible. In the meantime, he wanted to appear as the good guy, and was determined to fight Brandon tooth and nail, with a smile on his face, to win Ellis back for good. Asher knew exactly what he would have to do first.

51. WENDY

After

"I want to kill them both," Wendy vents, pacing at the end of the dock. She chews on a nail. She's fuming and seeing nothing but red. "I don't care if Daniel's your friend."

"He's not my friend—we're just coworkers, for lack of a better description," Aubrey says. He'd come by while Alexandria was wrapping Asher's sprained ankle and pulled Wendy aside, suggesting the lake as a spot away from others until she'd cooled down. "But you can't just kill either of them. I'm not saying I agree with what happened"— Aubrey holds his hands up—"I'm just saying that's not how things work around here."

"Mag said before we even went anywhere that anyone who wasn't entirely confident needed to stay behind. My best friend was nearly devoured because Rob's a little bitch and chained him out there. Daniel held me back and took my weapons away so I couldn't even save him."

"I'll get your weapons back, but you still can't kill them. Just try and relax. Asher's home, he's safe, and his ankle will heal fast; it's just bruised."

Wendy sucks her lips inward and puffs out her cheeks, trying not to scream. She stares out across the lake, attempting to focus on the small-town street they walked down on their first day at the park.

It's too far away for her to make out any details, but she remembers the boutique-styled shops and thinks further back to the day she was here with Ivy. She can't relate to the girl she was back then, focused on sorority politics and wondering when Glenn was going to propose. She rubs her ring finger as she thinks of Glenn for the first time in months.

"How's that relaxing thing working out for you?" Aubrey asks, stepping up alongside her.

Wendy laughs, but she is starting to relax. "Thank you."

"For what?"

"I wasn't doing anyone any favors by being in there getting everyone hyped up. At least Alexandria can mend them with peace of mind."

"Let's go." Aubrey leads Wendy to the tied-up paddleboats and helps her climb aboard one. He unhooks it from the dock and they peddle out across the lake. The boat cuts through the algae floating on top of the water, and fish trail them waiting for crumbs to be tossed overboard. They reach the middle of the lake and stop, allowing the boat to drift. "Sometimes, when I can't sleep I just slip out here and look at the stars."

"We're about five hours too early for that," Wendy says.

"Then look at the open blue sky. Just enjoy *something*. When was the last time you did that?"

"I had fun the night you found the beer."

"The night you turned me down for a dance," Aubrey says.

"I can't be that person for you. Not with everything going on, not with where my head is all the time."

"And that's fine, but be that person for yourself. You're wound so tightly. I know you did awful things while you were out there, you wear it all over your face, but you don't have to keep punishing yourself for it. You had to survive; you had to protect Asher."

"He protected me too," Wendy protests.

"Relax. I'm sure he did. I wasn't saying he's weak, but since you've been here, he's letting the road go. You're not. You need to forgive yourself."

Wendy looks up into the sun for as long as she can, letting the light burn spots in her vision until she has to blink and turn away. She doesn't know how to let go.

"Have you ever killed someone? Not someone that's infected?" Wendy asks. She knows she's crossing a barrier, asking a question she's not allowed to ask. But it's not as simple as Aubrey telling her to forgive herself when he doesn't understand.

"Most of us wouldn't still be alive if I hadn't killed someone that wasn't infected, not after the siege. Humanity is at war, and no soldier is going to live unscathed."

"I think I'd like to return to shore now. Alexandria should be done."

***

Wendy sits at a table in the empty restaurant, watching Tonya teach the kids sign language after Mr. Nichols's lesson, and mimicking the gestures with her own hands. It comes much more naturally to the kids, who are all eager to learn in order to better communicate with their friend, but Tonya winks at Wendy and repeats a phrase for her benefit.

"Miss Wendy, you don't have to sit back there by yourself," Jayden calls out, patting the bench between him and Frankie. Wendy blushes, embarrassed to be called out by a six-year-old, but she takes the kid up on his offer and moves down the table. "You can hear Miss Tonya better if you're closer."

Tonya teaches them a series of phrases and steps away, allowing Marie to take over and help the kids practice.

"It's strange, isn't it? I never thought we'd see kids laughing and playing and enjoying learning again," Tonya says.

"You do great with them, you and Mr. Nichols both," Wendy replies. "Do you think maybe I could help you guys out? Not with the sign language, obviously, but I want to continue learning that. But you're so happy around them, and the kids love you. I'd like to have that too."

"Of course you can."

Wendy explains that Aubrey investigated a greenhouse behind the park and found an entire supply of gardening tools and seed packets. The greenhouse was too far away from the castle for most people to feel comfortable trekking to and from, making it impractical to attempt to grow plants within the facility. By utilizing the flowerbeds lining the lake pavilion in front of the castle, they can use the lake for easy watering. Mr. Nichols teaches the lessons, Tonya teaches sign language, and Wendy will try to help the kids learn to grow and cultivate crops.

She will have a chance to create new life, and plant hope within the camp.

52. ASHER

Before

Asher gazed out the window from the breakfast table, watching the snow swirl downward. His father and Brady were talking about the football games scheduled for the day when his mom entered from the kitchen, carrying a plate full of pancakes.

"Bad news down in Florida," Sherrie said, placing the plate in the center of the table.

"Doesn't the bad news always start in Florida? That's where all the crazies live." Brady laughed and punched Asher on the shoulder.

"A little boy was rushed to the hospital last night," Sherrie continued as if uninterrupted. "He'd been complaining of feeling sick for a couple of days, but while the family was at church he lunged at his sister and tried to bite a chunk of flesh out of her arm."

"That's insane," Arnold, Asher's father, said while taking a sip of his coffee. "Do they know what caused it?"

"Not yet. His parents thought his initial illness was just from the change in weather and traveling, figured he was jet-lagged."

"It was probably bath salts—isn't that what the kids have been smoking these days?" Brady joked, stuffing his mouth at the same time.

"Come on, the poor kid is only eight years old. It's in ill taste to speak like that; we've raised you better." Sherrie frowned. "Besides, his mom is being looked at as well—she's apparently been feeling off for just as long. It could just be some bug going around. They're from New York City. With all the weirdos up there, you never know what you're going to catch."

"Or maybe they were smoking the bath salts together. They're all *progressive* up there; it could be family bonding." Brady stuffed another forkful into his mouth.

"Shh, here comes Paige with the kids. I don't want Max to hear you talking like that." Sherrie hushed her son as his wife walked in carrying one-year-old Kaylynn, with their son Max groggily trailing behind her. "Good morning! How're my babies doing?"

Sherrie stretched her arms out, taking Kaylynn and kissing Max on the head.

"He was refusing to get up, still fuming about not getting to go hunting yesterday. Not even the lure of opening presents could get him out of bed," Paige said, cutting a pancake into small bites. "I told him next Christmas he could go, as long as he behaved starting today."

"And no biting your sister if she gets better pajamas than you from Grandma and Grandpa." Brady laughed, earning more disapproving looks from his parents.

"Asher, you're being awfully quiet; what's going on with you?" his mom asked while trying to feed Kaylynn.

"What? Nothing, just tired I guess," he said, and continued eating. The meal tasted bland and unappealing.

"Were you up all night waiting for Santa to get here? Couldn't sleep out of anticipation?" Arnold laughed at his own joke.

"If by Santa, you mean browsing the Internet for porn," Brady said, eliciting a slap on the arm from his wife but another laugh from Arnold.

In actuality, Asher had been up worrying all night about how his family was going to react to his coming out. He'd spent the past week working up the courage to finally tell them, with Ellis acting as a life coach helping him through it, but each opportunity passed without Asher actually saying it. His mind was full of scenarios where his father kicked him out, his family disowned him, and he had to find a way back to Florida on his own.

"I'm gay."

A shriek escaped Sherrie's mouth as Brady gagged on his juice. Paige quickly covered her mouth, and Arnold silently stared at Asher.

"What's gay?" Max asked.

"Don't say that word," Paige reprimanded him.

"It's just a word, Paige, it's not going to kill him," Arnold remarked. He kept his head down, but calmly cut his pancake with his fork and continued to eat. Everyone watched carefully, awaiting instructions on how to react.

"You're not gay," Brady said.

"If he says he's gay, he's gay." Arnold shut down his eldest son. Asher listened for an undertone of disappointment, and although he couldn't decipher one, there wasn't any sense of approval either. Brady glanced from their dad to their mom, without acknowledging Asher, before wiping his mouth with a napkin and standing up. He retreated from the table, and a door slammed shut. Paige cautiously calculated the mood before deciding to follow suit.

"Maybe I should go check on him," she mumbled.

"Sit down and finish your breakfast. Brady's a grown man; he can handle himself," Arnold commanded. Paige quickly dropped back down, looking sheepish.

"Arnold," Sherrie intoned.

"What's gay?" Max repeated.

Nobody answered him, but Arnold shifted in his seat to look at Asher. They maintained eye contact as Asher fidgeted in his chair.

"You're my son. You've always been my son, and you'll always be my son. I don't like this; you know I don't like this. But nobody is going to disrespect you in my house." His voice rose with the last statement, his words carrying down the hall to Brady.

They hurriedly finished breakfast, only breaking the silence to compliment Sherrie on her cooking. Asher offered to clear the table, and as he was rinsing dishes in the sink, he felt someone's presence behind him. Turning off the water, he looked over his shoulder and saw his mom standing there with her eyes full of tears. She wrapped her arms around him.

"Are you okay?" Sherrie asked.

"Yeah, I think so. That went a lot better than I expected it to."

"Your dad might be a lot of things, but at the end of the day he's always going to love you; we all are. I want you to know this doesn't change anything," his mother said, rubbing Asher's arms.

"And Brady?"

"Brady is an idiot. But he loves you too, and he's going to come around," she said. "In the meantime, do what I taught you, close your eyes and count to ten, or thirty, however long you need. I want you to know how proud I am that you were brave enough to come forward and trust us with this. I'm just sorry it took this long for you to feel comfortable. I saw you struggling so many times and I wanted to help you, but I gave you your space because I felt you needed to handle this in your way."

"You knew?" Asher asked, in shock.

"A mother always knows her little boy's secrets," Sherrie answered.

"Why didn't you say anything? I could have used your help a long time ago," Asher said, bristling with frustration.

"I don't know, maybe the same reason you didn't say anything. I didn't know how. I figured the best thing for me to do was just be here when you needed me," Sherrie said, with a hint of remorse. She realized that her intentions, while good, were not helpful.

"I'm sorry. That's not your fault. I love you, Mom," Asher said.

***

Asher sat on the floor in his room the night before returning to Florida. His clothes were scattered all around him and he grabbed a shirt to fold and stuff into his suitcase. The rest of Christmas went by slowly, everyone tiptoeing around him and being polite. They spent the afternoon opening and playing with presents. Brady refused to speak to Asher, and Paige had been similarly quiet. Both were visibly uncomfortable watching Asher interact with the kids but did not verbally object to it. The next morning Brady and Paige packed up the kids and headed home before Asher had gotten out of bed. Brady claimed an unexpected issue at work needed his attention.

Asher's phone vibrated with a text from Ellis.

E: You ready to fly back tomorrow?

After coming out, Asher had texted Ellis and kept him abreast of his family's reaction to the news. Ellis was enthusiastic that Asher's parents received it better than expected and agreed that Brady would eventually come around. Otherwise, their texts were sparse, and it took Ellis increasingly longer to respond when Asher attempted to strike up a conversation.

A: Almost. About to overdose on family and I think it's time we take our breaks for a bit.

Asher folded a pair of jeans and stuffed them into his suitcase next to his socks. His phone vibrated again and he abandoned packing.

E: I bet. Do you have a ride home from the airport?

A: Yeah, Renee is picking me up.

E: Oh, okay. I was wondering if maybe I could pick you up.

Asher hesitated, writing two different texts and deleting both of them. Finally, he settled on a response.

A: If you wouldn't mind that'd be awesome.

E: Of course I don't mind.

**

"Next," the security guard called, waving Asher forward. He entered the X-ray machine and waited to be cleared. He lifted his bag off the conveyor belt and retrieved his shoes and belt from the plastic bin. The airport was crowded with travelers Asher had to continuously dodge as he made his way to his gate. He found an open seat and pulled out the yellow notebook, broke in the spine, and settled in to write. An old man violently coughed in the row of seats across from Asher, and the people sitting next to the man leaned away. Asher turned his music up and returned his attention to his writing.

An hour later, the gate attendant spoke into the overhead system, calling people to board the plane in sections. After settling into his assigned seat, Asher noticed an article headline on the newspaper the elderly woman next to him was reading.

"Excuse me, do you mind if I see that page?" he asked. The woman separated it from the rest of the paper and handed it over.

MORE VIOLENT OUTBREAKS IN GEORGIA

Police responding to a call of domestic disturbance from a neighbor at a Marietta, GA, house last night discovered the body of Anthony Healey, 43. Police are currently seeking Sarah Healey, 38, the wife of the victim, in what appears to be a homicide. Mrs. Healey was last seen at a neighborhood holiday party on the 27th where witnesses have described her as moody, aggressive, and sickly, descriptions that are out of character for the generally pleasant activist and charity worker. Full details have not been given to the public, but this is one of four recent homicides in the area that police are investigating under similar circumstances.

Asher folded the page in half and handed it back to the woman.
"It's sad, isn't it?" she asked.
"What is?" Asher asked back.
"What the world is becoming," she answered with a note of defeat.

53. ASHER

After

Asher adjusts the hat covering his face from the sweltering sun as he leans against the hard wall of the castle, the rifle draped across his lap and a two-way radio clipped to his belt loop. He sits atop one of the castle turrets and watches out over the park for signs of movement. During the day any sort of commotion is noticed right away, but at night it's more difficult to spot anything out of the ordinary. It has been five days since an attack. That attack came as a result of too many infected building up against a weak portion of the fence. In the two weeks since he'd bruised his ankle, nobody else was willing to venture out and pull the bodies away. Thankfully, the breach was during the day and spotted from one of the castle towers. Between the patrol and those with weapons skills, the breach was quickly handled, with confidence that none of the infected slipped further into the park without notice. Asher's shifts always started in the wee hours of the morning, and he could never spot any lights from outside of the park. No one uninfected has shown up since Rico and Jayden, and Asher is starting to wonder if human life beyond the gates is extinct.

There is a knock on the tower door leading to the stairwell and it slowly opens, revealing Wendy's face.

"Good morning," Wendy says, offering a plate of refried beans and crackers, "or, well, I guess it's lunchtime for you."

"Thanks," Asher says, accepting the plate and scooting over to make room for her. Every time he thought he saw something in the distance, he felt hope beginning to flutter in his chest, as he prayed that Ivy had finally shown up. But it was never her, leaving him unable to prove to Wendy that she had not killed her best friend. He found it impossible to believe that Wendy would be capable of committing the heinous act of cold-blooded murder, but he had never broached the subject again since she'd confessed to it. He won't tell her, but Asher secretly believes Wendy brings him lunch during every shift because part of her still hopes she will be greeted by the news that Ivy has reached the gates.

"Refried beans. Again," Wendy says, scooping up a mouthful with a cracker. People try not to talk about the rapidly shrinking food supply around others, but it was becoming more difficult with each day. Yuki had even stopped fishing to give the fish time to repopulate. Feeding forty people a day was depleting the lake. But every morsel had been scraped from the immediate three lands, and most from the next two lands.

"I overheard Mag telling George that she's sending out a team with Daniel and Aubrey for a food run today. They'll still have their radios, so if anyone catches anything up here they can be contacted to switch gears. But everyone is getting restless, and we need something different," Asher tells Wendy. He tries to think he's above complaining of boredom when he is lucky to even be alive, but he'd be lying to himself if he tried to pretend life is exhilarating. "Do you ever miss being out there?"

"Out of the park?" Wendy asks.

"Yeah. Don't you get claustrophobic in here?"

"Hmm . . . I guess maybe a little bit. But it's easier. It's safer."

"I know. And I'm glad for that, trust me, I am. I'm just worried that being in here is making us soft. I could hardly even run anymore when I got locked out of the fence. What happens if there's another attack like before we got here? Are we just biding our time? What about when food runs out for real and we're forced out of the gates? This is just temporary; everything is temporary."

"Asher, just because everything with Ellis—"

"This isn't about him. I just . . . I don't know."

He wrestles with telling her everything he's feeling, asking her for help clearing the fog and putting the pieces together. But just like with Todd he keeps it to himself, not wanting to burden Wendy with his fears when she has her own.

"You wish you had someone."

Asher glances up at her; she thinks he's talking about heartbreak, the temporary happiness he experienced before the outbreak. Not wanting to complicate things, he plays along, and hopes maybe she'll open up.

"No, I do have someone; I have six 'someones.'"

"You know what I mean. It's not the same thing."

"No, it's not."

"You're allowed to miss him." Wendy puts her arm around Asher's shoulder and pulls him in to her. "I hope you don't think you can't talk to me about him because of, well, you know."

"It's not that. I don't know, maybe it is. I guess I just don't really see what the point is. Why should I even waste my energy feeling anything?"

"Because your ability to feel is what keeps you separated from those things. All we have left is our humanity. And if we give that up, *then* you get to ask what's the point."

"I love our makeshift family. And my only opportunity to find someone died with the outbreak. There are too many other concerns; it'd be selfish of me to focus on trying to date," Asher says.

"You're far from selfish. And hey, I'm celibate too. Don't think that's reserved exclusively for you." Wendy laughs.

"Yeah, but you don't have to be. I've seen the way you and Aubrey flirt with each other." Asher smiles.

"Oh, shut up!" Wendy shoves Asher and they both laugh.

"He gave you two of his crackers yesterday."

"Well, round up the congregation, I've been swept off my feet and I'm getting married!" Wendy laughs, but a second later Asher catches her right hand rubbing her left ring finger, and her laugh dies out.

"Do you want to talk about it?"

"I think I better get going; we're going to try planting some of those seeds today to see if they're still any good. I'll see you in a bit." She grabs their empty plates and pulls the door open. Asher can hear her footsteps descending the metal stairs and jams the door fully shut to cut off the sound.

He picks up the binoculars and scans out and around his zone of the park, but nothing is out of the ordinary. He switches his focus to the parking garages in the distance, but they're as empty as ever. The sun rises in the sky and Asher checks his watch to see how much longer he has before his relief comes. Sweat rolls down his face, and he wipes his forehead with the bottom of his shirt.

After another twenty minutes, the door opens up again and he takes his leave as Jeffrey presides over the tower. Asher passes over the rifle, binoculars, and radio, and steps into the stairwell. Blue-tinted light streams in from the stained-glass windows in the walls. Although the windows serve a decorative purpose from the outside, they are in stark contrast to the plain interior of the turret, mirroring the differences between the park and the service area. The stairs end on a maintenance catwalk that intersects with another catwalk providing access to a different turret. Without any windows in the interior of the castle, watchmen have to use a flashlight or feel their way around to reach the ground level, but the batteries in Asher's light died the week prior, and lacking a spare set, he has had to suffice without one.

Halfway across the catwalk he hears the structure creaking. "Who's there?" he calls out.

A light flashes on and the beam hits him directly in the face. He throws up his hands to try to shield his eyes, and squints in an attempt to make out the figure behind it.

"Asher?" The beam is lowered. Craig stands on the intersecting catwalk, his face eerie and haunted from the shadows cast by the flashlight.

"I thought you had another two hours up there?" Asher asks. Watchmen shift changes were staggered as a precaution.

"Yeah, I would, but I was relieved early so I can join the food run instead," Craig says, moving toward the exit again. "I didn't realize you would be done now too—you scared the bejesus out of me."

"Sorry, batteries died in my flashlight," Asher explains.

"I'm worried mine are on their way out too. I only use it when necessary now, like when a voice calls out from the dark."

Craig reaches the intersection first but stops and waits for Asher.

"Don't use up the rest of it on my account; I know the way," Asher says, and Craig clicks off the light.

"Are you going to try and hold my hand if you get scared again?" Craig teases.

"Hey, you said I scared you."

"I could hear the panic in your voice, admit it." Craig laughs and nudges Asher's shoulder. After the conversation Asher had with Wendy, Craig's touch sends an electric shiver down his spine. He quickly pushes the thought away, trying to focus instead on feeling the drop-off for the stairs with his outstretched foot. The stairs end in a large room used for storage by the former maintenance and park restoration crews, with a straight shot to the exit door leading to the backlot behind the castle.

Craig reaches the door first and pushes the release bar. The sunlight floods into the room, momentarily blinding them both. Neither of them sees the woman standing on the other side covered in grime and blood. Asher reopens his eyes just as she attacks, sinking her teeth into Craig's outstretched forearm. Craig screams in pain and crashes backward into Asher along with the woman. Before Asher can react, the door closes and the room is plunged into darkness and he is pinned to the ground with the weight of both bodies on top of him.

"Get off of me," Craig cries out, twisting his body back and forth and accidentally slamming his elbow into Asher's stomach, knocking the wind out of him.

Asher struggles to free himself but isn't strong enough to leverage both of the bodies. He can hear the woman snarling between his own gasps for breath, and something warm and wet drips on his face. Craig's torso lifts up enough for Asher to push out from underneath him and scoot backward on his butt, kicking to shove both Craig and the woman away from him. Between being taken down to the ground and the ensuing scuffle, Asher has become disoriented and is unsure of which direction the door is, his ankle beginning to throb slightly.

He tries to run away from the wrestling behind him, but collides with a stack of boxes and crashes down to the ground along with the maintenance supplies, slamming his knee into the concrete floor. Items continue to spill out, a chemical smell burns in Asher's nostrils, and something shatters. When he attempts to get back up again, his foot slips in a puddle and he falls back to the ground, slicing his left palm open on a glass shard. Holding his hand in close to his chest, he gingerly feels around with his uninjured hand for dry, glass-free flooring to get his bearings on.

"Asher?" Craig calls out. "Asher, where are you?"

The sound of Craig's voice turns Asher's body to ice. He remains low to the ground. Asher is hesitant to give any further indication of his position; if the woman hasn't been fully taken out, it could mean his life.

"Asher, please," Craig says, his voice nearly a whimper.

Asher buries his face in the crook of his arm to force himself to not respond. He replays the scene of the woman's teeth entering Craig's arm like butter over and over, and he knows there is nothing he can do for his friend. Craig is living on borrowed time. A soft thud sounds nearby and Asher jumps into hyper mode. As nimbly as he can, he gets to his feet and steps forward. Another line of boxes block his path to the right, but he trails his uninjured right hand on them as a guide. He reaches the edge of the room and the hard wall as a rattling echoes around the room.

A beam of light ignites, landing like a spotlight a foot from Asher. He crouches down trying to avoid being seen, and it sweeps over the top of his head. Inhaling deeply out of relief, he makes his way in the opposite direction of the flashlight. His knee and ankle both ache, preventing him from bending his leg or moving quickly, and he has to drag his leg out behind him while keeping his right arm outstretched to feel the way.

"Please don't let me die alone," Craig calls, dropping the light to the ground.

Tears well up in Asher's eyes from the desperation in his voice. Although Craig is not visible, the light is coming from a position Asher gauges to be near the wall and possibly the exit door. Without anything to lose, and being consumed with fear, Craig could be blocking the only way out in hope that Asher will give in and help him. But if he is blocking the way out, then the way up and to a different form of safety is directly across from him.

Asher bolts away from the wall in the direction of what he presumes is the stairs. Since he's completely unarmed, speed is his only defense, and he has to make it before Craig or the woman finds him. Each step causes his leg to throb, and when he sets his foot down wrong, he loses balance and falls into another stack of boxes. The beam of Craig's flashlight swivels around the room in search of the source of the commotion, stopping three feet in front of Asher. The light lands on the edge of a box, forming a half circle, the rest of the light lands on the infected woman.

The woman was crouched down, ready to spring and attack Asher, until the light hit her in the face. She howls and shakes her head, changing targets and scrambling toward Craig once more. The light moves away from her, sliding across the bottom two stairs, as Craig runs for cover. In that last instant, before the woman moved, the fog lifted and everything finally clicked in Asher's head. He has to alert the camp before it's too late. Asher hobbles the last few feet and reaches out, wrapping his fingers around the metal support railing of the stairs. The metal of the bottom step cuts into his shins, but he holds his body up by the rail rather than falling down once more.

A resounding clang fills the room when he hops onto the stairs. Looking over his shoulder he watches the light perform a dizzying dance through the air as Craig tussles with the woman. Without either of them focusing their attention on him, Asher knows he has to move quickly before the noise distracts the woman away from Craig again. Each step rings out louder than the last, and when he reaches the top, the flashlight is stationary on the ground, illuminating only a blank stretch of flooring and a patch of the wall. Asher pulls himself along the catwalk with his right hand, endeavoring to minimize the volume of noise he is making, but it is futile, the need to reach one of the towers winning out.

He reaches the intersection where the catwalks split, as someone steps onto the bottom stair leading up to him, and then up to the second step. Whoever is trailing him is indiscernible in the darkness, the flashlight having been abandoned below, but they continue to climb as Asher stays stationary in fear. Coming to, he turns right, heading for Craig's watchtower with slightly less distance to cover. His loud footsteps cover the sound of his pursuer, preventing him from measuring the closing distance between them. At last he reaches the bottom of the tower, where blue light filters down.

The stained-glass windows only begin halfway up the spiral staircase, leaving the bottom half in near darkness. Asher immediately starts his ascent, propelled forward by the heavy breathing beneath him. Looking down is useless—the dark abyss only brings on a wave of vertigo. Asher shoves the service door open without bothering to knock. He tries to yell but barely whispers, "They're in."

He falls through the doorway and drags himself far enough away to kick the door shut again. He looks up into the frightened face of Rob, whose rifle is aimed at Asher. Asher uses the wall for support as he climbs to his knees, panting for his breath.

"Archon," Asher says. "We have to warn them."

Rob gives off no sign of understanding—his only movement is to raise the gun, keeping it focused on Asher. His two-way radio is clipped to his belt, and Asher takes a step forward, his hand outstretched, reaching for the device. Asher hears a loud bang and feels a forceful shove, slamming the outer half-wall of the turret with the small of his back. Looking down, Asher watches his shirt rapidly turn a dark crimson, and he feels faint and nauseous. His legs give out and his feet slip from under him as his tips backward over the edge. The final image he sees before losing consciousness is the sky pulling away as he plummets.

54. RICO

Before

The weeks after Rico's first adventure to Neverland passed in a blur. He missed an additional two days of class before returning to school and was bombarded with makeup work, but his teachers accepted a medical note from his mom. Neither Rico nor Chloe acknowledged the presence of the other when they passed in the halls. And although he hadn't communicated with Doug again while he languished in bed, Doug had been waiting by Rico's locker the day he returned to school. By midday they were skipping lunch to smoke in Doug's car. Rico found himself accompanying Doug to Neverland at least once a week, but never in the condition of his first visit.

It didn't take Rico long to track the flow of Doug's operation. Doug's cousin, Eric, supplied Doug with the goods (for a majority cut of the profits) and a list of pre-established clients to sell to. Although Rico still had doubts about whether he believed Doug's explanation for what he saw that night, he found it equally as hard to believe his memory, knowing how unreliable his brain would've been. Three weeks later, however, he met Holly in person for the first time, and the opportunity presented itself to uncover the truth.

"Well, look who it is, fellas," a loud voice boomed down the hall and into the living room. Rico turned his attention away from the screen, his avatar driving off the side of the road and into a lake. A girl with dirty-blonde hair down past her shoulders, wearing a dress that was purposefully too small, allowing her cleavage to burst forth at the top, danced into the room. Her heels clicked on the floor and she carried a bottle of tequila in each hand.

"Where've you been?" Eric dropped his controller onto the couch without bothering to pause the game. He wrapped his arms around her and lifted her in the air.

"Oh, you know me—I go where the wind takes me." She kissed him on the cheek. She handed one of the bottles to Eric and they twisted the tops off, clinked the bottles, and raised them to their lips. She glanced over at Rico, seeing him for the first time. "Who's your friend?"

"That's Rico. He works for Doug."

"You work for Doug? When did Douggie get people to work for him?"

"I've just been helping him out for a few weeks," Rico said.

"You high school kids." She laughed, taking another drink straight from the bottle. She swallowed and held her hand out in amusement. "I'm Holly."

Rico shook her hand in shock. Although she was blonde, the similarity in her appearance and Chloe's ended there. Holly's nose was longer and thinner, her jawline much more sharp, and her eyes slightly too far apart. Her hair was darker than Chloe's as well, and Rico guessed it would look more brown than blonde in poor lighting, on top of it being six inches too long. It also tweaked his mind that she had no inclination as to who Rico was, and while he might have been loaded before passing out, she should've recognized him as the boy sleeping in a puddle of his own vomit when she got out of Doug's bed in the morning.

"Weren't you here a few weeks ago? You look familiar," Rico lied.

"Me? No, I've been out west for the past two months," Holly said, brushing him off. "Peyote, that was an experience."

"No shit, you did peyote?!" Eric asked, his voicing jumping up an octave in excitement. Holly launched into a story about her experiences over the past two months, pausing for both dramatic effect and to drink. Eric lapped up everything she said, but her words blended together as Rico zoned out. His thoughts focused on a memory he started trusting: seeing a body roll over in the bed, blonde hair giving way to Chloe's face. He replayed it over and over with Doug's voice repeating in his mind, "Chloe wasn't in my bed. Why the hell would Chloe have even been at Neverland, much less in my bed? That's Holly, you jackass."

But unless peyote gave Holly the ability to teleport or astral project, there was no way for her to be at Neverland and out west at once. Doug had lied to him.

***

There was a bang as the front door slammed against the wall. Rico jumped directly from the stoop into the grass, stumbling as his legs shook from the impact, but regaining his footing to launch himself at Doug's back. Rico's shoulder slammed into Doug's spine and both boys flew face-first into the ground. Rico was burned on the cheek by Doug's cigarette, but remained unfazed by the pain. Doug twisted under Rico, trying to flip onto his back, but Rico shifted his own weight to hold Doug down.

"Get off me," Doug shouted, and thrust his hands into the grass to push up. Rico was caught unaware and slid partially off of Doug, giving him the leverage to flip over. "What the hell?"

Rico pulled his right fist back and punched forward as hard as he could, connecting with Doug's nose. There was a loud crunch as flesh met flesh, and a spurt of blood shot out.

"Fuck!" Doug screamed and grabbed his nose. Rico pulled his fist back again, preparing a second punch, but Doug kneed him in the groin. Doug pushed himself off the ground, regained his feet, and kicked Rico in the gut. Spitting blood out of his mouth, he leaned down into Rico's face and declared, "Now, I can continue beating your ass for the fun of it, or you can explain why I'm beating your ass."

Rico gasped for air.

"Jesus, Doug, what is going on out here?" Eric called from the open door, with Holly peering out from behind him.

"You slept with Chloe," Rico wheezed, holding his stomach.

"I thought we were past that?" Doug asked, squeezing the bridge of his nose to stanch the bleeding.

"You lied to me. You said it was Holly."

"Excuse me, what? You told him I had sex with you? Never in a million years, Douggie," Holly called out.

"You really should have let it go." Doug kicked Rico again, this time connecting with his arms protecting his stomach. Rico rolled onto his stomach, his words inaudible, muffled from speaking facedown in the grass. "I'm sorry, I didn't catch that." Doug theatrically put his ear closer to Rico's face.

"You were my friend," Rico slowly let out. Doug laughed and stood.

"No, you see, that's where you're wrong. We've never been friends." Doug pulled his cigarette pack out of his back pocket and flipped the lid. Most of the cigarettes were broken or smashed inside, but he found one that was only slightly bent and still in one piece. He held it between his blood-covered lips and lit it. He inhaled. "First, you were my customer. Don't get me wrong, a very prized customer. I liked having you hang around, throwing Daddy's money at me to get even with him. Made things easy."

Rico pushed himself up onto all fours, trying to stabilize his breathing. Doug used his foot to shove him back down to the ground.

"You went from paying customer to broke employee. You weren't much of a benefit to me anymore. But I still liked you a little bit. You were pathetic, but you amused me. And I could use you to do the shit I didn't want to do. And no matter what happened, you continued following me like a lost puppy." Doug took a drag on the cigarette and watched as Rico made another attempt to get up. Doug's foot swung into his stomach, knocking all of the air out again and causing him to see stars.

"Doug, I think that's enough," Eric said, no longer standing in the doorway, grabbing Doug's arms.

"It's all been business, Rico. You're nothing more than a transaction to me." Doug flicked the lit cigarette at Rico, missing by an inch.

"Get inside and clean your face up." Eric pushed Doug back toward the house. Holly descended the steps and grabbed Doug's arm, helping Eric pull him in.

"I think the bastard broke my nose," Doug said. He got to the top of the stairs and turned back to the yard, watching as Eric helped Rico to his feet. "Do you know my favorite thing about Chloe's naked body laying in my bed? The mole on her upper left thigh, the only blemish on her otherwise pure skin. It drove her crazy when I kissed her there."

Eric kept Rico steady on his feet, guiding him to the truck, and allowing him to ride passenger.

55. RICO

After

Rico sits on the rim of a large planter. The flowers that once grew inside are long since dead and gone. A gathering of people mill around, pairing off in groups of two or three, with their bags on their backs or slung across their shoulders, and hand weapons at the ready. He sees Yuki standing alone with an ax hanging by her side. He catches her attention and motions her over.

"You're going out gathering with us?" he asks her. She subtly nods in response and looks uneasily from face to face. "What's wrong? Are you scared?"

"No," she answers. "Nobody wants me to go with them."

"I do."

"You go today? You never go before," she says, and glances down at his duffel bag and tire iron.

"At least we're staying in the fences this time. Besides, not a lot of people want to go on runs anymore," Rico answers.

Daniel and Aubrey speak to Mag off to the side, and Rico tenses. He has avoided every interaction with Daniel since the fence, and a sense of agitation wells up every time he sees him around camp. Aubrey, on the other hand, is still trying to make amends for injuring Jayden. In the past week, Aubrey's brought the boy prizes from around the park, and continues to slip him and Marie special treats. Even though Aubrey still feels guilty for what could have happened, Rico and Jayden have long since forgiven him. The two men step away from Mag and approach the group.

"We were waiting for one more to join us, but he's taking too long, so we're going to go ahead and start without him," Daniel says, his raspy voice booming for everyone to hear. "When we leave here, we're going to go to the right. As many of you know we have not searched the buildings on that side of the park in depth, but the outsides have been cleared and there are watchmen up in the towers paying special attention to this side of the park."

Rico shields his eyes and looks up at the castle and the many turrets and towers, wondering if Asher will be one of the guys keeping lookout and having his back today. Daniel continues talking, and he turns his attention back to the instructions.

"Our main focus will be the restaurants, but some of you will be tasked with searching the stores. In the stores you'll want to look for food items like sunflower seeds, jerky, trail mix. Anything that hasn't gone bad yet; you'll know when you see them. Bottled drinks are a plus as well. We don't expect any issues, but you never know what you're going to run into so you should all be equipped with a weapon. We don't want to draw too much attention to ourselves so Aubrey, Ellie"— Daniel looks into the middle of the group where the girl Rico hit with the shotgun stands, previously unnoticed by him— "and I are the only three with guns. If you hear three shots from any of us, then get to safety and back to the camp as quickly as possible."

Daniel finishes up his rallying speech, and he and Aubrey travel through the pairs, passing out park maps with locations circled. Rico accepts a map from Daniel without meeting his eyes and opens it with Yuki to figure out where they are going. It shows a store near the front of the park, sending them the furthest from camp out of all of the groups. The smaller groups break off to get started and Rico jumps off the planter, shoving the map into his back pocket.

"Hey, Rico," Aubrey calls, jogging over to him and Yuki. "I was surprised to see you were joining us today."

"Yeah, I need some fresh air," Rico says, sliding the duffel bag strap over his head. Aubrey looks puzzled for a second before realizing Rico's grinning, and then Aubrey chuckles. "It's a joke, we live outside."

"Right. Where's Jayden—is someone watching him?" Aubrey asks.

"Tonya and Wendy took him and Marie with some of the other kids to plant those seeds," Rico says.

"Cool, well, if you need anything just let me know." Aubrey holds out his hand and firmly shakes Rico's and nods to Yuki.

"You ready?" Rico asks Yuki, and they head off.

They pass through the Germanic village, not paying the ghoulish carousel any attention as they hurry along into the neighboring area.

Yuki's face lights up as they step into a life-sized comic book. Rico has never made it this far into the park, and he looks around, mesmerized by the details. The buildings are covered in a variety of pop art images and figures. A large wall, made to look like a page from a comic book, depicts a fight between a superhero and a villain, with one of the bottom boxes missing the hero, allowing guests to stand in his place for a photo opportunity.

"Go stand over there and I'll take your picture," Rico says, nudging Yuki.

"That's racist," Yuki says, stone-faced and her voice flat.

She shoves Rico and laughs, running up to the box, pretending to punch the villain. She throws her head back, getting the hair out of her eyes, and smiles at Rico. He lifts his hands in the air forming a box with his index fingers and thumbs, and, pretending to take a picture, he makes a clicking noise with his tongue. With each click, Yuki changes poses until they hear someone clear their throat and turn to see a woman standing in the entrance of the restaurant across the way, her hands on her hips.

"Sorry," Rico says, holding his hand up in an apologetic wave. Yuki returns to his side and they hastily continue on, bursting out in laughter and grabbing each other for support as they cross a wooden bridge.

"She look so angry," Yuki says, covering her mouth to stop a giggling fit.

"Do you like comics?" Rico asks while looking around. The new land they have entered causes Rico's skin to tingle in discomfort. It was designed to look like a literal ghost town with large looming leafless trees surrounded by tombstones. A foreboding gate is chained shut in front of a Victorian-style house, the WAIT TIME sign hanging lopsided off to the side.

"Yes. I read them all the time in Japan," Yuki replies, nodding.

They pass another ride with giant pumpkins large enough to fit several people before spinning around each other, dizzying everyone up. Faces are carved into the backs of the pumpkins, leering at them as they walk by.

"If we finish quick enough up front maybe we can stop by one of the comic stores and snag you some to read. You can read English, right?" Rico says, picking up the pace to clear Spooksville as quickly as possible.

There's a gunshot in the distance and Rico reaches out, protectively using his arm to block Yuki, but she demonstrates speedier reflexes and is standing her ground and ready to swing her ax if needed.

"Do we go back?" Yuki asks.

Rico listens for a follow-up gunshot but there is only a tense silence. He shakes his head and says, "No. They told us to go back if we heard three gunshots. It could just be someone on the castle shooting something outside the park. Or maybe an animal got in or something."

At last they reach the portion of the park where their designated store is. The Ferris wheel looms large in front of them, with the store hidden in the shadow cast by the attraction. The glass doors are bolted shut and barely budge when Rico pulls the handles.

"Maybe in back?" Yuki suggests.

Walking around the building they find a path to the backlot and a metal door leading to what is presumably either a stockroom or a break room. Yuki turns the handle, and with a small grinding noise of metal on cement, the door opens, scraping along the ground. The dry, stagnant air wafts from the dark room, carrying with it the putrid smell of decay. The stench is more overbearing than what carries into camp from the fence, and Rico's breakfast races upward. Yuki covers her nose and gags, shoving the door closed.

"We can't go in there," Rico says, wiping his mouth on the bottom of his shirt.

"Maybe safer in the front?" Yuki says.

"Maybe," Rico says.

Without any other way to get inside, Yuki holds her ax in both hands, raises it above her head, and swings down into one of the doors. The glass cracks, forming a spiderweb from the point of impact. With a second strong hit, it shatters completely. They step through the door, crunching glass pieces underfoot. Sunlight seeps through the doors and windows, allowing them to monitor the stagnant surroundings. A hint of the smell from the back filters around the storefront but is not as pungent.

A large drink cooler stands next to the register and Rico treks directly to it, filling up his bag with as many bottles of water as he can carry. Yuki hops up onto the counter and drops down to the floor, disappearing from view. When she reemerges, she's holding a large plastic box full of batteries, small tubes of sunblock, adhesive bandages, and individual aspirin packets.

"How did you know that was back there?" Rico asks her.

"My family come on vacation here. My dad get very sick from ride and buys medicine from this store," Yuki answers, mentioning her family for the first time around Rico. One of the plastic tabs securing the lid on the box is broken, so she empties the supplies into her own bag. The only food supplies they find are bags of potato chips and candy bars, and they pack up as much as they can carry, including filling another bag they grab from a shelf.

"Here you go," Rico says, placing a tiara he found on Yuki's head. She clasps her hands up by her big cheesy smile, fluttering her eyelids while kicking back her foot, causing them to lose their composure for the second time. Their laughing is cut short when they hear gunshots from outside, continuing well beyond three. Rico grabs Yuki's hand. "We've got to go."

Running through the store, they jump through the broken door and land on the sidewalk. There are three infected swaying around the store. Not having time to think, Rico plunges the tire iron through the chest of the nearest one, twisting and turning his torso and head to miss the man's wildly swinging arms. He pulls the tire iron out again and stabs the man through the mouth. The man's body pitches forward, but Rico safely dodges out of the way just in time to watch Yuki swing the ax around over her head and bury it directly in the face of another infected man.

"Behind you!" Rico yells.

Yuki jerks the ax free and spins. The blade slices cleanly through the neck of an attacking woman, decapitating her and sending her head rolling through the shattered glass, landing a foot away from Rico and staring up at him with her teeth bared. The tiara sits, askew, on top of Yuki's dark hair, her bangs hanging in her eyes, and there is blood splattered across her face, arms, and chest, but she otherwise appears unharmed.

"Here, you don't want any blood getting in your eyes or your mouth, just in case." Rico steps up to her with a bottle of water. Yuki closes her eyes and leans her head back, allowing Rico to pour the water over her face and wash away the blood. "All done."

Not wanting to wipe her eyes with her blood-covered hands, she shakes her head and blinks until she can see again. "Where did they come from?"

"I don't know," Rico answers. "But the warning gunshots weren't from anywhere near here, so there has to be more of them."

While walking back to the spooky-themed land, Rico wonders why none of the watchmen caught the infected earlier and signaled to Daniel or Aubrey that they were in the park. They round the corner, and Rico's heart drops. There are at least twelve to fifteen infected roaming between the haunted house and the pumpkin ride, their attention focused in the direction of the shots, and another two are crouched on the ground feasting on one of the women from the camp.

Yuki drops her bag to the ground and charges forward with her ax before Rico can stop her. She chops into the back of one of the infected eating the woman, and when the other infected drops the arm he was taking a bite of, she expertly kicks him in the head with an audible snap. Yanking the ax free, she buries it into the neck of the one she kicked.

Rico rushes to Yuki's side but yelps when the woman grabs his ankle with her hand. She tries to speak but her voice is quiet and a blood bubble bursts from her mouth. Rico bends down low enough to hear her whisper, "Please, kill me."

Tears stream from her eyes and she chokes on her own blood. Using his tire iron, he grants her one last favor. The commotion has caused enough ruckus that the other infected turn their attention toward the duo.

"Can you climb?" Rico whispers to her, watching the crowd inch closer to them.

"Yes," Yuki answers.

"When I say go, run to the fence around the house and climb over it. I'll have your back," Rico instructs.

"No. We both fight," Yuki says.

They split off from each other and take opposite sides of the grouping, with Rico going left and Yuki going right. He silently prays while swinging and stabbing the tire iron to incapacitate as many of the infected as he can. Survival takes all of his concentration; he has lost sight of Yuki. A hand wraps around the strap of the duffel bag, yanking him sideways and off balance, and he misses the man he was swinging at by mere inches. Rico twists around, jamming the tire iron through the forehead of the teenager pulling the strap, and it releases its grip. He slips the strap over his head and swings the bag through the air, letting it soar away from the fight and bang into a metal trash can.

The reverberation from the impact catches the attention of the outlying infected, and they turn away to examine the source. Rico shoves the tire iron up through the jaw and into the head of the man he missed, following up with taking out the next two closest threats.

After finishing off the amassing danger, Rico puts his hands on his knees to catch his breath. He and Yuki are covered from head to toe in blood and in the center of a circle of bodies. He smiles up at Yuki and she returns the gesture, her white teeth in stark contrast against the dark red. Gunshots, intermixed with screaming, reverberate from the direction of the castle, and a large dark cloud of smoke is drifting into the sky.

"Jayden," he says. He gets a second wind when he realizes the camp has been breached.

"The bags," Yuki says.

"Who cares, we won't need the supplies if nobody is left to use them," Rico yells over his shoulder, running for the wooden bridge.

His feet pound against the planks—Yuki at his heels. They come to a quick halt in the comic book land. There are twice as many bodies now. Bullet holes in several of the heads suggest this was the start of the rapid gunfire, which has gotten even louder. But there is no sign of Daniel, Aubrey, or Ellie. Four of the infected slam their hands and fists against the restaurant door.

"Go," Yuki says.

"Someone is trapped inside there," Rico protests.

"Go!" Yuki demands.

"I'm not leaving you."

Yuki grabs his arm, shaking her head.

"Your brother," she says with care and concern.

"Okay." Rico nods his head and jogs away from her, sidestepping bodies and jumping over puddles of blood. He looks back once more before leaving the comics behind and catches the sun glinting off Yuki's tiara as she brings the ax down into the back of a woman's head.

56. ASHER

Before

The doors slid open and Asher stepped out into bright sunlight. He wheeled his suitcase behind him and shielded his eyes. He tossed his bags into the trunk, slid into the passenger seat, and was greeted by Ellis's face lighting up.

"Hey," Ellis said.

"Hey yourself," Asher countered.

Ellis pulled out of the line of waiting cars and followed the airport exit signs to the highway. Music played, and it required a large amount of self-control on Asher's part to not reach out and place his hand on Ellis's.

"How was your break?" Asher asked.

"Not as eventful as yours, that's for sure." Ellis laughed, and then added in a serious tone, "But I do want you to know I'm proud of you. It was brave of you to do what you did."

"Thanks. But I couldn't have done it without you. Being around your family and seeing how open and accepting they are showed me how things should be. And you showed me how happy I could be if I were honest and open." Asher caught the change in Ellis's posture. "Sorry, I didn't mean that to come out the wrong way, I just meant—"

"You don't need to apologize. I know what you meant. I'm glad I could do that for you; you deserve to be happy."

The ride was filled with conversations about the presents they received and classes starting in two days. They no longer had any classes together. Ellis shifted the gear into park but left the ignition on. There was an awkward tension in the air as both Asher and Ellis waited with bated breath, neither of them seeming to know what to do next.

"Would you like to come inside?" Asher asked.

"Sure," Ellis said, smiling again, and turning off the car. Ellis lifted Asher's suitcase from the trunk.

"I can get that," Asher said.

"Don't worry about it, I've got it."

"Thanks."

Mark's and Derrick's cars were absent from the parking lot, so Asher knew they'd have the place to themselves. Asher strode through the living room to open the patio blinds, and Ellis rolled the suitcase into the bedroom.

"Your pillow is still here," Asher pointed out, rejoining Ellis.

"I know, I realized it about two weeks ago." Ellis walked over to what had been his side of the bed and sat at the foot.

Asher looked down at his hands and picked at the skin on his thumb. After a minute he sat opposite of Ellis on the other edge. "How are things with Brandon?"

"I still don't know. A couple of times over break he drove back to visit, and I went up to him too."

Moments clicked into place and Asher understood the lack of communication and long gaps in their texting, his fears confirmed.

"I thought you wanted to use the breaks as, well, a break?" he asked, the hostility he tried to mask seeping out.

"I did. At least, I meant to, but there were times when I'd be bored, and when Brandon would ask what I was doing and if I told him 'nothing' he'd show up, or ask if I'd drive up," Ellis explained.

"And?"

"And we'd hang out. Sometimes it was fun and nice, and other times we'd fight and scream and yell. I thought everything was going to be simple and easy, but it's not. There's a lot of ground we have to cover, a lot of feelings that need to be expressed."

"How do you feel right now?"

"Confused. I thought I had things in check, and then I saw you today and I had to start questioning everything again. My mind is telling me that I owe it to Brandon to give things another shot, to make things work. There's so much history between us, and it wasn't as easy to just walk away from it like I thought it was going to be. It's not fair to him for me to just decide things are over when we could make it work if we tried, and I don't think I tried before ending it."

"That's a load of shit."

"What?" Ellis asked.

"You don't think you tried before? And if you really didn't try, then isn't that telling? If you cared and loved him *so* much then, wouldn't you have done everything you could to make it work? You would have stayed by his side. You keep saying that everyone around you deserves to be happy, except yourself. I think you tried for as long as you could, and it was exhausting and you fell out of love. But now you feel a sense of duty and loyalty, and you're willing to sacrifice your own ability to be happy for someone else. And that's bullshit." Asher narrowed his eyes at Ellis as he unloaded everything he had been holding back.

"I'm sorry you feel that way. You're free to have your own interpretation and thoughts, but you weren't in the relationship and can't fully understand what is going on in my head," Ellis said.

"I don't care what's going on in your head, I care about what is going on in your heart," Asher said. Ellis huffed a breath of frustration and flopped backward on the bed, resting his head on the pillow he had left behind. Asher hesitated but followed suit and lay down next to him. "Why did you want to pick me up from the airport?"

"I thought that if I picked you up and was around you again, then everything that has been so muddled would clear up for me," Ellis answered.

"And?"

"What do you think?" Ellis rolled onto his side to face Asher. Asher's eyes darted over Ellis's face, as if taking in his features for the last time and desperate to remember every detail. One minute slipped into the next, and slowly the toll of the conversation caused both of their eyelids to get heavy and start drooping. Asher blinked a dozen times to try to stay awake but exhaustion overcame him and everything slipped away.

The next time Asher opened his eyes, the room was noticeably darker. Ellis was still asleep next to him, and Asher slowly slipped off the side of the bed and tiptoed to the kitchen. He filled a glass with water, hoping the noise didn't cause a disturbance. He turned the handle and slowly opened the door to prevent creaking, and jumped a few inches into the air, sloshing water down his front, when Ellis was standing right in front of the door.

"Jeez!" Asher yelled, falling back into the door frame.

"Sorry, I wondered where you went." Ellis said, laughing. A phone vibrated while Ellis was getting his own glass, but Asher's remained silent and still in his pocket. Ellis returned and found his phone under the pillow.

"It's my mom; I promised I'd come over for dinner. Ivy's been staying with them since Thanksgiving and they're about to rip each other's heads off," Ellis said.

"Really? Why isn't she at her apartment?"

"I'm not sure; she won't tell anyone, but she's been moody, so I should really go." Ellis held his arms out for a hug. Asher could feel Ellis's chest throbbing against his own and maintained the hug for as long as possible. Neither of them wanted to release the connection, but when Ellis's phone went off again they accepted it as a cue and let go. Ellis turned to leave the room.

"You forgot your pillow," Asher remembered.

"I know," Ellis said, and walked out the door.

***

"Dammit!" Derrick exclaimed as an explosion rocked the television screen. He tossed the controller down on the couch and threw his hands up in frustration. Asher laughed and hit a couple of buttons on his own controller.

"And you guys thought I wasn't any good at this game," he said.

"You aren't any good at this game! You're supposed to kill the enemies, not me, we're on the same side," Derrick pointed out. "You're lucky Mark isn't back yet; he's going to be so mad when he realizes his online ranking has gone down because of you." Derrick picked up his controller again as his character respawned. They continued playing for another hour, and Derrick was even forced to congratulate Asher a couple of times as he got the hang of the game and defeated the correct side.

There was a knock on the door and Asher paused the game.

"Perfect, I need a new drink anyway," Derrick said, jumping up and running into the kitchen. Asher unlocked the door and was surprised to see Ellis standing on the other side.

"Hey, what are—" Before Asher could finish his question, Ellis lunged forward, placing a hand on the back of Asher's head and pulling his face forward, pressing his lips against Asher's. Asher released the door and pushed his lips forward while using his own hands to pull Ellis's hips closer.

"Don't mind me," they heard Derrick say as he passed through to the living room and returned to the couch. They broke the kiss and Ellis stepped back. Confusion and surprise flooded Asher's mind, rendering him speechless while trying to piece together the reasoning behind Ellis's sudden appearance and act of passion.

"I'm sorry, I know I can't just show up like this," Ellis said apologetically.

"Not that I disapprove, but why are you here?" Asher asked.

"Can we go for a walk?"

"Yeah, of course." Asher grabbed a jacket and they were outside and back on the path toward Asher's pool.

"From the time I left here yesterday I kept replaying everything you said in my mind," Ellis started. "And all through dinner I couldn't even focus on anything my family was saying because I just kept hearing your words. And they made perfect sense. Then this morning Brandon asked if we could meet for breakfast. The entire time I was sitting across from him all I could think was that he wasn't you."

As Ellis's words sank in, Asher allowed himself to feel a burgeoning hope. His breath caught in his throat, but his brain overloaded his body with thoughts of having been in this situation before. Ellis paused, and Asher couldn't tell whether it was to take a deep breath or for dramatic effect.

"Finally, Brandon asked me what was going on and asked if I had heard anything he said. And I hadn't—I couldn't repeat anything back to him. I apologized, pulled money from my wallet, and told him I couldn't be there. I walked out. I got in the car and called my dad, and I just broke down. And when I asked my dad what I should do, he told me to follow my heart. And that's you; it's been you since the moment we met. I could almost hear my dad smiling through the phone as he said, 'Good. You need him. He's good for you.' And I drove here."

"And your feelings for Brandon?" Asher asked, not wanting to fall back into the same situation again.

"My feelings for Brandon were that of nostalgia for what we had, and obligation. I locked them away before without dealing with them. But when I decided to actually confront what I was feeling, it was more of an idea of what used to be there. I tried to ignore it, but it overwhelmed me, especially from the time I saw you at the airport. I'm not suppressing my feelings for Brandon any longer, I'm letting them go."

Ellis opened the gate to the pool and they claimed their usual seats. Asher asked, "So what does this mean for us? What are you wanting?"

"I know we can't just start over and pretend none of this happened. I know I've compromised your trust in me, and I'll have to earn that back. But I want to move slowly and do things right this time, and I want to be with you." Ellis reached over and squeezed Asher's hand.

"I'd like that. You're right, we can't just ignore the past few weeks, but we can get through this together. Because honestly, I can't imagine being with anyone other than you. You make me feel safe and complete, and you give me the strength to face and overcome challenges," Asher said.

"It's just like our first date, except no drunk neighbor is passed out." Ellis laughed.

"I didn't realize that was our first date," Asher pointed out.

"Yeah, but that was the night I knew there was something special about you." Ellis smiled.

"Oh really? What brought you to that realization?"

"How shy and bashful you were when it came time to strip down."

"And I should have known by how readily you took your clothes off that you were going to be trouble." Asher laughed.

57. WENDY

After

"Good job, Jayden," Wendy croons, looking down into the evenly spaced holes he dug in the flowerbed. "Here, these are tomato seeds. Drop them down into the holes and then cover them back up, please, so Marie can sprinkle some water on them."

After handing Jayden the packet, Wendy turns her focus to the lake where Tonya stands on the paddleboat dock with the little girl, handing her the watering can they found.

"Miss Wendy, what about me?" Frankie asks, wiping his dirt-covered hands on his shorts.

"I'll come check now," Wendy answers with a smile, following him. They make it halfway across the pavilion when the gunshot sounds from the castle. Everyone jumps and halts. When Wendy looks down, she sees the eyes of the children on her and Tonya staring up at the castle. Marie looks up at Tonya, confused. "It's fine, don't worry, keep working."

Wendy nudges Frankie forward and continues to his dig site, waiting for Tonya to approach her. She gives him thumbs-up and a packet of green bean seeds before Tonya stops two yards away and she excuses herself.

"You don't think it's anything serious, do you?" Tonya asks.

"No, it was only one shot. There would have been more by now otherwise. Maybe one of them got too close to the outer fence and was within firing range? I'm sure whichever watchman it was cleared it with Mag or George," Wendy answers.

"You're right. I'm just on edge," Tonya says.

"Is Todd with the gatherers today?"

"No, he's on backlot patrol. I always hated him being a cop too and was nervous whenever he went to work."

Wendy squeezes Tonya's hand. "Do you want to run up to the camp and make sure everything is in order? I don't mind staying with the kids."

"No." Tonya returns to Marie. Wendy checks on Charlotte's progress and helps her plant and bury cucumber seeds. Marie is watering the seeds and the other three children are digging new holes when a round of gunfire bursts through the air again, but it does not stop at one shot. Instead, it continues, intermixed with yelling. Tonya lifts Marie off the ground and the girl drops the watering can. The other three children begin to panic, looking from the castle to the direction the shots are coming from, to Tonya and Wendy.

"That's not nothing," Tonya says.

"If I'm not back in five minutes get them on a paddle boat and get out on the lake and wait for me or someone else to come back," Wendy says.

"I want to come with you," Frankie pleads.

Wendy holds up her hand to stop him. "Stay here with Miss Tonya; I'll be right back."

"I want my mom," Charlotte screams.

"And Rico," Jayden says.

"I'll get them, I promise, but they would want you all to stay here," Wendy says.

"Be safe," Tonya says. "Come on, kids, let's get down to the dock."

Wendy bounds up the stairs two at a time. Camp is in disarray—people running back and forth, grabbing items, and dodging around each other as the gunshots carry on. Five infected people come around one side of the castle, unnoticed by the refugees.

"Look out!" Wendy screams across the camp but nobody pays her any mind. Charlotte's mom is stuffing items into a bag, oblivious to the woman stumbling up behind her. "Ashley! Turn around!"

There is too much commotion for Ashley to hear her own name. Wendy continues screaming and tries to dart across the camp but is slowed down by people bumping into her and blocking her path. A large body slams into her side, knocking her to the ground, and she rolls two yards into the side of an improvised tent, causing it to collapse down around her. Wrestling to get free of the tarp, she starts to panic and flail. Finally, her head bursts free and she gets her arms out of the wrappings, throwing it aside. She looks to the spot where Ashley was standing and is relieved to no longer see her, but when Wendy's gaze sweeps around the mess, she spots Ashley backing away from the infected woman, clutching her bleeding right shoulder, the color drained from her face.

Wendy regains her feet and seizes her hunting knife from its calf sheath. Flexing her fingers around the handle, she sprints up behind the woman and slices the blade through her throat. Ashley stares at Wendy, her chin quivering, in fear.

"Did she bite you?" Wendy asks.

"Please," Ashley begs.

"Did she bite you?" Wendy repeats.

Instead of answering, Ashley turns and runs, dropping the bag she was packing. Clothes and toys spill out of it, Charlotte's belongings. Wendy faces another infected, its body is emaciated and its flesh graying. She stabs the knife through its eye before kicking it away from her. A man runs up to the campfire and pulls out a burning log. He upsets the balance of the pot and it topples over, spilling boiling water that splashes up on the legs of other refugees. The man swings the log at one of the infected like a baseball bat and hits it in the chest, lighting its clothing on fire.

The infected person continues moving forward, reaching for the man and falling over on top of him. The burning log rolls along the ground, igniting a backpack as the man's screams fill the air. George stands in the open doorway of a store, watching the chaos with his hands covering his mouth.

"Where's Mag?" Wendy asks when she reaches him. He looks past Wendy without acknowledging her. Grabbing and shaking his forearm, Wendy says, "George, snap out of it."

He jerks away, the physical touch electrifying him, and his eyes drift to Wendy. He says, "They're being too loud."

"Stay in here; lock the door," Wendy says, shoving him backward into the store and slamming the door in his face. Half of the campsite is engulfed in flames; what is not burning is in shambles. Wendy checks the time on her watch and realizes Asher's shift in the tower has long since ended. Rushing across the street, she grabs the door handle of the store they live in and pulls, but it will not open. She keeps pulling at the handle with her left hand while knocking on the glass with her right hand and the knife. "Hey, unlock this door!"

Cupping her hands on the glass, she peers inside. People are gathered in a huddle along the back wall. Her eyes connect with Marsha's, and she beckons her to the door. Marsha shakes her head no without breaking eye contact. Wendy steps back from the door just in time to see the reflection of an infected approaching her. She spins around, swiping her hand with the knife out in an arc along the man's throat. He collapses at her feet.

The camp is essentially abandoned. Wendy watches the back of a man trying to crawl away, leaving a trail of bloody handprints, with his left leg on fire. She jogs up to his side, and he lifts his face to see who is approaching. His entire face is covered in scratches and blood, his lip is busted, and the pinky on his right hand is missing. It is Mr. Nichols, the elementary school teacher. The fire spreads up to his thigh and he tries to shake off the flames. There is a towel nearby and Wendy grabs it and throws it over his leg, doing her best to suffocate the fire and put it out. He rolls onto his back, and she hooks her arms under his armpits and drags him away from the camp and to the top of the stairs, propping his back against the railing.

"Mr. Nichols, are you okay?" she asks, getting onto one knee. His breaths are short and ragged, his head lolls from side to side. He mumbles a few unintelligible words and Wendy assumes he is going into shock. Reaching down, she grabs his right wrist and lifts it up to examine his hand. The flesh around where his pinky used to be is ragged and raw. The scratches in his face are deep bleeding grooves, three to four lines across. He is infected. She places the blade of her knife against his throat and says, "I'm so sorry."

58. ASHER

Before

"Hold on, turn up the volume." Asher reached across Ellis on the couch to grab the television remote. They were lounging at Ellis's parents' house, waiting for Ivy to get home, and the news was on.

"Cynthia Moore, a local woman, positively identified Sarah Healey as the woman that bit her left forearm," the newswoman said into the camera.

"Sarah Healey? I recognize that name," Asher said in confusion.

"Sarah Healey has been sought as a lead in a homicide investigation, believed to have murdered her husband before fleeing," the reporter continued. Asher knew her name from reading the article about her on the flight home from North Carolina.

"Wait, she's from Georgia. She made it all the way to Florida without being discovered?"

"No, look, it says on the bottom corner 'Reporting from Atlanta'"— Ellis pointed at the screen—"this is the national news not local coverage."

"Police attempted to apprehend Mrs. Healey, but she became aggressive. And after attacking an officer, she was shot in self-defense. We're investigating further. While we can't tie Mrs. Healey to any further incidents at this moment, there are similar cases that have been reported all over the country." Asher lowered the volume at the end of the segment.

"This is crazy. My mom was telling us on Christmas morning about a boy over in Clearwater that attacked his sister and bit her. The whole family was hospitalized for some illness or something."

"You didn't tell me about that," Ellis said.

"Yeah, well, I was distracted by things of slightly more importance that morning," Asher joked. The front door opened, and there was a rustling and a jingling of keys before the door shut again and footsteps carried toward the living room.

"Hey," Ivy said, her keys and purse dangling from one hand and a coffee cup in the other. She set her purse on the counter but kept her large sunglasses on, hiding half her face. Asher could distinguish the significant changes in her appearance from what small part of her face was visible. Her full cheeks had narrowed and her skin was pale, its glow diminished. "Where are Mom and Dad?"

"Dad's at work and Mom is upstairs," Ellis said, sitting upright on the couch.

"Great, as soon as I go up there she's going to try and corner me. I'm going to lock myself in the office; if she asks for me tell her I'm studying." Ivy retreated toward a room at the back of the living room and seconds later they heard a lock turn.

"Still no progress?" Asher asked.

"Nope. I even texted Wendy to ask what was going on and she never responded. I assume they had a huge falling out; it's just weird, because they're best friends and they've never fought like this." Ellis shrugged and relaxed again. Laurel descended the staircase, calling out for Ivy, but there was no response from the office.

"Did I hear Ivy get home?" Laurel asked.

Ellis hesitated before answering, but his eyes darted to Ivy's purse and his mom followed his gaze. "Yeah, she's studying."

Laurel rapped her knuckles on the door. "Ivy, I know you're in there." Music started playing through the door and a muffled response came out.

"I think this is our cue to leave." Ellis got to his feet, pulling Asher up with him. "We're heading out," he said to his mom and kissed her on the cheek.

"You're not staying until your father gets home?"

"Sorry, can't. We have plans with Asher's roommates tonight, and I didn't realize what time it was. Love you." They slipped out the door and raced across the yard to Ellis's car. Once securely buckled in and on the road, Ellis spoke again. "That was about to become a larger fight than I needed to be there to witness."

"I bet. Where to next?" Asher asked.

"We can head to my place; at least we'll be alone there," Ellis suggested. Asher agreed. His phone vibrated with a new e-mail from his dad.

> Ash,
>
> You know how much your mother and I love you, and I don't want you to ever lose sight of that. You're our son and we have a deep sense of pride for you. I can't imagine how hard it was for you to come forward with your proclamation when you were home, and how much you struggled with it. Although it does not change the way I love you, I must be fully truthful in admitting I have a hard time accepting it. I don't understand why you would choose this lifestyle for yourself and even after spending hours researching it, I can't make heads or tails of it. But I have found several programs that are capable of helping you through this time in your life and paving a path for change. I don't want you to think of money as an obligation or deterrence. I'm willing to do what it takes to help you overcome this issue. I've attached information and links for several programs and facilities that are familiar with cases such as yours, please read and consider them closely so that we can select the one you're most comfortable with. I'll never stop loving you.
>
> —Dad

Asher read the e-mail two additional times but refused to click any of the links his father had included at the bottom. His vision started to blur, and he gripped the car door for support.

"Are you okay?" Ellis asked.

"Pull over," Asher mumbled.

"What?" Ellis asked, glancing over and not understanding.

"Pull the car over," Asher repeated and released his seat belt. Ellis pulled off the road onto the shoulder and barely had the car at a complete stop before Asher shoved the passenger door open and teetered out. He took three steps and bent over, heaving and vomiting into the grass. Ellis watched from his seat and noticed the phone, the e-mail still open, on the seat. He reached out to pick it up but stopped. Instead, he unbuckled his seat belt and climbed across the console and out of the car. He approached Asher, crinkling his nose at the nauseating smell, and tried to avoid looking at the puddle on the ground.

"What's going on?" Ellis asked, grabbing Asher by the shoulders and examining his face. Asher refused to make eye contact but returned to the car and retrieved his phone. He handed it over and watched the color fade from Ellis's face as his eyes dashed through the e-mail. When he was finished reading it, he slowly looked up, aghast.

"Asher . . ."

"He wants to send me away," Asher said.

"You're not going anywhere. I promise you."

"He thinks that some doctor can *fix* me." Asher's bottom lip quivered and his eyes watered.

"There's nothing wrong with you; you're perfect the way you are," Ellis reassured him.

"He thinks I'm sick, like homosexuality is a disease that can be cured." Asher spoke more to himself than Ellis.

"You're not sick, there isn't anything wrong with you, and I'm not going to let him send you away." Ellis maneuvered Asher back into his seat, but kept his phone to prevent him from reading the letter again. He leaned into the car and kissed Asher on the forehead before returning to the driver's side. After buckling himself back in, he intertwined his fingers with Asher's. "You're not alone, you have me. I made you a promise that you'd always have me."

Ellis shifted the gear stick into drive and carefully directed the car back onto the road. Asher went directly for the bathroom when they reached the apartment to brush his teeth. After spitting out the mouthwash, he splashed water on his face, reinvigorating blood flow. He returned to the living room and curled up in a fetal position, the defeat washing back over him in waves. The small victories of the past month were reduced to nothing.

59. RICO

Before

Cold water shot out of the showerhead. Rico lifted his shirt in front of the mirror, inspecting the dark purple bruising around his ribs and stomach, cringing slightly when he poked himself in the tender areas. He locked the bathroom door and pulled the shirt up and over his head before stepping over the side of the tub and into the spray. The streams of water blasted against his skin, and he bit his lower lip to stop from screaming out. He adjusted the showerhead so the water sprayed against the wall, and he was able to wash his body and cup his hands under the water and pour it over the suds, a tedious and slow but effective process.

After gingerly drying off, Rico carefully dressed in the bathroom for a change, not wanting to take a risk of his mother catching sight of the bruises. He unlocked the door, turning toward the kitchen to force down some form of sustenance.

"Good morning, you're up earlier than usual." Melissa greeted him at the table. She was wearing her scrubs, and her hair was disheveled after a long night at the hospital. Rico passed her on his way to the fridge, but Melissa grabbed him by the arm. "What happened to your cheek?"

"It's nothing," he said, shaking her off and turning his face to hide the red burn from Doug's cigarette.

"It doesn't look like 'nothing.'" She stood for a closer look. "It looks like a burn mark."

"I messed up an experiment in chemistry yesterday and one of the liquids splashed up onto my cheek. It's fine—my teacher flushed it for me."

"All right, but I'm going to keep an eye on it while it heals. Why are you up so early?"

"Doug's not able to take me to school. It's the bus for me today," Rico said.

"The bus? Does the bus even know to stop at our house?"

"I guess we'll see." Rico pulled a bowl from the cabinet and a box of cereal off the top of the fridge, wincing as he stretched his arm out but recovering fast to avoid letting on that anything else was amiss.

"Take my car today." Melissa returned to the table and lifted a steaming mug to her lips.

"What about you?"

"I'm exhausted. I'm going to go to bed, and I don't have any intentions of going anywhere until after you're home. But you have to come straight home after school, no excuses."

"You're sure?"

"I'm positive. Just be careful. I'm going to take my tea to bed, and I'll see you when you get home. I love you." Melissa kissed her son on the cheek and left the kitchen. Rico finished eating and dumped his dishes into the sink, grabbed his backpack from the couch, the weight of which sent another shockwave of pain through his core, and snagged the keys off the hook.

He flexed his fingers around the wheel, after months of not driving, and placed the key into the ignition. The radio was turned up louder than expected, a sign of his mom's exhaustion, and Jennifer Lopez suddenly blasted through the speakers. He found a different channel but left the volume alone.

The painted sky was a foreign beauty; he was rarely awake to see the sunrise. He found his assigned parking space and reclined his seat, watching the blues become more pronounced through the sunroof as the music continued. Loud voices filled the parking lot and hundreds of students arrived in a steady influx. Rico shut off the car and pulled the key out of the ignition.

He knew that being upset, fueled by rage, and having an imminent cloud of doom following him would be justified and expected given the explosive and brutal night before and the throbbing in his abdomen. But, as he traipsed through the bright parking lot and breathed in the fresh air, he only felt a sense of hope, no matter how small. A chapter of his life had closed. The combined betrayal of Doug and Chloe finally gave him the shove needed to move forward. And he had no doubt that his serenity and newfound independence was aided by getting to drive once more. A peace spread through his bones as he stepped through the doors and into the school.

During the first two periods, Rico paid attention with genuine interest in class and took practical notes. He didn't spot Doug until he stopped at his locker before third period. Even with his new mood, Rico was pleased to see Doug's eyes were swollen and bruised from his punches. And although Rico might have imagined it, Doug's nose appeared slightly crooked. Doug avoided glancing down the hall toward Rico's locker and walked directly into the boys' bathroom to commence his selling for the day.

The lab was full of chatter when Rico entered. He took a cursory inventory of bodies around the room, but Chloe hadn't yet arrived. Rico claimed his seat and absentmindedly flipped through the book, distracting himself from watching for Chloe's entrance. The bell sounded and the class quieted down. Rico watched Mr. Evans write the experiment instructions on the dry-erase board, then his eyes darted to the left and landed on the back of Chloe's head. Mr. Evans faced the class, but before he could begin the lecture there was a knock on the door. All of the heads swiveled toward the intrusion. The door opened, and Principal Lance entered the room tailed by two police officers. Rico immediately recognized the second officer, Matty, his dad's best friend, and his stomach dropped.

"I'm sorry to disrupt your class; we need to see Enrico Martinez," Lance said. Every student turned in unison from the front of the class to the back, and Rico could feel twenty sets of eyes piercing his skin.

"Is everything okay?" Rico asked, his voice shaking.

"Please come with us, Mr. Martinez," the unfamiliar officer said, his gravelly voice stern and final.

"Matty, what's going on?" Rico pleaded. But Matty remained silent.

"Bring your belongings, Mr. Martinez," Lance ordered. The class-room was silent other than the squeak of Rico's shoes on linoleum. Rico dangled his bag from one hand and his textbook from the other. He followed Matty's lead and diverted his gaze from his fellow class-mates. The stern officer snatched the bag and textbook from his hands and handed them over to Matty. The officer grabbed Rico by the bicep and spun him around, pushing his face and chest against the wall. Rico screamed when his tender ribs hit the hard wall.

"Matty?! Matty!" Rico called, his voice shrill, humiliated in front of a room of peers. His arms were twisted behind him, and he felt the cool metal of handcuffs around his wrists, squeezed too tight and pinching his skin.

"Enrico Martinez, you are under arrest for the possession and dis-tribution of illegal substances. You have the right to remain silent; any-thing you say can and will be held against you in a court of law." The officer read him his rights, cutting off his pleas for help from Matty, and patted him down for weapons or other contraband, finding and removing only his phone and wallet in the process. Rico turned around and stared at the faces of the other students. They ranged from shock to humor until he locked eyes with Chloe, who looked sick and green, on the verge of fainting. He was jerked backward and shoved out into the hall.

The officer led Rico toward a side exit. As they passed the wing where his locker was located, Rico saw additional officers opening his locker. They were accompanied by a German shepherd and a photog-rapher. Matty held open the exit door, and Rico was pushed out into the glaring sunlight. Rico squinted his eyes, trying to adjust to the brightness, and stumbled on the sidewalk. Matty hustled in front of them to the police car parked at the curb, opened the door, and Rico was manhandled into the backseat. Rico tried his best to sit up with-out the use of his arms and jumped when the door was slammed shut. Matty sat in the passenger seat while the other officer walked around the front of the car to the driver's seat.

Rico watched out the window as they drove around the edge of the parking lot. They passed Doug's car, and Rico spotted him leaning against the trunk, his arms folded across his chest and a twisted grin on his face, full of satisfaction from setting Rico up.

60. RICO

After

A throng of infected surround the carousel, inching forward. Figures up on the second tier fire shots into the crowd when the horde gets too near. Rico walks close enough to distinguish Daniel and Ellie atop the carousel, with two other refugees cowering behind them sans guns.

Too many threats block the path to the castle for him to make the straight shot across. He can attempt to fight, but even with the frontline being taken out by Daniel and Ellie, it will be impossible to single-handedly push through the back. A bush next to him rustles and he braces himself, holding the tire iron up in defense. Aubrey's face appears between the bush and the wall.

"Rico?"

Aubrey grabs Rico's blood-soaked shirt and pulls him down to the ground and behind the bush as well.

"What the hell is going on?"

"We don't know. Everything was going fine until we heard the first gunshot," Aubrey says.

"So that wasn't you guys?"

"No. We radioed the castle, but only Rob answered and he didn't know anything. Then a couple of those things drifted into the park. We took the first few out easily enough without the guns, but they were like a freaking hydra. Every time we took out one, two more appeared. We retreated, but they started pouring in from everywhere. We didn't have a choice but to start shooting them, and the more you shoot them the more they're drawn to you."

"Why aren't you up there with the rest of them?"

"Got separated. Too many of them got between me and the group, so I stopped shooting, letting the others provide enough of a distraction so I could slip away. They've got to be almost out of ammo and I can't just leave them there, but there hasn't been a chance for me to get through to grab reinforcements."

"You don't know, do you?" Rico asks.

"Know what?"

"There's a ton of black smoke in front of the castle. I think the camp is on fire, but the breeze is carrying it in the opposite direction so you wouldn't see it from here. Whatever is going on is happening there too," Rico answers.

"Where's Yuki?" Aubrey asks, looking around when he realizes that Rico's alone.

"We think some people were trapped back there. She stayed to try and help so I could get back to Jayden, but I don't even know if that's possible now," Rico says.

They hear a yell, and when Rico and Aubrey peek out above the bushes, they see Daniel rip Ellie's gun from her and shove his own at her. He unleashes on the mob, firing the gun, throwing caution to the wind.

"He's going to get them all killed," Rico says. He thinks of his family, everyone he lost, Jayden. "We've got to do something."

The sunlight fades and the surroundings are cast into shadows. Rico and Aubrey look into the sky and see a large storm cloud has accumulated, blocking the sun. Sprinkles of water are followed by a torrential downpour. Blood is washed away from Rico's hair and face, the red streaming from his browned skin. Lightning crackles through the air, and a roll of thunder sounds from nearby.

The infected become disoriented as the thunder drums louder than the gunshots, and those toward the back of the crowd are unsure of the source of noise. Their clothes become heavy with water, weighing them down and slowing the pace of the thinnest and weakest of the bunch.

"Go!" Aubrey shouts over the storm. He shoves himself against the bushes to let Rico climb past him and remain hidden. Staying crouched, Aubrey readies his gun and begins shooting the infected blocking Rico's path.

Rico reaches the corner of the building where the bushes end. Red-tinted water flows by the bushes, pouring into a storm drain along with bits of flesh and a finger. Rico jumps out from behind the bushes, splashing into a huge puddle. The water floods his shoes but he keeps moving forward, slipping and sliding along the way. A woman lunges after him but loses her footing on the slick pavement and crashes. An infected man reaches out for Rico, but his head snaps backward and he falls over. Rico glances down as he passes the man—there is a fresh bullet hole in his forehead.

The third encounter requires Rico to defend himself, and he swings the tire iron at a small girl who is roughly his own age and is missing her bottom lip. The tire iron connects with her temple but slides out of his fingers, sleek with rain. Rolling across the ground, it lands in the outer rim of the crowd and is repeatedly stepped on by several pairs of feet. Rico jumps over the girl's body and runs for the castle.

His foot lands on the pavement at the wrong angle and he tumbles to the ground. One of the thinner men hobbles toward him, leaning over, and falls on top of Rico's back. Climbing to his knees, Rico tries to twist and pull away from the man as his hands slap against Rico's back, searching for a hold. There is a tight pressure on the right side of Rico's rib cage, and when he looks down, he sees the man attempting to bite through his drenched T-shirt. He elbows the man repeatedly in the head, while gritting his teeth and pushing up with his legs to stand, but his foot slides again.

A heavy force pushes the man closer to Rico, pressing his body further into the ground, but all of the weight quickly lifts away. Without having the man on him, Rico easily gets up and turns around to face Yuki. The tiara is missing from her head, and her hair is plastered to her face from the rain. She smiles and wrenches the ax from the man's back. She turns her ax against the quickly approaching threats, taking out the nearest four people, while Rico stands behind her, watching in awe.

The woman that stood in the restaurant door earlier frowning at them has a machete in hand and is vigorously slashing her way through the infected one by one. Daniel stands at the second-tier railing, slaughtering them methodically rather than mowing down a few with a spray of bullets. Aubrey is on his feet, no longer hiding behind the bush, and wiping them out from the back.

A gunshot resonates from the right, and Rico turns his attention away from the fight. Wendy stands twenty feet away with her feet planted and a shotgun in her hands. She cocks the gun and pulls the trigger again, blasting the side of the head off one of the infected.

"Where is Jayden?" Rico asks.

"He's safe. He's with Tonya and the other kids," Wendy answers. She pulls a pistol from her waistline and hands it to him.

Standing shoulder to shoulder, Rico and Wendy unload into the rapidly shrinking crowd. They step gingerly through the pile of bodies, closing in on the remaining threats.

"I'm out of ammo," Rico says. Wendy holds out the shotgun to him and reaches down, grabbing her hunting knife.

Within minutes, every infected has been decimated. The rain continues to pour, washing away their fear. Daniel and Ellie descend from the carousel alongside the two refugees and join Wendy, Rico, Aubrey, Yuki, and the frowning woman on the path back to the camp and the castle.

"How did they get in?" Wendy asks as they walk.

"We don't know. It's like they came out of nowhere," Aubrey answers.

"What happened back at camp? I saw smoke," Rico says.

Before Wendy can answer, they round the bend and see what remains. Black smoke tendrils continue to drift up through the rain but the flames have been doused by the weather. Several scorched bodies lay among the camp debris. The tarps are all burnt away along with the ropes, and several plastic chairs have melted. The tins used for boiling water are scorched but otherwise salvageable, and they set them upright to begin collecting rainwater. Rico follows Wendy, past Mr.

Nichol's body, down to the lake. Tonya, shovel in hand, stands firmly in front of the huddled kids on the end of the dock. Jayden sees Rico and takes off running, breaking away from everyone else. Ignoring the rain, Jayden sprints out from under the dry cover of the dock overhang and jumps into Rico's arms.

"I didn't know if you were coming back," Jayden cries into Rico's neck.

"I promised you, kid," Rico says, tightening his hold on his brother.

"Where's my mommy?" Charlotte asks Wendy when the rest of the kids and Tonya reach her and Rico.

"I didn't see her," Wendy lies, but her uneven voice betrays her. Rico looks at her questioningly but lets it go. He can surmise the truth.

"And Todd?" Tonya asks.

"Nowhere," Wendy says more firmly and honestly.

61. ASHER

Before

Dale slid by Asher and grabbed a wrapped stack of cups to refill the waning supply while Asher ground coffee beans to make a fresh pot. Asher turned the grinder off and tapped the side to release any caught bits. Once the coffee was brewing he grabbed a rag and scrubbed the espresso machine.

"Slow day," he said, glancing around the empty café.

"Yeah, no kidding. That's the first time all day I've had to refill cups," Dale agreed. Asher checked the clock and saw he only had twenty minutes left in his shift. He used the remainder of his time to refill the milk containers and sweep the floor as slowly as possible between a couple of orders here and there. At three o'clock, his afternoon relief arrived in the form of Shane, a freshman new to Cup O' Joe that semester.

"I'm clocked in, so you're good to go," Shane said, giving Asher a thumbs-up.

"I thought Samantha was supposed to come in?" Dale asked.

"She texted me this morning and asked if I could cover for her. I guess her roommate was sick yesterday, and then when she woke up today, she wasn't feeling well either and didn't want to spread it to anyone," Shane explained. "Was I supposed to check in with you and make sure it was okay? She told me it'd be cool."

"Nah, it's cool; I just didn't know." Dale waved him off.

"In that case, I'm out." Asher untied his apron and walked to the back to clock out. Outside the library, he unzipped his backpack to find his phone. A missed call from Brady was displayed, the first form of communication with him since Christmas. Asher dialed his brother, and Brady answered on the fourth ring.

"Hello?" Brady said.

"Hey, I saw you called. I was at work," Asher said, hoping he came off as friendly.

"Do you have time to talk right now?" Brady asked. Asher looked at the students milling around campus, and perched on a bench near a large fountain.

"Yeah, I don't have class or anything," he answered.

Brady cut right to the point. "Dad told me you didn't respond to the e-mail he sent you last week."

"Can you—" Asher stopped himself. He was about to ask whether Brady could blame him, but with Brady not speaking to him since he came out, he knew that, yes, Brady could blame him. Instead, he said, "No. I didn't. I didn't know how I was supposed to respond to that."

"Did you look at any of the programs we found?" Asher was thrown off by his use of "we"—he hadn't realized that Brady was in on the idea of sending him to "Pray the Gay Away" camp.

"Honestly? No. I'm not going to participate in any of those programs, so I don't need to look at them," Asher answered.

"I really think you should reevaluate your decision, Ash. We only want what's best for you." There was an indignant self-righteousness to Brady's voice, and Asher knew Brady wanted what was best for Brady's reputation, not for Asher.

"If you wanted what was best for me, you'd realize that I'm happy. This is the first time in a long time I've felt truly happy. I don't have to hide myself anymore or pretend to be someone I'm not," Asher said.

"You're an adult, Asher, you're free to make your own decisions. I just hope you realize how selfish you're being and how much you're hurting the family."

"Jesus! Do you hear yourself, Brady? I'm the selfish one? I'm not the one trying to get someone committed for a psychological evaluation and mind alteration." Asher could feel rage bubbling in his chest. He should've expected this from Brady. His mother's voice whispered to him to count to ten.

"I just want you to get better," Brady said, and he almost sounded sincere.

"There isn't anything wrong with me!" Asher shouted. He stopped counting in his head and was tempted to throw his phone into the fountain out of frustration. Several students turned to look at him and he slouched to appear smaller. "Does Mom know what you two are doing?"

There was a pause before Brady answered. "She doesn't agree with us."

"Well, there you have it. So you aren't thinking of 'what's best for the family,' you're thinking of what's best for you. Are you embarrassed by me, Brady?" Asher asked the question that had been on his mind since the moment Brady stormed away from the breakfast table.

"If you're not going to fix this, I can't have you around my kids. They can't be influenced by you," Brady said, effectively answering the question without a direct yes.

"Go screw yourself," Asher said, and hung up. He closed his eyes and counted to ten before unchaining his bike.

***

Ellis was waiting for Asher on the couch and watching Mark and Derrick play video games. Asher waved to him before stomping into his room and stripping off his work uniform. Ellis entered the room as Asher pulled up a pair of sweatpants. Asher ignored him and pulled a shirt from the dresser, but before he got his head through the hole, he launched into a retelling of the call with Brady.

"He doesn't want you around his kids?"

"Nope, says I'm going to 'influence them.' As if touching someone makes them gay. If anyone needs to be medically evaluated it's that twisted bigot," Asher said.

"It's going to be okay, they'll come around." Ellis reassured him with a hug.

"He's such an asshole," Asher responded, but he was exhausted and the fight was already slipping out of him. Ellis guided Asher backward to the bed, and when the back of Asher's knees hit the mattress, he fell over, Ellis landing next to him.

"You're with me, you're safe. Your friends are on your side, and your mom is on your side. Things work themselves out when you give them time." Right as Asher fully relaxed, Ellis's phone rang and broke the spell. "It's my dad, hold on. Hey, Dad."

Asher watched Ellis's jaw drop and his eyes flood with tears. Ellis staggered backward against the wall and the phone slipped from his hand. Asher scrambled to his feet and snatched the phone from the floor.

"Hello? Mr. Williams?"

"Asher?"

"Yeah. Ellis just dropped the phone—is everything okay?" Asher crouched to check on Ellis, who looked as if he had seen a ghost.

"I'm on my way to the hospital right now. Laurel is with Ivy in the ambulance; can you get Ellis in the car and bring him to Orlando Memorial?"

"Yes, of course," Asher said. The line went silent, and Asher slipped the phone into the pocket on Ellis's shirt. "Come on, we've got to go." He helped Ellis stand and grabbed his keys from the desk. Ellis started talking once they were in the car.

"Ivy took a bunch of pills."

"What?"

"My mom got home and found her on the bathroom floor. She called 911 and forced her to throw up."

"I'm so sorry, Ellis. She's going to be okay; remember what you just told me, things find a way of working themselves out." Asher squeezed Ellis's thigh, unsure if his words held any merit, and watched for signs toward the hospital.

"She's so stupid. Why won't she tell anyone what's going on? Why won't she tell *me*?"

"I don't know. But you can't think about that right now."

Asher pulled into the emergency room parking lot but couldn't find a parking space. He drove up to the door and let Ellis out before sweeping the lot for a second time. Finally, he pulled onto the grass. Asher entered the emergency room to a bustling crowd. All of the seats were occupied, and most of the walkways were blocked by those forced to stand and wait. From screaming babies to loud coughing and full-on arguing, there were a multitude of sounds assaulting him while he searched the crowd for Ellis or his parents. He sent a quick text.

A: I'm in the ER, can't find you . . . ?

A nurse squeezed past Asher and called out four different names. The crowd became agitated as people pushed and shoved past each other to reach the nurse and follow her through a set of double doors. Claustrophobia crept in and, mixed with Asher's concerns, caused him to feel swallowed by the room. He slipped back out the sliding doors to get some fresh air. His phone rang and Ellis's name appeared.

"Hey," Asher answered. "Where are you?"

"Hey, sorry, we're not in the ER. They had Ivy back in a room already when I got here, but it's family only," Ellis whispered into the phone.

"Oh. That's okay. Is everything okay? Is she going to be all right?" Asher asked.

"I think so. They pumped her stomach and think they got most of the pills out. She's groggy, though. We have to have some kind of meeting thing. We're waiting for someone to come talk to us."

"That makes sense. I'm glad they were able to get everything out, though."

"Me too. But we're not going to be leaving anytime soon. I don't want to be rude, but maybe you should go home? I don't want you to have to stand around waiting by yourself, and I can get a ride with my mom and dad when we leave."

"Okay. But only if you're sure. I don't mind waiting," Asher told Ellis, even though the last place he wanted to be was standing in or around the chaos of the ER.

"I'm sure. I'll let you know when we leave. I've got to go, though; I'm not supposed to be on my phone in here," Ellis said.

"I love you," Asher said, but Ellis had already hung up. He held his keys tightly in his hand and walked back to his car alone.

*****

"How is she doing?" Asher asked Ellis. They were alone on the patio of a coffee shop Ellis had suggested. Ellis pulled his sunglasses off and set them on the table, revealing the dark bags under his eyes.

"Better. She still won't talk to us about what happened, but the psychologist she's been seeing told Mom and Dad that they're making progress in her sessions," Ellis said.

"Anything from Wendy?"

"She returned one of my calls the other day. She told me she's sorry that this happened and hopes everything works out. But . . ." Ellis stopped to take a drink from his latte, cringing from the taste but needing the caffeine.

"But what?" Asher prompted.

"But she seemed more annoyed than actually concerned. I don't know, maybe I'm just imagining it. I just don't understand how they went from being so close to not even talking. Wendy didn't try to come by the hospital and hasn't been to the house," Ellis continued.

"But if she knew something, then she would say it, wouldn't she?"

"I don't know what to believe anymore. I never in a million years would have thought Ivy would swallow a ton of pills either." Ellis rubbed his eyes.

"How're you doing?" Asher asked. It was the first time they had seen each other in the six days since he'd dropped Ellis off at the hospital. Between classes, work, and Ivy, their schedules had been full.

"I'm all right. I'm staying at my place tonight, finally. I haven't gotten much sleep at home and I just want my own bed," Ellis said.

"That's understandable. Do you want me to come over?" Asher knew he was toeing the precarious line between helpful and intrusive.

"That's part of the reason why I asked you to meet me for coffee—I really just need a night to myself, free from any distractions."

Asher flinched at being lumped in as a distraction. If anything, he thought, distractions would be a welcomed reprieve, as it would provide Ellis a focus other than the devastating situation at home. But evidently they had different interpretations of Asher's offer.

"I understand," Asher said, not understanding at all.

"I'm sorry, I know that isn't what you want to hear. I'm just so drained, and I don't want to have to entertain or maintain a conversation. Or really even think," Ellis explained. Asher nodded.

"Don't worry about it, it's cool." Asher sat back in his chair, occupying his hands with his coffee.

It was apparent that both of them had finished their drinks, but they remained sitting without speaking, looking anywhere but at each other.

"I should probably go." Asher gave in. "I've got a paper I need to get started on."

"Me too. The needing-to-go part, not the paper." Ellis held out his arms for a hug and promised, "I'll see you soon."

They got in separate cars, and at the parking lot exit they waved to each other before turning in opposite directions. It struck Asher as odd how quickly he arrived home, even by maintaining the speed limit. The streets were mostly devoid of traffic, which was irregular for the area.

***

Asher locked himself in his bedroom and opened his computer to begin researching his paper. When he signed on to the intranet system, his access was impeded by a large alert. Clicking on the caution sign, he was redirected to a new page.

> Due to the increasing number of ill students, it is preferred that students only attend classes if in exceptional health. Faculty and staff are aware of the situation and advised to assist students, as possible, in maintaining curriculum outside of the classroom.

There were multiple links under the warning for resources available at students' disposal, both academically and for health purposes. Asher had received e-mails from all of his professors explaining that assignments could be turned in electronically if students were unable to attend the class periods, and one professor had outright switched the class to online only. Another e-mail from his boss relayed that all food and beverage facilities were temporarily suspended on campus, which, unfortunately for the employees, meant they were in a holding pattern before being able to return to work.

"Hey, did you guys see the notice from the school?" Asher asked, walking out to the living room.

Renee paused the movie she and Mark were watching and looked over the back of the couch at Asher. "Yeah, why do you think I'm not in class right now?"

"Are you sick?" Asher took a step backward.

"For all intents and purposes, we both are," Mark answered and held up a beer to toast himself before swigging it down.

"Derrick went to class, but he's been on campus since before the notice went out, so I think he figured he might as well stay," Renee said.

"We've gotten progressively slower at work over the past week, but I didn't think anything of it," Asher said. "Has there been anything on the news about what's going on?"

"Let me check." Renee switched the channel to the local news. They watched a report about the hospitals in the area reaching capacity, one of which suffered an attack by a man who'd turned violent and angry when the wait to be seen was exceptionally long. Other reports included preschools and daycares shutting down due to the weaker immune systems of young children.

The national news featured a live interview from New York City with a representative for the Centers for Disease Control and Prevention. He had salt-and-pepper hair, and his face was set and unreadable.

"—understand everyone's concern, we are experiencing similar reports here in New York City as well. But the key point we're relaying to the public is a need to remain calm. Panic leads to hysteria, which becomes a breeding ground for misinformation," Salt-and-Pepper said.

"But isn't it fair to say that this started in The City?" the reporter asked.

"No, we do not believe there is evidence for such a claim," Salt-and-Pepper answered.

"Reports place New York at the top of the list of infected citizens. Patient Zero, James Harrelson, was a resident of—"

"New York City has the highest population in the United States; it stands to reason that the numbers of those reportedly sick would be high. I cannot condone usage of words such as 'infected' and 'Patient Zero,' however, as they suggest a widespread pandemic."

"Well, you *are* calling in from a fallout shelter, so evidence would suggest you believe similarly," the reporter snapped back.

"I'm sorry, Miss, but I have to go." Salt-and-Pepper stood up and his feed cut out, but not before Asher noticed a symbol of an "A" inside a half circle on the wall behind the man.

"What is this, the black plague?" Mark scoffed.

"I don't know, has anyone died from it yet?" Renee asked. Asher retrieved his computer from his room. After minutes of fruitless browsing on different news sites, he searched "James Harrelson" and found an article from two weeks earlier.

UNKNOWN ILLNESS RAPIDLY TAKES LIVES OF YOUNG BOY AND FAMILY

James "Jimmy" Harrelson, aged 8, was the first of his family to succumb to an unknown illness at a hospital in Clearwater, FL. James Harrelson first appeared in the news after attacking his older sister, Meghan Harrelson, during a Christmas service at a local church and being hospitalized soon after. Doctors have yet to identify the exact cause of James's actions, only stating symptoms of an extremely high fever and acting out in a rage that was inconsistent with his general behavior. Meredith Harrelson and bitten sister, Meghan, were hospitalized soon after James, and at the time of this article all three have passed away.

Asher read the article to Renee and Mark, the line about Jimmy's rage-like behavior standing out. He keyed in a quick search of "Sarah Healey" and discovered the article he read on the plane describing her irregular behavior. Another search of "unknown illness" brought up articles detailing similar scenarios in growing abundance, not only across the country but internationally as well, with reports from England, France, and even India.

"Whatever this is, it's spreading like wildfire," Mark commented after hearing the other articles from Asher. The front door opened and all three of them jumped; Renee let out a scream.

"Whoa, what's going on in here?" Derrick asked.

"Sorry, you caught us off guard," Renee said.

"How was campus?" Asher asked.

"Dead," Derrick responded.

"What?!" Renee exclaimed.

"There was hardly anyone there—they issued a blanket sick excuse, so even people that aren't actually sick took advantage of it," Derrick said.

"Like you two," Asher pointed out, looking at Renee and Mark.

"We should have a party." Mark let out a loud belch.

"Yeah, everyone is sick, so we should celebrate." Derrick rolled his eyes and disappeared into his room.

"The world is falling apart, might as well be drunk to watch it all go down," Mark called after him.

Asher left Mark and Renee to their movie and returned to his room. He checked his phone but hadn't received any texts or calls. He debated whether calling Ellis out of concern would annoy him or touch him, but gave in and placed the call anyway. After five rings it clicked over to voice mail.

"Hey, it's me. I didn't know if you saw the news or the announcement from school. There's a pretty bad flu or something going around. I know you want to be alone tonight; I just wanted you to know I was thinking of you and that I love you." Asher hung up and dropped the phone onto his bed. Feeling overwhelmed, he collapsed onto the bed and buried his face into Ellis's pillow.

62. WENDY

After

The rain lightens up as they climb the stairs. By the time they reach the top, spots of blue sky and sunshine are breaking through the clouds. Wendy spots Marsha and a few others gathering ruined items into a pile, and looks over at the storefront where the entrance door now stands open. She scans the faces but none of them are Asher. A quick scan of the store reveals that it's now empty, but Wendy strides through to their sleeping space anyway.

Asher's pack is in its usual space—his baseball bat leaning up against it. She turns the pack upside down, spilling the contents on the ground. His flashlight rolls across the floor and the navy hoodie lands softly at her bent knees. She picks up the hoodie to stuff it back into the empty bag and feels something firm inside. Unwrapping the hoodie, she finds Asher's yellow journal covered in stickers. An elastic band holds it shut. Wendy carefully folds the journal back into the hoodie and returns it to the bag.

Approaching footsteps catch her attention and she regains her composure before turning to face Aubrey.

"You all right?" he asks.

"I don't know where Asher is," Wendy says, her voice shaking. "I haven't seen him since this morning when I took him food."

"We'll find him. He probably saw the infiltration and took cover in the castle." Aubrey pulls Wendy into a tight hug.

"Maybe. But his shift ended before the first shot. I can't shake the feeling that something's wrong."

"We'll sort it out," Aubrey says. "We're going back out."

"After what we just faced?"

"We haven't heard from the castle since the first shot, and then only one person answered our call. We don't know why we weren't given a heads-up on the attack, how nobody saw that many of them coming, or how they even got in. Nobody has seen Mag since we left this morning. There's a good possibility some of them are still wandering around, but Daniel, Ellie, and I are going to find as many answers as we can. We can't afford to chance anything. While we're out there I'll keep an eye out for Asher, I promise. In the meantime—"

Aubrey holds out a flask. Wendy graciously accepts it and takes a swig to calm her nerves. The warm liquid burns her throat and she hands it back. She follows Aubrey out of the store into the humid and rain-free camp. The smell of blood is overwhelming, even with the weather flushing most of it away. The opposite storefront door opens and George comes blundering out, gazing around the camp with his bug eyes, and mumbling.

"What's he saying?" Aubrey asks.

Wendy slowly approaches George and places her hand on his arm. Jerking away from her touch, he looks at her with caution but continues to mumble.

"It's okay, George," Wendy says, inclining her head to hear him better.

He continuously repeats the same word, or name: "Mag."

"Do you know where Mag is?" Wendy asks.

"Mag. Mag. Mag," he repeats.

***

The next several hours are spent dragging bodies from the comic land and in front of the castle into a pile near the carousel where they are being stacked up. Accustomed to Florida rains, the refugees stashed a large stock of dry wood in one of the stores, and they stack the pieces on and around the wet bodies.

Dragging her third corpse toward the pile, a flash of yellow catches Wendy's attention. She drops the body's legs and reaches down to its arm, pulling back the man's sleeve. A bright-yellow plastic bracelet, like one placed on patients at a hospital, circles his emaciated wrist. The cleanliness of the bracelet is in stark contrast to the muddled clothing hanging off the body, and it appears fresher than when he was infected. Wendy spins the band until a series of letters and numbers are displayed: SBJ1104.

She faces the pile, her eyes searching. An arm sticks out at an odd angle, the sleeve caught on the end of a boot, and a sliver of yellow is barely visible under the fabric. Abandoning the corpse she was dragging, Wendy charges toward the arm, ripping back the sleeve, and stares at an almost identical band. The only difference is the number: SBJ1127. Using her hunting knife, she slices the bracelet off and shoves it into her back pocket. She turns around to retrieve the first band and the corpse is gone.

"Wait!" Wendy calls out to a man hefting the corpse onto the pile. She cuts off SBJ1104 and places it in her back pocket as well. The man tosses the body into the mix and pulls Wendy back.

After squirting lighter fluid on the wood and the top bodies, Rico takes a match, lights a park map on fire, and throws it into the mound of corpses. Within seconds, the entire pile is engulfed and Wendy is overcome by the stench of burning flesh and hair.

"Wendy?" Marsha steps up, timidly wringing her hands. When Wendy watches her without responding, she continues, "About earlier, when I wouldn't open the door—"

"I get it." Wendy cuts her off.

"That's not me; I was just so scared," Marsha says.

"You had to protect yourself and the others in there. You did your job," Wendy says.

"But you protected us all. I don't know if I'll ever forgive myself. It was a lapse in judgment." Marsha bursts into tears.

"I forgive you," Wendy says with finality.

Marsha wipes her eyes and grabs Wendy's hand. "Thank you."

Night begins to fall, but the sixteen remaining refugees stand by the fire regardless of the smell, simply appreciating not being part of the bonfire of bodies. Nobody has eaten since morning but if anyone has an appetite, it goes unsaid, even by the children. A noise from the dark startles them all and they jump to their feet, braced and armed.

Mag is first to step into the circle of light cast by the fire, and someone behind Wendy gasps. Mag's hair hangs limply around her face, but the metallic sheen of the tape covering her mouth reflects the flames. She stumbles forward several feet, crashes down on her knees, and falls onto her chest. A line of rope binds her arms behind her back. She raises her head, her eyes moving from face to face looking for help, but nobody makes a move.

Next to step into the light is Daniel, his knuckles white from his grip on the gun, standing over Mag. Three more bodies follow him out of the shadows, two with the physical builds of men and the third, walking between the men, with a smaller and slight build. They have shirts thrown over their heads as makeshift hoods. Aubrey and Ellie are the last to come into the light, prodding the hooded figures in the back with their guns and then knocking them to their knees.

There are whispers through the air behind and around Wendy but she keeps her focus on Aubrey and the blank look on his face, giving away nothing.

"Today we lost several members of our community," Daniel begins. "Men and women were killed because of the careless actions of those we trusted to keep us safe. The watchmen on the castle have failed us, maintaining silence as they've watched us fight for our survival on the ground. Cowards granted positions of safety by a foolish leader. But her faults have caught up to her; she entrusted what is the most valuable position for our safety to the wrong men, and they have failed her as well by letting those things in."

Daniel reaches down, grabbing a handful of Mag's hair and pulling her head back. Three long red marks run down the side of her neck, smeared with blood.

"When we found her, she had already been scratched and was trying to hide. The woman that has led us all this time was ready to change, and kill us, because she was too scared to stand by the oath she took to do only what was best for the camp. I'm in charge now, and I am not afraid to do what it takes."

Releasing his grip on her hair, Daniel stands back up and steadies his gun. The sound of the shot rips through the air and Mag's head snaps forward to the ground. There is a scream and crying, but Wendy forces herself to remain still. Only when the blood pools around Mag does Daniel begin talking again.

"In our perimeter search we found multiple portions of the outer fence completely cut in half. Those creatures do not maintain the ability to handle tools—they are completely incapable of cutting through a fence so precisely, but someone wanted them in here. Someone wanted them to take us out, and we found them."

Daniel moves so that he is positioned behind the first and larger of the two men.

"These are the three that unleashed today's terror on us. Because of them, and the gross neglect of our leader, your friends are dead. Your family members are dead. And I will make them pay; I will make sure today never happens again. And now they will face what they've done. They will look into the eyes of those of us that remain, and they will know regret before they die."

Grabbing the shirt, Daniel tugs it up and off the unknown man's head. Messy, sweaty black hair frames his face and tape is wrapped entirely around his head, ensuring his scraggly beard did not cause it to become unstuck. His round eyes are dark to the point of appearing black, and like Mag he searches the different faces watching him for help.

Aubrey lowers his gun and reaches forward to pull the shirt off the female. Her hair clings to the inside of the fabric, and even once the shirt has cleared her head, her face is obscured by her dirty blonde hair. Unlike the man, she hangs her head instead of looking up at everyone. Daniel, visibly annoyed, grabs her by the chin and lifts her face, using his other hand to push the hair out of her eyes.

All of the air is sucked from Wendy's body, and her heart races in her chest when she sees the girl's face. It is the face that has haunted her for months, and she tells herself it's only a trick of the shadows and the flickering flames. There's no way. *She's dead,* Wendy thinks to herself, *you killed her*. But when the girl's eyes land on Wendy and widen in recognition, there is no mistaking who it is.

Ivy.

All at once every light turns on, glaringly bright against the black sky, and music blasts through all of the park speakers in a deafening roar.

63. ASHER

Before

The phone rang as Asher pulled the key from the ignition. Panic ripped through him when he saw "Mom" displayed on the screen.

"Hello?"

"Oh, thank God," Sherrie exclaimed. "I just saw on the news that your school was one of the first universities to shut down. They said that disease is rapidly spreading around the campus."

"Yeah, I got the notification this morning. Campus has been empty the past few days, so they just went ahead and told us all to stay home," Asher told her, "but don't worry, I'm fine. We're all fine at my apartment."

"That's good. Paige has been staying home for two days with the kids—Max was sent home from school for having a fever, and now their school is closed as well. Whatever he has passed to Paige; I'm on my way over to help out so she can rest. I've been so worried about you. Why don't you pack up a bag and head home? I'll transfer some money for gas to your account," Sherrie pleaded.

"Thanks, Mom, but it's not that serious. Mark is at the grocery store right now getting some food and stuff for the apartment. We're just going to hole up and play video games and stuff for a few days until it passes. I'll be fine."

"I would just feel better to have the family together right now," Sherrie said.

"I know. I tell you what, if this hasn't blown over a week from today, I'll drive up, deal?" The last thing Asher wanted at that moment was to be around Brady and their father.

"I guess," Sherrie conceded.

"I have to go, Mom, I love you."

"I love you too, Ash."

There was a chill in the air as Asher climbed the stairs to Ellis's apartment and knocked on the door. The minutes passed without any sounds coming from inside, and if Asher had not seen Ellis's car, he would have suspected nobody was home. He held the spare key in his hand, millimeters from the lock, and hesitated. He knocked one more time. Finally, he heard the lock turning, and Ellis opened the door.

"You're alive," Asher said. Ellis stood in front of him wearing gym shorts and an inside-out raggedy T-shirt with his hair disheveled, as if he threw the clothes on in haste. The bags under Ellis's eyes had deepened since the day at the coffee shop. Asher was bewildered, searching for signs that Ellis's poor health was from the stress of familial matters and not from contracting whatever sickness everyone had.

"Hey," Ellis said. He remained in the doorway, with one hand on the door frame and the handle grasped in his other hand. Asher noted the lack of excitement in his greeting.

"Can I come in?" Asher asked.

"That might not be the best idea."

"What's going on? I've tried calling you over the last few days, and I haven't heard back. I was freaking out, thinking you were sick," Asher said, his worry displacing his composure.

"Can we not do this here?" Ellis whispered.

"Do what?" Asher was mystified.

"I'm sorry, Asher, I really am. There's just too much going on right now. Between my family and yours, whatever is happening in the world, I just can't," Ellis responded.

"Are you breaking up with me?" Asher asked. Déjà vu set in, and he felt like he had been punched in the gut.

"I'm sorry," Ellis repeated.

"But I need you. You promised me." Asher tried to stop himself from begging but the words spilled out.

"God, can you try to *not* be selfish for like five minutes? Other people have shit going on in their lives, the world is crumbling, and you're only concerned with what *you* need?" Ellis shook his head. Down the hall a door opened and closed.

"Who's here?" Asher asked. Ellis moved back to shut the door, but Asher stepped forward and knocked it fully open. A black duffel bag sat on the ground right inside the doorway. Asher could hear water running as the shower started up down the hall. He looked up into Ellis's face and was fueled by rage. "And I'm the selfish one?"

"Asher," Ellis called out behind him as he rapidly descended the stairs. He cut across the grass, not bothering to use the sidewalks, and slammed the car door when he was safely in his seat. He punched the dashboard.

"Ow!" Asher howled and shook his hand as the pain raced up his skinned knuckles and into his wrist. Pulling out of the complex, he was astounded to see how many vehicles were on the road. It looked like the entire city was attempting to evacuate. He reached down and fingered the FM button on his radio and turned the volume up.

"—are grounded as the government puts a temporary suspension on air travel and closes all airports. Supermarkets have become battlegrounds as people turn physical in their desperation to stock up on supplies—"

A loud honk startled Asher and he regained his focus. He only progressed two miles in thirty minutes, in what was generally a five-minute drive. His frustration mounted even more when he looked down and his gas light was on.

"Dammit," he whispered, trying to look around the cars to see what the hold-up was, but there was no end in sight. At the next intersection, he turned off the main road, but the back road was similarly backed up. Aware that his car was running purely on fumes, he pulled off to the side of the road, parked the car, and turned it off. He scrolled through his contacts until he found Renee's number and dialed it. An automated response played back explaining that all circuits were busy and to try again later. He called his mom and received the same message.

He unbuckled his seat belt and left the car behind—his only option was to walk home.

When Asher finally came upon his complex, he was reminded of Christmas break by the emptiness of the parking lot. He entered his apartment and the air itself felt different, electrified. The moment Asher opened the door, Derrick jumped off a bar stool and raised a baseball bat.

"Whoa, it's just me!" Asher held his hands up in peace.

"Where the hell have you been?" Renee asked, stepping out of the kitchen holding up a skillet. "We've been trying to call you."

"I tried calling *you*; I got a notification that the lines were busy. Where's Mark?" Asher asked.

"Lock the door," Derrick said, climbing back up onto the stool and laying the bat across his lap.

"Mark is in his room," Renee said, lowering the frying pan. "He's getting some rest after the store. It was a nightmare."

"I heard about it on the radio. The streets are crazy too; I ran out of gas and had to abandon my car on a side road." Asher walked further into the apartment and dropped his keys on the table. "Why are you guys so tense?"

Before either of them answered, Mark's door opened and he stepped out holding a dark rag to the side of his face.

"What happened to you?" Asher asked. Mark lowered the rag to reveal four deep and long gashes running down his cheek, a rivulet of blood still leaking from one.

"Some woman tried to rip my face off over a case of water," Mark explained. He walked into the kitchen and opened the fridge. Asher noticed Renee and Derrick both lock up and step out of his way as he passed. He grabbed a beer and twisted the cap off, downing half of it in one go.

"Should you really be drinking a beer right now?" Renee asked. Mark glared at her. "I'm only saying that because the alcohol will thin your blood and won't stop you from bleeding." Mark lifted a second beer from the fridge and stalked back to his room, slamming the door behind him.

Mark stayed closed off in his own room to no complaints from anyone else. When he did emerge, he was moody and everyone kept their distance. A light sheen covered his face at most times too, but he wouldn't let anyone check his temperature. Any noise from outside raised their alarm and the atmosphere had a constant sense of high alert. After one day, the Internet ran increasingly slower, and on the second day it went out altogether. Nobody was able to place or receive any phone calls, and texts remained queued for sending without going through. Occasional arguments were heard from other apartments, but with so few cars remaining in the parking lot, Asher assumed most of the complex was abandoned.

On the second night, screaming could be heard in the parking lot. Asher kneeled on his bed and pulled the window blinds apart. A girl screamed from the stairs of a neighboring building as two guys wrestled on the sidewalk. One guy gained an advantage, climbing on top of the other, and began repeatedly punching him in the face. The girl covered her mouth in horror when the guy getting punched went still and stopped fighting back. The winner of the fight stood up and looked over at the now-silent girl. She let out one last scream and began running up the stairs, getting a head start as the brawler gave chase. A second later her call for help abruptly ended, and Asher released the blinds.

They didn't see Mark at all on the third day. The few times Renee, who had been sleeping on the couch, tried his door it was locked, and he didn't respond to her knocks. Renee, Derrick, and Asher sat in a circle playing a card game to pass the time and keep their minds occupied. Derrick and Asher exchanged looks frequently between Mark's door and Renee, neither of them wanting to ask the question that was on everyone's mind.

Asher opened his door on the fourth morning to find Mark standing in the middle of the kitchen with the refrigerator door wide open. He took a step forward and jumped when a hand grabbed his forearm. Derrick stood directly next to Asher's door, watching Mark as well. Asher opened his mouth to speak but shut it when Derrick shook his head in warning. Asher looked down and noticed Derrick's clenched left hand, his knuckles white.

"What are you guys looking at?" Renee asked, sitting up from the couch.

Her voice was a trigger and Mark shot off. He spun around, faced Derrick and Asher, and lunged toward them. Derrick thrust his arm out, shoving Asher backward into his door frame and then onto his bedroom floor. He threw his left arm up defensively to block Mark. Asher righted himself into a sitting position in time to see Derrick shove Mark back into the kitchen. Derrick turned and ran down the hall toward his room. Renee screamed for Mark, who jerked his head in her direction at the sound of his name. Derrick grabbed Renee and shoved her forward in front of him and into his room, slamming the door behind them.

Mark charged from the kitchen and down the hall, slamming his body into Derrick's door. Asher sat in shock, watching as Mark continuously attempted to break through the door, and realized that Derrick and Renee were trapped. The fifth time Mark shouldered into the door it shuddered and Asher heard it crack. Asher looked around for something to help and spotted the baseball bat on the dining room table.

"Mark! Hey, Mark!" Asher called out, holding up the bat in front of himself. Mark slammed into the door again and it splintered around the handle. Asher picked up an empty beer bottle and chucked it at Mark, shattering it on the back of his head. Mark slumped forward into the door and slid to the ground, stabilizing himself on all fours. His head turned to look behind him, and Asher gasped when he saw the animalistic rage and hunger on his face. Mark snarled and shot forward like a cannon. Turning on his heels, Asher raced back to his room, slamming and locking the door. He dropped the bat on the ground and threw his weight against his desk, pushing it away from the wall and in front of the door for reinforcement.

Asher's heart jumped into his throat when he heard a tapping on his window.

"Asher! Asher, it's me." Renee's voice carried through in an urgent whisper. Asher pulled up the blinds to reveal Renee, her face streaked with tears, standing in the bushes, looking terrified and constantly glancing over her shoulders. He unlatched the lock and slid the glass up, kicking out the screen. Before he could climb out, Renee was climbing in and closing the window again.

"Where's Derrick?" Asher asked, and was answered with a loud thumping noise, something knocking against his door, and three more thumps.

"It's okay, you can open the door," Derrick called from the other side. Asher and Renee pushed the desk away from the door. Asher reached forward and noticed the carpet under the door turning red as blood seeped in from the hall.

"Wait here," he urged Renee, and opened the door an inch.

"It's just me," Derrick said, peering through the slit. Asher opened the door another foot and looked down. Mark's body was twisted on the ground, blood pooling out from his face, and a blood-soaked skillet hung from Derrick's hand.

"Oh my God." Asher stepped back, covering his mouth and dry heaving. Renee dropped to her knees, screaming and crying, at the sight of her dead boyfriend. Derrick let go of the skillet and stepped gingerly over Mark to enter the room. He put his hands on Renee's shoulders.

"Look at me," he said, trying to get her attention. Asher collapsed against his bathroom door and watched Renee break down further.

"Don't touch me!" she screamed, pulling away.

"Look at me!" Derrick screamed back at her.

"You killed him! You killed him!" Renee looked Derrick in the eyes, her face contorted in wrath, and slapped him across the face. Derrick closed his eyes and steadied his breathing. When he opened them again, he was calm and spoke evenly.

"I did what had to be done to save you. He was going to kill us all. You know that. But you need to pull yourself together, and you two need to get out of here," Derrick said, directing the last part at Asher.

"Us two? What about you?" Asher asked.

"I can't go." Derrick let go of Renee. He held up his left forearm, revealing a deep bite mark from Mark's kitchen attack. "If a scratch did that to Mark in a couple of days, then who knows how quickly I'm going to be like that"—he motioned toward the doorway—"from a bite, and you two can't be here when it happens."

"You leave," Renee said, wiping the tears from her face. She moved from the floor to the bed. "If that happened to Mark in here, then it's worse out there. You leave."

"We don't understand how this thing spreads. But Mark's blood is all over the hallway, and if either of you stay here you're putting yourself at risk," Derrick argued.

"And it's not a risk out there?" Renee shot back.

"Derrick's right," Asher said, shutting them both up. "We can't put ourselves at risk by cleaning up the blood, and we can't just leave it there. And even if we could clean it up, there's no way you could mentally handle staying here and visualizing it every time you look down the hall. I won't be able to help but visualize it just by opening my door. We have to go."

"Where are we going to go?" Renee asked, her bottom lip quivering.

Asher remained silent. His parents' house was hundreds of miles away, but even if he had a way to reach it, there was nothing waiting for him there. If Max was infected and passed it to Paige, then surely Sherrie had contracted the infection during the ensuing days.

"You could try your place," Derrick suggested.

"I haven't been home in weeks," Renee said.

"We're aware," Asher said, "but it's a start."

Thirty minutes later Asher had his backpack loaded up with food items and water bottles, the baseball bat in hand. Having changed from his gym clothes, he was wearing a pair of jeans and a T-shirt with a light hooded jacket and a pair of running shoes. He found Renee sitting on the couch with her arms wrapped around her knees. She was dressed similarly but had the hood up over her head. Derrick's bag rested next to her, filled with additional supplies.

"Are you ready?" Asher asked. Renee wrapped her hand around the strap of the bag in response. She started down the hall to the front door, but Asher guided her to the balcony instead. "Let's go this way."

Renee slipped the bag's strap over her head and opened the door, choosing to wait outside rather than to say good-bye to Derrick. Asher approached Derrick's room, and the glass from the beer bottle crunched under his shoes.

"Hey," Asher said.

"Hey," Derrick responded, looking up from his bed.

"Thank you. Y'know. For, well—" Asher struggled to find the words for what he needed to say. His throat was scratchy, his mouth dry.

"You're welcome," Derrick said, allowing the flood of tears to start slipping from his eyes.

"I'm glad I got to live with you," Asher said. He gave Derrick a half nod and left him alone. He heard a sob break forth from Derrick's chest, but kept moving through the apartment to the balcony. He climbed over the railing and into the bushes before helping Renee over as well. Vultures circled above the body of the guy Asher watched get beaten to death. The sky was spotted with the black dots of other vultures in the distance.

***

Asher and Renee took to the woods for cover to avoid detection or danger, choosing to stay off the streets for the journey to her apartment. A snapping twig stopped them and they waited with bated breath for the source.

"It's just an animal," Asher said, "probably a deer."

They changed direction anyway, and searched for the road to familiarize themselves with their whereabouts. In the days since Asher had driven back from Ellis's, the town had become a wasteland. Gagging on the smell of death, Asher pulled his shirt up over his nose. The street was a cluster of abandoned cars and crashed cars—doors open, smashed windows. Renee pointed out a ransacked gas station with shattered windows.

"The world ended while we were playing cards," she said, kicking a rock and fading back into the trees.

There was an overwhelming stench of burning, and Asher's eyes started itching from the black smoke wafting through the woods. They tried to push forward, but once their lungs started burning they were forced to retreat. Choosing a different path, they stumbled from the woods and found themselves behind a shopping center. Asher pulled a water bottle out and swished some of it around his mouth before swallowing. He handed the bottle to Renee to do the same. They slowly edged around the building and were unsettled by a scream. Asher tightened his grip on the baseball bat and charged around to the front.

"Please, just let us go." Two girls stepped backward until they were trapped against a car. Judging by their appearance—one of the girls wore a sweater with Greek letters across the chest—they were college students as well. But five people were closing in on them.

"We have to help them," Renee said, but before they could act, one of the stalkers made a sudden move. One of the girls squealed as her attacker grabbed her hair. Two others grabbed her by the arms and pulled her in, surrounding her. Her screams became garbled, and then silenced, when her three attackers tore into her with their teeth. The second girl spun around and pulled on the car handle. In a lucky break the door opened and she clambered inside, slamming it shut behind her. The other two infected bashed the window with their bare hands, but before they could shatter the window, the opposite door opened and the girl emerged and ran off, disappearing behind another building.

"Come on." Asher pushed Renee away from the chaos. They noticed the black cloud of smoke rising in the distance as they hid behind the shopping center again, the source of the fire that chased them out of the woods.

"We can't go to my apartment," Renee whispered, "I think it's on fire."

"I know somewhere we can go."

After multiple roundabouts, backtracking, and dodging the sick, Asher and Renee emerged from the woods as the sun set and looked up at the building Ellis lived in.

"Are you sure you want to do this?" Renee asked.

"What other choice do we have?" Asher rebuked. He hitched his pack higher onto his back and checked their surroundings. The lot was clear of any obstructions and they crossed to the building. Asher climbed the familiar staircase, pausing at the third-floor landing and blocking Renee with his arm. The door to Ellis's apartment was open, the space beyond dark and hushed.

"Please don't tell me that's the apartment we're supposed to be going to," Renee said.

Asher nodded. They inched toward the opening and Asher stretched his hand out along the wall for the light switch. The electricity still worked and the fluorescent kitchen light flickered on. A knocked-over bottle of wine rested on the island counter next to a half-empty wineglass; the remaining contents of the bottle had spilled out onto the floor. A second shattered wineglass was on the kitchen floor in another puddle of wine. Aside from the broken wineglass, the rest of the kitchen and living room were in order. Asher checked the front door, the duffel bag from a few days earlier was nowhere to be seen.

"He's not here," Renee said, "but why was the door open?"

"Maybe he left in a hurry, didn't bother to close it behind himself," Asher answered. It was the only explanation he could think of that gave him hope. If looters had broken into the apartment, it would be ransacked. "We can stay here, at least."

Asher dropped his bag onto the table and Renee pushed the door shut. When it clicked, they heard a bump from the bedroom. Renee's momentarily relaxed face was replaced with fear, and Asher held a finger up to his lips. The bedroom door was slightly ajar but the room was dark. His hand trembled as he reached into the room, his fingers brushing against the light switch. He flipped it upward and kicked the door in simultaneously.

The carpet was stained a dark blood red, the center of the stain looking nearly black. An arm protruded from under the bed, chunks of flesh missing, and the shredded bird-embroidered sleeve was soaked crimson and no longer covered the skin. Asher's mind whirled with visuals of someone feasting on Ellis's body, recalling the sight of the girl attacked near the car, causing his stomach to flip, and vomit spewed out of his mouth and down his front. Then he could hear heavy breathing on his left; he could feel the hot breath on the side of his face, and he turned his head in time to see a large mass jolt forward. He swung the bat while dropping down, connecting and breaking through the wall and landing on his back. Ripping the bat free, he watched as Brandon regained his stance after crashing into the door. Brandon's features matched the animalistic nature that had consumed Mark, and he let out a guttural growl. His teeth were stained red, and dried blood was caked around his mouth and chin. Asher scooted backward, bracing himself with the bat as Brandon crouched to spring. An ear-splitting bang reverberated twice from behind Asher, and Brandon's torso jerked both times before he thudded backward onto the ground, unmoving. Startled, Asher looked over his shoulder to discover Wendy standing with her feet shoulder width apart, her arms stretched outward in front of her, and a gun in her hands. She lowered the gun and gazed down at Asher.

"You all right?" she asked.

"Yeah," Asher answered, climbing to his feet. "Thanks."

Renee peeked her head into the hallway, taking in the scene before retreating back to the living room.

"We shouldn't stay here," Wendy said. "You guys can follow me to my place; it's in the next building over." She walked around Asher and flipped the bedroom light off. As they were walking out of the apartment she hit the kitchen light as well before closing the door behind them.

AUTHOR'S NOTE

Thank you, reader, for taking the time to explore Deadland with me. But as with all great theme parks, there is mystery and adventure around every corner. The journey is only beginning for these characters, and as they discover their roles in the creation of a new society, you'll want to upgrade your ticket from a seasonal to an annual pass and return for another visit when the second installment is ready to launch. There's much more to come; more rides, more restaurants, and like a roller coaster, more twists and turns. As unexplored territory in Deadland is uncovered, further secrets of the past and present will be revealed. There are two sides to a park—what the guests experience and the tricks employees know—and there is always more to a story than what skims the surface. Sometimes people, and bodies, aren't what they appear to be. You can follow *Welcome to Deadland* on Inkshares and Facebook for news on the sequel.

Until the gates reopen,
Zachary Tyler Linville
#WhatIsArchon

ACKNOWLEDGMENTS

I have so many people to thank, and I'll start with the 687 of you that pledged to help *Welcome to Deadland* in The Nerdist Collection Contest on Inkshares. And to both The Nerdist and Inkshares, for without both parties being involved, I wouldn't have had such a wonderful opportunity to be a part of this growing community. I would like to thank my wonderful fiancé, Casey, for supporting me in pursuing my dream of writing. You encourage me and make me want to be a better person; you believe in me at times when I'm unable to believe in myself. Mom, Dad, Pam, and Drew, you're the best sets of parents a son could ask for and I couldn't be luckier than to have the four of you guiding me along a path to success. Thank you to Krystyn, Michael, and Tiffani. Even when we haven't gotten along, we've always had each other's backs and stood up for one another. And few things give me more joy than stomping y'all in races. Love you, mean it. To all of my grandparents, thank you for the weekend visits when I was a child, for teaching my parents and then me, and for your continuous loving support. To my cousin Courtney, for pushing and shoving and fighting alongside me each day during the contest and lighting a fire under me. And to my Mammaw Mag, to whom I dedicated this book, you taught me to tie my shoes, shell crab legs, and read. I hope you're proud of me.

ABOUT THE AUTHOR

Photo © Kelsey Lynch Ravindran

Zachary Tyler Linville is a winner of the Nerdist Sci-Fi and Fantasy Novel Contest. After receiving a degree in film from The University of Central Florida, Zachary went on to work as a costume assistant for TV shows and movies including *Boardwalk Empire*, *The Cobbler*, *Rob the Mob*, and *See No Evil*, and as a production assistant for MTV's *The Inbetweeners*.

He currently lives in Atlanta, Georgia, with his fiancé and pug.

LIST OF PATRONS

This book was made possible in part by the following grand patrons who preordered the book on inkshares.com. Thank you.

Amanda Blanchard

Andrew J. Ainsworth

Aunt Sandi

Becca Louise Stalling

Bleu Johnson

Candi Pender

Casey Ottinger

Cat Rixon

Christin Smith

Christina Tomasso

Christopher Tomasso

Cody Smith

Courtney Smith

Craig Campbell

Dave Barrett

Eoin Gorman

Erin Olinger

G. Lucht

Harmony Cadien

Holly Smith

Jana Linville

JF Dubeau

John Robin

John Tunningley

Jordan Marshall

Jossie Ann Garcia

Kate Tritschler

Kelly Ottinger

Kelsey Lynch Ravindran

Kim Greenwell

Kristie Boswell

Kristy van Treeck

Krystyn Linville

Lee and Pam Linville

Logan Annalise Judson

Megan Elaine Schuster

Mike Ferris

Mom

Patti S. Smith

Phillip Seng

Regina Taylor-Hines
Rhea Bieri
Richard Heinz
Rodney Henry
Ryan Smith
Sara Bailey
Scott Smith
Shaun Patrick
Shelley Russell Hanna
Stefanie Topping
Uncle Mike
Wanda Eley

NERDIST

Founded by Chris Hardwick, Nerdist is a many-headed beast. With a sprawling podcast network, premium video content, and a flagship site for breaking entertainment news, Nerdist is a nexus for passionate, intelligent, and engaged community to come together and celebrate their wonderfully nerdy interests. Whether it's *Doctor Who* or the science behind Iron Man's armor, if you nerd out about it, we do too.

Listen in or join the conversation at nerdist.com.

INKSHARES

 Inkshares is a crowdfunded book publisher. We democratize publishing by having readers select the books we publish—we edit, design, print, distribute, and market any book that meets a pre-order threshold.

Interested in making a book idea come to life? Visit inkshares.com to find new book projects or to start your own.